WHILE THEY SLEEP

Based on a true story

EDIE LIVESAY

Copyright © 2015 by Edie Livesay

While They Sleep
Based on a true story
by Edie Livesay

Printed in the United States of America.

ISBN 9781498439794

All rights reserved solely by the author. The author guarantees all contents are original and do not infringe upon the legal rights of any other person or work. No part of this book may be reproduced in any form without the permission of the author. The views expressed in this book are not necessarily those of the publisher.

Unless otherwise indicated, Scripture quotations taken from the Holy Bible, New International Version (NIV). Copyright © 1973, 1978, 1984, 2011 by Biblica, Inc.™. Used by permission. All rights reserved.

www.xulonpress.com

Dedication

This book is dedicated to:
My beloved sister Shari Iverson
Her husband Terry who is more my brother

*A little sleep, a little slumber,
a little folding of the hands to rest.*
Proverbs 6:10

Preface

In early 1970 Jillian Townsend had given up her life in the United States to come and live among the jungle Indians of Ecuador. Now she was suddenly aware that her silly dreams had brought her to the high sierras to work among the illiterate and helpless, but it was she who was feeling inadequate. The stark reality of where she was and the immense barriers she faced made her droop with concern.

All her romantic notions fled in the face of likely failure. All of a sudden she needed to get out of the truck. Even if she had to walk back to Quito she couldn't bear to sit another moment in the choking, claustrophobic atmosphere. Leaning forward, she was about to tap the driver on his shoulder when the bus turned a curve on the narrow road. She gasped in wonder at the scene before her.

Stretching for miles was the most beautiful valley she had ever seen. Clusters of villages, small forests of eucalyptus and fruit trees, silvery rivers, tall church steeples, and winding roads covered the valley floor. Around the edges, green rolling hills formed a ring and above them towered snow-capped mountains. To the right rose the perfect, cone-shaped dimensions of Mount Cotopaxi. To the left, with just a tip showing, was Mount Cayambe. Directly ahead, peering through the snowy white clouds, Mount Antizana glowed in the afternoon sun.

Forgotten were the dust and gas fumes of Quito, her claustrophobia, and discouragement. The foul odors and distasteful Ecuadorian culture fled from her. In the years to come, the first view of that valley would never fail to thrill her. It would live with Jillian for the rest of her life.

One minute the sour circumstances had been overwhelming, while in the next this new perspective uplifted her. She was traveling in an ill-constructed vehicle surrounded by the people she had come to love through literature.

Chapter 1

Jillian Townsend glanced nervously at her watch. Across the cobblestone street vendors sprawled on colorful woolen blankets. On the normally busy avenue there was no other sign of life. A siesta hour had brought the city to a standstill. The only sounds were the American/European hospital's muffled grindings of huge generators deep in the basement behind her.

Shifting her weight to the other leg, Jillian longed to sit on the steps leading to the building, but decided against the undignified act while wearing her best clothes. Wanting to make a good first impression, she had groomed herself carefully this afternoon. The visit to Pachuca could turn out to be an important step toward her future work in Ecuador.

Dressed in a tailored, lightweight gray suit trimmed with black facing and buttoned over a lacy white blouse, she felt satisfied with the impact she would make. Her waist length, light brown hair was pulled away from her face and piled atop her head, revealing a heart-shaped face, greenish brown eyes, and straight nose above a full mouth. Dainty black earrings and a matching necklace framed her frowning countenance. Black high-heeled boots adorned her feet.

Soft giggles dragged her attention back to the Indians now beginning to stir among their woolen goods across the way. The siesta hour was drawing to a close. Soon the sick and infirmed of Quito would arrive, bringing their sundry complaints to the resident doctors working at the hospital.

A telephone message had been taped to the front door of Jillian's apartment the previous afternoon. The note was from her new friend, Sandi Graham, inviting her for a weekend visit to Pachuca. It stated that she would meet her in front of the hospital by mid-siesta hour and escort her to the small village several miles east.

Sandi was a young nurse working in a privately owned orphanage on the outskirts of the Indian pueblo. Jillian had met the tall, dark-haired girl during a quiet lunch in Quito's city center. According to Sandi she was in a rush as each time she came to the capitol from her small village she was expected to complete many errands during a short day. Finally, in exhaustion, she had stopped in the cozy restaurant and recognized Jillian as an American. The mysterious bond that unites countrymen in a strange land extended to greeting and a friendship was formed. They lunched together over colas and ceviche. Now, days later the invitation on Jillian's door had not come as a surprise.

The cobblestone street was suddenly filled with honking trucks and jabbering pedestrians. Siesta hour had come to a close and as if the Indians had been lying in ready, they appeared in clusters moving toward the hospital entrance.

Jillian checked her watch again and sighed with discomfort as cars and trucks squeezed into a line along the curb. In amongst the sea of faces, suddenly one focused upon her. Hand upraised, the woman motioned to her from the street. Jillian was startled as the angry, stormy faced woman advanced toward her and then perplexed as she watched the impatient Indian push through the crowd and halt several feet away. Small, cold black eyes stared at her with contempt. The woman's slender, hooked nose and large-lipped mouth accentuated high cheek bones. Thick black, wavy hair combed away from her face gave her a manly appearance. As the woman pushed aside the crowd, Jillian could see that she moved with flowing grace, her broad shoulders sloping to a slender torso and thin legs. Held tightly in her grasp was the hand of a young girl who was being pulled along behind her. As the youngster caught up, she showed a quick and eager smile for Jillian, but as she moved forward to greet Jillian, the woman jerked her back.

"You Jill?" the woman yelled abruptly in English.

Chapter 1

"Yes," replied Jillian in amazement and dread.

She had expected Sandi. Who was this woman?

"Come," the Indian and child swung around and rushed away.

Jillian stood for a moment in astonishment but coming to attention, she quickly grabbed her belongings and dashed after them. After passing several parked vehicles, she slowed shifting her load from one hand to the other. Already the exertion of running while carrying her baggage was causing her to perspire under the woolen suit.

"Good grief," Jillian said out loud. "Where did she park the car?"

As they neared the end of the block and approached one of Quito's main boulevards, Jillian realized with a sinking heart that there was no waiting car. Moisture ran down her back and arms. A hairpin worked itself free, releasing a long strand of hair to hang limply over her shoulder. The overnight bag seemed to grow heavier with each step, and the strap of her purse dug into her shoulder causing her to lean off balance.

"I don't believe this is happening," she muttered aloud. "What a fool I was to wear a hot suit."

Glancing up, she realized the hostile Indian and her small companion had advanced a block ahead without a backward glance.

"Obviously she'd rather not be seen with me and I can't speak Spanish well enough to tell her to walk slower," Jillian panted.

Turning with sudden movement, the woman and child walked directly into the wide traffic-choked street. Dodging cars and buses with ease and experience, they crossed without difficulty while Jillian gaped in fear.

"At least you could have waited for me," she said as she gritted her teeth at the disappearing backs. "How am I going to get across this street and keep them close enough to see at the same time?"

Sharp stabs of anger rose in her. She debated whether to return home, but the desire to see Pachuca for the first time and visit her new friend, Sandi won out. In a split second, she grabbed at her swinging purse and jumped into the traffic. Honking vehicles swerved, barely missing her. Panicked, she found herself a vulnerable target in the middle of the street. Breathing deeply, she raced around one car, spurted between two others, and stood panting on the curb. The woman and child stood a block away, their backs to her, arms folded.

Puffing, Jillian reached them in a fury. She opened her mouth to scold them, but realized what a fool she would make of herself. Staring at their rigid backs for a moment, she dropped her overnight bag in defeat.

What's the use, she thought. Placing her purse beside the bag, she tried to adjust her suit. The child glanced around under black hooded eyes, a worried look wrinkling her brow. Jillian felt pity for her.

"Hola," she struggled in poor Spanish. "Mi nombre es Jill. Como te llamas?"

The child moved closer to the Indian and remarked shyly, "Leah."

Pointing to her companion, she added, "Y ella se llama, Lucia."

"Lucia," muttered Jillian.

Sandi hadn't mentioned Lucia by name. She nodded at the woman who in turn ignored her. Jillian shrugged. She had decided they would probably flag down a taxi for the drive to Pachuca, but her heart sank when a cab slowly motored past them.

"How we going?" she sputtered in faulty Spanish.

Much to Jillian's distress Lucia choked with laugher and Leah chuckled reflexively with the woman. As her face flamed with the humiliation of her bumbling efforts, her heart burned with anger. Gladly she would have returned to the hospital, but never would she let Lucia have the satisfaction. Stubbornly she pressed her lips together and brushed back long strands of hair from her face. Pulling on a deep draft of warm air mixed with dust and carbon monoxide, she decided to enjoy this so longed-for experience of mingling with the Ecuadorian peasants. She had waited too many years for this event to allow an ill-tempered woman to ruin it.

Another taxi passed, but Lucia ignored it. Jillian stared mystified. The wait was short-lived, however. Suddenly the woman darted onto the road to wave down a lumbering vehicle strongly resembling Noah's ark on wheels. The cab and bed appeared to have been constructed by a novice carpenter. Along the wooden sides of the vehicle, square openings had been sawed out to serve as windows. Eyes wide with disbelief, Jillian gasped as the vehicle sagged slowly to a stop. Its sides extended three feet beyond the wheels. The bus rocked under its weight like a ship tossed at sea. Several heads and

Chapter 1

arms of passengers pushed through the square openings, and a jam of young men held fast to the door, daring fate rather than wait for the next bus.

She stood aghast as Lucia and Leah trotted forward to squeeze inside the door. After yelling a few words to the driver, Lucia then turned, waving Jillian to follow.

Bending to retrieve her belongings, Jillian stumbled to the bus door. The woman grabbed the girl's bag with one hand and pushed Leah into the bus with the other. Latching onto a young man's arm, Jillian barely found a foothold on the bottom step before the vehicle moved slowly from the curb.

"This is ludicrous," she murmured fearfully, fighting her way passed the crowd gathered in the doorway. Dressed in layers of dark, heavy clothing, the passengers huddled beneath their ponchos and the brims of brown felt hats. Their tired faces testified to laboring long difficult hours, years of deprivation, and sickness. With an intake of air, she also realized they emitted a peculiar odor. In the years to come, she would grow accustomed to the heavy, smoky scent that clung to their clothing from the fires built on floors of their homes. Drifting smoke wafted throughout the small huts and upward through holes in the roofs. Chimneys were an uncommon sight in Ecuador's countryside. In a short time she would learn that they traveled on this dilapidated relic because the fare was half the usual rate.

Lucia commanded a young man to stand then waved the hapless foreigner toward the vacant seat. He stared bewildered at the spectacle she presented. A spectacle she was with long strands of hair laying over the shoulders of her wrinkled suit and hanging purse. Tottering on high-heeled boots, she stumbled forward. Clutching a woman's wide skirt, she crumbled to a wooden seat. Much to her surprise, it was nothing more than a slat nailed a few inches from the floor. The force of falling on the low bench pushed her knees halfway to her shoulders. Smothering a nervous giggle, she pulled her skirt down and tried to straighten her legs. Glancing around, she saw several pairs of eyes staring at her with undisguised curiosity. Sitting on makeshift buses posed no problem for short-legged Indians, but she stood a half head taller than most of the men.

While They Sleep

The woman beside her stood and pushed to the back of the bus. I must appear frightful to them, she thought. She smoothed strands of hair from her forehead and tried to pull her sticking clothes away from her wet back. Sliding to the vacant seat by the window, she made a grab for the sill. Desperately hanging on, she realized the seat slanted downward.

"This must be why everyone is hanging out the windows," she mumbled to herself. "They can't keep from sliding to the floor."

Sighing, she wondered again why she had come. Wearing billowing skirts, a newcomer fell onto the seat next to her. Jillian turned to her neighbor and with a gasp came face to face with a tom turkey. The bird showed Jillian his profile and glared at her with a beady eye. Settling contentedly on the woman's lap, his head jerked to and fro while his owner gave Jillian a shy, curious look. The woman, having satisfied her curiosity closed her eyes and fell asleep instantly.

Where was Lucia? Fear gripped her. What if she had already gotten off the bus? Jillian tried to wrench her body around to look behind her, but in doing so she slid from her seat and instinctively grabbed for the windowsill. The turkey's wings flapped in terror, and the woman's eyes and mouth snapped open in surprise.

Jillian pushed herself back onto the wooden slat and tried to pat her hair into place. Lucia has my overnight bag, she thought. I don't know where I am or if we will travel all the way to Pachuca in this horrible vehicle. Oh, Lord, how I wish I had stayed in my little apartment. Then fear turned to anger. How could Sandi have allowed this? She should have come after me in a car. This is no way to treat a guest.

Clouds of dust billowed through the open windows as the bus waddled onto a vacant lot and groaned to a stop. Several people pushed themselves to their feet, and carefully, Jillian unfolded, turning to look for Lucia. With relief she spotted the Indian and Leah elbowing through the milling crowd. Passing Jillian, Lucia nodded curtly indicating they were ready to disembark. With a great thrust, Jillian barged past the turkey and his owner. Flinging herself forward, she fell onto the back of a slumbering old man. He snorted in fright and all eyes turned toward her. Quiet snickers and giggles followed her to the bus door, down the steps, and onto the vacant lot.

Chapter 1

Through the dust left in the wake of the departing bus she realized with dismay that they were yet within Quito's boundaries. The city loomed behind them and stretching before them lay the Tumbaco Valley. Promptly Lucia and Leah turned their backs to her displaying their continuing indignation and disapproval.

Jillian made a face and grumbled softly, "It didn't take long for Lucia to turn the kid against me."

The highway appeared new, but the earth along its shoulders remained undeveloped. A layer of dust rose and settled each time a vehicle passed. Wind whipped the sandy mixture in swirls about the small waiting group. Jillian looked at her fine clothes already coated with powder and reached up to feel her hair. It was dry and gritty. She licked her lips and tasted dirt.

Lucia pulled off her sweater and wrapped her head, hiding her face from the wind. The child followed suit. Minutes passed. On two occasions the woman ran to the middle of the road to flag down buses only to watch the overcrowded vehicles slowly pass them by. Each time she returned to her spot, turning her back to Jillian without comment. Jillian glanced at her watch noting that an hour had passed since they arrived beside the hot, dusty road. She felt a desperate desire to cry.

Attempting to transfer the dirt from her hands to her jacket, she smeared it in streaks. A pain that had begun as a throb in her temples now spread across her head and down the back of her neck.

Just as she was seriously contemplating flagging down a taxi to take her home, Lucia darted onto the highway to block an approaching truck groaning under the combined weight of people and stuffed burlap bags. Jillian almost laughed with relief as it rolled to a stop. The vehicle appeared to be the progeny of a construction project from a local backyard. The hood was imprinted with a United States emblem, but the rear area could only have been constructed by an amateur. Fastened to a long, metal bed, a gigantic wooden box reached above the cab. Huge gunny sacks filled the long bed covered by a tarpaulin anchored by several huddled men.

Having been constructed with three benches, the cab was oversized with three doors lining each side. It overhung the wheels, teetering precariously under the movement of more than a dozen people

While They Sleep

inside. A door opened and three men jumped out. Running behind the truck to climb an attached ladder, they scrambled for vacancies on the tarpaulin. The driver waved Lucia and her companions aboard to sit on an amazingly small bench. Leaving her bag with Lucia, Jillian placed one foot on the high step and two hands on the doorjambs. Dipping her head to avoid bumping the low entrance, she hunched her shoulders down and with effort pulled herself forward.

Inside, the space between the rows of wooden benches was narrow and for a moment she panicked. There was little room to turn. Squeezing down, she saw that Leah was behind her. Lucia took up the rear and immediately leaned toward the window, while the child rested against the woman's arm, leaving Jillian with a sense of isolation. She glanced to her right and winced. Against her dusty skirt, a baby's foot tapped a contented rhythm as he sucked from his mother's breast. The same strange, smoky odor Jillian had endured during the bus ride assaulted her in waves; only now it mingled with scents of beer, sweat, and the baby's unchanged diaper.

How can they ignore these smells? How can they appear so comfortable? In front of her she watched a flea crawl across a man's neck and disappear beneath his collar.

Perhaps the strange, unfamiliar surroundings would have been acceptable to her, had she not slowly realized that she didn't understand a word of Spanish being spoken around her. In the space of a few miles she had suddenly entered a world of alien customs and language. Even with the weeks of Spanish study behind her, she could barely make out one word.

A strong sense of loneliness gripped her and she blinked back sudden tears. This wasn't what she had expected. Her faraway dreams and fantasies hadn't included indescribably filth and odors. Never had it occurred to her that the Spanish she had labored to understand and speak would be useless. She knew in an instant that for her, living among the country Indians would be impossible. This entire trip had been a mistake. The people she had come to help didn't need her at all. They were innocently cheerful in their poverty and ignorant of any improvement she could offer them.

What irony. Her silly dreams had brought her to the high sierras to work among the illiterate and helpless, but it was she who was feeling

Chapter 1

inadequate. The stark reality of where she was and the immense barriers she faced made her droop with concern. All her romantic notions fled in the face of likely failure. Nor would she be satisfied remaining in Quito as it was too large and complicated. Now, the rural area was simply too difficult a challenge to conquer. To her chagrin, these Indians didn't seem to realize they needed help from anyone. Their jabbering and laughter filled the cab with an air of festivity.

Swallowing the lump in her throat, she looked about the large, squat box they were riding in and desperately wished the woman at her right would turn her nursing baby the other direction.

All of a sudden she needed to get out of the truck. Even if she had to walk back to Quito she couldn't bear to sit another moment in the choking, claustrophobic atmosphere. Leaning forward, she was about to tap the driver on his shoulder when the bus turned a curve on the narrow road. She gasped in wonder at the scene before her. Stretching for miles was the most beautiful valley she had ever seen. Clusters of villages, small forests of eucalyptus and fruit trees, silvery rivers, tall church steeples, and winding roads covered the valley floor. Around the edges, green rolling hills formed a ring and above them towered snow-capped mountains. To the right rose the perfect, cone-shaped dimensions of Mount Cotopaxi. To the left, with just a tip showing, was Mount Cayambe. Directly ahead, peering through the snowy white clouds, Mount Antizana glowed in the afternoon sun. Forgotten were the dust and gas fumes of Quito, her claustrophobia, and discouragement. The foul odors and distasteful Ecuadorian culture fled from her.

In the years to come, the first view of that valley would never fail to thrill her. It would live with Jillian for the rest of her life. One minute the sour circumstances had been overwhelming, while in the next this new perspective uplifted her. She was traveling in an ill-constructed vehicle surrounded by the people she had come to love through literature. She almost laughed for joy as they descended to the valley, passing quaint villages and little mud huts surrounded by avocado and lemon trees, tall green eucalyptus forests and deep canyons. Church steeples pinpointing the main plaza lifted from the center of each town. Emaciated dogs searched for food while Indian women, babies tied to their backs with large cloths, trotted along the roads. Dressed in long, flared skirts, dark-colored sweaters and blouses, brown felt hats sitting squarely on their long, braided hair, they all appeared to be cut from the same pattern. The men, clothed in dark trousers, jackets and hats, hurried alongside with similarly dressed children trotting rapidly trying to keep up.

I'm here, she thought. *I'm really here. I can take anything as long as I'm here. Despite it all, this is what I want.* Turning to the young mother next to her, she smiled broadly, patted the baby's leg and received a shy smile in return.

An hour passed as Jillian tried to take in the scenery from every vantage point. Finally the cumbersome truck followed a sharp bend in the road, descending into a deep, wide canyon. In the distance, spanning the width of the canyon was the skeleton of a steel bridge under construction. With dismay, she realized they would have to follow the crude road down the side of the cliff to the bottom and up the other side. The lower they descended the narrower the road became. A terrible thought struck her. The truck was too wide! They would surely tumble into the river several hundred feet below. She glanced toward Lucia who had not shifted from her position at the window, and then to the others who also seemed unconcerned. The truck's swollen, distended side hung over the edge of the road; all she could see from her spot was open space. Slowly it continued downward, lumbering and tottering, its extended sides barely missing the high, steep cliffs. Its left wheels only just remained on the rutted road.

"This is no wider than a cow path," she muttered aloud grimacing at the lack of a guardrail.

After what seemed an eternity, the road turned onto a narrow ancient bridge. Jillian grabbed at the bench in front of her, staring over the driver's shoulder, as he slowly maneuvered the truck across thick wooden slats to the opposite side. Grinding down to a lower gear, he skillfully moved up the beaten track cut into the side of the steep cliff. Much to her distress ahead was a sharp, hairpin curve around an outcrop of the canyon wall. All laughing and chattering among the passengers abruptly came to a halt when the driver quickly stomped on the brakes. Raising his voice, he uttered a sharp, quick order. Doors flew open on Lucia's side of the cab, and several passengers dropped gingerly to the ground. Only she, the mother, baby,

Chapter 1

and chauffeur remained on board. Without understanding Jillian attempted to catch Lucia's attention, but the Indian ignored her, shutting the door in her face. Puzzled, she sat back on the bench.

Turning her head for a better view, she could see nothing. A voice called out and the truck driver let off the brake, slowly rolling backward. With a jerk, the vehicle stopped. Amid loud discussion, the passengers climbed back into their places. Jillian's woman companion jabbered and motioned in sign language that someone had placed a rock under the wheels so the truck wouldn't topple backwards over the edge. This procedure enabled the driver to ease the ungainly truck around the narrow turn and begin its ascent to the top. Jillian tried to lean back and relax. She had been clenching her fists and holding her breath again.

Straining for a better look, she gratefully saw the top of the canyon, however, as the vehicle rolled over a big hump, instead of thankfulness, she whimpered involuntarily in despair. Ahead, stretching for several meters was a lake of mud. Two large, old-fashioned construction tractors without drivers sat in the thick liquid.

As the truck pulled around a large boulder onto the new unpaved road to the bridge under construction, Jillian noticed a crowd gathered by the edge of the cliff. The driver stopped the truck before entering the mud and waited until a few curious passengers could jump from the cab. Babbling excitedly, the group by the cliff waved them over. Two men yelled into the ravine, then leaned forward to offer helping hands. A head slowly appeared from below the precipice. A man in a brown uniform grabbed the proffered hand and struggled up to the road. The newcomer brushed the dust from his pant legs and shook his head. Expressions of grief reached Jillian's ears.

Finally, the passengers began to wander back toward the truck. She tried desperately to pick out a few words, but nothing made sense. The driver muttered and sadly made the Catholic sign of the cross and reached for a dirty handkerchief. He blew his nose loudly and spit out the window. When everyone was again in their seat, the motor kicked into action, and the truck eased forward. With a sense of shock, Jillian realized they were about to ride into the mud. Her companions showed no concern as the rapid-fire conversation picked up in the small cab.

Fifty meters into the mud, the driver killed the motor while the chattering in the cab continued unabated combined now with the crying baby. The infant's mother automatically pulled a heavy breast from her blouse and stuck it into the eager mouth. Jillian sighed and glanced in the other direction. Lucia and Leah were still peering out the side window. Sounds of racing, chugging motors led her to believe that other trucks and buses had pulled up behind their truck. Slowly her discomfort and lack of understanding sapped her euphoria and she began to sink in despair.

Without warning, Lucia uttered a stream of unintelligible words and the passengers pressed to look out the windows. In response, the young mother beside Jillian unwittingly shoved her backward against the wooden seat. Stifling a gasp for breath, Jillian attempted to lean forward against the woman's weight which caused the baby lying on the mother's lap to slide forward. The infant wailed in fear as Jillian grabbed for the baby. Sheepishly the mother smiled, replaced her ample breast and straightened her blouse. Flushed with anger Jillian glared at the woman for her lack of courtesy. Fueling her anger even further, Jillian's fellow travelers seemed to ignore her predicament. She waited in fuming silence until after several hot, stuffy minutes she heard sloshing noises.

A man from the group at the cliff's edge appeared at the window and yelled up to the driver. After much conferring he turned to fight his way through the soupy mud. Climbing onto one of the big tractors, he moved it backward and carefully nosed the rear of the machine to the front of the truck. He then jumped down to attach both vehicles securely with a long cable.

Slowly they were able to climb together until the vehicles were free of the mud. With relief, ahead Jillian saw a newly paved road stretching to the base of the high, rolling mountains. Purring contentedly, the truck motor relaxed into a gentle idle while the driver descended to help release the tractor. Waving his thanks he returned to his seat and drove off as the tractor operator returned to help the next vehicle mired in the mud.

As they began the final leg of the journey toward the emerald ridged mountains, silent awe gripped her at the beauty that lay before them. The highest summits revealed land cultivated for farming. In

Chapter 1

the distance to the east, light from the sinking sun reflected from the tiny rooftops of small villages resting on the sloping hillsides.

Just as it seemed the truck was making better time, it bounced and jerked to a stop. The passengers groaned loudly when the driver opened his cab door and jumped to the road below. In a loud chorus everyone began jabbering again. Lucia pushed open her door and leaped from the cab with Leah following close behind. Watching from the small window Jillian saw a house in the distance and a church steeple towering behind. She assumed they had arrived.

"Thank goodness!" she muttered, grabbing her purse. She picked up her overnight bag from beneath the bench but stopped short at the closed, disgusted look on Lucia's face.

"No, no," the Indian frowned, shaking her head. Motioning for Jillian to be seated again, she turned her back and walked to the front of the vehicle.

Jillian decided that this time, despite Lucia, she would find out what had happened. Leaving her suitcase, she jumped from the truck and hobbled past a group of observers. Two men were in the process of jacking up the truck to remove a flat tire. Another man scurried from the back of the truck rolling a spare tire in front of him.

Ignoring Lucia's dark glance, Jillian took time to stretch and look around. She was hungry, needed a restroom and found herself too weary to stand. Selecting a lush, grassy knoll she sat, sighing heavily. Across the road a curious woman with a baby tied to her back, paused for a moment to watch the activity. A little boy carrying a load of towering corn stalks strapped to his back stopped behind her. Losing interest, the mother soon moved on. The boy lingered, watching them in the gathering darkness. Suddenly he noticed his mother in the distance and ran with the corn stalks bobbing above his head. He caught up with her, leaving the group behind.

Other than the chatter and laughter around the truck, the evening was silent. In a grassy pasture behind her the shadowy figures of grazing cows and horses grew darker as the soft sunlight quickly disappeared behind the mountain range she and her companions had left more than two hours earlier. The sudden darkness enveloped her with a sense of fear and loneliness.

I am certainly suffering mood swings, she thought. She adjusted her tired legs and looked longingly in the direction of Quito. She jerked to attention when Lucia called out her name. The Indian stood back and waited as Jillian clumsily grabbed the doorjamb to pull herself up into the cab.

They started off without mishap and, after what seemed a long time, turned left onto a cobblestone road. Through the darkness she saw small, dimly lit windows reflecting flickering candlelight. Stopping in front of an occasional hut, the cab gradually emptied. The narrow road ended abruptly and the tottering truck drove onto a wide avenue. A row of buildings lining one side faced a large plaza on the other. Several store entrances stood open, revealing disorderly shelves and groups of loiterers inside.

They traveled beyond the plaza, passing a few stragglers wandering up the steps of a church. Jillian noticed a school and basketball court barely visible under the pale street lamps. Several young people gathered in groups along the sidewalk talking and strumming guitars. The truck moved past a deserted marketplace and beyond the reach of street lights. Another short distance to the left and the truck stopped. Lucia dug in her pocket, counted out a handful of change and dropped it into the driver's hand. She opened the door and gently poked Leah awake. With a nod toward Jillian who was eagerly searching for her overnight bag and purse, she stalked up the driveway.

Bedraggled, sticky and dirty, her hair lying around her shoulders, Jillian was in dire need of a bath. With a groan she wondered what Sandi would think of her, but the relief of arriving and the hope of a place to rest caused her to hurriedly follow Lucia and Leah.

Chapter 2

The truck lumbered away as the three arrived at the top of the steep driveway and Lucia opened a large metal gate. Small floodlights perched on tall, wooden poles revealed a gray building on the left. Jillian remembered Sandi had mentioned a maternity clinic. They walked toward a two-story house sitting several hundred meters from the road. Every window glowed brightly as if to warmly welcome them. A door opened and Sandi ran toward her, yelling out greetings. Jillian laughed with joy at the sound of her familiar, native tongue.

"I don't know what was going on, but what a terrible trip we had," she moaned.

"We couldn't figure out what had happened to you," Sandi replied. "Usually we can make the trip in just over an hour because of the bridge construction, but you must have left Quito several hours ago. I called one of the places Lucia visited today. They told me she'd planned to be at home an age ago."

She turned Jillian toward the house, "Let's go. We made pizza just for you. Go ahead, get cleaned up. You must be exhausted and hungry. Then I'll find out from Lucia what happened."

Jillian picked up the small suitcase and said, "Anything would sound wonderful right now. I look terrible. Would you mind if I take a shower before we eat?"

"Come with me," said a smiling girl waiting for them at the front door.

"Jill, this is Flora. She works with us and will take your things down to the little house where you'll be sleeping as soon as you eat and meet everyone."

Jillian returned a smile at Flora with a greeting and offered her the suit jacket and purse, keeping the overnight bag.

"Now, follow me," Sandi directed Jillian to the bathroom. "Take a quick shower. Out here we don't have much water, just some that we store in a tower by the clinic for deliveries. Our water system is turned on each morning and we collect what we can. After that, if we have too many emergencies, it's just too bad."

In no time, dressed in clean blouse and skirt, Jillian found herself seated at a long dining table chewing on a dry, homemade pizza.

"We expected you long before this, so it may be a little tough, but I reheated it anyway. Here are some bananas and cookies. Sure hope this is enough."

"What about Leah and Lucia? Did they eat?" Jillian asked with her mouth full.

"Leah ate a bite while you were showering. Lucia will eat at the clinic. We usually just snack in the evening since we eat our big meal at noon. Now, you go ahead and I'll be right back."

Sandi glanced once more at the table setting, gave Jillian a big grin, and disappeared into another room. Jillian was left alone. She could hear muffled sounds of children and wondered how they would accept her.

Despite being tough the pizza tasted good. As she nibbled slowly on a banana, her eyes began growing heavy with the weariness of travel. Struggling to stay awake she studied the room. It was conservative and practical. Limp, faded blue curtains hung at the three aluminum-paned windows lining the east wall. Beige paint peeled from the plastered walls. Two faded pictures of animals in cheap ugly frames hung in a vain attempt to cheer the room. The table was nothing more than several long boards nailed to eight thick wooden legs covered with two pieces of oilcloth cracked with age. Folding chairs lined each side of the table. She was unimpressed. There was little to suggest that children lived here.

Jillian was startled out of a daze as the front door flew open and a tall, stocky woman lunged into the room. Her straight dark

Chapter 2

hair sprinkled liberally with gray and prominent front teeth drew Jillian's attention immediately. She wore black horn-rimmed glasses that framed soft brown eyes and long eyelashes. They were her most attractive features, but unfortunately, her eyes were easily overlooked because of a large nose and heavy growth of hair on her upper lip.

Jillian was alert and uncomfortable under the newcomer's steady gaze. The woman stopped to study the girl for a moment and then, with two large steps covered the distance between them to grab Jillian's hand.

"You must be Jill. I'm Marta Brewer. We sure had to wait a long time for you. We figured you would have to sleep in some Indian hut all night. Wow, would that have been a riot."

She was amazed to see the woman burst into laughter, slap her knee while pushing up her glasses to wipe her eyes with the other. Smiling back politely she wished desperately for Sandi. Where was she?

"Yes, it was a long and difficult trip. I still don't know everything that went on. I couldn't understand the Spanish," Jillian tried to explain.

For a moment the woman stared at her with a puzzled look, "You mean you don't speak Spanish? I thought Sandi said you were learning the language at school?"

"Well, I thought I knew a little, but this was totally different from anything I've ever heard," Jillian said as she watched the woman erupt into laughter.

Marta flopped down hard on a chair and rocked back and forth, fighting to catch her breath. She took off her glasses and ran the back of her free hand across her eyes. Feeling foolish, Jillian grinned wondering what was so funny. *Where was Sandi*, she thought again.

The woman opened her mouth to speak, but again burst into laughter sending a moist spray in Jillian's direction. Finding it difficult to look at Marta's face, she focused her attention on the woman's shabby tennis shoes and white cotton anklets.

Oh Lord, if you'll get me through this weekend I'll never return to this dreadful place, prayed Jillian fervently.

While They Sleep

Flora appeared at the kitchen door and asked in Spanish, "Señorita Jill, would you care for more pizza? If not, I will take your suitcase to the little house where you will sleep tonight."

Baffled, Jillian understood the words and replied, "No."

Laughing, Marta spouted off a few words in the local dialect, none of which made much sense to Jillian. Glancing covertly at Jillian, Flora winked. Sandi walked into the room followed by disgruntled Lucia.

She smiled at Jillian, "Well, you had quite a day and I don't think you still know what happened at the bridge."

She paused to look at Marta then turned to address Jillian, "You, Leah, and Lucia had a terrible trip. The commotion in the canyon was because a man who was working on the bridge fell and died. Two of the men in uniform were policemen from Puembo. The others were there to help recover the man's body."

"All the mud will be cleared away by tomorrow," continued Sandi. "We just hope it doesn't rain again like it did yesterday. Anyway, after all that, along with the flat tire, you must be very tired."

Marta began chuckling again, "You know what, Sandi? Jill couldn't understand anything that was going on today because she couldn't understand the country dialect. I've laughed so hard that I hurt. What a riot. This has to be the funniest thing I've heard in a long time."

Turning to Lucia the woman spoke several rapid words in the slurred sounding vernacular and giggled again. Lucia waited patiently in the doorway, looking at Jillian, a smirk tugging at her mouth, and then turned to leave the room. Sandi remained stone faced, anger narrowing her eyes.

Marta, unaware of sudden coolness, wiped her eyes with a handkerchief and heaved herself out of the chair, "I guess I'd better go check the kids. They'll be ready for bed in a few minutes. Maybe you'd like to come in and see them before I tuck them away, Jill."

Still chuckling, she walked out the door. Sandi sat down in the chair that Marta had vacated.

"Why was she laughing? Try as I might I can't see anything so funny," Jillian said to her friend.

24

Chapter 2

Sandi smiled, "Don't be bothered by Marta. She acts that way when she's nervous and trying to impress someone. She needs to feel accepted and doesn't know how to act around someone she just met. In so many ways she's unsure of herself, but when she speaks Spanish, she's secure. She can speak the language better than any American in this country. You must remember that it's very difficult to live and work here in the country away from your own people."

"Let me explain something to you," Sandi continued. "The Pachucan peasant speaks with a country dialect that is quite different from the Spanish you learned in the university. That is why some Spanish you understand and some you can't. What you hear is a mixture of Spanish and Quichuan and a lot of slang. Most of the Indians in this area are Quichuan. In this short distance from Quito there is a distinct difference. Many people born and raised in Quito have had more chance to attend school and have been taught by professors who speak a purer Spanish. You can usually tell where someone lives or has been raised in Ecuador just by the way he talks. After a while, words and dialects will become clear to you. Then it will be nothing more than you would call an 'accent.'"

Sandi popped a cookie in her mouth, "Flora speaks a purer Spanish because she is a very intelligent girl and has studied in Quito. She also speaks a bit of English and will be happy to practice with you, I'm sure."

Yawning, she stretched her arms above her head, "Don't let Marta intimidate you. You probably gave her a great lift."

Jillian laughed, "She did make me feel a little foolish for a moment. I hope you're right about being able to understand these people. What about Lucia? I don't know her, yet I get the distinct feeling she barely tolerates me. Why would you send her to pick me up in Quito? We spent the entire trip without speaking a single word to each other. She couldn't understand me and I certainly couldn't understand her."

At that, Sandi threw back her head and hooted with laughter, "You have been the victim of Lucia's dry sense of humor. She can speak English quite well. She has lived with Americans most of her life. But you see she's not very happy. Usually Lucia is the underdog.

She probably decided this was her chance to sit back and see how you would survive the trip."

"But I felt hostility from her. Why would she hate me before she gets to know me?" Jillian shook her head in wonder.

"Lucia's life was saved at birth by American missionaries who practically raised her. She was abandoned by her family and left at the door of the missionary's home. Unfortunately, it seems that jungle Indians are shunned as the lowest among social classes. So, despite all the help Americans have given her, she mistrusts them. She probably doesn't know how you would have accepted her had you known she's from the jungle and all the other negatives surrounding her upbringing," Sandi shrugged her shoulders. "I've tried to let her know she's accepted, but she continues to feel she's unwanted and accuses us being condescending. Can you understand that?"

"No, I certainly can't. I gave up my life in the United States to come and live with people just like her. I was inspired by the books I read about jungle Indians. It makes no difference to me how or where they were born and raised. I've lived for the moment I could simply touch a jungle Indian. How can such a class system exist that discriminates against them?"

"Tell me why not? It exists in the United States, doesn't it?" Sandi asked. "Class distinction is a way of life no matter where you go."

Jillian was silent for a moment, "I guess that prejudice hasn't been an issue with me. It is gratifying to learn Lucia is from the jungle. How did the missionaries save her life?"

Sandi looked thoughtfully at her guest, "She was illegitimate and premature. Although it happens a lot, it is still a terrible plight to befall any child in this country."

Standing, she patted Jillian on the shoulder, "We're just glad that you have come. I can tell you more about Lucia later, if you'd like. Now I hear the children singing. I try to spend a little time with them each evening before bedtime. Come with me. You will enjoy it."

Jillian wiped her mouth with a paper napkin and followed Sandi through the hallway into the living room. Several children dressed in pajamas were sitting around the room. They saw her and their eyes grew large with pleasure. Smiling broadly, she nodded her head to them.

Chapter 2

Sandi showed where Jillian should sit. Obediently, she walked across the room to a davenport near a blazing fireplace. A small girl with straight, black hair, seated at the end of the couch looked up at her out of the corner of her eye. Jillian turned toward her and smiled, excited as the child moved closer, reached out, and took her hand.

Abruptly Marta yelled, "Look at me, all of you. We will sing a couple more songs and then I will introduce our guest who is visiting for the weekend."

Delighted, Jillian realized the children could understand English. To her right, two boys whispering in Spanish came to attention when Marta loudly clapped her hands.

"Tommy and Peter, I will only speak to you once more. Now let's sing. What song would you like to sing, Leah?"

Leah smiled and glanced over at Lucia, who was slumping in a chair frowning, her chin resting on her chest. Leah looked at Marta, mumbled a few words, and everyone bust into a song in Spanish. As they sang Jillian studied the sullen Lucia. The resentment she felt earlier for the Indian lifted to be replaced by pity.

After the singing Jillian was introduced to each child. She smiled at the girl holding her hand in a tight grip. Marta noticed and glared at the youngster until reluctantly she withdrew her hand.

"Jill, you are sitting next to Susana. Although she is a big girl of six, she may try to take advantage of you and not leave you in peace," Marta said sounding almost irritated.

Susana moved away and bowed her head. Puzzled, Jillian looked at the girl, then to Sandi who was sitting on the floor next to Tommy and Peter. Sandi merely smiled back.

Pointing to each child, Marta continued, "Elizabeth is my firstborn. She is a twin, ten years of age. Her mother kept her twin brother. Leah is next. She is eight and the result of a rape."

Jillian winced.

Pleased with Jillian's reaction, the woman's eyes twinkled behind her horn-rimmed glasses, and she continued, "Paul is six. His mother decided she didn't want him. You've met Susana. Frank is six. His mother is dead and his dad has too many mouths to feed. Tommy's mother didn't want him either. He's four. Peter is five and illegitimate. His mother is too busy for him, if you know what I mean."

She chuckled and winked, "Sara is two. She has a twin brother. Her parents preferred the boy, so they kept him."

She pointed at the door, "Then there's Lydia. She's already in bed. You'll see her tomorrow. Anyway, she's only one year old and my pride and joy."

"What a handsome group of children," murmured Jillian, smiling at each of the black-haired, brown-faced children now facing her with curious, dark eyes.

"Okay. It is time for bed," said Marta gruffly.

Lifting her head, she yelled, "Flora! Flora, it's time to have the children brush their teeth!"

Sandi jumped to her feet and led them out the door. One by one they filed out, smiling shyly at Jillian until only Lucia, Marta, and Jillian remained.

Marta leaned back in her rocking chair, unabashed pride glowing in her face, "What do you think of my children?"

"I'm impressed with them," Jillian said sincerely. "They seem so well mannered and well adjusted"

A smothered chuckle came from Lucia's direction and Jillian turned to see the familiar smirk working around her mouth. Ignoring Lucia, Marta continued to beam. She vigorously rubbed her hands together.

"If I have to say so myself, the fine characteristics you see in my children are because of the way I have raised them," then the glow disappeared and a dark frown wrinkled her forehead. "However, if by chance you notice any ill manners in them, you can almost always point your finger at Lucia. She delights to take all the good I do for my children and reverse it. She ruins them. You will notice this especially in Leah and the boys. Did you see the way Leah mumbled when I spoke to her? That happens every time I let her go to Quito with Lucia. You would think she's retarded. She acts like that to get Lucia's attention. I could just scream."

Marta glared at the Indian. The smirk on Lucia's face disappeared and her chin dipped again. Jillian searched her mind for something to say and felt foolishly blank.

Marta stared directly at her guest. Then she opened her mouth to explain further, but in a sudden burst of fury, Lucia leaped from

Chapter 2

her chair. Lunging toward Marta, she rattled off a torrent of angry words in Spanish. Jillian gasped, expecting the nurse to fearfully cry out, but instead, the woman calmly watched Lucia stalk out the door slamming it behind her.

As if nothing had happened, Marta said, "You came at an exciting time for the town of Pachuca. This Sunday they are having their annual fiesta celebrating the village's anniversary. You will perhaps see great crowds and hear loud music, but we usually don't make it a practice to mingle with the heathens."

Dumbly, Jillian nodded her head and decided she would question Sandi more about this strange woman.

Marta stood, yawned widely, and walked to the doorway, "I must tuck in the children and give them their goodnight kisses. They won't sleep well without a kiss from me, you know."

Smiling proudly, she left the room.

Chapter 3

Jillian looked imploringly toward heaven and shook her head in wonder. Ignoring a leaden feeling in the pit of her stomach, she glanced around the room. *Nothing special in the way of décor,* she thought. On the wall a baby picture hung at an angle. Furnishings consisted of a small rug in the middle of the wooden floor, a cheap green davenport, and two matching chairs. Marta's rocking chair sat on another thin rug. A television perched on a crudely constructed stand in the corner. Curious, she rose to open a door opposite the fireplace. Turning on the light switch, she saw two large boxes loaded with toys.

"This must be the playroom," she whispered.

Returning to the sofa, she longed for a bed. All the glamour she had expected to find in an orphanage seemed distant from this house.

Muffled noises sounded from the rooms above. She heard a child cry and a sharp command, then total silence. Moments later she heard thumping footsteps and doors clicking shut signaling the children were tucked away. Jillian watched the dying fire until Sandi appeared in the doorway.

"Everything you will need is in the guesthouse where you'll sleep tonight. You'll be alone in the little house where you can sleep as late as you wish in the morning. You must be so tired," she said as she led the way through the dining room. "I heard how cramped the truck was. I've never ridden on the buses or trucks from Pachuca because Marta has a pickup and I have a jeep, but I hear about it each time

Chapter 3

Lucia travels to Quito. I'm sorry I didn't pick you up today, but only one of us can be away from the maternity and outpatient clinic at a time. Here, we'll go through this door."

They passed through the kitchen and Sandi opened the back door.

"It was Lucia's day off, so she went instead. Watch carefully. There are two steps. We had a light back here, but the bulb burned out. Lucia hasn't gotten around to replacing it. We can only buy bulbs in Quito," she explained as she turned to wait for Jillian who was feeling her way. "There's no walkway yet. Here, take my arm."

"Thanks, but I'm all right," Jillian assured her.

They moved at a slow pace down a small incline. Away from the large, shadowy house the sky shimmered. The moon had not yet risen, but the sky glowed with millions of flickering stars.

"I've never seen the sky so beautiful," exclaimed Jillian stopping to look upward.

Sandi paused to stand beside her friend as she softly explained, "You are on the equator and at almost ten thousand feet altitude as you know. Perhaps that makes a difference, but anyway, since we're in the country, away from the city lights, the darkness only accentuates the beauty of the stars. Many times I have found that sitting in the starlight helps make my problems seem insignificant."

Jillian considered asking Sandi if her problems concerned Lucia and Marta, but decided to wait until she was more rested.

Instead, she sighed and remarked, "I have never heard such stillness; just a dog barking in the distance. What do I smell? It is so sweet."

"Oh, it could be hay or alfalfa. Perhaps you smell the fruit trees. We're in the middle of farmland. There are several eucalyptus trees nearby, too," she explained as she pointed east. "Behind us there's a hacienda. You'll see it in the morning."

She chuckled with delight, "Take advantage of these sweet smells. You may find yourself in a few situations where they aren't so pleasant. The guesthouse is fairly new. We built it for a place to get away. Once in a while we take a day off and have no particular place to go. It's nice for reading or for grabbing a catnap."

She felt in the pocket of her nurse's uniform for a key and inserted it in the door, "You can only open the door with a key. It will never be unlocked so no one can walk in and bother you. Keep it with you."

Sandi stepped ahead and flipped on the light switches. Jillian was met with a closed, musty smell and wondered when the house had last been aired. Leaving the door open, she walked through the tiny entry. To the right was the bathroom. The gray cement walls appeared new and wet. A toilet, open shower, and sink had been crowded into the small room. To her left was a square room containing a stuffed chair and two straight-back chairs pulled up to an old scarred table. This room also had not been painted.

Directly ahead, Sandi pushed open a door to reveal the bedroom. Here, cement walls had been painted a pale yellow. Dingy, faded blue flowered curtains covered three windows. Two hospital beds placed end to end barely fit into the narrow room. On the opposite wall a long bureau was pushed up beside the door leading to a tiny closet.

"You'll have to sleep on a bed from the hospital in Quito. We were able to buy a few from them for the clinic and ourselves. You'll find them comfortable because you can adjust your head and feet as you want."

Jillian noticed her purse and jacket had been placed on the bed beside some folded towels and a washcloth. Now there seemed little to say.

"Perhaps you'd like to read before you sleep. If so, you'll find a few books on the window ledge in the next room," Sandi explained. "But now, I must get back to the house to be near the children. We have a woman ready to deliver in the clinic and since Friday is Lucia's day off, Marta needs me to be close by. She lives in a little house next to the clinic and will be there to help the patient when she is ready to deliver. Marta is going to need my help, so I must go to the clinic when she signals me by a bell system Lucia set up. I think you should rest. We'll have all day tomorrow to talk."

"You say there's a woman who's going to deliver a baby tonight in the clinic?" Jillian asked.

She couldn't believe Sandi's relaxed manner.

"Sure. We have deliveries in the clinic all the time. Some times more than one a night," Sandi explained. "You've probably never

Chapter 3

had the chance to see a delivery. If you'd like, I can run down here to call you when the woman is ready. That way you can see the delivery, too. Would you like that?"

"Oh yes. Please call me," pleaded Jillian. "Now I'll not be able to sleep at all."

"She might deliver in the middle of the night. Remember, you've had quite a day," Sandi pointed out. "Can you manage getting up that early?"

"Yes. Please call me," Jillian said excitedly. "I'll be in bed fifteen minutes from now."

Sandi left the key on the bureau saying, "Remember the key. Lucia has the spare. I don't think it would be a very good idea to wake her up to ask for hers, do you?"

They giggled together as Jillian shut the door behind her friend. She found a bucket of cold water close to the sink and remembered how scarce it was in Pachuca. Brushing her teeth, she ignored the rust-colored water and the small bugs in the corners of the bathroom.

The sheets were fresh and white, but the bed was cold and damp. With delight she discovered there was an electric blanket and turned it on high. Do wonders never cease? Who would imagine an electric blanket?

Sleep came slowly. Thoughts of the trip to Pachuca and her meeting with Marta rolled over and over in her mind. The excitement of meeting the children and the upcoming delivery pushed sleep from her, but eventually the thoughts mingled and became unclear. Her subconscious replayed Lucia's leap at Marta and the woman's apparent unconcern. The children sang as they ate pizza and bugs crawled up the walls. A loud pounding at the door brought her to a sitting position. She couldn't believe she had fallen asleep and yet she felt drugged.

"Jill, are you awake? Jill!" Sandi pounded.

"Yes, I'm awake," Jillian answered sleepily.

"You'd better hurry. You might miss the delivery. I have to run. Just walk up to the house and follow the cement sidewalk to the clinic," Sandi said hurriedly.

Miserable from the abrupt awakening, she resisted the temptation to lie back. It would be so easy to drift off again. Perhaps she didn't

While They Sleep

want to see the delivery after all. What if she got sick? Slowly she climbed out of bed and found her slippers, shaking them to loosen any hidden bugs. She turned on the light and wrapped herself in a robe she found hanging in the closet. Grabbing the key, she walked into the night. There was a chill in the air and soon she was shaking uncontrollably from the excitement and cold.

In the distance, bright lights shone from the clinic windows casting shadowy movements on the curtains. She walked the distance, opened the door, and entered a sparkling clean kitchen. Gleaming white counters and cabinets lined one wall. A stainless steel sink was housed under a window opposite a new four-burner stove and washing machine. This is Lucia's domain, she remembered Sandi telling her.

Jillian followed a stream of unintelligible noises amidst groaning and moans. A strong, unpleasant smell grew even stronger as she approached a room beyond the kitchen. Still shaking by the sudden awakening and chill, Jillian leaned against the wall for a moment, her stomach unsettled by the odor of blood and childbirth. The respite helped, and feeling a little better she walked to the doorway of a brilliantly lit room.

Marta, donned in a white surgical robe and gloves stood at the end of a birthing table. Her thick hair fell around her face as she leaned forward to gently massage the patient's abdomen. A darkskinned woman, nude from the waist down lay on the table, her legs elevated in stirrups. In her agony she turned to see the newcomer, a desperate look on her face. Without comprehension, she stared for a moment, then in terrible helplessness she screamed, her back arching upward.

"Push! Push!" Marta yelled in Spanish. "That's right. The head is closer now. I can feel it."

Jillian could make out enough words to understand.

The pain passed and the patient relaxed, breathing heavily in exhaustion. Marta looked up and saw Jillian. Her eyes conveyed tenderness and love she'd not seen at their first meeting and for a moment she almost looked attractive. She marveled at the woman's strange, complex nature.

Chapter 3

Marta grinned, "You are about to see the most wonderful miracle that God can perform. This is when I feel closest to Him. You know, I have delivered about one thousand babies in this clinic and we've never lost a mother."

She leaned her back against the wall, being careful not to touch anything with her gloved hands.

"Excuse me," Sandi appeared behind Jillian in the doorway pulling a bassinet behind her. "Everything is ready in the main room, Marta. Hi, Jill, I see you made it. I wondered if you could wake up."

A sudden scream drove the nurses into action. Sandi stepped onto a small stool next to the table and placed her hands on the woman's abdomen above the baby bulge, as Marta moved into position at her feet.

"Push, push with all your strength," encouraged Marta.

Jillian held her breath as the woman strained and Sandi pressed on the bulge above. In a moment everyone relaxed, and a big grin crossed Sandi's face.

"You've never seen this technique before, have you? We use only a shot of Darvon on these patients. We haven't any other pain killers, so you can imagine the torment they endure," Sandi said as she turned from Jillian back to Marta. "How's the baby, Marta?"

"It is close. Just a couple more pushes."

The nurse adjusted the bucket at her feet with the toe of her shoe and leaned toward the patient, now covered with glistening sweat.

"It will take only another push or two," she explained in Spanish. "If you try with all your might this next time, perhaps the baby will appear."

Sandi translated the conversation to Jillian, as she focused on the mother. Marta pushed the bucket even closer to below the edge of the table, catching the liquid dripping from the birth canal.

Gasping, the patient began to bear down and the nurses jumped to attention. Jillian clenched her fists and jaws until she ached from tension.

"Here it comes, push!" Marta yelled.

The new mother uttered a long, tortured scream and with a great effort, forced the baby's head into view. Spurts of liquid accompanied it, drenching the front of Marta's gown. Quickly Marta grabbed a piece of sterilized cotton to wipe the infant's eyes.

"Okay, now just one more push and it will be here."

With another tremendous effort, the shoulders appeared and the baby slid out covered with a thick, greasy white material. Marta turned him over, holding him high by the ankles. Suctioning his mouth with a sterilized suction, she cleared his passages, and startled him into crying.

"You have a little boy. Oh, he's a nice one," Marta chuckled with glee as she clamped the umbilical cord.

Sandi quickly placed a pin clamp closer to the mother. With a snap, Marta cut the taut cord and plopped the baby in the readied crib. Sandi quickly covered him, wiped his face, and pushed the bassinet into the next room where she would give him his first warm bath.

Instructing the mother not to push again, Marta tugged gently on the cord until the placenta separated from the womb wall and slid into the bucket. She lifted it, examined it carefully for tears, and satisfied, placed it again in the bucket. Clearly pleased, she turned to Jillian who was now sitting on a stool watching through parted fingers, feeling quite faint. Marta dampened a washcloth and placed it in the girl's hands.

"Wipe your forehead. Your nausea will soon pass," she laughed.

Jillian giggled with embarrassment, "Thanks. I'm much better."

Standing on shaky legs, she walked toward the door, "I want to see the baby."

Watching Sandi finish bathing him, gently drying the little body, she shook her head in wonder as she handed him to her.

"Here, you can dress him," Sandi said as she pointed to a small, blue flannel gown.

"Oh," exclaimed Jillian. "Don't leave me. He's so little."

Sandi chuckled and left. *He's just ten minutes old*, Jillian mused. *Shortly he and his mother will be in bed together and the lights will be turned off. Marta and Sandi will quickly fall asleep, but I doubt that I will be sleepy. I think I have just seen something that will forever change my life.*

Chapter 4

A balmy Saturday passed rapidly. Jillian saw little of Marta and Lucia, but she talked with Sandi as they watched the children at play. The two friends sat comfortably in a large sand-pile littered with toys, running their hands through the warm grains. Occasionally, one of the children came over to hug Sandi or rest on her lap.

"It is so clear how much these children love you," Jillian commented after witnessing another endearing hug.

"Yes," Sandi fixed her gaze upon them and muttered wistfully, "Isn't it amazing how much love they can show when it's reciprocated?"

Jillian looked quizzically at her friend, tempted to ask her what she meant, but Sandi had fallen silent.

After the midday meal, the two took a short walk during the children's nap. Jillian recognized an earnest desire in her companion to serve the residents of this distant land, denying herself many conveniences as well as close contact with her family. She understood this, for the same desire had also drawn her to Ecuador. However, when Jillian laid her head on the pillow that night, she had a gnawing feeling that Sandi was hiding something from her. Could all her cheerfulness be a veil for sorrow? During their walk she gathered enough nerve to ask about her relationship with Marta and Lucia, but a shadow seemed to pass over her and Sandi carefully skirted the issue. Jillian pondered this until sleep overcame her.

Sunday dawned brightly. The air was filled with the songs of birds and crowing of roosters. Looking at the battered, ticking clock on the bureau, she noted it was barely six o'clock. Lying back on the pillow, she stared at a crack in the ceiling. A crack in a new ceiling, she wondered drowsily. Where had someone dug up those ugly curtains? She pushed them back to gaze out the window at fields of green wheat. Thrust into the deep blue sky, the Andes Range loomed behind the guest house.

Concentrating on two huts that appeared as specks in the distance, she imagined what the lives of the families were like. When a woman delivered her babies, where could she go for help? Did she perform the birth alone in her cold house? Or what if someone became ill? There probably were no doctors nearby. What about witchdoctors? She had heard there were a few in the area. What happened if someone died? Did they bury their loved ones in the mountains or in a communal cemetery?

In the distance she heard strange music. What was it she heard, flutes and trumpets? There was also the sound of an unknown instrument. The melody was almost drowned out by the heavy drum beats. The sound died and all she heard were the bird's songs. Suddenly the peculiar music reached her ears again, floating in and out on the waves of the breeze. She hopped to the floor and scanned the horizon. Marta had mentioned a fiesta in Pachuca. *Certainly they started it a bit early,* she thought.

Standing on the doorstep, she looked toward the town of Pachuca but saw nothing. She dressed quickly, grabbed the key and walked passed the main house and clinic. Approaching the property gate, she watched as crowds of people passed below on the road. Everyone seemed to be in a state of anticipation, speaking and laughing softly among themselves. The men led, with the women following and the children close behind. Thin dogs sniffed their way in and out of the groups searching for food. A woman saw Jillian and returned her wave and gave her a shy smile.

With sudden inspiration, she tried to open the gate enclosing the private compound area and found it lock. Hiking her skirt above her knees, she climbed over the white picket fence and found a secluded rise above the road. She removed her sweater, placed it on the damp grass and sat to listen to the music. A whistling firecracker burst overhead releasing puffs of smoke that drifted off in the breeze.

Chapter 4

An hour passed before she felt compelled to return to the main house for breakfast. She was anxious to see the children. Approaching the house, a child's cry of terror halted her. Thinking someone was hurt, she rushed to open the door. Sobbing, Tommy scampered up the stairs with Marta screaming after him. The alarming scene paralyzed Jillian until she noticed Lucia watching her from the dining room doorway. Gaining her composure, she walked passed her and went into the crowded room. Sandi sat at her place, a frown clouding her face. She glanced up to see Jillian and affected a quick smile.

"Hi. Find a chair," Sandi invited. "Breakfast will be ready in a moment."

Jillian pulled out a chair next to Susana.

"Tommy is going to get a spanking," the child across from Jillian leaned forward and looked at Lucia out of the corner of her eye, then lowered her voice. "He spilled water on the bathroom floor when he was washing his hands before breakfast."

Jillian waited for more information, but Susana began drinking from her glass of milk. Puzzled, she looked around at the other children, then toward Sandi who was now helping Elizabeth serve scrambled eggs and toast. Everyone but Lucia was ignoring her. The Indian stared at her unflinchingly until Jillian felt a wave of fear sweep through her.

Lucia doesn't disguise her hatred for me, she thought. *She treats me like an intruder. What a strange and terrible household.*

In that moment Jillian forgot the wonders of the morning and the miracle of the baby's birth. She longed to be back in Quito.

In some far room Tommy was crying and she cringed. Without a word, Sandi finished serving the children and everyone ate in silence. The strain of unspoken words was visible on their lowered faces.

Marta appeared in the doorway and sat down at her place. She sighed, smiled at Jillian, and tore into her food. A few moments later, Tommy entered the room, sat down, and attempted to swallow spasmodic sobs.

Marta gently admonished him, "Be quiet, Tommy, and eat your breakfast."

Jillian watched the child eat without appetite, sobbing in hiccups.

"Flora, come here." Marta leaned back and yelled into the kitchen.

The maid stood in the doorway, looking toward Jillian, "Buenos días, Señorita Jillian. Si, Señorita Marta?"

"Flora, go in the downstairs bathroom and clean up that mess on the floor. I told Tommy not to play in the water and when I went to find him, there he stood with water dripping all over the floor. He'll never learn."

Tommy looked up, a deep red flush creeping across his face, "Mommy, I didn't play. The soap slipped and I tried to catch it."

Marta fastened her eyes on the boy, stood, and walked toward him. Terror gripped him and a sob stuck in his throat. She slapped him.

"If I said you were playing, you were playing. Don't you ever talk back to me, especially in front of a guest."

A burning anger toward Marta pulled Jillian from her chair and she stepped toward Tommy. She was shocked to see Sandi's eyes plead with her not to get involved. Reluctantly she returned to her place. The only sounds were the little boy's sobs. The sudden tension made her stomach churn in rebellion and she couldn't finish eating the food on her plate. Closing her eyes, she waited for the emotion to pass. Sounds of gulping food forced her eyes open. Marta was filling her mouth as if nothing had happened. Jillian turned toward the end of the table. Lucia was still watching her with a smile similar to the one she had seen when she'd first arrived in Pachuca.

Hostility had disturbed the warm, placid morning, and breakfast was completed in silence. Even when the children drifted away, Jillian felt heaviness in the room from unspoken words and unshed tears.

Sandi retreated to her room, while Marta and Lucia walked to the clinic and disappeared behind closed doors.

At loose ends, Jillian went into the playroom and surveyed the scene. Eight pairs of eyes turned in her direction. She was struck by the combination of delight and caution in them. Pulling a stool against the wall, she sat, preparing to watch them play. Immediately Susana stood, ran shyly toward her on tiptoes, and without a word sat at her feet. With a surge of affection, Jillian moved the stool aside to sit on the floor.

As if a signal had sounded, the room's entire population ran toward her, touching her face, feeling her hair, hugging her neck, and planting kisses on her cheeks.

Chapter 4

Overwhelmed by the demonstration, she laughed aloud and gasped for breath. Encouraged, the smaller ones ran to bring gifts of toys, while the older children sat in contented bliss until a soft, urgent voice cut through the noise and Elizabeth looked up to see Flora place Lydia on the floor.

"What did Flora say?" Jillian asked. "I couldn't hear her."

"Oh, Mommy doesn't like us to..." Elizabeth began, her voice trailing off. "Flora just said not to make so much noise and not to bother you so much."

"But I don't mind. You don't bother me a bit."

Bewildered, she noticed the older children back away and return to their games. From across the room, they looked enviously at the younger children still clinging to her. Feeling uncomfortable, she said her good-byes and with all eyes watching her, left. Frustrated, she fled from the main house to her room and sank down on the hospital bed.

Staring at the crack in the ceiling, she sighed in despair. This is a terrible place. It was a house filled with pain and fear. She was thankful the weekend was almost over.

Drifting in and out of sleep, the time passed until a gentle knock pulled her to a sitting position.

"Jill, are you in there?"

"Is that you, Sandi?"

"Yes."

Jillian swung her legs over the high bed edge, hopped to the floor, and opened the door.

"Do you want to come to dinner now?" Sandi asked

"Not if it's a repeat of this morning."

"I'm sorry about that, Jill. Please come. This is our best meal of the week."

"Is there a chance we can talk together after lunch?"

Sandi hesitated, "Of course we can, if not after lunch, then sometime this afternoon." She grinned sheepishly, "I guess I've had my mind on a few things, and I've left you alone unintentionally. I'm sorry. Yes, we'll have that talk. Perhaps there are a few things you should know. I'll see you in a minute. Okay?"

She waved and walked toward the house. Jillian frown and then shrugged. She splashed cold water on her face and combed her hair. Checking the skirt and sweater top she had worn that morning, she decided they would pass for the afternoon, too.

As Sandi had promised, great care went into the preparations for Sunday's midday meal. Jillian felt hungry for the first time since her arrival. Fried chicken, baked potatoes, corn on the cob, and a large green salad were consumed with gusto.

Like that morning, the room was silent and oppressive, but she decided to let nothing bother her until she talked with Sandi. Lucia sat in a dark mood, picking at her food, while Marta ate hungrily, her eyes riveted to her plate. Sandi seemed anxious for the children to finish and go down for their afternoon nap. Finally, she ushered out the last child and disappeared. Jillian ate the remainder of her homemade banana ice cream, wondering why Sandi was behaving so strangely. After waiting several minutes for her friend to return, she walked to the guest house.

She was reading when she heard a pounding at the door. Sandi stood in the doorway with suspiciously red-rimmed eyes, but entered smiling.

"Marta would like for you to go with her to the fiesta today. She wants to show you a little of Pachuca life."

"Go with Marta?" Jillian asked stupidly. "Are you going?"

"No, I must stay here. Lucia is going to the plaza to look around. She will probably stop to see a bullfight. Of course Marta doesn't know that. She has so many objections to Lucia going off to fiestas. Anyway, Lucia asked me to stay here so she'd have a chance to sneak away."

"Who else is going?" Jillian asked, dreading to be alone with Marta.

"I think just you. Why don't you go? Maybe you can get to know each other a little."

Sagging with disappointment, she muttered, "I don't want to get to know her."

Sandi watched her for a while then said quietly, "We'll talk later. I promise."

Chapter 5

Marta drove her new pickup into the center of Pachuca. Jillian was stunned by the hordes of people lining the streets. The quiet, proper Indians she had seen that morning were now creating a great deal of noise. Studying the groups at closer range she saw that many of them held whiskey bottles.

This was her first opportunity to see the town in daylight. She noticed the weathered, aged houses, public buildings, and roads. The church stood back from the street, crumbling and in need of paint. A modern addition had been built onto the ancient building. At one side of the long walkway leading to the church door, a section of land had been set apart for large family tombs.

Assembled on the walkway was an orchestra of weary, dark-skinned Indians, some of whom banged on drums, while others played trumpets and flutes. A small group of Indians danced, weaving in and out of a circle performing a strange stomping motion. Their exaggerated plodding movements revealed their drunkenness. Bobbing babies strapped to their mother's backs slept or watched their siblings play games alongside the dancers.

Impatiently, Marta honked the horn and slowly maneuvered through the crowd, urging the dancers aside.

"Get out of the way," she howled, poking her head out the window.

"Perhaps if we turn to the right and go around the plaza, we'd be able to get through. The crowd is thinner down there," suggested Jillian as she tensely gripped the armrest and leaned forward.

Marta snapped her head around and laid on the horn. She put the transmission into reverse and moved backward at a snail's pace until she could manipulate the truck around the corner. Making impatient gestures, she finally found a place at the curb, and sighing deeply, stopped the motor.

"Oh my, what an experience this is. We probably shouldn't have come to town. I always feel peculiar when I get too close to their revelries," Marta said as she laid both hands on the steering wheel and shook her head sadly. "But I just wanted you to have a chance to see what I have to deal with here in Pachuca. It's not easy, Jill, living with all this drunkenness, sickness, and debauchery."

"Don't you find pleasure among the people at all?" Jillian asked, wondering why Marta had made a commitment to them if she didn't want to be a part of the culture.

"Child, I'm not here to enjoy. I'm here to help. You will learn fast enough that there is nothing to enjoy. There is nothing but hard, hard work. The hot sun, the indifference and a broken heart for a thankless job are your rewards. But who else will do it? Who wants to live this way?"

"I do. That's why I'm here," Jillian said passionately.

Marta threw back her head and laughed.

"Oh, my dear, how many times have I heard a young thing like you come to Ecuador and speak such commitments, such honorable ideals," she said as she shook her head and looked at the plaza. "Come back and talk to me in ten years. I guarantee you will be burned out."

"I don't think so. I really wanted to come to Ecuador. This decision wasn't made overnight," Jillian assured Marta. "I planned this as my future for many years."

The noise from the orchestra became louder as the small band moved around the plaza to interest more dancers. Jillian turned in her seat to gain a better vantage point.

"A fiesta is just another excuse to drink," Marta explained as she studied Jillian carefully. "Liquor is the ruination of these people."

After no response from Jillian, Marta sat back to enjoy the warmth of the sun. Fascinated, Jillian watched the large family groups milling about eating roasted potatoes, pork skin, and drinking bottled beer.

Chapter 5

"Do you come from a large family?" Marta asked breaking the silence.

"I have one sister, Shari, and two brothers, David and Ken, all of them married. Right now all I have is one nephew named Russell. He is Ken's son and my darling," Jillian said with a smile. "I have wonderful parents who support me completely, but Russ was the hardest person for me to leave at home. He will soon be three years old."

"If it was so difficult, why did you leave him?" Marta asked.

"How can you ask me that? You're here," Jillian said as she studied the nurse. "Maybe I should ask you the same thing. Why are you here?"

Marta gave the girl a defensive look, "You don't have to question me. I'll be glad to tell you. It was my duty. I understood the need when I heard about the poverty and disease running rampant in South America. I volunteered and sacrificed."

"I don't see this as a sacrifice," Jillian said passionately. "It is more of a blessing to be here."

"Oh, you are a dear innocent child," Marta answered as she unleashed a high-pitched giggle that caused her thick hair to bounce.

"Marta, I am not a child. I am old enough to understand that I'm here to do what I can to help. I have no intentions of returning to the United States, at least not for a long while."

"Ah, I see you've left a door open, however," Marta said giving the girl a coy look, her leg thumped nervously. "You know that most people who have such good intentions don't remain. They usually leave at the end of the first year."

"Perhaps they have a good reason. This lifestyle can't be suitable for everyone," she said as a weary tone in Jillian's voice brought relief to the tension that had been building between them.

Perceptively, Marta noticed and laughed easily, "We are glad to have you visiting us. I hope that you won't stay away after this weekend. Whatever caused you to choose Ecuador?"

"I read a book about the Ecuadorian jungle Indians, in particular the Jivaros and Aucas and haven't been the same since," Jillian said with renewed excitement in her voice. "It affected me enough to quit my job and move here."

45

"Do you know what you'll be doing in the future?" Marta asked. "Will you be moving to the jungle?"

Jillian's heart began beating rapidly, "I'm not sure right now. A door will open for me, I'm sure. Perhaps you already know I come from a strong Christian background. That is one of the reasons I have an interest in these people."

For a long moment Marta remained quiet. She seemed to be studying the dancers, who were weaving their way down the cobblestone road.

"You know, these people don't understand birth control methods. That's the problem here," Marta explained. "Liquor and too many births keep me busy in the outpatient and maternity clinics."

Jillian glanced at her. Maybe Marta hadn't been listening, but more likely she had lost interest in the conversation. Because of her growing interest in the children and desire to be a part of the Pachuca community, she was beginning to be concerned how Marta felt about her. In spite of Lucia and Marta and the extreme emotions she had witnessed, she was beginning to care for the children and this little village. But should it matter how Marta feels? Visions of the children sprang into her mind. Maybe she could help them somehow. She needed somewhere to put down her roots. She was tired of waiting for a place to work. Afraid to suggest she might join Sandi in her work with the children, she sat back and tried to relax.

The unfolding drama and primitive customs that made up this strange and backward country was more than she could have imagined the previous week. It was evident that Quito was becoming modern with ideas and ways of living adopted from America and Europe; the modern coupled with the ancient. Quito's residents had been shaped by tradition, but were feebly attempting to break the bonds that held them to the past and change the face of Quito. But in these mountains and beyond the eastern ranges, deep in the jungles, the life of the Ecuadorian would remain forever unchanged. Jillian felt deeply moved to have been given the opportunity to become one of them. She reflected on her good fortune to be in a tiny pueblo almost ten thousand feet above sea level, a few short miles from the equator, studying the lifestyle of these people she had grown to love through library books.

Chapter 5

She was pulled back to the present with the appearance of a shy woman holding an infant in her arms. Marta stuck her head out the window and conversed in rapid Spanish.

Turning to Jillian, she explained, "The baby needs an injection for a high fever. I've told her that she must go to our outpatient clinic because I didn't think to bring any medicine with me. Sandi or Lucia will be there to help her."

Jillian smiled to herself, imagining Lucia watching the bullfights at the corner lot behind the marketplace.

"What is that group passing in front of us?" she asked as her attention was drawn to several young men dressed in matching white gym shorts and tee shirts.

The tallest man carried a volleyball under his arm and in the midst of a jovial conversation, turned to the pickup and gave Marta a hostile look.

Marta shrugged, "They are the dregs of this community; never working, always playing. They are the children of landowners."

Jillian watched the tall man and was struck by his beauty. Almost a head above his companions, he commanded attention. His hair was lighter than theirs, his eyes almost a light brown. She was fixed on his well-proportioned face gracing a straight nose and soft, full mouth. She would enjoy watching him talk, she knew. But his antagonism toward Marta pressed his mouth into a thin line and his eyes darkened like hard stones. He stopped and waited for a group of girls to catch up with him, and in a possessive way, reached down to lay his free arm across the shoulders of one attractive and vivacious teenager. Her long, shining hair caught the sunlight and gleamed as her healthy face reflected pride and love. Slim and graceful and well-proportioned, she seemed within marriageable age. Jillian was glad to see that at least this young woman appeared to have enjoyed good nourishment and love.

The girl hugged him, looked up into his face, and saw his stern appearance. Following his glare, she saw Marta and pulled him toward the waiting group of young people.

"Who was that attractive couple, Marta?" Jillian asked.

The look of despair on Marta's face surprised her.

"Covering it quickly," Marta chuckled. "Who? Oh, that was Rolando and Elena Martinez. They live across from the marketplace, two of the more well-to-do residents here in Pachuca."

"Are they married?" Jillian asked.

"Oh my goodness, no," Marta said quickly. "They are brother and sister. It's a mess really, not normal at all. He acts like he's married to her, almost like he's afraid she'll get away from him or something."

"She looks old enough to be married in this culture," Jillian observed. "Look at all the young women with babies on their backs."

Marta sat in silence for several seconds. Jillian waited, hoping she would tell her more.

"She's too young for marriage. She's probably only thirteen or more likely fourteen in another month or so," Marta added and another long silence followed.

"Are their parents living? Why does he act so possessive?" inwardly Jillian shrank against the fierce look Marta gave her.

"Yes. Their father is a drunkard. The night Elena was born Rolando was unable to get his father to drive them to Quito for the delivery. These people don't have a bit of sense. So her mother chose to have the baby in a witchdoctor's home. As a result, she suffered a stroke and has been an invalid ever since. I guess because of that, Rolando raised Elena. I don't know. They have family in Pachuca, uncles and aunts, but for some reason, Rolando wanted the responsibility," Marta added "Silly, the whole thing is silly."

On the contrary, Jillian was feeling great admiration for the young man, but she gulped, fearful of her next question, "Why did he look at you with such hostility?"

Marta assumed an expression of innocent surprise, "You must be mistaken. He didn't look hostile to me."

She sighed deeply and reached for the ignition key, "I guess we'd better get back to the house."

For Marta the subject was closed, but for Jillian the atmosphere was now so charged with emotion she couldn't let it drop from her mind.

They pulled away from the curb when a sudden series of shouts caught their attention. A terror-stricken man ran out in front of them waving his arms causing Marta to stomp on the brakes. She waited

Chapter 5

for him to approach the window. Jillian looked where the man was pointing and saw a woman hobbling toward them, clutching her abdomen.

Marta spoke rapidly to him. Then he turned to help the woman over to the passenger side. Opening the door, he boosted the woman onto the seat and Jillian scrambled closer to Marta as the horrible truth dawned on her, the woman was about to deliver a baby.

"Jill, listen to me. This woman's baby is trying to emerge right now. If she pushes, we'll have it born on the floor of this cab. Grab hold of her legs and keep them together until we get back to the clinic," Marta commanded. "The last thing I need is blood on my new pickup seat."

Dismayed, Jillian stared at Marta hoping her last comment was an exaggeration. She reached down and saw the woman's dirty, stained legs where her water had soaked her limbs and clothes, and hesitated.

The man climbed into the rear of the pickup and sat near the window of the cab. Laying on the horn, Marta pulled into the street. Startled, drunken Indians lifted bleary eyes to the truck and moved clumsily away. When the pickup neared the end of the street, the woman suddenly screamed and threw herself backward against the bench seat. Her legs flew up and Jillian fought to hold onto them.

"Grab her legs, Jill," Marta shouted. "Grab them!"

"Oh, God, help me," Jillian prayed as she struggled to gain control, bending over to grasp the woman's jumping ankles.

Cautiously the truck plowed through the crowds while Marta leaned on the horn and screamed in Spanish for the crowd to part.

She began chanting to help Jillian from becoming hysterical, "Keep those legs together. Keep those legs together."

The woman went into another contraction as Marta told Jillian, "We have nothing with us to cut the cord if the baby is born. If we don't get it breathing, it could die. Jill, hold her legs together. We've got to get her to the clinic."

Jillian fought the writhing woman as they drove to the outskirts of the crowds, passed the marketplace, and turned toward the clinic. Marta suddenly hit the brakes barely missing a man and two boys trying to guide an errant herd of bulls back into the outdoor stadium.

The bewildered animals milled about in all directions, confused by the honking. Marta was furious.

Jillian crouched, terrified by the woman's thrashing legs as another contraction shook her. The truck's fender pushed a frightened bull against the mud wall that lined the narrow road. Turning, the indignant animal ran in front of the truck and butted the wall. Marta pounded on the window behind her. The man leaped from the pickup bed to the nurse's side.

"Get those animals out of the way," she screamed.

Croaking, Jillian pleaded, "Perhaps we ought to let the baby be born. Can't it be harmed this way?"

"I don't know," Marta said with frustration. "Just hold on. We're almost there."

"Oh, Lord, I can't much longer," Jillian prayed out loud.

"Don't push, Señora. Don't push," Marta exhorted. "Look, we can get by the bulls now. Let's go."

She drove off with the patient's husband running behind. Reaching the entrance of her property, Marta gunned the motor and turned up the steep driveway between two high mud walls. Two huge, stray bulls blocked the closed gates. Marta stomped on the brakes to avoid colliding with them. They turned their large heads in bland observation.

"Oh no," howled Marta, pulling at her hair.

Jillian trembled from the strain of holding the woman down.

Gasping for breath, the patient's husband ran up from behind the truck and threw himself at the bulls until they moved away. With a flick of the wrist, he flung the bolt aside and the two gates sprang back. He leaned against the mud wall as Marta pushed on the gas pedal. The truck jumped forward and stalled. Backing to the bottom of the drive, the perspiring nurse pumped the pedal until the motor roared to life and lunged forward just missing the man flattened against the wall. The truck raced to the clinic with Marta pushing on the horn. Lucia opened the door and peered out. Jillian sighed with relief as Marta jumped out, rushed to her side of the truck and opened the door.

"Take your wife's arms," she commanded the nervous husband. "Jill, you grab her legs."

Chapter 5

Lucia held the door open as the nurse ran in, followed by the husband and Jillian carrying the patient. At the labor room door they stopped, stunned. Beside the delivery table stood Sandi garbed in a white uniform in the midst of another birth.

"Where shall we go?" cried Jillian.

"Put her on a bed. This one is occupied," laughed Sandi.

"In here! In here!" Marta yelled.

Jillian and the man lumbered forward with their heavy cargo and entered the patient's ward. Just as she plopped on a bed, Marta grabbed the baby as it popped out.

Jillian walked to another bed, slumped onto it and sobbed, "I can't believe what just happened."

She wiped at her eyes while tears of relief rolled down her face.

"I just pray the baby is all right," moaned Marta as she washed and clothed the crying infant. "We'll have to hope the trauma wasn't too much for him."

Meanwhile Jillian left to find Sandi rinsing off her bloodied gloves. On her hands and knees Lucia was cleaning the labor room.

"Looks like you had quite an afternoon, Jill," Sandi grinned, tossing the gloves into a bucket to be washed and sterilized.

"I'm surprised to see everyone at home," Jillian muttered, moving closer to the nurse at the sink. "Why is Lucia here? I thought she was up at the plaza. Why was the gate closed? You know, that was the last straw."

Sandi checked to see if Marta was within earshot, "Lucia was out, but I sent someone up to the stadium to get her. When she arrived, there were twenty bulls in our front yard."

She giggled, giving Lucia a mischievous look, "I wish you could have been here to see her chasing twenty bulls around in circles. About the time she scurried one out and returned to get another, the rascal wandered back into the yard."

"What happened?" Jillian had to laugh, picturing the scene.

Sandi gasped for breath, "It finally took their owner, his son, and Lucia to herd them out. Then they shut the gate."

"I think we met your bulls in the road, Lucia," Jillian chuckled and turned to leave.

Sandi wiped her hands carefully and followed her, "After the children are in bed tonight, why don't we have our talk? Right now, perhaps you would be willing to help Flora and Elizabeth with the dinner? I'll be there shortly."

"Sure. I'd be glad to," Jillian answered.

As she walked out the door, Lucia glanced up from the floor she was cleaning and smiled. This time, Jillian noticed there was no disdain in her look.

Chapter 6

With the last child in bed, Marta and Lucia departed for the clinic and Jillian was left alone. Climbing the stairs, she knocked on Sandi's bedroom door.

"Come in," Sandi greeted her warmly.

Jillian found a chair beside a small oak desk and pulled it forward to face her friend. Sandi was sitting in bed, leaning on a propped pillow with an old magazine open in her lap. Suddenly her foot jerked and she made a grab for it.

"Oh dear, I'm being eaten alive by fleas tonight," she peered under the covers and carefully rolled them back. "Don't move. I'm going to catch this fellow."

Her hand crawled slowly to her shin. The room turned silent as both girls held their breath. With great concentration she reached out and snatched the culprit. Staring at her pinched thumb and forefinger, she parted them slightly with exaggerated slowness. Placing her other thumbnail over it, she squashed it between her nails and flicked the flattened pest into the air.

"There. I don't know why I take the trouble. I feel like I'm covered with them. It's a losing battle," she grinned engagingly. "Perhaps I like the challenge of my wit and skill against theirs."

As if to prove her words, Jillian watched a flea meander across Sandi's shoulder and shuddered, trying not to think of the critters crawling under the blankets. Replacing the covers, Sandi looked thoughtfully at Jillian.

"I'm glad you came. I have some things on my mind that perhaps we should discuss," she hesitated, searching for words. "As I told you in Quito, I have been thinking of moving to Costa Rica to study advanced Spanish. I don't know, but I feel there is something special in store for me."

"Why would you need more lessons in Spanish? You sound very capable right now," Jillian asked.

"How do you know that I speak good Spanish?" teased Sandi. "Are you an authority?"

Jillian scratched her nose and grinned, "Not exactly. Any headway I thought I had made at school in Quito flew out the window on the trip to Pachuca. But already I'm understanding more and more by listening to Marta and the patients."

"Good. I think it was the experience you had on the trip here that confused you. I think you will be all right as soon as you become more secure."

She cleared her throat and Jillian noticed her agitation, "Do you know yet what your future plans are?"

Jillian shrugged her shoulders, "No, I really don't. I'll complete this term of schooling, but I haven't thought beyond that."

"When is the end of the term?" Sandi asked.

"The middle of March," Jillian responded wondering why her friend was so interested.

"What are your feelings about the work here? You probably feel something for the children, don't you?" Sandi asked Jillian watching to see her response. "You seem to have an interest in the mountain people."

"Yes," Jillian replied slowly, choosing her words carefully. "I do like the children and could even come to love them, but my heart is in the jungle. You know that."

"You have to pass through the mountains to get to the jungle. There is a terrific need here with these children. I need a strong and capable person to take my place. I thought you could be that person," Sandi said biting her lip.

Jillian felt her heart thumping, "All that is true, and it would be so easy to admit that I've considered living in Pachuca since coming here, but I have to be honest with you."

Chapter 6

She almost faltered under Sandi's intense gaze, "There are things going on in this household that I can't understand."

A shadow crossed Sandi's face.

"If I were to consider it, I must know what's going on," Jillian continued as she watched Sandi's face. "It won't be easy to reach a decision, but what you say may help me."

The nurse's fingers played with the magazine, "You have all the qualifications. You come from a good, solid family background. The fact that you're here proves that living among these people is your number one priority."

Jillian nodded and Sandi continued, "Actually, the first problem we have is not whether you'll be willing to work here. It is convincing Marta that she needs help. She feels that she and Lucia can handle everything. Of course, she knows better and I know better. She's just more comfortable working without outside help."

"Why does she take in children? I have the feeling it's the children she's not comfortable with," Jillian asked.

Sandi raised her eyebrows, knowing what she shared next could make a difference in Jillian's response to her suggestion to work with Marta and Lucia.

"Frankly, I don't know why she has the children. Maybe it's her way of getting attention from her sponsors, but she has them and believes that she can make them miraculously perfect. Of course, we know this is foolishness. No child is perfect," she said nervously fingering the blanket.

Now they were moving closer to the crux of the matter, "Do you feel she is too strict on the children? Is it necessary to spank a little boy for dripping water on the floor?"

"I'm not going to say anything against Marta. She's given her life to these people, and she's a very good nurse. Years ago she came here before there were any conveniences in this part of the country. She went through difficult training and chose a hard field. I could show you some very nice homes in Quito where Americans live. She could have chosen to live there, but she chose this area," Sandi carefully explained.

"You'll notice that she spends very little money on herself or the house," Sandi continued, her eyes focused on Jillian. "Most of it goes to the children. You ask why she's strict with the children. I would say it's probably because she wants to perform her job well. I don't like it any more than you do. I was raised in a loving family where everyone was happy and our obedience was nurtured. Apparently, from what little I know, Marta has never experienced real love from her parents or siblings. I think she must have suffered in her childhood and doesn't know how to display love. So she resorts to the only method she understands, heavy discipline."

"You sound as if you're defending her actions," Jillian said.

"I can't feel any differently," Sandi said. "I respect her."

Jillian studied her friend wondering if she was being completely honest, "Why do you think she needs someone like me to take your place?"

"I don't think she realizes yet that she and Lucia can't handle everything. Something would have to go, the outpatient clinic, the maternity clinic or the children. She'll soon know this. I think that she will believe, as I do, that you are the one to take my place."

With her head hung low, she shielded her face and muttered, "I must be leaving soon. I'm no longer at peace here. There must be something else for me in Costa Rica."

She lifted her head and with a pleading voice asked Jillian, "Would you at least consider the possibility that you will fit in and be able to care for the children?"

"How can I promise you this when I'm not sure that Marta will accept me?" Jillian asked honestly. "I can't do anything about that."

Hiding her face in her hands, Sandi began to weep great gulping sobs.

Shocked, Jillian scrambled for tissues sitting on the nightstand and placed the box in her hands, "What's the matter? Why are you crying?"

"Because, Jill, I'm not being truthful. I fear for the children. Something isn't right in this house and I don't know for sure what it is," she dabbed at her eyes and moaned in despair. "I've tried talking to Marta, but she somehow avoids the issues. We've come to the point where I can barely look her in the face. I've written her letters hoping she'd have to understand how I feel."

Chapter 6

Sandi giggled despite herself, "I even bought a book for her on parenting skills and scribbled what I thought were good points on the borders. She was furious with me. Yet how can I allow myself to think bad things against her?"

Her crying renewed and she took another tissue, "Why does she do the terrible things she does? Why is she destroying these children?"

"Hasn't anyone noticed this before? Am I the only one who has stayed here and wondered why she's so strict?" Jillian asked sharing her friend's concern for the children.

"You weren't supposed to see what happened this morning. You surprised us all by coming in the front door. Most people who come to visit come for an hour or two and then leave," Sandi shared as she breathed heavily through her mouth and flopped down her hands on the bed. "The children aren't punished constantly. It seems to go in cycles. The visitors who have come have seen the results of her work among these people and they leave singing her praises.

"Who knows? Maybe nobody notices anything about the children except how good they are. I've come to the conclusion that most people don't really notice terrible things going on right under their noses. It is as if they are asleep and while they sleep, content in their own worlds, children languish in institutions lonely, sick, and starving for love and attention. This may be a small corner of the universe, Jill, but I refuse to sleep. I refuse to let the suffering pass me by. I won't leave these children alone without genuine care, but I can't let Indians in other countries go without medical care either.

"I've been handicapped here. Primarily, I'm a nurse and I intend to bring sick people back to health for the rest of my life. I'll live in places where no one else wants to go. I'll live in the jungles, in huts crawling with bugs, use outhouses, and eat native food, anything to fulfill the need I have to help the suffering humanity while others sleep."

Jillian blinked back her own tears, "But, Sandi, that's how I feel. I don't care about a life of ease. I want to help people."

She leaned forward, "Please let me think this through. If God wants me here, He'll open all the doors and there will be no doubt in anyone's mind."

While They Sleep

Sandi blew her nose and sighed heavily, "One more thing you must consider. If you decide to stay you must never reveal any opposition to Marta. Try to support her and if possible grow to love her. In that way you will avoid a lot of problems that I've blundered into. Just agree with whatever she says. You'll keep her happy and protect the children. She won't do crazy things to them if you're around."

"What do you mean, 'crazy things?" Jillian asked, really concerned about what Sandi was sharing.

"I don't mean crazy exactly, but sometimes she loses her temper and does things without thinking," Sandi quickly added. "She's in charge here and believe me no one will ever usurp her authority."

A thoughtful pause turned into a lengthy silence and then Jillian said, "I want to talk to you about Lucia. I really don't understand her. She has given every indication that she hates me, but today she actually gave me a friendly smile."

Sandi shrugged and blinked her red, teary eyes, "Lucia is someone I don't understand yet myself. I've lived with her for several years and she's still a mystery. I know Marta has complete control over her. Lucia idolizes Marta to the point where I think she might even kill for her. A missionary family brought her out of the jungle when she was nothing more than an ignorant Indian girl. They felt it was time she was introduced to the working community in Quito. The American hospital accepted her and trained her in medicine. The only schooling she has had was a six-week course in the hospital in Quito where you met Lucia last Friday.

It was very difficult at first because she had lived in the jungle. She had never turned a door handle or turned on a water faucet. Just getting in and out of a vehicle was a terrible culture shock for her. Everything she knows is from experience, and you can believe me when I say that she has learned a lot. Marta was a nurse in the hospital at that time and took a liking to her. When Marta moved to Pachuca she brought Lucia with her. But even with all this, Lucia is a very sad woman."

"Sad?" Jillian exclaimed with a skeptical grunt. "I call her scary. Why she almost attacked Marta the other night. Marta accused her of spoiling Leah and suddenly Lucia jumped out of her chair. I thought for a minute she was going to beat her, but Marta just went on talking

Chapter 6

to me as if nothing had happened. Lucia disappeared all day Saturday and until this afternoon I feel she acted like the world was against her."

Hitting her forehead with the palm of her hand Sandi gave Jillian a frustrated look, "I'm so tired of hearing about Lucia and Leah. There is a very strange bond between them. I don't quite understand that either. When Marta was on vacation in the United States several years ago, Lucia attended Leah's delivery and made the decision on her own to take the child in. Lucia and Leah adore each other. The girl's mother is deaf and mute, and as the story goes, was raped. Marta has never cared for Leah, maybe because she had no say in her coming here or maybe because she's jealous of the bond between Leah and Lucia. I don't think the child is very bright, but I wonder if she's faking that for attention. I wish a stateside doctor could examine her."

She shrugged and adjusted the pillow, "We often see outbursts from Lucia. She has dark moods and loses her temper. This never seems to have an effect on Marta because she knows that Lucia would never hurt her. She just goes off for a couple days and when Marta starts to miss her, she goes after her. They make up and all is well again."

Smiling, she lowered her voice, "I can't help but think that Lucia fakes her anger so they can make up. It's her way of getting attention. You say she smiled at you. She's softening toward you."

Nodding her head, she blew her nose again, "Now, to answer your question about Lucia. I don't think Lucia hates you. She dislikes guests because they take Marta's attention away from her. If you hang around a little, she'll get used to you. When you can find time, you should talk to her. Perhaps you two can become friends."

"What would you think could happen if I really tried to become friends with her? From what you've told me, they seem to be a rather strange couple and probably wouldn't care for a third party trying to entrench herself," Jillian asked her friend as she pondered this unusual situation. "Or maybe, that's just what they need, someone to get in the middle so the intensity of their relationship can be shared with the third party."

"You can try. It sounds like a good idea if it works. In fact, I've often wondered if I could do that. But Lucia is a little too much for me and I don't have the emotional energy to handle both of them," Sandi shared candidly as she threw her hands up in the air. "Anyway, spend a week or month thinking about this. It's January and I won't be leaving until someone comes to take my place. You'll be out of school in March. Now, I think you'd better be getting to bed. You'll have to get up early to go home. We'll take you to the train so you won't have to take the bus through the canyon. I'll be in touch with you."

Chapter 7

The night after seeing Marta Brewer sitting there in her brand new truck, Rolando Martinez suffered a restless night filled with memories he had long since tried to suppress with alcohol. That night the memories were so clear, it was like it happened yesterday.

When Rolando was a month into his eleventh year, his mother's labor pains began one late Sunday afternoon. As her pregnancy had been monitored by a doctor in Quito, it became Rolando's responsibility to find transportation. Until this pregnancy, his mother had chosen to remain at home to birth her previous nine children. Helped by a neighbor she had little trouble, but her last produced a stillborn child and a slow recovery. To avoid any further complications, she chose to deliver this baby in a hospital.

"You'll have to find your papa, Rolando," his mother told him between labor pains.

As expected the boy was informed by friends in Pachuca's central plaza that his father had been invited to a party further up the mountain. Late that evening he found him too drunk to accompany his wife to Quito. With a great sense of urgency, Rolando hurriedly descended the pathway alone, running through the plaza and home. He found his mother on the sofa groaning with pain. Kneeling beside her, he wiped her sweating face with the edge of the blanket.

"I sent Geoff to find someone with a truck to carry me to Quito," she gasped.

While They Sleep

Rolando paced the floor, returning to the window to search for Geoff. Each time his mother cried out he covered his ears wincing with sympathetic pain.

Eight-year-old Pablo burst through the door as his younger brother Roberto followed on three-year-old legs.

"Mama, we went to the clinic to find Olivia, but no lights are on. It's all dark," Pablo knelt by the sofa. "The nurse is away from the clinic. Maybe we can go down to see the American nurse."

She shook her head, "No. She won't help me. We all know the gringa nurse won't help anyone who has not gone to her for prenatal care."

Grasping the blanket, she groaned through another contraction, "Maybe I should have gone to her. I never thought I would have this baby without help."

"Pablo, you and Roberto go!" Rolando ordered. "Go to find a midwife that has not been drinking this afternoon. Go up the mountain. Mama and I are going to see if the foreign nurse will deliver the baby."

Turning to his mother, he knelt by her side, "Mama, we have to go to the American clinic."

"It's raining, Rolando. It's raining hard," Roberto yelled from the door.

"Just go. Don't worry about a little rain now. Go!" commanded Rolando.

The boys dashed into the street as Rolando brought a poncho to his mother. Pulling her to an upright position he wrapped her warmly. She swayed and he planted his feet in an attempt to embrace her thick body without losing his balance. A contraction gripped her driving her to a crouching position. Rolando gritted his teeth when she screamed.

"Mama, the pains are coming closer. The baby could come right here and I don't know what to do," Rolando said with wisdom beyond his years. "We must go."

Rearranging her poncho, he tugged at her arm. As they stepped out the door the stinging pellets of windswept rain soaked them before they had crossed the road. Darkness settled around them hiding the familiar scenes. His mother walked slowly, stumbling against the pelting torrent. Guiding her arm, he attempted to wipe

Chapter 7

her face with the palm of his hand. Puzzled he brushed his hand across her mouth again.

"Mama, is your nose bleeding?" he said with fear.

"My head hurts so," she groaned with a sob. "If only I could deliver this baby."

Rolando trembled aware of his mother's high blood pressure. Rage toward his father engulfed him. By rights, his father should be driving his wife to Quito instead of lying in a drunken stupor somewhere in the foothills.

Stopping a moment to let her rest, she leaned heavily against his small frame, "Mama, please, we must go on."

"I can't," she wept in despair. "I can't go on. A pain is coming. I must rest."

"But it's too cold and wet in the rain," he pleaded. "Please try to go on. It's not far now."

"I can't. You go and find the nurse," his mother told him weakly. "Ask if she will come and help me."

"I'm afraid to leave you," he sobbed. "Where will you stay? There is nothing but mud and rivers of water."

"Leave me. There is little time. We can't worry about where I stay. You must find help soon," she said with an urgency that scared Rolando. "Hurry now!"

Hot tears mixed with cold rain ran down his face. Shaking with fear he fell to his knees and moved forward until he reached the edge of the uneven cobblestone road and found a patch of wet grass. Pulling off a frayed sweater he spread it out.

"Mama," he called. "I found a spot for you. Stay until I return. Don't move from here. It's so dark that a car may hit you."

His body shook making his speech difficult. Guiding her to a reclining position, he wrapped the poncho around her and tucked in the edges. Then as though the shackles had been cut free, he ran through the darkness toward the clinic. Rain ran off his head in streams and down his short-sleeved shirt soaking his pants and shoes. Dogs barked from a hut behind the high-walled mud barriers as he sought a moment's shelter beside a gate. His fear and weariness were put aside with the thought of his mother lying helpless and vulnerable to untold dangers.

"Oh God, please help me. It's so dark," he cried aloud.

Suddenly he saw a bright light through a large crack in the common mud wall that surrounded all properties close to the plaza. Feeling his way, he ran his hand over the steep side until he found a branch growing from the structure. Praying it would hold, he pulled himself up to the crack where clods of dirt had worn away. Then running with renewed strength he fought the deep pools of water gathering on the sides of the road and arrived at the metal gate that stood at the top of a steep entrance between two high, dried mud walls. The heavy doors were always left unlocked for patients seeking help. Gasping for breath he hurriedly pulled them open.

A dim light glowed through the window of the gray two-story building. Someone would be there. A long white picket fence divided the width of the clinic barring access to a clump of buildings several meters in the distance. The inner entrance to the maternity hospital was used only by the American nurse and her helpers leaving the clinic patients access to the door facing the road.

Rolando yelled with all his might and pounded on the window. Dogs barked anxiously in the distance. Finally he saw movement in the clinic. After a long, agonizing wait, the door slowly opened.

A woman in her mid-forties appeared, stern and disapproving. The boy fought a rising panic as he viewed Lucia. Contempt showed in her small, cold, black eyes. Her hooked hawk nose accentuated large lips. With short combed back black hair, wide shoulders and small breasts she could have passed as a man.

"What do you want?" she asked angrily as she squinted at him.

"Please come with me. My Mama is having a baby," he despaired at the anxiety in his voice.

"Well I'm not going out in the rain to see your Mama," the clinic door slammed shut.

Rolando beat on the closed door bringing on another chorus of barking dogs. In a state of panic he ran to the end of the clinic and yelled. It had stopped raining, but was growing colder. With an effort he tried to control his shaking.

Just as he was about to give up, he saw the door of a house at the end of the long sidewalk open. The light from the house revealed a woman's shape. He caught his breath with hope as he realized

Chapter 7

she was walking toward the clinic. Time seemed to stand still as the shadow moved under the field lights and again into darkness. Running back to the patient's door, he heard the far entrance open and close. Heavy footsteps approached and the door opened quickly.

Strange tales had circulated far and wide about Marta Brewer. Even with a neglected brush of hair above her mouth and chin, she appeared more feminine than Lucia. She was an American nurse who had arrived in Pachuca twelve years earlier and decided to make it her permanent home. Even though she claimed to have stayed to support the nationals, she remained aloof and mysterious. Stories were passed from hut to hut that she was wealthy due to connections with the United States and in turn this caused her to be a subject of awe.

He felt he could trust her more than Lucia, sensing the nurse had some measure of compassion. Marta's soft brown eyes could look kind at times. Her competent hands caused many a woman to continue delivering babies at the clinic. Now with renewed hope, Rolando greeted her.

"Buenos noches, Señorita. Please come with me. My mama is on the road in great pain. She's about to deliver a baby. She needs your help."

The woman hesitated a moment seeming to contemplate the situation.

"I can't help you. It's raining and I must not catch cold. I have patients in my clinic. What if I become ill? Anyway, I understand your mother has been seeing a doctor in Quito. Why doesn't she go there?"

"Because we couldn't find transportation to Quito tonight," he felt his throat choke with tears and fought them, blinking hard.

Lucia peered over Marta's shoulder and snickered. The nurse turned and without a word stared at the Indian. Finally, Lucia shrugged her shoulders and walked away, stung.

"I'm sorry, but I just don't go out on clinic calls and I don't like to deliver a baby when I haven't given the mother prenatal care. This and because it's rainy and cold," she said squinting down at him. "My goodness, Rolando, there you stand without a coat. Why can't your parents care for you? Sometimes I believe you people would rather live like animals."

Rolando couldn't believe his ears, "But my mama, she's close to delivery and she's ill. Her nose is bleeding and she said her blood pressure is up."

"All the more reason why I can't help you. Now please leave me alone," Marta said. "I have my patients to care for."

The door shut and Rolando sprang to life ramming his fists on the clinic wall, "I hate you! I hate you! Why did you tell us you came to our country to help us? You are nothing but garbage."

Spitting on the door, he screamed, "I will never forget this."

Turning, he ran down the soggy pathway. Upset from his encounter he no longer realized how cold it was. Out of breath he scrambled up the road, slipping and falling until he finally reached the spot where he'd left his mother. Softly he called her, then more loudly. Falling to the road, he moved on his hands and knees to the mud wall.

"I must not be in the right place," he said as he crawled further.

He called again, "Mama! Mama, where are you?"

He stood and walked several meters in both directions, "Mama, please answer me. Mama!"

Panic enveloped him. Could she have died? Thinking he might faint, he rested against the wall a moment. From deep within, large sobs rose to rack his body. What if she crawled out on the road and a car hit her? What if dogs attacked her? What if she delivered the baby alone and had to take it to a neighbor. He screamed in hysteria. Dogs barked as he moved on his hands and knees the length of a block. Soaked, cold and distraught, his head swam with exhaustion.

"I've got to think," he panted, trying to relax. "Could she have returned home? No, she was too weak. It's impossible."

The thought gave him hope. Rising to his feet he started back to his home. He burst through the front door and when not finding her on the sofa he ran into her bedroom. It was empty. Yelling through each room, he found no one. Fear gripped him totally and he fought the urge to vomit.

Without thinking of a coat he ran from the house and up the block to the main plaza. Olivia, the village doctor's aide lived in a large aged two-story dwelling built of dried mud blocks and wood. It stood in a central location directly in front of the main plaza, leaning at a

Chapter 7

comical angle where it had settled after being buffeted by two hundred years of fierce winds, rainstorms, and occasional earthquakes.

Rolando pounded on the door and yelled out a greeting. After a long wait, it was slowly opened by an elderly, heavyset man wearing a stained, cheap business suit frayed with age. His mouth opened in a wide grin revealing two remaining teeth. Don Eduardo went through all the maddening greeting formalities.

Anxious to ask if his daughter, Olivia was home, Rolando rudely interrupted.

"Why no, Rolando, I haven't seen her," he replied, pursing his lips thoughtfully. "Now, where did she go? Let me see. Yes, she was here for a while today. You know, I think she decided to go to Quito tonight. Or, was that last night? No, wait. She might be up at my son, Cesar's house."

The old man spoke slowly, squinting up his eyes and scratching his chin. Rolando pressed his hand to his face, stifling more rudeness.

Breathing deeply, he asked, "Actually, I'm looking for my mama. She's ill and I thought perhaps Señorita Olivia might know where she is."

Shifting his weight from one foot to the other, Don Eduardo suddenly clapped his hands together.

"You know, I think I saw your mama go to the church tonight. Wasn't she your mama I saw?"

But Rolando was gone. Don Eduardo stared after him, shrugged and yawned. Rolando knew of one place he could ask. Someone was always present at the corner store where much of the town's activities were discussed over beers and bottled sodas. He ran the half block to the corner.

Chapter 8

One naked light bulb hung from the store's ceiling in a vain attempt to light the room. Shadows darkened the crowded, uneven shelves that held meager staples along with rows of liquor bottles in various shapes and sizes. On the floor, barrels of rice, flour, sugar, and salt stood open as if in invitation to the scores of flies that lit on every exposed surface. A large cupboard set in the dried mud wall held several round chunks of soft, white salty cheese. Each was decorated with specks of dirt and sand having been carelessly added when the curd was separated from the whey. Tall cabinets of wood and glass set on the floor with assorted buns and rolls available for customers. Two thin dogs watched from the doorstep in hopes the cabinet doors would be left ajar.

Ernestina, the store owner had recently bought a small black-and-white television set, a source of the villager's awe. As Rolando ran through the door, he started with fright at the sound of a siren. Realizing it was coming from the television, he bobbed his head nervously.

Several children sat on the filthy floor staring at an American program dubbed in Spanish. Pushing past the group, he approached a girl standing behind the counter.

"Buenos noches. Is your papa or mama here?" he asked.

Grudgingly she acknowledged him, "Si. Wait here."

Her eyes remained riveted to the television as she moved away.

"Please hurry and call them. It's very important," urged Rolando.

Chapter 8

She looked at him resentfully and walked to the back of the room.

Absently he glanced impatiently around the familiar room oblivious to the falling patches of plaster from the mud walls and shelves in disarray. The uneven wood floor was worn and muddied from heavy traffic that frequented the store all that day. The action on television captured his attention for a moment. Two American actors were carrying guns while sneaking into a building somewhere in a far off country called, he thought, the United States of America. Snapping to attention, he saw the girl return.

"I don't know where papa is, but my mama is coming," she said as she returned to her spot behind the counter and leaned on her elbows.

Through a narrow opening covered by a thin blanket, a pleasant-faced woman emerged. Her hair was caught with a rubber band at the base of her neck, a sweater wrapped around the stocky build due to having borne many children. Her kindly face broke into a wide smile.

"Buenas noches, Rolando, what are you doing out on a night like this without a coat? You must be cold. I will get a poncho for you."

As she turned, he grabbed her arm. "Buenas noches, Señora. Please. I'm not really cold. I'm looking for my mama and wondered if you had seen her tonight."

"Your mama? No," the kindly woman asked. "She's not at home?"

He shook his head, fear renewed, "No. She started her labor pains tonight and I don't know where she went. I hoped maybe you had seen her pass."

"Would she have gone to your uncle's house?" the store owner asked.

"No. They would have sent a messenger," Rolando said, frustrated. "Anyway, she was too weak to walk up there."

Ernestina thought for a moment and finally brightened, "Why don't we go up to the saloon? Maybe someone there knows something. First I'm going to get you a poncho and we'll walk together."

She stepped behind the counter and into a shadowy corner and stooping she plucked up a dingy, faded poncho.

"Take this," she said as she returned to him and draped it around his shoulders. "I was going to have my daughter wash the clothes tomorrow, but you might as well use it tonight. Come chiquito."

Turning to her daughter she said, "Watch the store a little longer. I'll be right back."

Without looking at her mother, the girl grunted her consent.

Glancing at the sky Rolando noticed the rain had passed, but the sky remained cloudy. He moved swiftly beside Ernestina as they passed the bakery, a small restaurant, and then turned into the saloon.

Blaring music greeted them as they climbed the broken cement steps leading to the surprisingly bright interior. Stale air and the smell of beer assaulted the boy. He followed Ernestina, picking his way between the rows of littered tables surrounded by bleary-eyed Indians. Some had fallen asleep, sprawling backwards on their chairs while others had slipped to the muddy floor in drunken stupors. One young man staggered to a battered record player in the corner to replay the only available record. The mournful tune blared as he returned to his table and dragged his companion to her feet. They danced halfheartedly in the corner, leaning on the other's shoulders, as the woman's baby strapped to her back slumbered.

Ernestina walked directly to the kitchen located in the back of the saloon. Pushing aside a curtain blocking the doorway, she yelled out greetings.

Rolando's head swam with exhaustion, but he followed reluctantly, longing for fresh air. What chance was there he'd find his mother in this place?

Movement at the back of the dimly lit kitchen proved to be a woman. She was thin and wiry. Harsh exposure to years of fierce equatorial sun rays had etched a network of wrinkles on her face. She looked aged and yet Rolando knew her youngest daughter was about to enter grade school.

A huge pot of new potatoes bubbled on a small kerosene stove. Plates of chicken necks, heads and feet, along with ropes of intestines sat waiting to be cooked over an open fire on the back patio. Indians awakening from drunken stupors would soon have to face the long walk up the mountains to their huts and would need food for strength.

The kitchen was narrow and long, stretching into darkness. A lopsided table, one leg shorter than the others, precariously balanced a pile of dishes, several pots and pans and a large bowl of cold, greasy water that was dripping onto the dirt floor forming a mud puddle.

Chapter 8

The woman stood under the only light wiping her hands on a dirty sweater. She met Ernestina with a handshake.

"Buenas noches. This is a pleasure. What brings you to our home?"

Returning the obligatory greeting, Ernestina replied, "Rolando is looking for his mama. Did you or any of your family see her pass by? Her labor pains started tonight, but no one knows where she is."

Wiping the sweat from her face with a filthy apron tied at her waist, she replied slowly, "No, I don't remember seeing her tonight, but come to think of it, about fifteen minutes ago, someone came here asking for water. You know the old lady who lives below the plaza and gives out cures? Her son came running for a bucket of water saying they had an emergency."

Ernestina bit her lip thoughtfully, "We might go down there and just peek in. What do you think, Rolando?"

He shrugged and sighed, "I guess we might as well because I don't know what else to do."

Looking up hopefully, he asked her, "You will go with me?"

"Of course, dear one," she smiled, patting his shoulder.

Pushing through the crowd in the saloon, they quickly reached the entrance and walked back past the corner store. They crossed the street and walked through the plaza into the darkness of the neighborhood beyond. It was cold, black and silent, a direct contrast from a few hours earlier when the streets had held throngs of people buying, selling, drinking and dancing. Terror struck him afresh as he remembered his mother being alone.

Ernestina sensing his fear walked confidently beside him, reaching for his hand in an effort to calm him.

"Do you remember what house she lives in?" he asked, comforted.

"I think it sets behind her daughter's house about a block from the plaza. We must be here now, I'd guess. It's difficult to see clearly," Ernestina said. "Wait a moment and I'll call out."

Leaving the muddy road, they cautiously walked toward the walled structure that separated the road from the hut. Ernestina felt along the bumpy surface until she came to a small gate. Yelling greetings, they waited for a reply. She called again. At the third try a menacing growl sounded from the direction of the house. A dog barked at them until eventually a door opened and a man walked onto a cement step.

"Quien es?" he said holding a candle in his hand.

"Buenos noches. It is Señora Ernestina from the corner store and Rolando Martinez. We are sorry to disturb you, but can you tell us if you have seen Rolando's mother? We are hoping she may have been brought here tonight because she is about to deliver a baby. Can you tell us anything?"

With a small grunt he turned to go back into the house. They waited impatiently until the old man finally returned to open the gate.

"Step in," he called cupping his hands around the candle flame, he mumbled an order to follow.

Turning he led them around the house and down an uneven pathway that led to another small hut directly behind. There was no step, as the floor of the house became an extension of the dirt pathway.

Stepping inside, Rolando noticed the room was stacked high with burlap bags containing grains of corn ready for sale. The old man held the candle high and walked to a door in the opposite wall. He slowly opened it, motioning them to follow. Flickering candles brought a shadowy light to the inner room and revealed several chairs lining the walls. As Rolando glanced throughout the room, he saw two elderly women sitting together, each holding a bottle of beer. It was a typical hut, the room with one small window. Thick walls made from dried mud were constructed around a mud floor. It had no ceiling, but wood beams held the dried mud tile in place to form a roof. Repeated cooking over the years had blackened the beams. Long cobwebs streamed from the tiles.

Ernestina questioned the two Indian women as the old man silently walked out the door, "Buenas noches, Señoras. Can you tell me if Señora Martinez is here tonight?"

They jerked their chins forward to point in the direction of a room that lay beyond.

Rolando ran to the door, but Ernestina held him back, "No dear. Let me go in. I will see first if she is here and what condition she is in. Wait just a moment."

She paused at the door, carefully pushed on it and poked her head inside as Rolando peeked from behind her arm. More candles

Chapter 8

flickered, dimly lighting the room. Three beds, a bureau and a bed stand had been crowded into the small area. A shelf on the wall held yet another candle that sat beneath a picture of the Madonna. Two women knelt by one of the beds. Rolando saw his mother resting quietly there.

Ernestina left Rolando and stooped slightly over the bed. The two midwives looked up at her without curiosity, "Buenas noches, Señoras, I have been looking for Señora Martinez."

The two women rose to make room for her so that she could kneel.

Placing her mouth close to the patient's ear, Ernestina whispered, "Buenas noches. Your son has been very worried."

At that moment, Rolando's mother gasped and screamed out, arching her back to push down.

One of the attending women grabbed a feather and thrust it in her hand, "Blow on the feather. Blow on it. Blow. Blow."

Señora Martinez grabbed it and blew, relaxing as the pain eased, "It's taking longer than I expected."

She attempted a smile. Strong smells of sweat, childbirth, and tight quarters were almost more than Rolando could bear. He considered returning to the outer room, when his attention was drawn back to the bedroom as he listened to Ernestina questioning his mother.

"How did you get here? Rolando has been looking everywhere for you."

Attempting to arise on her elbow, his mother glanced at the doorway and spoke with effort, "He left me close to the American nurse's clinic. I was lying on the side of the road when a small car passed. I didn't move, but the car returned. A nice man from Tababela told me he was going to look for someone in the plaza. He almost passed me by, but his son noticed something by the side of the road. He was so insistent the man returned to look. I directed him to my house and asked the man to send the children up to where my husband is spending the evening and then he brought me here. I remembered that sometimes the Señoras can help with deliveries."

Rolando's desire to be close to his mother overcame his revulsion at the strange sights and smells. Creeping forward timidly, he observed the bedside table. On it sat a candle, several bottles, chicken feathers, a basin, knife, and thread. Pondering on these items, he realized Ernestina had noticed him. Rising she pushed Rolando into his mother's outstretched arms. Then she pulled him back and put her arm around his shoulder.

"Come with me. Your mother needs her rest," Ernestina told him. "You can either go to where your brothers are staying or you can go to the outer room."

Just then another scream rang out and Rolando grabbed at her arm, terror in his eyes, "I'll stay in the other room, but please warn them her last delivery was difficult and that she isn't feeling well. Her headaches have been very painful."

"I'm sure she has already told them, Rolando. I'll go back in to keep an eye on her while you wait out here," the kindly store owner promised.

Rolando seated himself, wrapping his arms tightly around his chest to warm himself as the poncho did little to ward off the chill of the room and dampness of his clothes. He fought to keep his teeth from chattering as the tension of the long evening overcame him. The two elderly women were fast asleep, chins drooping on heavy woolen ponchos. Several empty bottles and glasses lay scattered on the dirt floor.

Why don't they go home and go to bed? he thought, resenting their intrusion. Despite the chill, he soon found himself drowsy. A scream from his mother jerked him to an upright position and set his teeth to chattering again. An hour passed, the screams occurring closer together until finally he heard loud frantic talking and a baby's cry.

In a short time Ernestina came to the door, smiling, "Come."

Rushing to the door, he tiptoed into the room. Plastic pails sat at one side of the room, rags piled beside them. The smell of blood and other unfamiliar scents were strong and sickening. Greeting the ancient midwife and her daughter, he approached the bed where his mother rested. With a fearful heart he knelt and sought her hand.

"How is she?" he asked Ernestina without turning from his mother.

"Fine," she smiled. "She seems fine now. Outside of suffering a lot of pain and a terrible nosebleed, it was a good delivery."

Rolando reached out and patted the sleeping woman's face. She slowly opened her eyes, smiling up at him.

Chapter 8

"You are such a good boy, my darling son," she squeezed his hand and slept.

"Now, Rolando, would you like to see your new sister?" asked Ernestina.

"Sister," his eyes lit up in surprise. "You mean I have a sister?"

"Why are you so surprised?" Ernestina asked him smiling.

"I never thought of having a sister," Rolando explained. "I only have brothers."

"Come with me," she took his hand to help him rise and led him to a basket on the floor.

Holding a candle for him to see, she smiled, "There she is."

He knelt by the basket. Looking down, he turned his head quickly as tears rushed to his eyes. Embarrassment burned his cheeks because the women were watching him, but this was his sister and even in the red and wrinkled state of new birth, she was beautiful to him. A love swept over him that he had never before felt, a powerful blending of emotions. A surge of possessiveness and joy caused him to feel lightheaded.

Rising he wiped tears from his eyes and laughed. Ernestina laughed with him, relieved the ordeal had ended so well.

"Come," she said. "We must be getting back. Your mother will stay here tonight, but she wants you to get home and see that all is well there. You have to remember that no one knows where you and your mama are."

He looked again at his sister and then thanking the two women heartily, he promised to pay them as soon as he could speak with his papa. Leaning over to kiss his mother's cheek, he felt a stronger love for her than ever before in his young life.

Ernestina and Rolando walked back through the plaza as if a dream. He kept telling himself he had a sister. It had never occurred to him his mother would have a baby daughter after having so many sons. He shook with emotion as they crossed the plaza and Ernestina explained to him the events of the night.

The streets were deserted and dark, only a dim light glowed above the entrance to Ernestina's store. She banged heavily on the door until at last her daughter irritably peered through a crack and allowed them entrance.

While They Sleep

"Gracias," Ernestina said at the retreating girl as she shuffled through the curtained opening in the back. "Come, Rolando."

She lifted the curtain aside and they entered a small room. A sagging green sofa and matching chair sat in the center and a few straight-backed chairs lined the painted mud wall. A large dish cabinet, scarred and aged completed the living room setting. One light hung from the fly-speckled ceiling. There were no windows.

Ernestina invited him to sit on the sofa as she disappeared into an adjoining room. Her chatter sifted back to him. When she returned to the room, she brought two cups of steaming milk and a platter of cheese. She spooned sugar into both cups and handed one to him. Sipping his, he realized how hungry and tired he was. The cheese was strong and salty, the milk rich and sweet. Drowsiness overtook him. He fought the temptation to close his eyes for a moment. She noticed this and invited him to stay the night, but he declined the offer.

"I must see if papa is home. He should know about the baby."

Anxious to leave, he thanked Ernestina, embarrassed and uncomfortable knowing he couldn't reimburse her properly. She sensed his discomfort and waved him on. He started running toward home, barely missing a dark object on the sidewalk. Slowing to check, he squinted into the darkness. A woman was laying on the dirty curb, a weeping child alongside her, clutching a baby wrapped in a linen blanket.

Stooping, he recognized the child, "Carlos, is that you? What's wrong?"

"I can't get mama home," the boy sobbed.

Rolando shook the woman's shoulder until she muttered for him to leave her alone. How well he understood this predicament. Many times he had been responsible to guide his drunken papa home.

"Carlos, all I can say is you must take the baby home and put her in bed or she'll be ill. Here, let me see if I can find the key to your padlock at home."

Fighting revulsion he felt in Carlos' mother's pockets until he heard the sounds of keys. Pulling them out, he thrust them into the boy's hand.

"Here they are. Go home," Rolando told the boy. "I'll tell Señora Ernestina to send someone to take your mama home."

Chapter 8

He waved away the boy's faint thank you and returned to the store.

"Go along home, Rolando. I'll see that Carlos is taken care of," Ernestina said kindly. "His mama can stay with me all night."

Rolando ran for home, thinking of his beautiful baby sister and made a vow that never would he be in the same predicament Carlos found himself tonight. He had no premonition of the impact Carlos would someday have in his life.

In the morning he woke to discover his mother had suffered a stroke which left her entire right side paralyzed. Nothing was ever the same after that day.

Chapter 9

It was the incessant talking outside his bedroom window that pulled Rolando from a deep sleep filled with dark, oppressive dreams. Two fat black flies buzzed against the pane in a vain effort to escape. A ray of sunlight streamed from a gap between the two uneven, faded cotton curtains and glanced off a small mirror hanging on the flaking, whitewashed walls. Heavy, humid air left him breathless and nauseated. The pillow and bed felt clammy as he turned his sweat-soaked body. His mouth was dry, bitter-tasting, his head and heart pounded. Lifting himself on one elbow, he groaned. Focusing on his two brothers still in the bond of sleep, he watched Geoff's mouth hanging open, a muscle twitching in his cheek and eyes fluttering. Roberto lay with his arm across his eyes in an unconscious attempt to keep out the sunlight ray glancing off the mirror onto his face. The talking outside paused a moment and Geoff snored softly.

Rolando passed his hand over his face and tried to sit up. The nausea and dizziness increased so he sat for a moment until he felt safe to stand. It took a minute for him to remember today was Sunday. That meant it was market day. That explained the noise outside.

The Martinez house lay directly across from the open market. Only on Sundays could the residents of Pachuca and neighboring hills and valleys buy fresh meat and produce. Hours before dawn, merchants laid out their wares on long, rickety wooden tables. Ripened tomatoes, carrots, potatoes, beets, and green beans placed side by side with rows of oranges, lemons, chirimoyas, and taxos adding color

Chapter 9

to the simplicity and poverty. Along the mud brick walls women with sleepy-eyed children laid combs, batteries, threads, and colorful yarns on the woolen blankets. Trucks filled with thin pigs, sheep and cattle had been backed into a makeshift corral and unloaded. The animals were made ready for slaughter by husky ranchers.

At dawn the market filled with people who had walked throughout the night, descending from the mountains that surrounded the town of Pachuca. As the sun spread over the sleepy village, the excitement of friends meeting, the clanging of church bells, the squealing of helpless pigs, and the motors of buses and trucks brought life to an otherwise lethargic people. This eagerness would by afternoon change into drowsiness brought on by drinking beer in local saloons or by the droning of lengthy church mass. One day a week the Indians attempted to forget the dreadful toil of grubbing an existence from the thousands of steep hillsides that make up the Andes Mountains in Ecuador.

Yawning, Rolando pulled on his pants and buttoned them. Yanking a towel from the bedpost, he searched a drawer in the scarred bureau for a clean T-shirt. He padded through the door, down the hallway to the back entrance that led to a small patio. Directly in line with the house was a squat one-room dwelling built of large, dried mud blocks crumbling with age. Decades before a deep oven had been built into the wall which now was stacked with old mattresses, tires and sacks of rags. The roof had been layered with chipped, weather-beaten mud tiles in a futile attempt to keep out the heavy rains. Hamsters, part of the Indian diet, scurried about nosing among stored debris for grass and corn stalks tossed in for their feeding.

Hens scratched in the dust between rows of corn stalks, clucking in contentment while keeping a watchful eye on their baby chicks. A thin cat looked up from licking his paw and made a move toward Rolando as he plodded by, then changed his mind and returned to the sunny spot by the weather-worn rabbit hutches lining the mud wall.

Moving to the back side of the patio where water was running out of a faucet into a cement vat, Rolando pushed a tub of soaking clothes to one side. He placed the towel and shirt on an extended branch that had grown out of the hardened mud wall dividing the Martinez property from their neighbors.

While They Sleep

He was oblivious to the beautiful morning. The bright sun was almost overhead now. A dark blue sky to the west was quickly changing to light powder blue. White, lazy, puffy clouds gathered in the east throwing shadows on the rolling green mountains that towered above the drowsy town of Pachuca. A patchwork quilt of tiny farms rose to the summit, a day's journey by foot away.

He dipped a metal cup into the vat of water and filled a bowl. Finding a bar of soap behind the tub of clothes, he wet his face and lathered the bar.

"Rolando, oh, I'm so glad you're awake. Mama said if you come in I can give you breakfast," came the voice of a twelve-year-old girl as she burst through the back door and ran across the patio, long black braids dancing on her back.

She threw her arms around his waist.

"Watch out, Elena, or you'll have soap all over you," his throbbing head caused him to wince involuntarily.

"I don't care," she said as she pulled him down and put her nose in the lather. "I'm just glad you're up. Mama said I can go to the party with you this afternoon."

His heart warmed and he had to laugh at the spot of soap on her face. Even with a tendency to stoutness, she moved quickly, her large dark eyes sparkling with excitement. He adored her.

Elena was still his only sister in a family of male siblings. From the day of her birth, she had a lively charm that had won his heart completely. He could deny her nothing.

Leaning down, he kissed her nose lightly erasing the soap, "You know what happens when I take you to parties. All the other girls are ignored."

"Oh, you are silly. Hurry, come and eat," she said laughing as she vanished through the door.

Rolando shaved, stripped to the waist, and washed, trying to push nagging thoughts from his mind. Liquor was beginning to hold him in a tight vise. It was a curse that held many in this downtrodden village. Few escaped the degradation either directly or indirectly. Liquor destroyed families, sent young men to early graves, and turned beautiful girls into old women.

Chapter 9

Because of the economic effects on the family, only the fittest of children survived the poor diet they were forced to eat. Money went to quench the thirst of their fathers and mothers. Half of the village infants would die before their first birthday. This Rolando knew, as of the ten children his mother had borne, only five had survived.

He despised his weakness. Only his unusual height and fair complexion, unusual in an Ecuadorian Indian, had set him apart from others his age and allowed him the honor of leadership among his friends. He cringed at the thought of his feeble willpower. It resulted in his drinking himself into a stupor each weekend. But if Elena were to go to the party with him, he determined tonight would be different. He felt uplifted and breakfast began to sound good.

Pulling on the clean shirt, he then combed his light brown hair, absently unaware of his masculinity. His large brown eyes, soft mouth and straight nose, combined with a perfectly curved chin and jaw brought more than his share of attention. At times he took advantage of this, but basically he loved his family and friends, and when sober was careful to show them care and to involve himself in their lives.

Grabbing the towel and bending to pet the cat who had casually wandered closer, he sighed. He decided to tell Elena it would be better she not go to the party as there would be too much liquor and carousing. He dreaded the argument that his announcement would ensue.

She had a cup of hot milk waiting on the old wooden table placed in the middle of the small kitchen. Pushing a jar of instant coffee toward him as he seated himself, she also placed fresh cut buns spread thick with butter and chunks of white cheese bought at the bakery that morning.

"Where's Pablo?" he asked wondering at the whereabouts of his younger brother.

"He left with his friends hours ago. They're probably playing soccer," she said as she placed the sugar bowl closer to him.

Slowly stirring the hot coffee mixture, he watched her movements, "Elena, it's probably better if you don't go to the party with me. If I take you, you'll only be able to stay for an hour. Tomorrow is school."

Her reaction startled him. She spun on her heels, hands on hips.

"Oh!" she yelled, her eyes flashing with anger. "That's not fair. Roberto is going to stay."

"Elena, my love, Roberto is fifteen. He's old enough to stay out later than you. Anyway, many times he leaves early," Rolando said as his voice trailed off lamely, already feeling he had lost the argument.

"I don't care," she snapped. "I have to go. I want to go and stay the whole party."

He stared at her mystified.

"Anyway," she continued, eyes now sparkling with tears. "I don't want to stay home tonight. You know that on Sundays Papa is always worse."

Sighing inwardly, he started to relent, hating confrontations with her, "Go talk to Mama. Maybe you can spend the night with Aunt Mariana. You can go to school from there tomorrow."

Jumping with delight, tears still bright in her eyes, she kissed his cheek and ran from the room. He sighed audibly, knowing she was right. Their papa was always worse on Sundays, but her actions puzzled him. He had a nagging feeling that Elena was hiding something from him. Why was she so eager to go to this party? She had shown little interest in past parties.

Perplexed, he shook his head. The fact of the matter was, for the past few months she was having mood swings he didn't understand. One day over a cup of coffee, his Aunt Mariana tried to explain that Elena was growing up and with that came changes his sister was experiencing both mentally and physically. The conversation had embarrassed him.

He had long ago determined Elena would never grow up in Pachuca without being educated. Rolando looked on the ruin in his town with dismay. Girls married at age fifteen to boys so young they knew nothing more than to work as peons. The majority of marriages were forged because the girl was pregnant. Many couples had six living babies before they were married ten years, more if all the children conceived had lived.

Tiny white, wooden coffins were sold daily at the local carpenter's front door. Couples lived in mud huts, cooking and sleeping on floors, their only escape being liquor. If he had to spend every minute

Chapter 9

of his life protecting her, he would be more than happy. He would see to it she would never have to worry about her future.

"Rolando, Mama said it is okay. I can go with you to the party this evening and then to Aunt Mariana's for the night," Elena said happily as she danced a jig in the kitchen. "Let's change clothes and go play volleyball until then."

He shook off his daydreaming and picked up his coffee cup. It was no longer hot. Gulping the tepid liquid, he felt better after his breakfast. Reaching over to mess her hair, he smiled his approval.

"Come on, let's go," he said eagerly, Elena's excitement was contagious.

Laughing, they walked out of the kitchen arm in arm.

Chapter 10

Now suddenly it seemed, at age sixteen, Elena Martinez was lovely. Having lost her childish stoutness, she was slim and small. Her black hair pulled back revealed an oval face with large black eyes and a sensual mouth. Her abundance of energy often exploded in laughter, joy, affection, tears, frustration, and temper tantrums at a moment's notice. Rolando delighted in her. In one year she would complete high school, and his dream for her to obtain a university education was coming closer to reality. At an early age Rolando learned he could not depend on his father, who was now in a continual state of drunkenness. Despite this, Rolando and his brothers had managed to buy a flatbed truck. They built sides on the rear bed, and then placed a sign on the planks to advertise the use of their truck for hauling materials such as cement blocks, bricks, tiles, sand, and topsoil.

Rolando's own schooling had been sorely neglected since the family depended on his financial support. He was determined that following the graduation of each of his siblings, he would finish school and then find work in Quito. Now his obsession to see Elena settled was as severe as ever and until that time he would not consider leaving Pachuca. As for marriage, there was no time. His days were filled with seeking work and delivering materials in the truck.

He could no longer turn to his mother as she was unable to leave her room. After the birth of Elena, she hadn't regained her strength and from the day they brought the baby home, Rolando, with help from his Aunt Mariana, had cared for the child.

Chapter 10

In the beginning his mother joined them for meals and evenings in the living room, but the time between these visits became lengthy and she took to sitting by her bedroom window facing the green mountains. It seemed she never tired of watching the little brown huts on the hillsides, remembering the people who lived in these homes and through her memories they became the center of her existence.

Rolando suffered with the changes in his mother. He remembered her before his sister's birth as a vivacious woman on whom he was dependent. She was always active in the small village both in school affairs and civic duties. From her garden she took vegetables to the market to sell each Sunday. Her household had been run with pride and enthusiasm and in turn a great amount of love and respect from her children gave her a sense of accomplishment and contentment.

One ambition Rolando's mother held stood out from the rest. She wanted all her children to graduate from the university in Quito. In the years of her youth, before the highway to Quito had been laid with concrete, she traveled by truck to high school with her two brothers and one sister along deep rutted roads. Her parents were ridiculed for the value they placed on their girls in a culture where women were only worthy to bear children. As if in defiance to society, the two girls graduated with honors in a class dominated by boys.

He grieved for his mother and wondered whether her life would have been different if the American nurse had helped her that night. Now, many years later she had left her chair by the window and retired permanently to her bed depending on others for her care. His mother's illness was the despair of his life as he helplessly watched her dying before his eyes. It broke his heart not to be able to share his pride in Elena as she grew into an intelligent and attractive young woman.

The most important day of Elena's sixteenth year had arrived. Her Saint's Day which would be celebrated with greater festivities than her birthday. For weeks the party had been in the planning stages. Aunt Mariana and Uncle Hector had offered the use of their home for the occasion and would host a dinner and dance.

Having returned home early from school, Elena was nervous with excitement, willing the hours to pass quickly. A local seamstress had completed a new dress, a knee-length green velveteen creation which had been copied from a borrowed European magazine. Unable to wait another moment, Elena washed at the tap behind the house, scrubbing her face in the cold water until it was glowing. Brushing her strong, white teeth, she rinsed her mouth and dropped the toothbrush in an old plastic cup and carried it with her to the house. Rushing to the bedroom, she took the green dress from a hanger, pulled it over her head, and belted it to her waist. She brushed her hair, tying it back with a dark green ribbon. Rolando had purchased a pair of poorly made shoes in a Quito dress shop and Aunt Mariana had given her a pair of earrings and a necklace. Glancing in the mirror on her dresser, she smiled at her reflection and bounded to the door.

She found Rolando in back of the house combing his hair, his eyes squinting in an attempt to see himself in a small cracked mirror hanging on a pole.

"Aren't you ready, Rolando? I can't wait for you. Do you mind if I go ahead?" Elena said impatiently.

He turned his face in an effort to see the back of his head in the mirror, "Will you please be patient? Why do you want to arrive early? Your brothers and guests aren't coming for an hour or so. They won't begin without you."

"I just can't wait. Anyway, you are too proper. What's wrong with being a little early? Oh! Someone is at the door," she said all in one breath as she disappeared to the front of the house and found her two cousins on the doorstep.

"We came by for you, Elena," they announced, turning her around. "You look so nice."

She twirled in a circle, showing her pleasure and they each grabbed one of her arms pulling her to the door.

"Come with us," they said excitedly. "We want to show you the preparations."

Clapping her hands, she cried, "Yes, I'll go, but I must tell Rolando first."

She skipped to the back patio, "Vanessa and Susana are here. I'm going with them now."

Rolando sighed, "Okay, but be sure to stop and see your mother before you leave."

Chapter 11

Without enthusiasm Rolando completed dressing for the party. He had hoped it could be a small family affair instead of a gathering of Elena's school companions, but since it was her sixteenth saint's day, the family let Elena choose her own guests.

He put off his departure until he felt certain his brothers would have arrived at his aunt's house. Looking in on his mother and the young neighbor girl he had hired to watch her for the evening, he passed his father sleeping on the living room sofa and shook his head. The elder Martinez had stumbled in earlier that morning, collapsing in a stupor. Rolando could see little chance of his father attending the party and wondered if his absence would bother Elena. He shook his head again and walked out into the blazing afternoon sunlight.

Grade schools had dismissed at noon and now the streets were almost deserted. Everyone was indoors eating the main meal of the day before siesta time. Slowly walking toward the plaza, he waved to a few stragglers playing basketball in the schoolyard. Passing Don Eduardo's house, he glanced in the open door and saw the heavy, elderly man spooning hot soup into his mouth. Waving to Ernestina at the corner store, she greeted him with a wave in return. The saloon was silent and empty, the doors to the variety store across the worn cobblestone road were closed, and the few mud huts along the roadway were quiet and sleepy looking. Pachuca was shut tight against the heat of the day as the occupants relaxed through the siesta hour.

Pachuca, situated on the equator had survived centuries of a blazing sun, hurricane-force winds, and torrential rains. Now in the year 1973, it remained a small community of one thousand residents, nestled at the nine thousand foot level in the Andes Mountains. Without giving it any thought, Rolando was unaware of the town's ugliness and decay. Deterioration touched everything: the houses, roads, vehicles, and people. He had heard things were better beyond the mountains, but his limited imagination allowed few fantasies. On one or two occasions he had felt panic about the sleeping culture and wondered if he was being sucked into a way of life from which he'd not be able to break away. However, this day he paid no more attention to the poverty and filth than he did the breathtaking beauty of the mountain ranges surrounding the town on three sides or the vast valley lying before Quito in the distance.

As he drew close to his Uncle Hector's home, he glanced at his watch realizing it was still early. The house had been built of oven-baked brick fifty years earlier and then plastered and painted now a faded blue. More recently, indoor plumbing and a toilet had been installed, adding to the prestige of the family. Two acres behind the house boasted chickens, pigs, fruit trees, and corn.

Rolando walked through the front door without knocking, "Buenas tardes, where is everyone?"

"We're in the kitchen," came a voice from that direction.

A small dark-haired boy ran into the living room, "Hi, Rolando. Mama's in the kitchen. We're going to have a party."

Rolando swept his cousin up in a hug and kissed his cheek, "How is my boy, Francisco?"

"Fine. Mama is cooking for the party," Francisco announced as he grabbed his hand and pulled Rolando to the kitchen.

"I wasn't sure you would make it on time," said a middle-aged, slender woman with graying black hair cut short and curled.

She beamed up at him as he planted a kiss on her cheek.

"It looks like I am early," he said smiling after Francisco as the boy ran out the back door.

He turned to watch his aunt Mariana stir chunks of potato in a large skillet on a four-burner gas stove, an appliance rare in these parts. The kitchen was bright and airy. Green plants lined the sills and

Chapter 11

climbed the window frames. The floor was laid with blue tile blocks; the counters covered with thick linoleum. Cabinets and drawers had been built by a local carpenter, and then painted a blue that did not match well with the floor. One of the more modern homes, it was envied by the townspeople.

Mariana pinched salt from a bowl and scattered it over the potatoes as she chattered about the party. The maid, a young Indian girl walked in from the back patio carrying a bowl of toasted corn. Rolando greeted her and grabbed a handful of the corn, stuffing the grains in his mouth.

"Rolando, will you do a favor for me and go out behind the house and find Carlos? I need his help," requested his aunt.

"Right now," he replied, his mouth full.

Stretching he swallowed and reached out to pull his aunt's hair affectionately. Outside, he went to look in the chicken house.

"Carlos, where are you?" Rolando called out.

"Here I am. Buenas tardes," came a voice behind him.

He swung around and saw Carlos carrying a large gunny sack filled with ears of corn. Following him were Rolando's two cousins and sister. He greeted Susana and Vanessa and turned to Carlos.

"Buenas tardes. Will you be able to go to the house now? My aunt needs your help," Rolando asked.

"Si. I'll first put this corn in the shed," the boy said as he adjusted the bag on his back and walked away.

"What are you girls doing out here?" Rolando asked. "I thought you'd be in the house looking over the preparations or at least helping in the kitchen."

"Oh, we were just walking under the trees and happened to see Carlos in the field. Aunt Mariana told us we were in the way," the girls laughed with Elena as she explained. "You arrived early after all."

"I thought dinner would be ready and everyone would be here," Rolando explained. "Ah, Francisco's yelling. The bus must be coming."

"Yes, he's been waiting all afternoon for it," Vanessa called as she and the other girls ran for the house.

Rolando arrived in the living room as the bus pulled up before the gate. Several girls, along with Elena's brothers spilled out the

While They Sleep

door, through the gate, and into the house. There was much excitement with greetings, hugs, and waves. Rolando met his brothers with a smile and look of relief.

"I'm glad you finally got here," he said to them.

"What do you mean? We thought you would be anxious to join the girls in their games and dances?" Pablo teased with mock surprise.

"No and I won't because it's obvious it's you they want," Rolando chuckled at his brother's discomfort.

Pablo's shyness was a delight to the girls.

"Are you ready? Dinner is served," Uncle Hector yelled in an effort to get everyone's attention.

He started guiding the children into the dining room. Aunt Mariana and the maid made several trips from the kitchen to the table bearing plates piled high with fried pork strips, fried potatoes, roasted corn kernels, cooked hominy, and pieces of cheese.

"Come to the table," Aunt Mariana called over the noise. "Take a piece of paper and fill it with food. Come, form a line."

She directed them into a single line and then returned to the head of the table, face rosy from effort and pleasure. No one used plates or utensils, as food was placed in a butcher paper and popped into the mouth with fingers. The living room soon filled again, every chair taken, some of the girls spreading their paper filled with food on the floor.

Uncle Hector and the maid passed a bottle of cola, along with a few glasses which would be shared from friend to friend. Rolando, Geoff, Roberto, and Pablo stood along the wall eating great amounts and tolerating the noisy chatter. Aunt Mariana stood by the table snacking, but also keeping an eye on her guests. When she saw they were eating at a slower pace, she filled two pieces of paper to overflowing and called the maid.

"This is for you and Carlos. He can sit with you in the kitchen if he would like. Later we will clean this table."

She clapped her hands, motioning to Susana and Vanessa. They jumped to their feet and ran from the room, returning with a pile of gifts. Color rose in Elena's face as the girls placed the packages in front of her.

Chapter 11

Rolando leaned against the wall, watching her as she opened the presents. Carlos and the maid stood in the doorway interested in the proceedings. Elena's cries of pleasure over a trinket, sweater, ribbon, doll, and a record by Julio Iglesias brought laughter and clapping of hands. He thought Elena was more attractive than he had ever seen her.

Gathering up the wrapping papers, Aunt Mariana asked the children to move the chairs back so they could begin the dancing. Rolando had no desire to stay longer and motioned his brothers to the door.

"Why don't we walk to the plaza and see what's happening. Maybe we can play some basketball," he suggested.

In agreement they left by the front door.

Chapter 12

A few minutes before sundown Rolando returned to his uncle's house alone, his brothers having departed for home. The house was quiet and cluttered, the children having caught the bus back to Quito. He noticed his uncle slumped down in an overstuffed chair sipping a cola. Rolando patted him on the shoulder affectionately, again thinking how different his father was from this man. How could brothers be so dissimilar?

"There you are, Rolando. Elena? No, I've not seen her for a while. Perhaps she's in the kitchen or better yet, maybe in the girl's bedroom," Hector told Rolando.

He found the maid washing dishes in the kitchen, "Hola. Have you seen my sister?"

The girl absently wiped the greasy counter and shrugged her shoulders, "About an hour ago, I guess. Señora Mariana sent me to your mother with dinner and I haven't seen Elena since."

He thanked her. At his cousin's bedroom, he knocked and waited. Receiving no answer, he opened the door and peeked in. No one was there. Noticing a light under his aunt's door, he tapped on it lightly.

A soft voice invited him in. His aunt and Francisco were sitting on the bed, pillows propping them up, watching a television program on a small black and white set.

"Why, Rolando, I thought you had left for home. Are you all right?" asked his aunt.

Chapter 12

"I'm fine. The boys went home to their studies, but I need to check with you about Elena staying here tonight and going to school with her cousins tomorrow. You don't happen to know where she is, do you," Rolando asked.

"I thought she was with the girls in their room. Don't I hear them now?" Mariana responded.

Vanessa and Susana walked into the room and abruptly stopped, surprised looks on their faces when they noticed him.

"Oh!" gasped Vanessa, coloring. "When did you get back? We thought you had gone home."

"Vanessa, what's the matter?" her mother asked, puzzled by the girl's expression.

"Nothing at all," snapped Susana, glaring at Vanessa.

Rolando frowned, "Where is Elena?"

"Elena? She's no doubt in the kitchen or in the bedroom looking at her gifts. She did say she wasn't feeling well. Perhaps she is lying down, or perhaps she has left for home. The party was very tiring for her," Susana spoke rapidly as she looked from Vanessa to her mother and back to Rolando

He watched her with curiosity, then gently pushed the girls aside and returned to the girls' bedroom. No one was there. Momentarily a small fear nagged at him, but he shrugged it off with a smile and headed for the kitchen.

Behind the house, the equatorial dusk was fast approaching with darkness on its heels. Moving quickly to the chicken house shed, he found it filled with roosting fowl cackling their displeasure and shifting positions nervously. No one was else was there. Turning, he looked out over the cornfield. Where was she?

Carlos must have left for home by now, so I can't question him, he thought idly. Perhaps Elena did decide to return home thinking I had gone on.

He turned his attention to the restfulness of the hour. The winds which blew each afternoon had died and as he walked under the taxo tree, he inhaled deeply the fresh scented air. He loved the combined smells of animals, topsoil, and fruit trees and wished he could capture these few short minutes and live in them forever. Reaching high to grab a taxo, he bounced the orange fruit in his hand, then pocketed it, thinking of the delicious drink it would make later in the evening.

Yawning, he stretched realizing the last minutes of daylight were quickly running out. He glanced over the fields again and held his breath as a movement caught his eye. Along the mud wall at the end of the property a small shed had been built to store an old tractor and other discarded objects. Squinting, he waited for the movement to reappear, but all was still.

"Must have been a cat or opossum," he said under his breath.

Turning, he started for the house, but paused unable to push aside the nagging thought he had seen someone. Walking to the hut, he stopped when he heard whispering. Creeping closer, he looked around the corner and caught his breath in shock and disbelief. Dizziness swept over him as he leaned against the small building, certain his knees would give out.

Elena was sitting on the ground, her head on Carlos' shoulder. The young man was kissing her forehead. Smiling, he raised his head and spotted Rolando. In a flash, Carlos was on his feet, but before he could react, Rolando had grabbed Elena. He slapped her hard and then pushing her behind him, he reached for Carlos in a blind fury. Elena screamed and held the side of her face while the boy tried to reach her. Rolando hit him, the force of the blow knocking Carlos to the ground. The big man bent over and grabbed the boy up by the shirt, holding him close to his face. Speaking coldly and softly, he gritted his teeth.

"If you ever touch my sister again or if I ever see you near her, I will kill you. Do you understand?" Rolando threatened as he pushed Carlos to the ground again.

Elena, crying and trembling tried to kneel beside him. Rolando grabbed her arm, squeezing so hard she cried out in pain, "And you, young lady, we are going home."

He pushed her passed the house with little concern if someone saw him, and led her home, not once releasing her arm nor speaking. Arriving at the house, Elena jerked herself free and lunged in the direction of her bedroom, slamming the door after her. Rolando glanced around knowing his family had already settled for the night. There was no movement.

Chapter 12

Now reality set in. He felt crushed, betrayed, confused, and angry. His cousins had known where Elena was and had covered her secret. Marching out to the street, he wandered for an hour. He needed to think, to calm himself before speaking with his sister. Sitting in the darkness of the plaza, his anger turned to remorse and he decided that surely this problem could be resolved. Returning home he thought suddenly of his father with a flicker of hope then snorted in disgust.

"He's either asleep or gone. There's no sense talking with him anyway. How could he understand?" Rolando reasoned out loud.

Knocking at Elena's bedroom door, he spoke softly, "Let me in."

After a moment's hesitation, she opened the door. Her party dress was crumpled and dirty. She had been weeping. All anger and self-pity disappeared as Rolando watched her wipe her hands on the dress, a lost look on her face.

"Elena, come here. Sit down," Rolando said calm now. "I want to explain to you how I feel and why I did what I did."

She sat beside him, her eyes red and swollen, hands folded in her lap. He felt a sharp stab of pain combined with a wave of love and compassion. She looked so young and confused.

"I don't know how to explain this," he started out slowly, choosing his words carefully. "You see, you just can't get involved with a boy like Carlos. Don't you know what kind of a family he comes from? He doesn't know who his father is. I'll never forget the night you were born. I found him late at night on the street with a baby tied to his back. What was he doing there? He was trying to drag his drunken mother home. I helped him because he was so desperate."

Rolando paused looking into her eyes, "Elena, I've known Carlos all his life and I've never known his mother to be married. Oh yes, she has four children and no telling how many times she has been pregnant. She picked up each of their fathers at street festivals or parties. I don't believe she's ever gotten pregnant while sober, so she probably doesn't remember who the fathers are. You want to get involved with a boy like this? What are you thinking of? Haven't I taught you better?"

Alarmed, he suddenly stopped. Instead of anger or confusion, he saw maturity and steadiness in her eyes. In a flash, he realized she was no longer a child, but had become a woman.

Speaking evenly, she looked directly in his eyes, "I love Carlos. I have loved him since I was twelve years old. Do you remember that Sunday afternoon I went with you to that party at your friend's house? Remember when you weren't going to let me go with you and I begged so? I cared very much for him then. He told me he would try to be outside waiting. I met him and on that day four years ago we declared our love.

"Yes, Rolando, when I was twelve years old I knew he was the man, not a boy like you keep calling him, but the man that I'm going to marry. I don't understand how you know so much about what his mother does, but it doesn't matter to me how she lives. Carlos is the gentlest, finest, most honest, and upright man I know except for you. I know I always said I would wait to marry, but that was because you have been so good to me. You've stayed home and even refused to date so I would finish high school. I will finish. I promise you we don't plan to marry until I graduate."

Surprise and fear were building in him so rapidly he felt his head and heart would burst from the pressure.

"Elena, you can't possibly think of marriage. Have you considered what he does for a living? He works for our aunt. He's a peon. What does he earn each day? It's not enough to put proper food on the table," Rolando said.

The pressure was dissolving into a mixture of disbelief, frustration, and fear.

Standing, he walked to the door, "You will not marry him. If I ever see you near Carlos, I will kill him. He means nothing to me. My life means nothing to me if you choose to ruin yours. Now, get in bed."

He didn't sleep until dawn. The fact he had been unaware of something of this importance going on for so long left him shaking his head in wonder. How long had his cousins known? Surely Aunt Mariana hadn't been in on this deception. Why would Elena choose Carlos, of all people? He didn't mind her marrying. In fact he hoped she would, didn't he? Perhaps she could find someone educated and influential from Quito.

He turned over in bed. Perhaps if he were truthful he could admit he didn't want things to change. Time was moving too rapidly. What

Chapter 12

hurt the most was that Elena had kept a secret from him for such a length of time and that he had been an outsider.

He finally slept, but woke feeling a sense of dread and with a headache that caused his head to reel with pain. Elena stood at the kitchen counter, her back to him as he picked at the breakfast she had prepared. No words were spoken as he played with his coffee cup while trying to think of something to say. Finally, with a sigh he rose and walked to her, putting his arm around her. With a sob, she turned and wept on his chest.

"I see you decided not to go to school," he said gently.

She nodded her head, nestling in his arms.

"Come on, Elena, let's go to Quito together. We'll spend the day in town, buy some lunch, and have time to ourselves. Okay?" he suggested as he searched for a napkin to wipe her eyes.

She attempted a small smile.

"You'll have to wait until I change my clothes," she spoke softly.

"Take all the time you need. I have some unfinished business I must take care of first. It will be about an hour and then I'll return."

Nodding, she left the kitchen. He watched, his face softened with love, but in an instant it turned dark and hard as he clenched his fists.

"It's time to take care of Carlos."

Looking at his watch, he grabbed a sweater and left the house.

Chapter 13

Carlos pulled on his boots and slipped his arm into an old jacket. He grabbed a freshly baked bun from the table, poured coffee into a tin mug, and carried both outside to a bench leaning against the front of the house. Shivering in the chilly air, he dipped water from a bucket and poured it into a bowl to wash his face and splash a little on his hair. From a window ledge high in the mud-walled house, he took a bar of soap wrapped in newspaper and a razor. Careful to avoid the wound Rolando had left on the side of his face, he shaved and combed his hair. Slowly he ate the bread and drank the coffee, letting the warmth spread through his chilled body.

It was cold, the sun still hanging low behind the mountains, but it promised to be a beautiful morning. He looked down on the road from the rise where his two room house sat. Indian women wrapped in ponchos from their heads to their ankles carrying heavy burdens strapped to their backs were walking rapidly toward the plaza a mile from his home. Men hunched in smaller ponchos or jackets, hats low on their heads rushed to their respective positions as peons, thankful they were able to earn a few sucres each day despite the grueling labor.

Carlos carried the bowl around the side of the house and threw the dirty water on the onion patch. After replacing the bowl, soap, and razor he took his cup and returned to the house. He shook his sister and brothers awake. His mother, Laura had left for work two

Chapter 13

hours before daylight joining a group of Indians harvesting potatoes in a field several miles north of Pachuca.

"Wake up. I've got to leave for work. Joel, Jerman, wake up. There's coffee on the fire and I bought bread. Be sure to eat before you leave for school, and you boys had better collect water from the road faucet. Perhaps you should bring three buckets back home. Yolanda, you can peel potatoes for lunch. I'll run home before you boys return from school and light the fire. I don't want you to touch the matches. Mama will be home around three o'clock, so try to have your homework finished and the dinner ready for us. Okay?"

He checked the boy's clothes and hurried out the door before someone noticed the bruise on his cheek. Carlos, like so many poor Ecuadorian Indian children had acted as a mother to his siblings all of their lives. The baby girl who had been strapped to his back the night of Elena's birth had died. In the wee hours of the morning she had awakened, whimpering with a high fever. Two days later she was dead.

For some time, it had an effect on his mother and she worked hard caring for Carlos. However when he was nine years of age, she arrived home late one night, drinking heavily, in the company of a young man. Carlos had buried his head in the blankets and tried to sleep while his brother Joel was conceived. Since the father was still studying at the university in Quito, he failed to return and claim his child. Carlos quit school to care for the baby as his mother had to return to the fields for work.

Two years later his brother Jerman was born. Jerman was followed a year later by an infant girl who died after the life span of one week. Yolanda arrived close to Carlos' fifteenth birthday. The small room which made up their home was becoming crowded and the time came when Carlos decided he must look for a larger space or perhaps a house to rent. After a few weeks search he found a two-room mud hut on a small rise above the road leading to Pachuca. In this area wealthy residents from Quito invested in land and crops. To protect their interests, huts were built in full view of the property and families were hired to live on the land to guard against thievery.

In a matter of days he had his family settled in larger quarters. They could live there rent free with the stipulation that someone would always be home. There was no electricity or plumbing, but he was pleased to see the property had an irrigation ditch that could be used for laundering and bathing. One Sunday he found a man in the market selling straw mats. Until the family was able to afford a larger bed, he and his brothers slept on the floor and Yolanda slept with her mother. There was one small window in each room, but candles supplied the majority of light for homework. They cooked on the floor and every two or three days gathered fire wood.

As Carlos left the house, he checked to see if there were enough potatoes left for dinner and pondered what else they could eat. It was Friday and there would be no meat in the stores. Inadequate refrigeration limited the supplies of perishables and until the weekly slaughter of animals on market day, the poverty-stricken Indians lived on starches. Carlos decided they could eat soup flavored with bouillon, fried potatoes, and boiled rice.

He had taken another bun and withdrawing it from his pocket, he started munching. His throat closed in anger. He was already tired from lack of sleep. How dare Rolando humiliate him in front of Elena? It was no secret among the townspeople that Rolando drank too much and his father was an alcoholic. Both had low morals. Mixed with the rage, he was concerned that Elena might have been abused upon arriving home.

What had Rolando told her? He wasn't sure how much Elena knew about his family life and his heart ached with pain at the thought of her negative reaction. Sometimes he could hardly bear the fact that his mother brought young men home when she was intoxicated. Sometimes he hated her, but most the time he could see the intolerable burdens she bore and he pitied her. It was the love he felt for his brothers and sister that kept him home realizing they still needed him, although he admired the strength they possessed. They soon could survive without him. His dream was to make a new life for Elena and him, to live deep in the country area, to farm, maybe someday to own an acre or two.

When his mother was pregnant with Joel and Carlos had been forced to leave school, he was able to find work with Elena's uncle. After the baby was born, he cared for the child until his mother returned home from her job in early afternoon. He would then work

Chapter 13

until dark tending the crops and animals belonging to the Hector Martinez family. He had worked hard and developed into a fine looking young man, dark of color, medium height with a strong build. Seeming alert to potential problems, he was cautious and smiled infrequently. However, when he was able to relax with a companion, he showed a wonderful sense of humor. His smile was one of his greatest assets, lighting his black eyes, and crinkling his entire face. His laughter rang loud and true, compelling his companions to join in.

Carlos had known Elena all her life. He first developed an interest in her when he was fourteen and she only age ten. From that time on she gradually became one of the most important individuals in his life. She wove her way through his dreams and he wanted her. When she was twelve, he realized she cared for him and as a result, they fell in love and began to make plans for the future.

Elena often spoke of her brother's obsession for her. Carlos had expected opposition to their union, but nothing like Rolando had displayed the previous evening. He felt his only chance for a life with Elena pivoted on a conversation with her brother so he could lay out his plans for their future. He hoped he would be able to do that in the next few days.

The shortest distance to the Martinez home was a narrow path which ran alongside an irrigation ditch between two mud walls. It was always his hope to arrive early for a glimpse of Elena in case she had slept over at her cousin's house. Chewing the last of the bread, he knelt to dip a drink from the ditch. Refreshed, he rose, wiping his hands on his jacket and began to run. Perhaps all was well. She may have already explained to Rolando that he would love and provide for her. Perhaps she would be waiting at her aunt's house for him. These thoughts drove away all anger and anxiety.

Rounding a bend, he spotted Rolando and one of his cousins leaning against the wall faces set in stony anger. He stopped suddenly, his heart lurching with fear. There was a possibility he could fight Rolando alone, but not both men. In order to save face, he decided against turning back. He walked ahead, trying not to show concern. Approaching them, he nodded good morning and continued to pass. Rolando thrust out a hand and grabbed Carlos' shoulder.

"Where do you think you're going?" Rolando asked in a low threatening voice.

Carlos shook his shoulder free and glared into Rolando's face, "I'm going to work. Where do you think?"

"Not to my aunt's house. You're through there," announced Rolando.

"Don't you think it's your aunt's place to fire me, not you? I'll go talk with her," Carlos said as he moved to walk away.

Sneering, Rolando grabbed Carlo's arm and pulled him back, "If I ever see you on the street in front of my aunt's house, I'll beat you. Stay away from that house and my house. Do you understand?"

"What will your uncle think if I don't show up for work?" Carlos asked. "They'll be expecting me."

"I don't think it will be too hard for them to figure it out. I'll speak with them about your relationship with my sister. You know they would be against something like that as much as I am. I could vomit when I think of you touching my sister. How do you dare think she could love scum like you?" Rolando said through clenched teeth.

Again Carlos shook free, asking, "Why am I scum? You can't tell me one thing I do that isn't upright and honest. I never come home drunk because I don't drink. I always pay my bills. I don't have girlfriends all over town and that's more than I can say about you and your friends. Why am I beneath you?"

They stood like angry bulls ready to charge until Mario left his position and stepped up to Carlos, "Well, for one thing, you smell. Where do you take baths? In sewer water, huh? Your mother lives like the rats in the garbage. Tell me, who is your father?"

He laughed, "How about the fathers of your sister and brothers? Where are they?"

Snickering, Mario's eyes lit with delight, knowing he had hit a raw nerve. Looking to Rolando, he expected a smile of appreciation, but backed away when he received a hard glare.

Meanwhile anger drained from Carlos to be replaced with despair.

"You've got the wrong kind of blood. You're too dark for my sister," Rolando spoke with less force, but his voice still held authority. "Stay away from Elena, or anyone else in my family. Better yet, stay away from the main plaza. There are several stores in this area where you

Chapter 13

can buy food. I don't want to see you anywhere near our house. Do you understand?"

"Have you spoken to Elena about this? Has she expressed her desire never to see me again?" Carlos asked. "I love her and she loves me. She's told me so and I want to marry her."

Unprepared, Rolando's fist caught him against the mouth, knocking him down. Blood flowed freely from his lip. Automatically he checked for broken teeth.

"What does it matter if you kill me? If I can't be with her, I don't care if I live. I love her," Carlos declared passionately.

Rolando grabbed at his hair and jerked him to his feet. Pushing back Carlos' head, he stood over him.

"If you show up in town, I'll not only ruin you, I'll ruin your mother. You don't realize what a family like mine can do to you. Think of all the relatives I have in Pachuca and Quito. They work in the schools and in the government. They own the fields where your mother works. I could go on and on. You'll never survive. In the first place, your mother would lose her job. Second, you'll never find work. Your brothers will suffer in school. Not only will they find it impossible to pass a day without someone causing them trouble, they will never graduate from one class to the next. Oh, we can do lots of things. That's just the beginning."

Rolando pushed him again and Carlos lost his balance, falling backward.

He watched and then turned to Mario, "Let's get out of here before I get sick."

In humiliation, Carlos turned face down on the grass for several minutes. He heard a pig grunting on the other side of the wall. Birds sang and he felt the sun warming his back. Carefully he sat up and put his head in his hands, swallowed hard against a knot in his throat and struggled to breathe. Then he cried, not so much for the humiliation or the unfairness of being a poor Indian or for having a mother who cared little about her reputation or even for the frustration of knowing there was no way out. He cried for Elena. Being at school, she would have no idea Rolando had waited for him this morning. In his heart he knew she still loved him and he could do nothing about it.

An hour passed and finally he got to his feet and returned home to sit in the dark front room. Yolanda was behind the house caring for the chickens. What a life for his sister. At five years of age she carried water, cared for the animals, washed dishes, and swept the dirt floor. She was learning to cook and wash the smaller articles of clothing in the ditch water. There was no money for toys. She was fortunate to have shoes.

He couldn't think straight. His emotions were so raw he wanted to scream. He had to see Elena, but how? Rolando would not change his position, he was sure. Part of what the man had threatened was true, part exaggerated. His family was large, but not as influential as he had stated. Faced with this predicament Carlos could not involve his own family. That would be taking a big risk for his own gain. He'd have to explain to his mother he had decided to look for a better paying job, perhaps on a hacienda somewhere. He'd start looking tomorrow higher in the mountains.

"Carlos, what happened? Why are you home? What happened to your face?" Yolanda ran to him, breaking into his thoughts and sat on the bench, staring at him.

"Nothing, Sweet, just a problem that shouldn't concern a pretty little girl. Anyway, I thought I'd come back home. We'll fix a nice dinner and have something hot and ready for you, Mama, and our brothers. Okay? Why don't we go out to gather wood so Mama won't have to worry about doing it?"

A sudden emotion ran through him and he threw his arms around her, hugging her tight, "I'm proud of you. You work so hard and don't have a chance to play."

"When Joel finishes his schooling and can stay home, I will get to go to school and then I'll play. Jerman told me there are toys at school. There are even swings and a slide. Think of that, a slide. I'm not sure I know what a slide is, but Jerman tried to explain. I don't think I'd be scared, but he says I will be. What do you think?" she talked so fast he had trouble following her.

She looked at him eagerly.

"I think you'll be able to handle almost anything that life sends your way, little one," Carlos said full of love for his little sister.

Chapter 13

"I peeled the potatoes. They're setting in water. What else shall I fix?" Yolanda asked.

"Here's a little money. Why don't you run down to the store and buy garlic, also some of those flavored cubes for soup. Let's see. Do we have enough rice? You know what we can do? Let's make popcorn. That's what we'll do for a surprise tonight. Now get along. When you come back we'll look for fire wood."

She danced out the door and he followed, walking behind the house, absently passing the chickens and pigs. The family was allowed a small plot of land in front of the house and a section behind, large enough to grow a few crops and raise animals for meat or to sell. Rabbit cages lined the mud wall which served as a boundary.

Descending the rise where the house set, he walked through a field of corn until he reached the end of the property where a stream of water ran from east to west. It was shady and cool, sheltered from the sun by tall eucalyptus trees that arched like umbrellas, casting refreshing scents and long shadows. Sitting on the large rock the family used for scrubbing laundry, he sighed with a deep sob. It was no use. There was no way to see Elena unless she came to him. That seemed improbable now. Rolando would watch her more carefully or he would convince her she could not be happily married to him.

Perhaps he would have to let a few months pass and then when Rolando turned his attention to other interests, he would set up a chance meeting. But how could he wait that long to see her? His heart felt like lead in his chest. When Rolando had found them last night, they had been planning their future together. She had been in the process of preparing the speech she would present to her mother and brothers informing them of their engagement.

He had intended to talk with Elena's uncle in hopes of persuading the man to hire him as foreman on his harvesting crew. The Martinez family had a great deal of land, not only in Pachuca, but high in the mountains several miles inland. He had planned to ask if he could oversee the work, not only at harvest time but during the planting season.

Now their dreams were dead. With the extra money he would have earned he could have given Elena the home and attention to which she was accustomed. If only Rolando hadn't stepped in.

"Oh, God, help me," Carlos prayed as he held his head and wept.

It was useless. What if Elena forgot him? Would she find someone else? Perhaps by the time he could marry her without her parent's consent, she would no longer care for him. After all, she was only sixteen. What chance was there that Rolando would feel any different when she came of age? Well, tomorrow he would look for another job. He'd make money, enough to care for her. He'd buy her a home that would be more comfortable than the house she lived in now.

Chapter 14

A shrill scream broke the heavy silence. None of the eight children sitting at the large, crude dining room table moved. Some held raised spoons motionless while others kept their heads bowed and eyes closed. Lucia glowered and plopped a tea towel on the table to blot some milk that was steadily forming a small pool on the yellowed linoleum floor. She looked accusingly at Leah, who stared into her plate.

Leah jumped involuntarily as another scream pierced the stillness followed by the whack of a belt again bare skin. Wincing, she slowly pushed back her chair and rose, balancing herself carefully on trembling legs. She held tightly to the chair, and then moved toward the living room door. Leaning against the naked plaster wall, she gasped desperately in panic. Leah didn't fear the punishment as much as she feared the woman. Peeking around the corner of the door frame, she saw six-year-old Frankie sitting on the floor with his arms grasping his knees. A long leather belt lay on the floor.

Marta stood over him yelling, "Look at me, you fool."

He lifted his head wearily and looked at her. Several red stripes ran down the length of his back. One stripe extended to his ear, where a trickle of blood glistened. Marta kicked the boy with her toe.

"Get up! It's not so much that you spilled the milk, but that you lied and said you didn't do it. I will not tolerate a liar in my house," Marta said in anger.

At that moment she swung around and spotted Leah watching with fearful eyes.

"What are you doing in here?" she bellowed. "This is none of your business unless you want to be next."

"I-I-I," the girl sputtered, close to fainting. "Mommy, I'm sorry, but....but, Mommy, I spilled the milk. Frankie didn't do it. Mommy...I did."

Tears clouded her eyes, "Please, don't be angry."

The wildness in Marta's eyes fled. In its place was the dead look of one held in suspended animation. The only sound coming from her was her heavy breathing. Finally, she raised a long finger at the girl.

"You wait right here," she said contemptuously.

Springing into action, she grabbed the boy. He whimpered as she held his chin tightly in her hand.

"Why didn't you tell me who did it?"

When he didn't reply, she pushed him away.

"Now get out of here."

Paralyzed with terror, Frankie hesitated as Marta moved toward him again.

A low voice interceded, "Leave him alone, Marta. He tried to tell you, but you were too busy accusing him of lying to listen."

Lucia gestured to the boy and a look of tenderness crossed her face, "Come to me, Frankie, and I'll dress you."

Marta pushed him toward her. Frankie stumbled toward Lucia as Marta, now subdued turned to look out the window. Carefully, Lucia helped him with his shirt and led him toward the door.

"Come now. You must eat," she said as she nudged him gently. "We'll wash your face and ear after dinner."

He gagged at the thought of the cold soup and moaned as Marta began screaming at Leah.

The nurse pulled Leah by her long, black hair passed the dining room door and headed up the steps to the second floor. Upstairs, she led the girl to her bedroom and threw her on a cot.

Standing over her, she placed her hands on her hips and panted heavily, "If you say a word, I'll whip you with the hose. Now, sit up."

Shaking uncontrollably, Leah lifted herself up and sat on the edge of the bed. Crossing the hallway with determined steps, Marta reached

Chapter 14

for a smooth, thick leather belt hanging on the wall and returned to the room, softly shutting the door behind her.

"It's all I can do not to beat you until you bleed. How dare you embarrass me in front of the children? You're an evil and deceitful liar, just like your real mother. You're the result of her dark ways. I don't know why I had to be saddled with you. I can hardly bear to look at you. Now, turn and lie on the bed face down and don't turn toward me," Marta threatened.

Leah turned and buried her face in the pillow, clenching her jaw. The woman stood above the cringing form and in swift motions brought the belt down with force across the child's buttocks and thighs. Jerking, Leah cried out and tried to defend herself.

"Did I tell you not to turn toward me?" she pushed the girl down and hit her again. "You will stay here until I'm ready to let you up. Don't expect dinner. We'll let you pay for the milk by not eating a couple meals. Next time, you'll see that we don't play at the table. We eat."

Marta watched the child for a moment then left the room, replacing the belt on a large nail protruding from the wall. Plodding thoughtfully to the bathroom she washed her hands, combed her hair and smoothed her blue nurse uniform. Her reflection in the mirror showed a thin glimmer of perspiration across her heavy features. She wiped her chin as a satisfied smile settled on her full lips.

Gladly she accepted praise by her peers and supporters. She was a good mother and worker among the people of Ecuador. Marta Brewer's orphanage was well organized and inhabited by nearly perfect children. To be acknowledged far and wide as a wonderful, accomplished woman was more than she had ever dreamed. Her name was known and admired in this country and in her native land, America.

In her youthful fantasies, she had hoped that one day she would be successful, but it hadn't taken her long to learn that in the United States she could never find the power and attention she craved. Now, in Ecuador, she had influence over many people.

Deep in thought, Marta slowly walked down the steps to the dining room. She was well aware of her children's fear of the discipline she administered, but she had come to the conclusion early on that only through strict disciplinary measures would they become proper adults. Someday they would return to thank her.

While They Sleep

Crossing the small hallway downstairs, she entered the dining room to find each head bowed. She sat and ordered them to look at her. In silence, she scanned each face until slowly her chin began to quiver. Tears filled her eyes and rolled down her reddened face, dropping onto her nurse uniform. With quavering voice, she spoke in an unnatural high, nasal tone.

"You children don't understand how I hate to punish you. It's not my fault. I have to repair the damage that others have inflicted upon you," Marta said sadly.

Tears began to flow anew as she sobbed into a large, worn handkerchief, "I've tried with my whole heart to bring you up properly, but there have been others working behind my back, tearing down what I have tried to build. I'm glad Sandi has decided to leave. Let's just hope that she was able to get her exit papers today. When she's gone, we'll start over fresh and things will improve, I'm sure."

Sobering abruptly, she glared at Lucia, who was now sitting at her place at the end of the table.

"And you, Lucia, you are the worst one yet at the way you spoil the boys and Leah," she sighed heavily. "Look what just happened. Oh, I should never have taken in the boys and Leah."

Groaning, she blew her nose loudly into the handkerchief and ignored the angry flicker in Lucia's eyes, "I have so much more trouble with you boys than I do with the girls. I would have no problems with the girls at all if Sandi and you, Lucia, would leave them alone. I'm counting the days until Sandi leaves. Oh, why can't people just leave me alone with my children?"

Her voice choked with emotion again as she leaned forward to rest her head against her hands, "You all should be ashamed! Your poor Mommy, you treat her as if you don't care for her at all."

She lifted her head as large tears dropped from her chin. Grabbing for the soggy handkerchief, she removed her glasses to wipe her eyes.

Suddenly Elizabeth jumped to her feet, rushed toward Marta and threw her arms around the woman's neck, her legs dancing with emotion.

In a small, trembling voice, she proclaimed, "I love you, Mommy. I love you!"

Chapter 14

Two of the younger children stood beside their chairs, considering the same move, while the others remained motionless in their places.

Marta sighed deeply and gently pushed Elizabeth toward her chair, "Okay, okay, that's enough. You can go back and finish your dinner. Then we'll forget this ever happened."

One by one the children finished their meal and waited in silence until permission was granted to leave the table. Frankie struggled against the lump in his throat, as he swallowed the last of his soup and bread. A trace of a sneer formed at the corner of his mouth as he watched, under hooded eyes, Elizabeth leave the room. Politely he requested leave of the table and followed the girl to the living room where the hour before bedtime was spent watching television or playing in the playroom. Inside the door, he took her arm and pulled her close.

"Stop that, Frankie, or I'll tell Mommy on you," Elizabeth whispered.

"You make me sick. You always run to her when she cries," he glared at her. "Why do you tell her you love her?"

She stared at him in wonder, "I tell her that because I do love her. She's our Mommy."

"She's not our Mommy. My Popi lives above Pachuca and your real Popi and Mommy live in Yaruqui. How can you call Marta Mommy?" Frankie said as he shook his head with frustration.

"Our parents don't want us. You've heard Mommy and Lucia say that. They gave us away," Elizabeth said as she put out her hand. "Anyway, you've seen what kind of houses we would live in and what food we would have to eat if Mommy hadn't accepted us. It's better for us here. I wouldn't want to live in a mud house, would you?"

"Yes, if I could go away from her," Frankie said.

Elizabeth looked at him with disgust, "You don't know what you're talking about. You're still such a baby."

Her body grew rigid, "Why don't you leave then? Go when no one is looking."

He gave her a defeated look, "Because I wouldn't know where to go."

"Knock on your Popi's door. See if he wants to let you in," Elizabeth added.

He watched her for a minute than turned toward the playroom adjoining the living room. Sitting in the corner, he looked up at the sky through the aluminum-paned windows. How he wished he could run away to the mountains behind Pachuca, up where the birds float on the wind, where children run and play without fear. Maybe the houses up there were small and dark, but they had more warmth than this place. They were warm from the fires built on floors and from bodies living close together.

Lucia once told him that the natives were not very clean, and the food was scarce. After the sun went down they had no light, except from candles, and everyone went to bed early for warmth. He had heard Sandi telling Jill all about Lucia the day they sat in the sandbox. Lucia had never had much of a family life. When she was a little girl she had wandered through the jungles from one mission station to another. Her stepfather had never wanted her. Then when she was older, the missionaries took her to Quito and left her at the American hospital. That's where Marta had found her and Lucia came to live with her. Perhaps Lucia's real Popi had died. She was always unhappy. Even so, Frankie thought, living in a native home could never be any worse than living here.

Two year old Sara ran to Frankie's side and daintily dropped a red block in his lap. A small smile played on his lips.

"Thank you, Sara," he patted the block and handed it back. "Why don't you go play with Peter? Look, there he..."

Frankie froze when the door opened and Marta entered. Her attention was immediately focused on Tommy, who in tears, was struggling to grab a toy from Susana.

"Tommy, what are you whining about? What? What did you say?" she barked, walking into the adjoining room. "I'll give you something to cry about, if that's what you'd like to do."

Frankie sank lower in the corner as she pounded across the floor, yanked the hapless Tommy to his feet and sent him scurrying into the playroom. The dejected boy sat down close to Frankie and wiped tears from his eyes.

Through the open door Frankie watched Marta seat herself on a rocking chair with a plop. Looking around she counted heads, "Where's Frankie?"

Chapter 14

"In the playroom," exclaimed Elizabeth, running to the woman's side and pointing toward him. "Do you want me to get him?"

"No, he's alright," eyeing Lydia, Marta pushed the girl aside, grabbed the startled infant and placed her in her lap.

Still sulking from the manner in which Marta had spoken to her, Lucia walked in and sat cradling her head in her hands. Marta, oblivious to Lucia's mood, spoke pleasantly to her, but Lucia remained silent. Unaffected, the nurse shrugged her shoulders. It seemed to Frankie that Lucia was always in a huff.

Settling back to watch television, Marta issued an order for Elizabeth to turn up the volume. Sandi poked her head inside the room. All the children turned to her, their faces bright with joy. Lydia squealed with delight, straining against Marta's arms. Sara rushed from the playroom with outstretched arms as fast as her chubby legs could carry her and Tommy followed slowly. Sandi dropped to her knees and gathered Sara in a hug. The older children moved slowly toward her, but kept a close watch on Marta who, in turn, glared at Sandi.

"Oh, I missed you, Sweetheart," Sandi planted a kiss on the child's cheek.

Sara hugged the girl's neck tightly, prompting the other children to rush over.

"Get away before you crush her to death!" Marta dumped Lydia from her lap and brushed back the circle of little bodies. "Leave Sandi be or I'll send you all to bed right now."

Sandi leveled a look of disappointment at the nurse and glanced at Lucia.

Smirking, pleased at the battle over the children, Lucia remarked, "They were just glad to see her, Marta. Why can't you leave them alone?"

"The attention spoils them. You know how I feel about prolonged hugs. And need I remind you that no child is to be picked up or carried past the age of three? We all know that babies manipulate adults just to get affection. They're hard enough to manage without all this added excitement," Marta declared firmly.

Sandi found a place on the davenport.

"Go on, children," she sighed. "Go on with your playing."

Sitting back, she said, "Marta, I leave next Tuesday. I will be able to obtain my salida by the end of the week."

While They Sleep

An unrestrained smile lit Marta's face, "The government will be able to give you your exit papers this quickly?"

Sandi's eyes swept the clusters of children, "I guess that means by this time next week I'll be gone."

A frown creased her brow, "Where are Frankie and Leah?"

Elizabeth motioned toward the playroom, "Frankie's in there and Leah is in her bedroom."

Standing, Sandi walked toward the darkening playroom and flipped on a light switch. She spotted him sitting in a corner and stooped beside him.

"Hi, Frankie, what are you doing in here by yourself?"

"Nothing, Auntie Sandi," he said, smiling sadly. "I just felt like sitting here. I was watching the clouds."

She sat close to him and put her hand on his back, pulling her hand away quickly when he winced. A rush of love swept through her as the little boy was choked with tears and involuntarily sobbed, but he continued to look at the golden hues of the rapidly disappearing sunset.

As she reached out to gently hug him, he gave a little cry. Fearing punishment from Marta, he jumped with fright and pulled away from her.

"Please, don't. She'll see us."

She inspected him at closer range, "Why was your neck bleeding? Just a minute. Turn around."

She lifted up the back of his shirt and pressed her lips together in disgust at the sight of his wounds.

"I don't know," he muttered.

She rose to her feet and walked back to the living room. Marta ignored her while attempting a conversation with Lucia.

"At least you could have tended to the wounds on Frankie's back and cut behind his ear, Marta."

A look of surprise crossed the nurse's face and she looked accusingly at Lucia. The Indian glared at Marta, walked into the playroom and took Frankie by the hand. She led him out the door without speaking a word.

Chapter 15

Deliberately Sandi surveyed each of the children, then climbed the steps to the second floor and entered Leah's bedroom. Flipping on the light switch she found the girl lying face down. Sadly she brushed back the child's hair and felt the dampness on her pillow.

"Oh, Auntie Sandi," Leah whimpered with relief.

Kneeling, Sandi spoke softly, "I want to see your back, honey."

"It's all right. It was my fault," Leah said as she licked her dry lips.

"Turn on your side so I can see," Sandi said, fearful of what she would find.

She raised the child's shirt and shook her head at the black and blue welts across the small of her back and upper legs. Tears filled Sandi's eyes as she bent to kiss the wounds.

Replacing the shirt, she touched Leah's cheek, "Can you sleep?"

"No, I'm not very tired," Leah managed a smile.

"Have you eaten?" Sandi asked.

"No, I don't want anything. Really I don't. Auntie Sandi, please don't bring me anything," Leah pleaded.

Sandi gritted her teeth against the knowledge of what had happened. Rising to her feet, she fought the temptation to run into the living room screaming at Marta against her cruelty, but she had tried that in the past. Sandi had even spoken with a lawyer about putting the children up for adoption. To her despair, she learned that Marta's hold on the children was secure; she could keep them if she wished because the parents had left them in her care. Sandi suspected the nurse had used her influence and money to ensure that her position in the community and authority over the orphanage remained unquestioned.

Now she was leaving. Stress and emotional pressure had finally worn her down. In her room at the end of the hall, Sandi sat on the bed deep in thought, pain twisting her heart. With a start, she looked up and saw Marta standing in the doorway.

"I came up because I thought you would be in Leah's room. I don't want her disturbed," Marta said pointedly.

"I've already been in there, Marta. What could Frankie and Leah have done to deserve such a whipping?" Sandi asked sadly.

"Believe me, they deserved it. I just wish you would stay away when I'm disciplining them."

"Well, I know you won't listen to what I tell you, but I think from a health standpoint you should not whip a child across their kidneys. That's dangerous and painful. Also, Leah needs some water. Her lips are parched," Sandi added. "As a nurse you should know better."

Marta stood in silence. Sandi knew she could reach the woman with health warnings in a more profound way than by criticizing her discipline measures.

"Okay. I'll take her some water," Marta stood with her hands on her hips and glanced about the room. "Did you bring my mail?"

"Yes, of course," Sandi said as she pulled a handful of envelopes from her purse and handed them to her.

Marta giggled as her eager fingers tore at the envelopes, disregarding the letters in a search for checks.

"It looks like the contributions will be heavy this mailing. I was getting a little worried that some of my friends had forgotten me. Hey, I'll get to the correspondence later," she giggled again and looked at Sandi joyfully.

Sandi sighed and left the engrossed woman to return to the living room. Lucia was seated in her regular place. She saw Frankie who appeared much happier, speaking with Tommy.

"Why don't you do something when Marta starts punishing the children, Lucia?"

"What can I do?" Lucia pouted.

"Stop her," Sandi said simply.

Chapter 15

Laughing sarcastically, Lucia said, "Why don't you?"

Her head dropped to her chest, "What do you suggest I do?"

Shaking her head, Sandi watched her for a long moment, then moved to the sofa, seating herself just as some of the children came running to surround her. Above their heads, she continued watching Lucia. When had she ever seen her happy?

"What happened to Frankie and Leah?" Sandi asked.

Tommy jumped up from his conversation with Frankie and ran to her. He leaned against her with eyes full of love as she hugged him.

"Frankie fell down and hurt himself, Auntie Sandi. Leah did, too. That's why she's upstairs," Tommy said nonchalantly.

She shook her head in disbelief, looking over Tommy's head at Lucia. The Indian gave her a defiant look, challenging her.

"It sure seems that the children fall and hurt themselves a lot," Sandi said.

Marta appeared in the doorway, "Get away from Sandi. You're all going to bed. I'm gone one minute and there you are, tearing at her."

A throbbing pressure expanded in Sandi's head. These poor children, they receive so few demonstrations of love or praise. Their attention is usually negative gained from a scolding or a beating.

"Go on, darlings. Get ready for bed," Sandi said with a sigh.

Immediately they stepped back, ready to run for the bathrooms.

"Two at a time. Two at a time," screamed Marta. "Flora is waiting upstairs. Wash your faces and hands, brush your teeth, and get into your rooms. Paul and Tommy, you're first. Go on."

In twos, they exited at Marta's command until the room was empty and quiet except for the three adults. Misgivings assailed Sandi as she made herself more comfortable on the sofa. Perhaps leaving the children alone with these two women was a terrible mistake. Was Jillian their only hope? Could she bring a balance to this home?

"I spoke with Jill today, Marta," Sandi stated.

The woman's attention riveted on Sandi, "How does she feel about coming here to live?"

"There's a good chance. She'll come again to visit the end of next week, if you still want her to," Sandi said. "Her school term ends this week and she'll want to rest and maybe travel a little."

"No. I want her to come here this weekend. I want her here tomorrow night. I must talk to her before she makes plans to do something else. I want to talk to her about the benefits of living here, but she must understand the rules too" the nurse said as she rubbed her nose in thought. "I'll call her tomorrow. Maybe we can arrange a ride with someone else, maybe with the American school children who study in Quito and live on the other side of Pachuca."

"Why do we want her here?" Lucia muttered. "It's better when we're alone."

"Who is going to watch the children in case of an emergency? What do you suggest we do when there's a delivery in the middle of the night or when we're working in the clinic? Tell me that," Marta cocked her head toward Lucia and smoothed her lap. "Flora has too much to do with all the cooking, cleaning, and laundry. I agree with you that we can get along better without outside help, but there is a limit as to how much we can do in the time that we have."

With a frown, Sandi glanced at Lucia who was fidgeting with frustration. She knew the Indian felt threatened. Lucia had never cared for her, always needling her, reminding her that she was an outsider and not considered one of them. Now she was faced with another newcomer.

She rose, her mind was in turmoil. Her only desire was to be as far from them as possible, and yet she needed to be close to the children for their sake. It bothered her that she had not been completely honest with Jill about the problems here, but she was certain she was the right person for the position and that she would be able to handle the pressures. In fact, she was so certain that she had bought airline tickets for Costa Rica that day. Jill would be able to care for the children and stand up to Marta also.

"Leave Leah alone, Sandi. I gave her some water. She's tired and needs her sleep," Marta commanded.

"Good night," Sandi glanced at Lucia smirking back at her and walked from the room, tears smarting in her eyes.

She just wanted to get away.

Chapter 16

A rain shower during the night enhanced the brightness of Friday morning. The mountains showed a lush green and the dark blue sky replaced the gray tumbling storm clouds.

"It looks like a painting," Sandi muttered to herself.

She often wondered how this part of the world could be so beautiful. Perhaps it was the high altitude, being so close to the heavens, to God. There was no smog to obscure the sharply defined lines of the mountains, trees, and verdant growth. She loved Ecuador. Life was so simple beyond the high mud walls that Marta had built around her property. Seldom had she had the opportunity to visit the townspeople on the other side of the big gates.

Marta discouraged casual contact with the natives, fearing disease from parasites, fleas, and lice. She believed crossing cultural boundaries only invited unnecessary complications, but Sandi was beginning to suspect that the lengthy discourses against the dangers and the evils of the outside world were nothing more than the fears of an insecure woman; fears that she would lose her grip on her small empire.

Glancing at her watch, she saw that it was nearly six o'clock. Each morning at seven the children's doors were unlocked. Only then were they allowed to leave their beds. Sandi would spend this hour cooking the cereal, pouring milk, and setting the table.

Lucia entered the back door, mumbled good morning, and brushed past Sandi. She was still angry that Jillian was coming this evening and that Marta seemed too eager to accept her. She had let it be known that she had a foreboding feeling that nothing would ever be the same again once Jillian was installed in Pachuca. As much as it distressed her, when questioned, she couldn't deny there was something about Jillian she liked. It was just that she hated change.

When Sandi received no answers from Lucia to the polite inquiries about her night's rest, she lapsed into silence.

Marta entered the house and climbed the stairs. Small voices and footsteps sounded overhead and soon children started appearing in the dining room doorway. Peter poked his head around the kitchen door and smiled up at Sandi. When she returned the smile, he held out his arms for a quick hug.

"Good morning, Peter. I think you'd better get up to your chair," she said, turning to see if Lucia had noticed, but was relieved to see she was staring out the kitchen window.

As the children scrambled to their chairs, Marta seated herself, "Good morning, Sandi. I hope you slept well."

"Thank you. I did. How about you?" Sandi replied.

"Well, you know how it is sleeping in the clinic. There's someone knocking on the door all hours of the night. We had a patient come in just after I fell asleep. We were up most of the night. That's the trouble with sleeping in the outpatient clinic. They go there first. Then I must get Lucia up over at the maternity clinic. So instead of just one person being awake, we both lose sleep."

She shook her head, the thick hair flying, "Poor Lucia had to listen to the groaning and screaming all night. At least I can escape by going back to my little house."

Now Sandi understood part of the reason for Lucia's dark mood, she hadn't slept well.

The back door opened and Flora walked in carrying a pail of fresh milk she had bought at a local hacienda.

"Buenos dias, Flora. Please help bring in the breakfast," called Marta.

Placing the milk on the counter, the maid rushed to help Lucia and Sandi serve the bowls of hot mush. Glancing covertly at Peter, she gave him a warm smile and quick wink. He was her favorite.

Marta saw them and glared down at her bowl. The look on her face revealed she was going to have to watch Flora more carefully,

Chapter 16

knowing the maid's favoritism toward Peter and tendency to spoil him. She banged her spoon on the table.

"I need your attention. Frankie, do you hear me? Stop your whispering. I'd like to talk with each one of you." She hesitated a moment for their full attention. "Now, this evening we will be expecting company. Auntie Jill is coming to be spending time with us."

Their eyes sparkled, but they remained silent.

"I don't have to remind you that the belt is ready and waiting for anyone who misbehaves. I have the reputation that my children are the best behaved and I will do all in my power to see that it continues. During the dinner hours there will be no talking or playing. Heaven forbid, don't spill your milk."

She stared at Leah, and then searched each face slowly, "Of course, if there is no playing at the table, no milk will be spilt. However, I'm not worried about our dinner hour as I am at times when I can't keep an eye on you. There must be order the entire time that she is here. If I see or hear of any mischief, you will not soon forget what will happen after she leaves. When she comes I don't want you pulling at her or clinging to her. I get so sick at the way you climb all over guests, Susana. I want it to stop. You don't have to hold someone's hand or touch them constantly."

The child's eyes wavered under the hard stare.

"I can see no reason why, at your age, you still need to hang all over people. I'm sure that's why you are such a spoiled child."

Marta looked over to the kitchen doorway where Flora, Lucia, and Sandi stood watching. The message had been for them also. Tormented by the demonstration of affection between the women and the children, she was hoping to see signs of shame.

Lucia sighed and turned away. A long silence followed until Flora took her leave and Sandi sat down to eat her meal.

"Do you understand?" Marta asked.

"Yes, Mommy," they replied in unison.

"Do you understand what will happen if I see one of you trying to get attention from Jill?"

"Yes, Mommy."

"Frankie, I don't want anyone to see your neck. Come here for a moment."

The boy carefully placed a piece of bread on the table, rose obediently, and walked to Marta's side. Gently pushing his head down, she inspected the nick left by the belt blow. A hard scab covered the ugly black and blue stripe.

"Come with me. I'll put a bandage on it," Marta rose and took the boy by his hand, leading him to a large bureau at the end of the room.

Opening a drawer, she withdrew a first-aid box and deftly removed a bandage from its wrapping and placed it on the wound.

"There now, no one will notice. And if they do, they'll think you were scratched."

She glanced quickly at Sandi to gauge her reaction and led Frankie back to the table.

"Jill will be here after school tonight and will be curious about everything. There's no sense in her knowing what happened to you, Frankie."

Sandi frowned, her body stiffening.

"Tommy, what happened to Frankie?" Marta asked.

The boy's eyes darted from her face to Frankie's and back again, "Frankie fell down."

Sandi pressed her lips tightly together.

"Good," smiled Marta. "Leah?"

Leah faced her, a flicker of defiance in her eyes and then slowly lowered her head, "He fell."

"That's fine," Marta said as she grinned, satisfied. "There's no sense in upsetting Jill until we can find out if she'll stay. Then the rules will change. Are you through with your breakfast? Then get down and get washed. School will start in a few minutes. Be ready to walk over there when I say so."

One by one the children left the table. The smaller ones wandering to the playroom, while the eldest groomed themselves for morning sessions at a small, two-room building on the edge of the property.

Sandi pushed back her barely touched plate of food and with a heavy heart plodded to her room. She heard Marta climb the stairs and rap on her door.

"Come in," Sandi said softly.

Marta pushed open the door, "Well, the kids are off to school."

She remained in the doorway appearing to search for something to say, "I know you've heard this a thousand times, but it doesn't hurt to

Chapter 16

hear it again. It's worth handpicking teachers and bringing them from Quito each day to teach my children. Can you imagine the incapable teachers of Pachuca teaching even the most basic studies? I shudder to think of the outcome for the future of this town."

Sandi groaned to herself. Marta's lengthy ranting and ravings about the incompetent teachers in Pachuca's public schools frequently left the listener wondering if any worthwhile student could ever come out of them. A long silence followed and Sandi fought to remove the involuntary frown that clouded her face.

"You didn't eat your breakfast, Sandi," Marta challenged.

"I wasn't hungry," Sandi said flatly.

"May I speak with you for a minute?" Marta moved inside the door without waiting for an answer and found a place beside Sandi on the bed.

"I suppose, but I should go downstairs with the little ones," Sandi stood hoping to escape the ensuing conversation.

"They'll be all right. Flora is there," the older woman cleared her throat and patted the bed beside her. "Sit down for a minute."

Reluctantly Sandi chose to sit on the chair by her desk and forced herself to face Marta. Looking into her eyes was difficult. For months she had played a game of deception and evasion, unwilling to admit that it might be selfishness that was causing her to flee from the depression and sadness of the orphanage. The only thing that had kept her was the children. When her attempt to free them legally from their virtual prison failed, she knew she could never be at peace. Was that selfishness?

"What is it you need?" she asked politely.

"We must talk about your departure. While waiting for the delivery last night, I had a lot of time to think."

The eagerness was difficult to hide in Marta's voice, "You will be leaving this coming week. Lucia and I will be alone with the work."

Sandi smiled inwardly at Marta's feigned sadness, "I'll fly to Costa Rica for a week, then on to the United States for a month before returning to Central America for good."

Marta licked her lips, "I spoke with Jillian. She is willing to spend an entire week with us, but now I wonder if perhaps she might remain here. What do you think?"

"I told you the other night that I think there's a good chance. I'm satisfied that she wants to find a permanent home in Ecuador and to work with these people. I'm sure she will try to follow all your rules, Marta, in an attempt to please you," Sandi said as she tried to stifle the sarcasm.

"Please me with the rules?" Marta asked with a frown. "Sandi, I know you must feel that I'm too hard on the children. I'm sure that your attempt to remove them from my home was done with the best of intentions."

Resting an arm on her lap, she crossed one hairy leg over the other.

"We've been through this, I know but it still hurts me a lot. I know you must feel I'm too hard on the children," she repeated, "but I can't always remain as mild tempered as you. Sometimes my mind feels numb with the pressures that are with me day and night."

Sighing deeply, she hesitated, "But of course that's something only I and I alone can understand. How do I explain what I go through or how I feel to someone who's always in control of her feelings? The sun always seems to shine on you, while there seems to be nothing but problems for me."

Tears glistened in her eyes.

"I do understand the load you are carrying," Sandi's heart sank at what could be a tearful outburst from Marta. "I've told you often that you should cut back on the hours you spend each day in the outpatient clinic."

Impatience pushed Marta's voice to a higher pitch, "How can I do that? Surely you know how patients are treated in the government clinic. The doctor's helper, what's her name? You know who I mean, the one who helps out when the doctor is gone? She's worthless. What's her name? Oh, yes, that's right, Olivia."

Her hand swept the air in disgust, "The responsibility for a dozen deaths would be on my shoulders the first year."

Sandi pressed her lips together at the exaggeration and sensed now was the chance to say something that she had been avoiding, "Have you thought that maybe the reason you have taken on more than you can handle is because you believe the people who support you expect it? The letters you write are more appealing because of all you do, but I can't believe that your friends would want you to overwork. On

Chapter 16

the other hand maybe it's good. They need to know you are working beyond your strength."

Ignoring Marta's narrowed eyes glaring suspicion, Sandi continued, "A newsletter full of results isn't worth having poor health."

"Is that what you really think?" Marta's voice rose and her hand dug in her pocket for a handkerchief. "That I work myself to the limit so I can send a good newsletter to my friends? Thank goodness God knows my only interest is to serve the people of this country."

"I'm sorry, Marta, but…"

Ignoring Sandi, the woman stood and plodded to the window, twisting the handkerchief tightly in her hand.

"I just want to be a part of this country," she whined.

Turning suddenly, she glared at Sandi and stormed, "How can you attack me in such a way? Sometimes I feel that no one understands me."

"Marta, I'm sorry. I'm trying to understand and help you," Sandi said in frustration.

Marta was hysterical now, grinding her jaw, eyes fixed in a wild stare, and waving her arms frantically. Tears flowed down her face.

"Perhaps it is better that you leave soon," she choked.

Shocked, Sandi watched and with a sudden revelation realized for the first time what Marta craved more than anything was approval. Withholding mild revulsion, in a conciliatory gesture, she patted the nurse's shoulder and put her arm around the sobbing woman's neck.

"I'm sorry," Sandi said trying to sound sincere. "Truly I am sorry for how I must have sounded. I should never have inferred that your motives are dishonest. Everything will work out. Jill will be here tonight and we can talk over her plans."

She paused, "Now I think that the children need some attention and you should be on your way to the clinic."

Marta noisily blew her nose, wiped at her eyes, and stepped out the door.

Shaken by their confrontation, Sandi rubbed the back of her neck. She would forever feel a sense of guilt for bringing Jillian here, but what else could she have done? To leave the children alone with Marta was unthinkable. If she had to sacrifice someone, it would be Jill.

Chapter 17

It had been eight months since his confrontation with Carlos and Elena. Rolando was having difficulty sleeping again. There was no way of telling what time it was so he carefully pushed back the covers so not to wake his brothers and tiptoed out the door. Feeling along the wall he found the kitchen entrance and pushing a stool aside felt on the shelf for a match. Holding it close to his watch he saw that it was three o'clock. His head was groggy as he had been drinking that afternoon and now he needed another drink.

Prepared for emergencies, two pints of liquor sat in the old unused kitchen. Creeping into the night he slowly pulled on the big wooden door, wincing at the protesting squeaks. Hamsters stirred in their sleeping places as he lit the candle and placed it in the holder he had carried with him from the kitchen and balanced it on a stack of burlap bags. Behind a pile of broken pottery, he found the whiskey.

Sitting on the floor, he blew out the candle and put the bottle to his lips. Hearing a noise, he looked up and saw a figure in the doorway, a flashlight in hand. Rolando shielded his eyes against the blinding light.

"Who's there? Put out that stupid light," Rolando growled.

"It's Geoff. What are you doing in here?" the boy asked as he doused the light.

"How did you know where I am?" Rolando asked his brother.

"You left the door open. If you aren't careful all the hamsters will get out," Geoff answered in a disapproving voice

Chapter 17

"Well, shut it then," Rolando muttered under his breath relighting the candle.

Geoff pulled it shut and stood above Rolando, "Why are you sitting here in the middle of the night? What are you doing sitting here in your underwear and drinking that whiskey?"

"Why are you bothering me, Geoff?" Rolando answered his brother's question with a question in an attempt to cover his disgust and embarrassment.

"I heard you were to drive the truck for someone today," Geoff said. "You didn't show up. Were you ill?"

"Yes, I was very ill," Rolando answered ruefully. "I spent the entire afternoon in the saloon drinking myself ill."

"Rolando, how can I help you? If only you would tell me what's bothering you," Geoff touched his arm hesitantly.

"How can I tell you what's wrong if I'm not sure myself," Rolando answered as he rubbed his face and sighed. "Thank you, Geoff. Maybe I'll be able to talk with you when I get my own mind straightened out. Sometimes I feel my emotions are greater than my body can contain and I'll explode. Drinking helps and for a short time I have some peace."

Geoff squatted beside him for a moment then patted his brother's arm again, "Let's go back to bed. You're cold. Leave the whiskey here."

"No, you go. I'm all right," Rolando answered softly. "I'll stay here for a while. I've got to think a little. Please, go."

"Then I'll bring your clothes and a blanket," Geoff said as he reluctantly returned to the house.

Rolando watched daylight peek through the cracks in the roof and remained sober. Later that day he combed his hair and shaved. Walking to his Aunt Mariana's house, he knew he could find answers from her. After his mother's illness and depression had left her helpless and liquor had claimed his father, Rolando relied more heavily on his aunt and uncle. Of all his relatives, he trusted them as parents.

Mariana was behind the house feeding the chickens. A look of delight lit her face as he approached.

"Why, Rolando, I'm so glad to see you," she said warmly as she reached up to kiss his cheek. "Please come in the house. I have coffee, bread and cheese left from our breakfast. Are you hungry?"

He nodded, smiling as she tossed the rest of the corn and grass to the chickens. Wandering toward the house, she took his arm.

"Are things alright at your house today? I must go to see your mother this week, although I must admit I'm almost more worried about your father than your mother," his aunt inquired. "At least she seems content."

"Things are the same. As you know, I hired a girl from the village to care for Mama all day as she never leaves her room. Papa is here and there, I never know where. He comes and goes and sometimes I don't see him for days. I wonder how we make ends meet. I told you that we had to sell another piece of property a mile up the mountain. How else could I keep Elena and the boys in school? If we didn't have that property, I'd have to stop their education," Rolando admitted as he looked at his aunt sadly. "But, Tia, it makes me sad to sell property that has been in the family for generations."

She motioned him to the table, "You still have several acres further up the mountains, don't you?"

Pulling out a chair, he sat, "Yes, but I hate parting with each plot. If only the time would come for Elena and the boys to graduate. They could help with the family business and she could begin taking care of Mama. I would be able to go back to school and then work at a real profession. There is no way I can stop what I'm doing until then."

She prepared coffee, sliced bread and cheese, then sat across from him as she stated, "I feel there's more that is bothering you. You have had these responsibilities for years. Why are you so troubled now?"

He ran his hands over his face as he shared his frustration, "It's Elena. These past eight months have been difficult for us. I don't know what to do with her. The school principal sent me a note yesterday saying she is failing her subjects. I couldn't believe it. She's never had problems in school. In fact she has worked harder than her brothers."

When his head drooped in despair, she reached over to touch his hand, "Querida, you will never know how much I admire you. You have raised that girl from birth and cared for your brothers. You

Chapter 17

have put them through school without help from your parents. I think you have done a wonderful service to them and to us, your aunt and uncle."

Lifting his head, Rolando smiled at her, "I could never have raised them without help from you, Tia. We did it together. I've turned to you for help hundreds of times over the years. All of this would have been without a moment's regret if only I could understand what has happened to Elena."

Mariana bit her lip, hesitating several moments before she said, "I think she still loves Carlos."

Suddenly furious, he sprang to his feet, "No, that's impossible. That happened over eight months ago. How could she still think she loves him? In the first place, she doesn't know anything about love and in the second place, he isn't worthy to look at her, let alone touch her."

Enraged he set his jaw as he struggled to control his anger.

"Sit down a moment," his aunt said calmly. "You may have raised Elena and again I'll say you accomplished so much, but frankly you don't understand anything about a girl in love and I believe the problem with Elena is exactly that. She loves Carlos and she's suffering due to the separation. Have you noticed her eyes? They're sunken and she has lost weight. She looks ill, and quite honestly I'm concerned."

"Has she said anything to you about Carlos?" Rolando asked. "Does she talk to her cousins?"

"Elena has changed so much that she hardly visits anymore and when she does, she doesn't talk or laugh as she did in the past. If she talks about Carlos to her cousins I don't know it. I've been thinking of asking you if there is anything I can do to help you. My fear is that Elena is ill."

"She's ill, but I am, too," Rolando admitted tiredly. "It is affecting my whole life. Do you think I did the wrong thing in separating them?"

"No, you did the correct thing," Mariana assured him. "Class distinction in our society is important, and even though we are all Ecuadorians, we live on a higher level. We are landowners and in the town of Pachuca we are a principle family. Our relatives own homes throughout the plaza area. We all have cattle and crops. People like

Carlos work for us. We have superior blood flowing in our veins. There is no way we could have approved of a marriage between Carlos and Elena, but when a young girl is in love she doesn't see any difference in people or classes. She loves Carlos because of who he is, a handsome, well-mannered man. Hector and I were impressed with him and his work while he was with us. It is a shame he hasn't returned to work since the day of Elena's party. He disappeared and when I became concerned I was told he is working at a hacienda further up the mountain. Perhaps he's afraid of seeing Elena."

She smiled at him knowingly, "Or perhaps he now understands the differences in our families after you spoke with him. I know you explained to him that he couldn't have a future with her in your usual gentle manner. Knowing Carlos, I don't think it is because he has a lack of respect for you, but out of love for Elena that he hasn't come back."

Rising again, Rolando walked to the window and stared at the mountains above Pachuca. For a fleeting moment an overwhelming longing to escape to the hills, to hide in the brush and canyons, to lie along springs of water, to never have to face the hurts and problems of life swept over him. He was sick of the burden on his shoulders and of the lies he hid from his precious aunt. Sighing, he remained with his back to Mariana.

"Then you really believe Elena is still in love with him. How can she be at her age?" Rolando asked his aunt. "You'll never know how this surprised me. It's something I never considered."

Mariana carried the plates to the sink and looked up at him, "Carino, I have something important to ask you. Please don't be offended. I feel I must ask if you are having a problem with liquor. Are you drinking too much?"

Caught off guard, he managed to control the jerk of alarm, "No. I have no problem with alcohol. Sometimes I can't sleep and I drink a little to make me sleepy, that's all. You can understand that, can't you?"

"Geoff told me he had to carry you home the other night," his aunt told him with concern. "He came here looking for you and when I told him I hadn't seen you, he searched until he found you in the

Chapter 17

saloon. Oh, Rolando, you have to be careful. This is what happened to your father."

Controlling his anger against Geoff for troubling his aunt, he laughed and pinched her cheek, "Don't worry about me, Tia mia. I'm taking care of myself. It's Elena I worry about. You know, maybe I'll approach her differently. Maybe I can persuade her to do some things with me socially so she'll forget that boy. Surely in time all of this will pass."

She gave him a hint of a smile with a negative shake of her head, "You don't understand women, do you? Perhaps it's possible for men to forget or leave their loves and emotions behind to look for other relationships, but it's a great deal harder for women, I believe, especially if they are really in love. Elena won't forget Carlos quickly."

"That's it!" Rolando said suddenly as he snapped his fingers. "I have a friend in Quito. I'll ask him to throw a small party; just a small fiesta and I'll take Elena. He has a couple of nice brothers. Do you think I could get her interested in another fellow?"

"It is worth trying," his aunt nodded.

"Thanks, Tia. I do love you," he grinned.

She wrapped her arms around his waist, "I love you, too. Very much."

He returned home, took the truck on two runs and waited for Elena's return from school. Time passed slowly. He visited with his mother, but found her uncommunicative. He left her side after only a few minutes. Making a cup of coffee for himself, he slowly sipped it at the kitchen table, deep in thought. His anger toward Geoff involving their aunt in his drinking problems had passed. He made a resolution not to drink today and maybe not tomorrow. The thought that he would become like his father terrified him.

Hearing Elena in the doorway, his heart quickened. They would have an hour alone before their brothers arrived from school, as he had sent the young maid home early. Noticing him, Elena stepped into the kitchen and with a start he realized how hollow her eyes looked and how listless she acted. Why hadn't he noticed this before now? Elena's school uniform seemed to hang on her. Seeing her every day, the change was less obvious. But what bothered him the most was her quietness.

"Elena, sit down," he said with concern. "I'll get you a cola."

She dropped her books on a chair as she answered, "No, I can get my own. You stay there and I'll bring you one."

"How was school today?" he asked hoping to get her to admit she was having trouble.

"Okay I guess," she shrugged.

Rubbing his hands together, he took a deep breath, "I have a good idea. Do you remember the friend of mine who lives on the south side of Quito? Remember when we went to visit him on his saint's day two years ago? Well, I thought maybe we could visit him again. He has two brothers you got along well with, remember? I thought perhaps you'd enjoy going with me. We can have dinner and maybe dance a little afterwards. What do you think?"

Turning from the small counter, she placed a glass of cola beside his cup and looked at him, "No, I know what you are doing and I have no desire to go with you."

As she started to leave the kitchen, he got up from his chair and took her arm.

She jerked away, eyes flashing, "Rolando, you will not choose my friends for me. I'm old enough to know who I want for a friend. Now, if you'll excuse me, I want to visit Mama."

He stood, stunned, then slumped in his chair. *I'm losing her*, he thought. *What am I going to do? Perhaps I've already lost her.*

The familiar depression settled on him and he pushed the cola away, rising to his feet. Anger replaced depression and he stomped to the old abandoned kitchen. They found him two days later sprawled on an old bed in a small hut a mile up the mountainside. Vaguely he remembered being with a woman. Geoff and Uncle Hector half-dragged, half-carried him as he fought to resist them. They were able to bring him under control. Not wanting the townspeople to see his condition they placed him beside an irrigation ditch and wash him as best they could. Guiding him to his uncle's house, Aunt Mariana gave him a little to eat and put him to bed. Geoff walked home and returned with clean clothes for his brother.

The next morning Rolando woke with a terrible headache, but felt hungry.

Chapter 17

"I'm sorry," he winced with embarrassment. "I guess I have no excuse."

His aunt fried two eggs and cut bread for his breakfast. Placing the food in front of him, she laid her hand on his hair and brushed it back affectionately.

"Yes, you do. You have never had a chance to live a normal life. You've cared for others more than for yourself. I think one solution to all of this is that you find a girl, get married, and settle down. Stop sacrificing yourself for others."

His aunt placed her hands on her hips, frowning down on him, "Sometimes I think you like to live a life of sacrifice. Look at all your friends. They are married and have children and what are you doing? You're living like a monk just to care for your sister. You can't do that any longer. Elena loves you, I know that, but she was willing to leave you to marry Carlos. Did you really believe she would remain single for you? Not a chance. She would still desert you for Carlos if she had the opportunity. It is not because she doesn't love you. She's just more selfish than you are, or shall I say, perhaps willing to be a little more human, just as we all are."

"I'd like to be married," he said, spreading butter on his bread. "Do you think I don't wonder what it would be like to have children? It's just that every time I meet a girl I think I could love, the responsibilities at home pile up and I put off my own happiness for another year. How can I possibly think of marriage? I am doing what I must for Elena and Mama. Elena will graduate someday from the university and then I will have my own life."

Mariana dropped beside him and took his arm, "By that time you will be in your thirties. Where will you find a girl who will wait that long? Who is the woman you were with yesterday? Do I know her?"

"I guess so, but she means nothing to me," he scowled, embarrassed. "I don't remember much."

He buried his head in his palms, "What's happening to me and my life?"

"Everything will be all right," his aunt assured him softly. "I spoke with Elena."

His head jerked up and he stared at her, "You did?"

Patting his shoulder, she stood, "Yes, last night. She feels bad about the way she treated you. I have an idea she stayed home from school today and will be waiting for you. Why don't you run along and see if I'm not correct?"

He crammed bread in his mouth and hugged her, "Thanks Tia. I'll see you later."

Mariana was right. Elena was waiting and without a word she walked into his arms.

He held her face in his hands, "Are you okay?"

"Yes, and I'll go to Quito with you, to the party," she said gently.

"No, that wasn't a very good idea," he smiled.

"Aunt Mariana is worried that I'm ill. She thinks something is making me ill, Rolando. I don't want to treat you the way I did the other day. I love you and appreciate all you've done for me," Elena admitted warmly. "It's just that I have no desire to get up in the morning. I honestly don't know what's wrong."

"Could it be that you still care for Carlos?" he asked gently.

It was the first time since Elena's saint's day that Carlos' name had been mentioned between them.

Sighing deeply, she left his side and sat down then suddenly burst into tears, "I don't know. I haven't seen Carlos since the day you found us. Perhaps that's part of the problem. If he loved me as I love him, why didn't he try to see me? No matter what you said to him, if his love was as deep as he declared, surely he would have tried, wouldn't he?"

She wiped her eyes with the back of her hand.

With a surge of relief, he began to understand, "Is that what's bothering you?"

"Yes," she said relieved she could finally confide in her beloved brother. "We were going to get married. He had such grand plans. How could someone tell me he loves me with his whole heart and I never see him again? I know he's in the area. My friends who live near his house have seen him. Sometimes I think I will walk to his house, but I know you have forbidden me to do that and I respect your wish, but oh how I want to find out if Carlos has found another love."

"Perhaps that's what happened. Perhaps he didn't love you as you loved him. I guess there are different degrees of love," Rolando

Chapter 17

said trying hard to control his joy. "Just remember this. I love you. We all do, your brothers, our aunt and uncle, cousins and our mother. In time you'll forget what has happened. I don't expect your feelings to change overnight, but please, Elena, try. For your sake and mine, don't let it affect your schooling. You've come so far and done so well."

She smiled through her tears, "Thank you for your patience. I will try. Perhaps you're right. He just wasn't worth my faithfulness all these months, but still, it hurts so much."

Another rush of tears choked her as she turned for her bedroom.

The relief he felt was tremendous. Walking out the back door, he stood in the sunshine and thrust his arms upward. All was well. Out of sheer joy, he found two bottles of whiskey and emptied them.

"I'll not need you, I guess," he told the empty bottles as he threw back his head and laughed out loud, causing the maid to leave hanging the wash to stare at him in amazement.

Chapter 18

At the last minute, Sandi offered to drive Jillian from Quito to Pachuca. After the siesta hour the young nurse gathered her exit papers and airline tickets and dropped by Jillian's apartment.

"Thank goodness you decided to come to Quito today," Jillian grinned, climbing into the jeep. "I don't know if I could face another truck ride this soon even if it is with the missionary children."

"The embassy called me shortly after breakfast needing me to pick up my exit papers. It's my pleasure to take you to Pachuca. I wish I could have done it the first time," Sandi said to her.

"Actually now that I experienced that terrible ordeal, I'm glad it happened. I gained a lot of enriching memories," Jillian admitted with a smile.

Sandi let out a hoot of laughter, "Well, that's one way of looking at it."

She sobered and smiled sadly, "This is the most beautiful valley in the world you know. Hopefully you'll learn to love it as I do."

Overcome with excitement, Jillian knew an important door was about to open for her. She sat forward in the battered jeep as Sandi drove through the Tumbaco Valley telling stories of her experiences.

Encountering no problems, they arrived in Pachuca within an hour. Marta relented, allowing the children to greet their guest as she entered the house. Jillian gathered them to her with hugs and kisses, pleased with the nod of approval from Marta.

Chapter 18

Lucia mumbled greetings and headed for the clinic while Sandi stood back, clearly delighted with the demonstrations of love and Marta's leniency.

At breakfast the next morning Marta informed them that she and Sandi would be attending a farewell luncheon for Sandi at a missionary compound in Pachuca that afternoon.

Jillian peeked at Lucia as it was announced that she would be in charge of the children and Lucia would oversee the clinics. Lucia failed to look in her direction but continued to focus on her breakfast.

When Sandi and Marta drove off the property, Jillian relaxed with a grand smile, exhilarated in the sheer joy of belonging. With Flora's help she fed the children their lunch and put them down for their naps.

She spent time with Flora in the kitchen, but her mind was on Lucia. Was this the time to see if there was an opportunity to begin a friendship with her? What if she was not invited to work in the ministry here? Would this be the only chance she had to approach her? Her interest in Lucia was becoming stronger with each passing hour. She was determined to become her friend.

Strolling slowly to the clinic, her heart beating fast, she entered the maternity clinic. Loud groans came from the patient's area.

"Lucia, where are you?" she called out.

No answer.

"Lucia!" she called again louder.

The labor room was empty. Turning, she rushed into the main ward. All the beds were made except for one in total disarray. She was alarmed to see a huge puddle of water by the bed. Where was the patient? Where was Lucia?

A scream emitted from the bathroom. A young woman, squatting on the toilet was straining in contractions.

Jillian grabbed her arm and fumbled in Spanish, "What are you doing? You should be in bed."

Expressionless, the tired woman looked at her through sweat-soaked strands of hair. Unable to move the patient, Jillian ran in panic to knock on Lucia's door. No one answered. She ran upstairs to the attic but found no one. Flying down the stairs and out the front door, she ran to the outpatient clinic. Throwing open the door, she ran through Marta's bedroom and into the main room. Lucia looked up impatiently. An old man in great distress was sitting on a stool beside her.

"What do you want, Jill?" Lucia demanded.

"I'm not sure, but I think there's a problem in the clinic," Jillian explained. "The patient is sitting on the toilet. It looks like her water has broken."

"So what? Maybe she needs to use the bathroom. I have a big problem here that needs immediate attention," Lucia said impatiently. "Go on back and try to get her into bed. I can't come right now."

"But she's on the toilet and her water has broken. What if the baby is born in the toilet? It will drown. Can't you leave him for a moment and help me?"

Sighing loudly, she dropped an instrument into a white metal container, "I'll make this man a little more comfortable and be right there. I'm sure the patient isn't ready yet. She would have rung the bell if she was."

Jillian raced back to the maternity clinic. The expectant mother's groans were louder now.

Rushing into the bathroom, Jillian gasped, "Oh my goodness. What are you doing?"

The woman was sitting back on the toilet clawing desperately at the emerging baby's head.

"Please come with me and get in bed," Jillian sputtered in English.

Uncomprehending the woman pushed her away and continued her attempt to reach the baby's head, "Where is Señorita Marta?"

Frightened and angered, Jillian fought the urge to cry. When Lucia hurried through the door, she almost fainted with relief.

"Oh, hurry. Hurry! The baby is coming out," Jillian screamed running ahead of Lucia.

She rattled hysterically, "It's falling into the toilet."

Lucia burst passed Jillian and with incredible strength picked up the woman, dragged her to the labor room and pushed her onto the table.

"What were you doing on the toilet?" she yelled at her. "Are you so stupid that you don't know that your baby was almost born in the toilet? We have a bell beside your bed. What do you think it's for? Why didn't you ring it?"

Chapter 18

She displayed forcible pounding on the button of an imaginary bell, "Now there is a mess all over the floor. Okay, push. I've got someone waiting for me in the other clinic. Push! Harder! Okay. That's better. Here it comes."

Feeling weak and shaky, Jillian leaned against the wall, "Thank you for getting here in time."

Frowning, Lucia looked up at her, "Why were you so excited? So, the baby would have been born in the toilet. It's just one less person having to grow up in this godforsaken country. You can believe me, he would have been better off drowning."

Disgust tempered Jillian's relief. How unthinkable. She would never have gotten over such a tragedy. But watching the tenderness Lucia was showing as she cleaned the patient and put her to bed, she had to smile. Lucia's bluster was a cover-up for the nearly fatal birth.

"I'm glad you're here," Lucia conceded.

She found a bassinet and some clean clothes for the baby. Pouring warm water in a basin, she tested it with her elbow.

"Now, if you will bathe the baby, dress him, and give him to his mother, then clean up this mess, I've got to return to my patient. Why don't you stop over there afterwards? I'd like to talk to you and I think you'd like to see what I'm working on."

With that, she left the clinic.

Bathing the baby, Jillian stopped to admire the delicate, olive-skinned beauty, wrapping the long black silky hair around her finger. She inspected the top of his head to see if the mother had inflicted any damage during the time she had spent on the toilet. No injuries were showing. After dressing the little boy, she tucked in the mother and with a sense of pride handed her the infant.

"Would you like a cup of anise water for your pain?" she asked the shy, smiling woman remembering this is what Lucia had offered other patients.

After serving her the hot-flavored water, she again checked the baby and with insight she realized she had saved its life. This exhilarating thought rushed her through the clean-up and followed her to the outpatient clinic.

Lucia was yelling when Jillian entered, "Hold still! You can't move. Hold still!"

The patient waved wildly and pushed at Lucia, who stood above his tilted head. With one hand she poked a small penlight up his nose; the other hand held a long tweezers. Beside her stood a small table with a metal basin, some cotton, and alcohol.

Out of the corner of her eye, she spotted Jillian and called to her, "Come here. Look at this."

Experience had already taught her that Lucia delighted in seeing her discomforted. She hesitated then moved slowly toward the old man. His unwashed condition assaulted her nose, causing her throat to constrict.

He gasped as Lucia poked the tweezers up his nose and removed a bloody mucous-covered object.

"What is that?" she croaked in horror, feeling her stomach rise.

Swallowing her nausea, she stared down at the basin where Lucia had discarded her treasure, "Is that a fly?"

"Yes. Apparently a fly laid her eggs up this man's nose while he was sleeping or whatever. That's not too hard to believe considering that there are millions of flies in this country," Lucia explained as she continued to work on him.

"Didn't he realize what was happening?" Jillian asked unable to understand how such a thing could happen.

"He's just an old man who didn't know something was wrong until his sinuses became very infected. When he could no longer breathe they dragged him in here," Lucia shook her head and swabbed at the bloodied nose. "Imagine how he felt when the larva started moving around in there. Who knows what they fed on? Anyway it's obvious they were in there long enough to hatch into small flies. At least they seem to be all dead now."

"Why did he let it go so long?" Jillian asked disgusted yet amazed at what she was watching.

"There is another one. These people don't come around here until their eyes are rolling back in their heads," Lucia said sadly. "Then they expect miracles."

"I've got to go," Jillian said. "I need to check on the children."

Lucia, looking highly pleased with the effect she had created, chuckled, "No, stay a minute. I want to talk to you."

Chapter 18

She grunted with the effort of fighting the waving man's hand, "I'm going to be through here in a few minutes. Hand me that basin so I don't have to turn around."

Jillian hesitated but decided she'd rather stay and make Lucia believe she was strong rather than provoke her disdain by leaving. Girding herself, she took a deep breath, picked up the basin, and held it out.

Lucia spoke gently with the man to relieve his discomfort. The minutes passed while several more flies and larva were removed from his sinus cavity.

"I got as many out as I could. It might be that we've removed all of them, but you may have to come back again," she told him.

Dropping the tweezers into the basin, she stuck the penlight in her blouse pocket and proceeded to pack his nose with cotton. Then she opened the front door and called out. An elderly woman lost beneath layers of ponchos shyly padded in, and politely greeted Jillian and Lucia before turning to her husband. With great concern, she comforted him, arranging his poncho and holding his hand. He dug into a pocket with his free hand for a few sucres and importantly paid his bill.

After they departed, Lucia cleaned the room, discarding the basin's contents and used swabs. Working in silence, she replaced the alcohol and put the tweezers in another metal basin to be sterilized. Jillian waited without comment, anticipating what Lucia wanted to tell her, but to her surprise the Indian turned to leave the clinic. Perplexed she took Lucia's arm.

"What was it you wanted to talk to me about?" Jillian asked.

"I've changed my mind," Lucia said tersely, pulling her arm away.

"No you haven't," Jillian said kindly. "What is wrong?"

Jillian could see the struggle Lucia was having with the decision to walk away or stay and reveal what was on her mind. Several seconds passed and finally she slowly spoke, with deep sighs and hesitations.

"It's hard for me to accept people, especially foreigners. I've been mistreated by many people, some of my family members, but mostly foreigners who think they're better than Ecuadorian Indians, especially one who is from the jungle. Maybe someday I can tell you how they have treated me, but you act like you care a little," Lucia said sincerely. "I just wanted to say that I'm glad you came here."

Delighted, Jillian responded, "Lucia, I promise that you can trust me. I'm also very happy to be here. The fact that you're an Ecuadorian Indian makes me proud to know you."

Lucia turned quickly and walked away, but not before Jillian glimpsed bright tears in her eyes.

It was later that evening after the children were in bed when Marta approached Jillian for a talk, "I'll only take a minute of your time."

She pulled two stuffed chairs forward, facing the warm fireplace. Regretfully, Jillian saw Lucia and Sandi leave for the maternity clinic. Her heart was beating rapidly.

"We need to talk about your future, Jill. Perhaps if I discuss some of my thoughts you can add to them," Marta said looking directly at Jillian.

I don't like her, thought Jillian. *I simply don't like her.* Fearing her eyes would betray her, she fought to bring a smile to her face.

"What I first need is to know is if you have thought about your plans," continued the woman. "How do you feel about moving to Pachuca? Have you considered working with me?"

She paused and adjusted her body weight and patted her waist line. "Whew, I ate too much. Anyway, I'm without Sandi now that she's leaving in a couple days. If you choose to work in another location, I'll have to start a search for someone else right away. I hear you've been putting more effort into your Spanish these past few weeks. That's good. Maybe you can take more lessons in Quito. However, we'll talk about that later. Normally I'm a loner, but after much thought I realize there's no way that Lucia and I can do the work alone."

She paused again for a long moment then leaned back and laughed gleefully, "I haven't had a chance to ask you. Were you with Lucia at all this morning? I'm afraid she's very unsociable. It sounds like I'm bragging a little, but so far I'm the only one who can handle her. Everyone I've left her with in the past has told me the most horrid stories."

She continued grinning and pulled off her glasses to wipe them with a crumpled handkerchief, "One of the main reasons I left you

Chapter 18

two alone was part of your initiation. I wanted to see if you two could find a way to be civil to each other. Oh well, we'll discuss that later. Right now I'm more interested in your decision about staying."

Jillian smiled inwardly. Lucia and the children were her reason for staying. Hopefully her relationship with them would override her growing dislike for Marta.

"If you are certain that I'd be an asset to this work, I'd like to stay more for the sake of the children. What a shame it would be for them to be separated from Sandi's care and not have someone to take her place. Right now that's the most important issue, the children. You're in the outpatient clinic and Lucia is with the maternity patients, so the children will need someone here. I'll be glad to stay. I have my Spanish books and I'm picking up the accents just listening to Lucia. Maybe from now on we'll speak only in Spanish to each other. I'd really like that," she grinned innocently. "And please don't worry about Lucia and me. We got along just fine this morning."

A strange look crossed Marta's face and several seconds passed before she cleared her throat and spoke, "I'm glad to hear that. Jill, you're going to have to understand what I'm going to tell you. If you work here I'll expect you to respect me as the authority figure. I've had a few problems in the past. We're going to have to put this out in the open right now."

Her chin quivered. Searching on her lap, she found her linen handkerchief and burst into tears, crying in a high nasal pitch.

"No one shows me respect. No one. I must have a promise from you that you will respect and honor my requests. Just a year ago Sandi's parents were here," she said with tears running down her face. "They felt I discipline my children too much. Think of it!"

Marta's tears fell freely and she blew her nose loudly, "I've saved these children from death's door and just because I want them well mannered, I'm told that I'm too strict."

She pounded the chair arm, rose, and paced in front of the fireplace before seating herself again, "Too strict! They wouldn't think too strict if they could see how these children would act without a strong hand guiding them."

Swinging her head toward Jillian, she demanded, "Can you imagine?"

Dumbfounded Jillian watched the pathetic woman and nodded.

"I know what they would be like," Marta continued sobbing. "Do you know what I did? I'll prove to you how easy I am to get along with. Sandi's parents suggested that they care for the children to give me a break. They thought if they could have the children under their care for a while it would prove that lack of discipline would improve their behavior. Well, I did it. I stayed away from the kids for several days. Lucia and I even took our meals in the clinic. It was hard on me. I felt as if the whole world was against me. I'll tell you, only Lucia stood by me. She really did. She's the most faithful friend I have."

Marta paused for effect, "Do you know what Sandi's parents did? They hired a lawyer to grab my children away and adopt them out. I was horrified. I prayed and pleaded with God to protect us."

Her arms waved dramatically, her piteous wide eyes begged for Jillian's understanding, "Do you believe me?"

Jillian nodded again.

"Finally when I couldn't stand it any longer I went to Sandi's parents. Everyone was against me, even Flora. Then it struck me. All of a sudden it struck me that this is my house and I am the authority. My mind was suddenly clear. My relief was beyond words. When I realized that I had been duped, I told them to get out immediately. I am the authority in my own home and I will be always. No one will ever take my place with my children. I hope you understand what I mean," Marta said as the tears dried and her brown eyes flashed with anger.

"Jill, if you want to stay in this house, you will have to promise me tonight that you will follow my orders, the most important being that you will discipline the children as they need it. I will not have spoiled children in my house. They are totally out of line right now because Sandi has spoiled them to death. You should have seen them after Sandi's parents left. Unbelievable! Just look at Lydia and horrors, at Sara. Sometimes I'd like to strangle them. Leah has been ruined by Lucia, but what can I do about that? I have a hard time liking Leah anyway. I never chose her. Lucia took her in when I was in the states on a shopping trip for the work here."

She sighed deeply, "Your job will be to obey orders and see that the children are turned into respectable adults. Well? How do you feel?"

Chapter 18

Jillian sat for a moment, thinking quickly. *How can I ever feel respect for this woman, let alone have fellowship with her? I know if I leave the children under her influence for long, there will be no hope for them. What if Marta finds someone else who treats them cruelly or would leave them in a few weeks? They would have to get to know someone else. They are already nervous wrecks. But if I stay, I may be able to contribute something positive to their development. How could Sandi have put me in this position?*

"I think that I will be able to do what you ask, but as far as I see, the children aren't as spoiled as you say. Infants do cry and babies do have needs. It's natural for children to protest or even fight sometimes. But that doesn't mean they're spoiled," Jillian said as respectfully as she could.

"My children will not cry. If they do, I will expect you to spank them," Marta said firmly. "Do you understand?"

Now she began to comprehend the tremendous pressure Sandi had been under and she wondered if she would ever be able to protect these children.

"I promise that I will do whatever is necessary to see they grow up to be respectable adults," Jillian said truthfully.

"Good," beamed Marta. "I can see that you and I will get along just fine and will be able to spend many good times together."

A warning signal went off in Jillian's head and she began grappling with words. The last thing she wanted was forming a friendship with this woman.

"Perhaps, but I've found to have a good working association it's probably better not to have a close friendship," Jillian said with a boldness she did not really feel.

Marta was shocked, "What do you mean? I can't live with you under those circumstances."

An unpleasant undertone entered her voice, "You said that you got along well with Lucia, or at least you implied that. Do you mean that you could be a friend of hers but you can't with me?"

"Lucia is my peer. You aren't. You said yourself that you are the authority," Jillian reasoned as the pressure to explain was growing heavier. "I don't know you very well. Besides that, you have already placed me on a different level than yourself by demanding that I obey your orders. Even though I have promised to help you, I can't completely agree to all your methods of discipline. No doubt children need it as much as they need love, but I have to say that when discipline becomes lopsided, there will be problems in the future."

"Oh, now I understand," said Marta shaking her head. "You have been talking to Sandi, haven't you? That's one reason I advised her not to spend much time with you. I knew she'd try to change your mind about me."

That's why Sandi kept to herself so much, thought Jillian. "I'm sorry that you felt you had to keep Sandi from me. She has nothing to do with my feelings. I've always felt this way. As far as Lucia is concerned, I think underneath all of her bluff, she is a very nice person. I've been told she is depressed and despondent all the time, but while you were gone, I found her to be a kind and gentle person. We had no trouble at all."

Concern deepened the lines on Marta's face as she stared at Jillian and after a moment spoke softly, "Jill, you will have to stay away from Lucia. She is not your peer. Of course, you two must act friendly. If you don't, you will have problems. But you see Lucia is in a different class. She's an Indian. Worse, she's a jungle Indian, the lowest class there is in Ecuador. Listen to me and I can teach you a great deal. It's not proper to make a close friend with Indians."

She leaned closer, "Keep this uppermost in your mind; don't befriend an Indian on a companionship level. Lucia must remain in her place, or I'll never be able to handle her."

Jillian sputtered in disgust, "That's impossible for me to understand. What is all this class business? It doesn't matter to me in the least if someone has high cheekbones, dark skin, black hair, and eyes. What are most important to me are the person and their character. Marta, I've given up everything I love at home, my family, my church, and all my friends for this one reason, to live with these people. Then to my surprise, upon my arrival, I'm informed that I must not be friends with them?"

"I didn't mean that exactly. You just can't be on an intimate basis with them." Marta slapped her knees in agitation. "Goodness, what do you think I'm trying to do? I'm just saying, not an intimate relationship. You'll ruin Lucia, Jill. I warn you."

Chapter 18

"Maybe it's not a good idea for me to be here," Jillian said with concern. "We are already arguing."

The nurse tossed back her head and laughed, "Arguing? You think this is an argument? Oh my dear, this isn't an argument. This is a normal conversation."

She cleared her throat, "I think I'm going to like you a lot, but we must get this straightened out. There will be no close friendship between you two. You can talk and continue to practice your Spanish with her, but always keep in mind that she is like a child and can be influenced very easily."

Her face softened, "One day you may be able to speak the language as well as I do, but listen to me. Unless you understand the customs, you will never gain a foothold. I've been here for many years and I'm still trying to understand these people. They constantly amaze me. How can you expect to understand the class distinction in just five or six months?

Trying to push back a tremendous resistance rising in her, Jillian leaned back and closed her eyes. How she wished she could flee from Pachuca, never to return, but right on the tail of this thought she saw the faces of the children. Could she submit enough to Marta for their sakes? She knew in her heart what her answer must be. Glancing at the woman patiently waiting, she nodded her head.

Jillian rose, feeling the meeting had come to an end. At the door, calmer now, she turned to speak.

"I did a lot of thinking and praying about this decision. I will give my notice at my apartment in Quito as soon as possible. I do appreciate you asking me to live here with the children. I know that you could probably handle things by yourself and it pleases me that you have put this much faith in me," Jillian said remembering Sandi's advice to her. "I'll try my best because of the trust you have given me."

"Thank you, Jill. Perhaps we can pick up your things in Quito this week and bring them out," Marta offered. "I know we're doing the right thing."

"Well, I believe this is what God wants me to do," Jillian added.

Marta stared into the dying embers without comment.

Outside, Jillian paused to lean on the doorjamb, breathing deeply. Anxious to see Sandi and Lucia, she walked halfway to the clinic before realizing the building was in darkness. A glance back at Sandi's window showed it was darkened, too. The meeting with Marta had taken longer than she expected. With a sense of loneliness, she wandered to the guesthouse, hoping she too could sleep.

For more than an hour she tossed and turned, struggling to find peace in her heart, but Marta's words bothered her. Maybe she was right. After all, she had lived here for many years, working with the people, speaking their language, delivering their babies, and curing their diseases. Maybe the cultural barrier was too great to cross. Maybe Lucia was too much of a child to deal with. Truly, she had shown her worst immature behavior on their first encounter. How could she, Jillian compare her scanty experience and knowledge of the culture to what Marta had gained over a quarter of a century? Maybe I have too much pride, she thought. I'm new at this language and culture. I've never raised children. Maybe I have too much zeal and no wisdom.

She pounded her pillow to make herself more comfortable and lay back. Holding her breath, she thought she heard a small noise. Then a tapping at the door brought her upright.

"Who is it?" Jillian called out.

"Shhh. It's Sandi. Keep the lights off, but open the door."

Jillian jumped from the bed and slowly turned the bolt. Peeking out, she saw Sandi standing in her long robe, shaking in the chilly air and casting eerie shadows on the guesthouse wall.

"Let me in," Sandi pushed her way inside and felt her way to the bed. "I'm freezing."

"What's wrong?" asked Jillian, following her.

"I just wanted to see you, but I had to wait until Marta went to the clinic before I could leave the house," Sandi said quietly. "I thought she'd never go home."

"I'm glad you came," Jillian said sincerely. "I didn't know if we would have much time to talk before you leave."

"I know. I have to get right back. Sara has a tummy-ache tonight. I think the children are upset by the changes all of us are going through. But I just had to know what you told Marta," Sandi said urgently. "Are you going to stay here in Pachuca?"

"I told her I would," Jillian answered with a small smile.

Chapter 18

Sandi let out a small yelp of delight, "Oh, thank you, thank you. You can't imagine how happy you have made me."

"I don't know if it's a good idea or not, but I'll try," Jillian said as she hoisted herself up on the high bed and sat by her friend. "There are a couple things that bother me a lot. Maybe you can give me some insight."

Sandi shrugged her shoulder, "I'll try."

"In two conversations I've eluded to the fact in one way or another that I've a strong Christian background and that I pray. Both times Marta ignored me. She acted as if I hadn't said anything," Jillian asked bringing her major concern to the forefront. "Will this ever become an issue?"

"I don't see why. I think she's open to religious things. When I'm home I go to church and have told Marta this. She doesn't seem to care," Sandi brushed the subject aside. "What was the other thing?"

"What is the relationship between Marta and Rolando Martinez?" Jillian asked.

"What?" Sandi turned and studied Jillian's dark form in the dim light. "Why in the world would you bring up Rolando and Marta? How do you even know about him?"

"Do you remember when Marta and I went to the plaza the last time I was here?" Jillian asked. "During the fiesta Rolando and Elena, his sister passed our truck. Rolando gave Marta a very hostile look. It was almost a look of hatred."

"There are some Ecuadorians who don't like Marta or foreigners, so that attitude isn't too unusual," Sandi said hoping to bring this thought to a close.

Jillian shook her head, "No, there was more to it than that. It was obvious that it bothered Marta a lot. There must be more to it."

"It's probably a rumor more or less, but the townspeople claim that because of Marta's neglect at the time of Elena's birth their mother had a stroke that left her partially paralyzed," Sandi said.

"Neglect?" Jillian asked. "Marta said that their mother went to a witchdoctor for the delivery."

"She did but from what I hear, Marta had to refuse to help her because she wasn't feeling well and that their mother had not come to the clinic for prenatal care. However, the people say Rolando's mother was left on the road to die, but eventually made it to the midwife's house," Sandi said sharing what she had heard. "Marta thinks that all midwives are witchdoctors."

"So that's it," Jillian paused. "I was struck by how nice looking they are."

"Yes, but Rolando drinks too much. I've driven through town and seen him and his friends in the plaza, drunk as skunks," Sandi said. "But there you are, his father is a drunk. too."

"That's too bad," Jillian said shaking her head as she thought of the handsome young man and his sister.

"Yes it is. Well, I've got to go," Sandi grunted as she hopped off the bed. "Thanks again for staying. No matter what Marta told you, follow your heart, Jill. She has a bark bigger than her bite."

Sandi stepped outside pulling the door closed behind her.

"That's easier said than done," Jillian replied to herself.

Chapter 19

A few days later Sandi rode off the property in Marta's truck. It was anticlimactic after watching her weep her way through the morning. Already Jillian knew how Sandi must feel because her own emotional ties were threading deeper as each minute passed.

During lunch, the depressed children had picked at their food and searched Sandi's face in hopes she would change her mind. They sobbed during her good-byes and all the way to their bedrooms at nap time. Surprisingly, Marta stood back watching without criticizing their emotions. She was too delighted to see Sandi leave to make a scene.

Jillian had hoped to visit with Lucia, but the woman needed to be in the clinic and didn't want to be disturbed. *I'll go to town while Marta is in Quito with Sandi and Lucia is recovering from Sandi's departure*, she thought excitedly. She found Flora and told her she would be back in an hour, and walked through the gates and up the road to town.

Walking lazily, she absorbed the early afternoon's sunrays that were beating warmly on her back. Her thoughts were on Sandi. Jillian couldn't imagine how the nurse could have made the decision to leave Ecuador. Surely things weren't that bad.

There was little movement on the streets as the townspeople were enjoying the main meal of the day. A dog sniffed at her heels and returned to his doorstep. She passed the magistrate's office and stopped to peer into the government outpatient clinic. Chuckling softly, she could see in her mind's eye, Marta recoiling in horror. Disappointed that most doors were closed for the siesta hour, she walked on, passing the long, brick schoolhouse and crossed the street to the plaza. She sat on one of the stone benches.

A young girl appeared on the balcony of the house across the street, carrying a plate of food. She had been told that was Olivia's house, the government doctor's aide. Jillian watched the girl return empty-handed and descend the steps.

An elderly woman peered out the door of a store, then stepped to the curb and dumped a pan of dirty water. Wiping her hands on a flared skirt, she stared at Jillian momentarily and returned to the house. In a moment the door opened again and several heads craned to see her.

A young male Indian turned the corner at the end of the block and leaned against a building, digging food from a brown paper container. He examined each piece before popping it in his mouth, and then cleaned his hands on his shirt.

She sat in wonder looking at the old mud-block houses and cobblestone roads surrounded by the lush mountainside, still astounded at her good fortune. As she drank in the beauty of this aged pueblo, she noticed a man astride a large, brown stallion come to a halt at the elderly woman's store. He dismounted and dropped the reins to the sidewalk, strode to the store and removed his hat. Jillian was surprised to see he was very tall and had thick gray hair. She had only seen pictures of Ecuadorians with gray hair and they were usually Ecuadorian governmental officials. She watched him knock on the door, open it carefully and step inside. Within minutes he exited, sack in hand and stared in her direction. Leaning down to pick up the reins, he gingerly mounted the stallion.

When she realized he was going to pass her, she held her breath and tried to look away. But before he was halfway across the road, she saw his dark eyebrows, blue eyes, large and bright. He stopped directly in front of her and lifted his wide-brimmed hat in greeting. A long straight brush of dark lashes set off their blue color, and she stared into them foolishly. Attractive and distinguished, she placed his age to be mid-forties, but his face was youthful, so maybe it was the gray hair that aged him.

Chapter 19

"Buenas tardes, Señorita," he nodded toward her.

"Buenas tardes, Señor," she responded

With a smile he nodded again and walked his horse passed her. It took a minute for her to realize she was again holding her breath. Afraid he would have stopped to converse with her, after he passed, she wished he had. She watched him ride toward the magistrate office and dismount. Much to her pleasure, he turned to look at her before entering the building.

"Buenas tardes," came a voice right next to her.

"Oh!" yelped Jillian.

Startled, her hand flew to her heart. Face flushing with shock she turned to see a young man standing beside the bench. Her first impression was that he was immaculate. He was short, very thin, wore glasses, and sported a trimmed beard. In his hand he held a doctor's satchel. His other hand lay on the breast of his neatly ironed shirt and perfectly knotted tie. Completing his outfit was a crisp, snow-white doctor's coat. His fingers were long and nails manicured.

"I'm sorry for frightening you," he said with a small bow. He apologized in educated Spanish. "May I sit with you?"

Jillian shrugged, uncomfortable. Then he smiled, lighting up his face, his black eyes lost in a host of laugh lines. She couldn't help but smile back.

"My name is Philip Rios. What's yours?"

"Jill Townsend."

"Jill Townsend?" he struggled with the difficult last name and they both laughed. "I'm very glad to meet you, Jill Townsend."

He stuck out his hand and cautiously she took it. It was soft and warm. The clean smell of a recent shower rose to meet her.

"Do you live in Pachuca, Philip?"

"I was going to ask you the same thing," he laughed again. "No, I live in Quito, but I have a medical clinic in the next pueblo. I also teach medical students in the governmental hospital in Quito each morning, so I am able to bring medicines to the clinic in Pachuca each day."

"You look too young to be a professor of medical students," teased Jillian.

Philip laughed with delight, "Perhaps I am young, but I am fortunate enough to have studied in Europe and the hospital needed me to pass on many of my experiences."

He grinned again, "Do you live in Pachuca and if so, where have you been?"

His personality was contagious.

She giggled with him, "Yes, I live here. Down at the end of the road with Señorita Marta."

Sobering, he frowned, "The American nurse?"

"Yes," replied Jillian, puzzled by the reaction. "Do you know Marta?"

"A little. We've met on a couple occasions. Actually I hear more of how she feels about the medical profession in this country," Philip responded. "She doesn't respect us very much."

"No, she doesn't," Jillian admitted, thinking that Marta was probably mistaken about Philip.

"Where is your family?" Philip asked changing the subject.

"In the United States. We live in Oregon, which is the most beautiful state on the continent. I have a very nice family," Jillian shared. "Maybe they will come to visit me someday."

"You speak good Spanish," Philip complimented her.

Jillian chuckled, "You don't have to say that. I just speak the basic words right now."

He shrugged, "I understand you." Turning his head sideways, he pursed his lips, "Are you a Señorita by chance?"

"If you mean, am I married? No, I'm not. I mean yes, I'm a Señorita," she laughed.

He laughed with her and relaxed in an exaggerated manner, "That is very good news. How would you like to marry an Ecuadorian and become a citizen?"

"And who would you mean?" she asked her eyes twinkling.

"May I visit with you at the Señorita's house?" Philip asked.

The question was like cold water thrown on their teasing. She had never discussed with Marta her chances of a relationship with a man, but somehow she knew the nurse would not like it.

She shook her head, "I don't think that would be a very good idea."

He looked hurt, "I think I understand."

Chapter 19

He reached into his back pocket and removed a card from his wallet, "Here is my card. On it is my house number in Quito and also the clinic in Yaruqui. Call me if you need me and I'll come."

He picked up his bag, brushed off the back of his pants and coat, and held out his hand.

"By the way, the man on the horse, his name is Eric Perez. He's a hacienda owner and is a very important young man in this part of Ecuador. His gray hair makes him look older than he is. He's actually quite young to be an hacienda owner and he's not married," Philip said and with a lopsided grin, he turned.

She watched him walk to the government clinic before returning home. She decided not to mention either man to Marta.

Chapter 20

He was tired. Unsaddling the horse, he led her to the railing and secured the rope. After wiping her flank and brushing her, he paused a moment to pet the big head. Untying the mare, he led her to the enclosed pasture and unlocked the gate. The horse trotted to her companions, nuzzling them before settling down to chomp on the sweet grasses.

Discovering the water in the trough was low, Carlos brought several buckets of water from the well beside the barn. Fatigue made him weak and he wondered if he could walk the distance home.

During the weekend two horses had escaped from the pasture below the hacienda and he had been tracking them all day. After a fruitless search and some vague information from peons on the trail, he presumed they had traveled southeast along the sides of a canyon and up into the mountains. He planned to get a good night sleep and try again the next day.

Departing early, he wrapped himself in a poncho and pulled his hat low. He continued to question people on the roads and nearby homes, but no one had seen the stray horses. An hour later sunbeams reached the top of the canyon and warmth spread through his chilled limbs. He stopped to remove his wraps and eat the bread he had stuffed in his pockets and to drink from the ditch beside the road. The way had been laid with smooth rocks making travel easy; however an hour from Pachuca, the road became a path of hardened ruts, rocks, and tufts of grass. Billowing clouds of dust, a testament

Chapter 20

to the lack of rain, compelled him to tie a handkerchief around the lower part of his face.

Guiding his horse down into a small canyon, they crossed a wooden bridge and emerged on the other side, enjoying the cool shade. Turning away from the canyon, the road widened, a surface of smooth rocks proved Hacienda Palugo was near. Two men on horseback passed, nodding their greetings.

"Please wait," called Carlos turning to approach them again, "Buenos dias. Have you by chance seen two stallions without riders in these parts? One is brown with a white patch on his face and two white front legs, the other all brown with a black mane and tail."

The two men cordially told him no and continued on their way.

The rock-laid road ended abruptly and took a direct right turn narrowing to a trail alongside a deep canyon. To the right rose a sheer mountainside, towering hundreds of feet to the sky. On the left there was a sheer drop of two thousand feet to the river below. Peons had labored throughout the years constructing the pathway connecting haciendas and towns, despite the mountains, the huge rocks and the rains that triggered mud slides to cascade into the deep ravine.

Carlos dismounted to lead his timid horse along the narrow treacherous pathway. He picked his way around sections that had disappeared into the abyss below. Several yards ahead, he could see that the road had remained intact and he sighed in relief when they reached it safely. He traveled several miles before cobblestones appeared once again, acknowledging he was close to another hacienda. Stretching high in the saddle, he saw a group of houses. With a yelp of delight, he nudged his horse into a fast trot that took him into the yard. Dismounting, he embraced the shady coolness offered by the trees.

Several women sat on a long porch that ran the length of the main house. Corn was grown past the maturity stage, the grains large and ready for roasting. Piles of golden corn seemed to fill every vacant spot. Leaning their backs against the house wall, the women were husking the corn cobs, dividing bad grain from good. The good grain would be taken to Quito and sold for seed or roasting corn, the bad used as animal feed.

Carlos tied his horse to a porch railing and glanced at the women, hoping for someone to call him forward. They were silent as he approached, then with relief he spotted a woman sitting on a stool in the foreground who looked familiar.

"Buenos dias," he said with a slight bow.

The woman studied him carefully, wondering from where he had come, "Buenos dias."

"My name is Carlos Tapia. Perhaps you know my mother, the Señora Maria Laura Tapia from Pachuca."

A smile lighted the woman's face and she stood, wiping her roughened dirty hands on her apron. Corn kernels flew in every direction. She then held out her hand as her smile widened into a grin revealing few teeth.

"Of course we know her. We call her Laura. Often we have worked together. I do hope all is well with your family."

Carlos opened his mouth to reply just as a baby began to cry. For the first time he noticed an infant wrapped in a dirty, white cotton blanket lying behind the stool and as the mother glanced to see if all was well, she seemed to forget her visitor. Lifting the baby, she sat on the stool and continued to draw out a breast, placing the nipple in the infant's mouth. Satisfied, the small bundle settled into a relaxed position, sucking noisily.

The woman smiled again, "You're a long way from home. What brings you to us?"

Carlos pointed over his shoulder, "I'm looking for two horses. Did you by chance see any strays in the last two days?"

"I have not," then she raised her voice so all could hear. "Have any of you seen two stray horses pass by?"

All muttered negatively, the girls whispering with giggles among themselves eyeing the uncomfortable young man.

The woman turned back, "Perhaps you should find the hacienda owner. He knows almost everything that goes on in these parts. Maybe one of the hired men saw your horses," she coughed without covering her mouth.

"Thank you for your help. I'll look for the owner," Carlos turned as the woman tucked her heavy breast into the stained blouse and carefully placed the baby behind the stool again.

Chapter 20

He knew the poor little creature would lie all day wearing the same soiled rag for a diaper until the mother could get home to remove and wash it. Walking the length of the patio, he looked for someone to help him. The large hacienda sprawled behind the road. Giant eucalyptus trees formed a canopy over the principal buildings, small corrals, pig sties, barns, chicken coops, rabbit hutches, and a new stone dairy.

Pasture land extended as far as the eye could see up the high, rolling mountains behind the complex. Herds of cattle and caretaker huts dotted the hillside. In front of the grand house there was a crossroad, the left branch leading several miles away to the Pan American highway and Quito, and the right to the high summits of the Andes Mountain's eastern ridges. Eventually the latter would end in the jungles of Ecuador. If the horses had wandered that far, he would never find them. Directly ahead was the dangerous road back to Pachuca. He dreaded the return home and knew he must not be caught on the canyon's ledges after dark.

To the right of the house he found a large mud-walled barn. Looking into the shadowy light he saw mounds of corncobs, sacks of husked corn, an old abandoned plow, and a new pickup. A noise made him turn his head to see a battered tractor move slowly into the yard. A small, dark peon edged the machine close to a tall tree, turned off the motor, removed his hat, and yawned. Jumping down, he stretched and then noticed Carlos.

"Buenos dias or rather buenas tardes. What can I do for you?" he asked.

"My name is Carlos Tapia. I work for the Hacienda Hermosa in Pachuca. We've lost two horses. Have you seen them by chance?" Carlos asked.

"No, not me. I've been out with this tractor for the past two days, plowing the fields in the east pastures. If any horses passed by up there, it would have been impossible to see," he yawned again. "The owner of the hacienda will be coming for lunch. Maybe he can help you, but I doubt it. He's been very busy overseeing the wheat planting. I'm sorry that I can't help you. Hasta mañana."

He walked off, yawning again as two little girls yelled with delight and ran toward him, calling, "Popi, Popi!" Carlos smiled as the children darted into their father's arms.

He pondered what to do next, wait for the owner or travel to the hacienda further east, or perhaps return to Pachuca. He decided to find a spot to eat his lunch and had turned toward his horse when a large brown stallion galloped into the yard and stopped alongside the tractor. A tall man dismounted and walked toward him, smiling. Striking blue eyes peered out from beneath a wide-brimmed hat. Thick grey hair curled around his neck. He spoke with an educated dialect and walked with a confidence that heralded him as the hacienda owner.

"Buenas tardes. May I help you?" he held out his hand and stared at Carlos. "Have we met? My name is Eric Perez, owner of the Hacienda Tulcachi."

"Buenas tardes. No sir," Carlos took his hand and introduced himself. "I work as acting foreman of Hacienda Hermosa in Pachuca. I regret I haven't had a chance to visit with you before this. However, I am very impressed with your hacienda. My family has eaten your cheeses. They are the best in these parts."

"Gracias," his blue eyes twinkled. "Now what may I offer you, a drink or perhaps a bit of lunch? The cook will have it completed I'm sure. Please stay for an hour before your return to Pachuca. I'll show you where you can wash and refresh yourself."

"Gracias," Carlos said thankfully.

Eric Perez took him to a small shed where a wash room had been set up. When they had taken turns, Eric ushered him into the main house and took the lead, motioning him to follow. The entrance was a narrow passage leading to a lengthy porch that ran along the four sides of the house. Several arched openings revealed a large outdoor patio surrounded by the house. An old stone fountain stood in the center, a few broken benches had been placed at random among wild flowers, tall weeds, and green bushes flourishing in abundance. Towering trees cast shadows lending the area a gloomy, unkempt look. A balcony decorated with arches and wooden railings ran along the four sides of the house on the second floor. At the end of the porch stood a grand staircase and it was up these steps Eric Perez led Carlos.

Chapter 20

The upper floor was lined with doors and at one he stopped. Pushing the double doors open, he stepped inside and flipped on a switch.

Carlos followed, entering the cold room, its faded green walls climbing to a high chipped plaster ceiling. A simple wooden-backed divan sat along one side with two matching chairs against the adjoining wall. A single light bulb hanging from a long electrical wire and a bright sunbeam from the doorway provided the only lighting. It took a moment for Carlos to realize the room was larger than it appeared because the majority of it lay in shadow.

He sat on one of the chairs while Eric tossed his hat on a squat coffee table, laid Carlos' hat and jacket alongside, and plopped down on the divan.

A small girl appeared in the doorway smiling shyly, "Buenas tardes, Señores. They told us you had arrived. May I bring you something to drink before lunch?"

Eric motioned to the girl and she ducked quickly out of sight leaving the men sitting in uncomfortable silence. Carlos was hungry as he had eaten little more than bread that morning. He tried to put thoughts of lunch out of his mind as he turned his attention to the host.

Eric was observing him. As the young man's black eyes met the bright blue eyes, Carlos felt an unfamiliar stirring as if something passed between the two men. He looked away, shaking off the feeling, afraid it had only been on his part. One thing he would never forget was his station in life. To entertain the thought that a wealthy landowner and he, a poor Indian could become friends was foolishness and would be opening himself up to heartbreak again.

The moment passed and they began to chat about unimportant matters until the girl appeared with a tray and set it on a side table. She poured the drinks and handed each of them a glass, stepping back to see if they were satisfied. The cola was lukewarm, but tasted good to the thirsty traveler. Carlos and his host emptied the first glasses quickly and the girl hastened to replenish them and then left the room.

Eric relaxed on the divan and sighed deeply while Carlos longed to question him about the stray horses. Social decorum obliged him to wait until he was asked the reason for his presence at Hacienda Tulcachi.

The subject had turned to the wheat planting in process when a stout middle-aged woman bustled through the door projecting a greeting. She wore a scarf that pulled her hair away from a handsome kindly face prone to laughter and compassion. Eric introduced her as Isabel, his housekeeper and cook, but Carlos noted a tone of affection in the man's voice. She flashed Carlos a motherly smile and disappeared into the shadows of the room. Opening double doors that led to a small balcony, she then thrust back the shutters of two deep-set windows on each side of the doors engulfing the room in bright light.

Carlos relaxed as he looked at the high green mountains through the foliage of the eucalyptus trees. A strange emotion settled in him, a tie to this old house, to the confident landlord sitting on the divan and to the cheerful cook.

Eric reached out for Carlos' empty glass. The boy was aware that he studied him and was surprised at the emotion he felt when their eyes met. He knew this encounter was important and that he would again meet with Eric. As he pondered this, Carlos glanced quickly at the older man only to notice the touch of a smile working across his face. Carlos grinned and turned his head to scrutinize the room.

It had been neglected. Wall cracks showed mud brick under paint, the floor's wooden planks worn unevenly. A large bureau stood against one wall and a dish cabinet squatted beside a window. The walls were bare except for a bobcat head trophy and a perch that balanced a realistic stuffed bird appearing anxious for flight. On the floor a huge stuffed tortoise lay in a lifelike crawling position, compelling Carlos to look more than once at the reptile to see if it was moving.

But the most impressive item in the large room was the dining table set. Built of dark polished walnut, it gleamed as a mirror. Hand-carved, each leg ended in an eagle's claw. The table edge gracefully curved to give an exquisite oval effect. The chairs were high-backed with an eagle in flight carved into the top and with the legs extending its talons. Elegant arm rests expanded beyond the tooled leather seat and curved downward.

Carlos was limited in his appreciation for the fine craftsmanship. He noted none of the richly carved features. However, he was struck with the contrast of wealth and poverty combined in one room. Smiling, he thought of the wide span separating wealth and poverty

Chapter 20

presently deep in conversation as though the two had been friends for years. Unfortunately, he was the one without worldly goods. If Señor Perez hadn't made him feel at home, just being in his company would be an unbelievable situation. He smiled again, thinking of how his family would thrill to his story this evening.

Eric misinterpreted the smile and beamed with pride, "I bought the table in a town up north. I don't know how much you have traveled, Carlos, but the men of San Antonio produce wood carvings of the finest quality. Everything from small items to bed frames, picture frames to amazing chess sets. If you play chess, we must get together for a game."

He looked hopefully at the boy, as Carlos nodded, having no idea what a game of chess was.

"Anyway, the table was expensive. It's much too grand for the hacienda but for some reason I didn't want to put it in my house in Quito. That would be the proper place, however, my heart is here in Tulcachi so this is where we put the table."

Carlos made an appropriate statement, enjoying the way Eric talked. He watched the cook place a linen cloth over one end of the table and add silverware she had removed from the cabinet.

"Please, be seated," Eric moved to the far end of the table and motioned Carlos to his left. Isabel positioned a stained cloth napkin next to the silver, and perplexed Carlos eyed it not understanding its purpose. He watched and imitated Eric as the man opened the napkin and laid it on his lap.

"Have a nice lunch, sirs. I will send two girls with the food if you are ready," she clasped her hands, awaiting the reply.

"Si, Isabel. We are ready," Eric said fondly.

Giving Carlos another smile, the woman left the room and shortly two young girls brought trays laden with soup bowls and a tureen. They set them on the bureau and filled each bowl, placing them before guest and host. The soup was thick and hot, made from ground corn, seasoned with garlic and salt. Leaves of cabbage, potato halves, and pieces of corn lay on the bottom.

They ate hurriedly and the maids replaced the bowls with large plates piled high with rice, potatoes, and meat. Dishes of hot sauce were placed in front of each plate and salads of cooked cauliflower, peas, potatoes, and hard-boiled eggs tossed with mayonnaise were placed to the side. Never having seen so much food at one sitting, Carlos ate to his heart's content, carefully avoiding the salad.

Eric noticed and chuckled, "My cook is from Quito. When I'm in Tulcachi she stays with me and prepares the same type of meals here that she would there. You probably have never eaten this kind of salad, but in Quito we eat a lot of it. My brother brought a few ideas from the United States about salads. However, eating fresh vegetables like the rabbits eat isn't my idea of good food. My mother, who is American, has lived in South America for so long she has forgotten her love for stateside salads. It's surprising how many Americans eat raw food. It's disgusting. I'd rather die of starvation. Can you believe many Americans eat their meals without rice?"

Carlos was astonished, "How can anyone live without eating rice? Surely Americans must be hungry all the time."

"Oh no," Eric laughed. "They have foods you cannot imagine, in an abundance that would cause your head to ache if you had to make a choice. Americans are strange people. They have so much, yet many of them will spend most of their lives complaining they have so little. Of course, I'd complain too if I had to eat their salads. They are funny, too. They strive to compete to find new and different methods to save time and energy, yet many of them half kill themselves running through the streets in rain or hot sunshine to get sufficient exercise. They are strange people. I will never be able to live among them. I'll take the peaceful way of life right here, though they would call it backward and primitive."

One of the maids removed the plates and replaced them with bowls of figs cooked in a brown sugar sauce and two plates of white salty cheese. Cups of steaming coffee with hot milk and sugar were set beside the bowls. With that, the maids stepped back to wait for dismissal.

Eric surveyed the table and motioned for the girls to depart, settling back in the chair to sip his coffee.

"Take the cigarette for an example. We have had smokers in this country for hundreds of years, but certainly not like we do now. I personally believe it was American and West European influence that caused many Ecuadorians to start smoking. It's what is called a 'fad'

Chapter 20

in English. You will notice in Quito almost everyone now smokes. They believe it is the proper thing to do. What makes it complicated is the average Ecuadorian doesn't care for the American, but we desire to do the things they do. We want to look like them. You try to understand that. We want to dress like them, style our hair like theirs, entertain ourselves as they do, smoke as they smoke and eat the foods they eat. Dios mio, we now have hamburgers and hot dogs in Quito.

"What next? You don't know what a hot dog is, do you, Carlos? Anyway, on one of my trips to the States, what do I discover? Americans are now spending millions of dollars every year on cures to stop smoking. They diet, starve themselves, run around half nude, and have some of the craziest hairdos I've ever seen. In the years to come Ecuadorians will discover what Americans are doing and will again follow their example. Have you seen some men in Quito with hair to their shoulders? You don't go to Quito? Well, years ago that was popular in the United States. Next thing you know our young people will want to be too thin and madre mia, if that means we have to start eating raw salads, I might live in Tulcachi for good. Sometimes I wish my brother wouldn't bother me with what goes on in the States. It just confuses me."

Carlos had several questions to ask concerning the man's family, but he remained silent. He knew nothing of the United States. In his imagination Americans lived in another universe. Someone had told him they were all millionaires and had many worldly goods, more than any other people on earth. This was beyond his imagination and now he listened to Eric with fascination and amazement. Moreover, he had heard that all Americans owned homes with dozens of rooms and a swimming pool for each family. This had occupied his mind for days knowing each village in Ecuador shared one pool in the town proper for bathing and washing clothes. It was public property and for the families without water supply in their homes, the pool became a center of importance. To have a bathing and laundering facility beside each house and a bedroom for each person was more than he could imagine.

Abruptly, Eric interrupted his thoughts, "I've been doing all the talking, Carlos. Tell me something about yourself."

Carlos blinked, startled, "There's nothing to tell you. I've been very interested in what you've been telling me. But, as you know, I work at the Hacienda Hermosa. I live just above Pachuca with my mother, two brothers and a sister. My life is not so interesting. Tell me, does your father live in Quito?"

"My father died several years ago. He lived here in Tulcachi with my mother, my brother and me, until he became too ill to manage a hacienda. This beautiful old house is about three hundred years old and has been on my papa's side of the family for that long. My mother, as I said is American, but she was raised in this country, the child of missionaries. Outside of a few years when she attended school in the United States, she has always lived here. Her nationality explains the color of my eyes. My only brother is a doctor who lives in New York with his wife and four children."

"My life is here in Tulcachi, even though my family has a lovely home in Quito. Because of my mother I commute each day except during planting and harvesting seasons. Then she lives alone with hired helpers," he sipped coffee and smiled at the young man. "You are not married, Carlos?"

A hot flush deepened his dark coloring and he adjusted his position on the chair, reluctant to discuss Elena and the embarrassing emphasis of his poverty, "No, sir, nor do I intend to marry. I have interest only in work and my family. You have not mentioned a wife."

"I've never married, much to the distress of my mother. It is unusual for a man living in Ecuador not to marry, but now I'm no longer young so it's something I'll not plan to do. Many years ago I loved a young lady very much, but just before our marriage she fell ill with a disease that baffled doctors in this country. Back in those days, we believed she would regain her strength with rest, but by the time we realized its seriousness, we were unable to help her. Our two families were devastated and I just have not been able to find anyone to compare with her."

He sat, lost in thought and then brightened, "The biggest shame of all is there is no one to take the hacienda when I die. That's the only regret I have," he studied Carlos, seeming to wait for a reaction and when none came, he laughed. "I worry little about this as I feel

Chapter 20

there are many years yet for me to live and enjoy all that God has given me."

Carlos was fascinated with the man and his seeming interest toward him, but he was also aware of the lateness of the hour. He didn't want to appear rude, but he needed to find the horses and return to Pachuca before dark.

Eric must have felt the shift in unspoken communication because he pushed back his chair and rose, "Well, my friend, this was a pleasure. It's seldom I have guests here in Tulcachi."

Carlos stood, "I appreciate your invitation to lunch. When I stopped at your hacienda I didn't realize such an honor was waiting."

Pausing to gaze on Carlos for a moment again making the young man feel he was being scrutinized, Eric smiled and then reached up to rub his tired eyes. For the first time Carlos noticed fatigue on the tall man's face.

"You're a long way from home, son. I haven't asked you why you came this way. Actually, I didn't want you to leave. But now the hour is late and there are many things I must do. Is there anything I can help you with?" Eric asked Carlos.

"I'm looking for two horses that escaped from the Hacienda Hermosa. After searching all day without success yesterday, this is the likely route they would take, but so far no one has seen them."

Carlos gave a general description of the horses.

Eric shook his head slowly as if in thought, "No, there have been no reports of stray horses. If they went up the mountain, they could be many kilometers from here by now."

He looked at the dismay written on Carlos' face and patted his shoulder, "Why don't you go home? Come back tomorrow if you don't find them. Perhaps I can send a boy with you up the mountain. If I don't see you by noon, I will know all is well. Now you would be wise to return on the road leading to the Pan American highway instead of the road from Pachuca. You already know the horses aren't on the back road since you would have come here that way. It's a longer distance, but much safer."

Nodding, Carlos agreed, "Yes, that's a good idea. Thank you again for the lunch. If there is anything I can do to repay you, please stop by the Hacienda Hermosa. I would be happy to see you again, but now it does seem to be getting late."

"Yes, you must be anxious to be on your way. Sometimes I begin talking and don't know when to stop. Let me show you to your horse," Eric led him outside.

"Your horse will be in the corral, fed, and watered," he motioned in the direction of the barn and a small boy ran from inside the door toward an enclosure to the left of the now vacant porch and soon reappeared with the horse.

Carlos held out his hand, "Thank you, Sir."

Taking his hand, the tall man smiled, "I feel we will meet again soon. You will always be welcome here. God go with you."

Carlos mounted his horse and trotted to the road, turning toward Quito. Glancing back, he saw that the boy and Eric had disappeared, giving the hacienda a deserted look. The road to Quito turned north through a small community with many huts and side roads. Relieved, he noted the way was laid with cobblestones. Leaving the protection of the trees, the fierce midday sun beat down on him. It would be another hour before the clouds rolled in from the east, easing his discomfort.

A mile from the hacienda, he met a peon on horseback. Greeting the man, Carlos questioned him concerning the stray horses. He was shaking his head when another man joined them and was informed of the situation.

"Have you spoken with Señor Perez?" the newcomer asked Carlos politely.

"I have been to the hacienda searching for the horses, but no one seems to have seen them," said Carlos.

"Hmmm, I wonder if they are the same two horses my neighbor found in his cornfield last evening. If they are your horses, you'll find them about six kilometers up the mountain, in the first hacienda. You know, if you don't claim them within two weeks, the hacienda owner will be able to claim them."

Carlos began to feel new hope. He thanked the horsemen and contemplated the situation as they moved away. He could travel to the distant hacienda now, but that could take three hours round trip easily with another three hours to travel home, or he could return

Chapter 20

tomorrow with help. A glance at the sky showed the late hour and he decided the return to Pachuca to be the more prudent choice.

After arriving and caring for his horse, he walked the mile from Hacienda Hermosa to his home, considering a plan for the next day. He had decided he would not bother Eric Perez any further. He would send his brothers to the house of a boy who worked with him on occasion, requesting his appearance before dawn. They would travel the longer, but safer road to Tulcachi and beyond to secure the horses so they could return home early in the afternoon.

Satisfied, but exhausted, he arrived home. His mother was stretched out on her bed sleeping, his brothers bent over their homework, straining to catch the light from a flickering candle. Carlos interrupted their concentration to send them to Fausto's house. Happy for an excuse to leave their studies, the boys grabbed their jackets and ran for the door.

Carlos stripped off his sweat-stained shirt, tossed it on a bench, and found a clean, tattered undergarment in a two-drawer end table. Gathering water from a bucket in the corner, he washed outside, shivering in the cool refreshing evening air.

"Do you want dinner, Carlos?" Yolanda asked him from the doorway.

"Just bring me some soup after I'm finished here. Is it still hot? I'm too tired to eat anything else," Carlos said, thinking just how tired he really was though it had been an exciting day of surprises.

Walking into the back room where he slept with his brothers, he climbed into the double bed he had purchased during the past year. Yolanda followed him and stood beside the bed with a bowl of soup. Gulping the hot liquid and vegetables, he handed the empty bowl to her and rolled over in bed, not realizing another thing until he awoke before dawn.

Chapter 21

It was still dark when he descended the crude steps from his house to the road below and found Fausto waiting. The small boy with thick, straight black hair and slanted eyes above broad high cheekbones stood shaking with cold against the embankment. His face was creased from a constant effort to ease the sun's glare in his eyes and from the worry that plagues Indian children who never have enough to eat. At age fourteen he had the build of a ten year old and the face of an adult.

The cold was penetrating and Carlos had thoughtfully brought a warm jacket for Fausto. Grabbing it with gratitude, the boy wrapped himself in it. A quarter moon drifted over Quito in the distance to the west and the dense scattering of stars lit the road before them. To take their minds off the cold during their walk to the hacienda, Carlos explained his need for the boy's help.

Approaching their horses, the animals shied away, reluctant to be caught. Wanting to please, Fausto sprang to life and ran after them with a rope. Laughing, Carlos followed the boy's shadowy form in the approaching daylight until they were able to corner the horses and slip ropes over their heads. Pulling the animals to the barn, they saddled them.

A peon, roused from his sleep in the back of the building yelled out, "Who's there?"

Chapter 21

"Carlos and Fausto," replied Carlos. "We're going over to Hacienda Tulcachi. We think the horses are in the mountains. Please tell the rest of the men we'll return this afternoon."

The peon grunted and turned over, snuggling in a blanket. Carlos checked his gear, strapped a knapsack containing lunch to the back of his saddle and searched through a pile of old blankets and ponchos until he found a piece of material for Fausto to place around his head to keep out the cold.

Pulling his knitted cap down over his ears, Carlos grinned at the boy, "Come on. If we want to be home before dark tonight, we must find the horses quickly."

They followed the Pan American highway for five miles and crossed a large canyon by way of a newly built bridge. Continuing on their way, they reached the partially paved road that took them south through several ravines. Despite the tremendous drops in elevation, the young men felt safe on the wide road and they were struck with a sense of adventure that bordered on gaiety.

A mile from Hacienda Tulcachi, Carlos suggested they stop for a midmorning break near a stream shaded by tall trees. Removing their jackets and other wraps, they ran for the creek, falling on their stomachs to drink deeply of the cold water. The horses followed, drank their fill, and then wandered, munching on the thick grass.

From the worn knapsack Carlos pulled a large object wrapped in brown paper. Yolanda had prepared lunch and now he shared cheese, bread, and bananas with the boy. Jars of cola completed the meal and as Carlos watched Fausto eye the package, he wrapped the remains and gently reminded the boy they would need the rest for lunch later in the day. Stuffing the package and jars back into the knapsack, he felt pity for Fausto, knowing he came from one of the poorest families in Pachuca. He understood the boy's hunger and for that reason invented small chores to put him to work

They resisted the temptation to remain under the shady trees and with reluctance interrupted the lazy grazing of the horses to continue their journey. After an easy mile they reached Tulcachi and Carlos thought of the previous day. In fact, he had thought of little else all morning. Walking the horses past the buildings, he waved to the women on the porch and searched the area with his eyes hoping for a glimpse of Eric. He was disappointed not to see him.

They passed the small trail that Carlos had traveled the previous day and stopped before the road leading to the high mountain range. With a deep sigh, he smiled at the boy and with a jerk of his head forward, they prodded their horses into a trot. For several meters the road was paved, making the ride easy. However, the ascent soon became pronounced, causing the horses to slow. The men let the animals settle into their own paces, knowing the ride ahead would be arduous.

By this time, Carlos had other concerns. He had been filling his mind with thoughts of Eric, ignoring a growing fear they would find the horses at the first hacienda, a farm owned by Hector and Mariana Martinez. He had taken care to avoid Elena's family since the morning of his encounter with Rolando. His agony had been complete and he wondered sometimes if he could live with the hurt and loss. Only the love of his family and hatred for Rolando kept him alive. Never would he give his enemy the satisfaction of running away. In the early days he had been on constant alert for a glimpse of Rolando's immediate family, but it eventually became evident they were also avoiding him. He knew the day would come he would have no choice, but to meet them and he desperately hoped it wouldn't happen today.

In the past, he had fantasized that he and Elena were together again. During the first days of their separation she filled his thoughts as he created and discarded plans to carry her away from Pachuca. He visualized fighting the entire Martinez family single-handedly to win her. His suffering would be so severe all would be forgiven and forgotten, but then reality always set in. He had others to consider. Secondly, it was the painful knowledge that Rolando was right. He was trapped in a social class from which there was no escape.

Eventually thoughts of Elena ceased to dominate his day. He would always care for her, but now there was no desperation to see her or no temptation to run away with her. Other priorities cropped up and simply pushed her from his mind until the day came he didn't hurt as much. Long ago he acknowledged she would be better off

Chapter 21

without him and he rebuked himself for instigating the friendship in the first place.

Lately he had begun to put emotional distance between himself and the girl and had even considered dating another young lady. Mercedes lived in an old two-room house a few hundred yards from his own. The front room was used as a small store that carried a variety of dry goods, hard candy, chewing gum, and school supplies. An interest in the girl had been aroused on Saturday afternoon while he was buying a pencil for Joel.

Startled, he became aware of the lingering touch of her hand and the look in her eyes as he passed the sucre to her. He had seen that look in Elena's eyes many times. Counting it as foolishness, he ignored her and set his heart on his work. However, he was surprised when frequent thoughts of Mercedes began creeping into his mind. Longings for love and warmth made her more intriguing and as a result Elena was soon lost in a maze of confusion and his unfilled need to become a husband and lover.

Now, as he drew nearer to the Martinez hacienda, he decided he would no longer allow his wounded pride to rule him and he would no longer remain alone. He would visit Mercedes this very evening.

The midmorning sun beat down and the winds flung dust in their faces, forcing them to tie handkerchiefs around their noses and mouths.

Two hours passed before they reached the main buildings of the hacienda. Stopping to pull off their kerchiefs, they noticed a large pickup loaded with alfalfa pulling out from the long graveled driveway. Carlos rode to greet the two men inside and asked for the foreman. With waves of their hands they showed the boss was in the barn at the end of the long driveway. A barking dog rushed out, but turned in the opposite direction, tail between his legs when a large, dark middle-aged man walked rapidly from the barn to meet the riders, yelling at the mutt to retreat.

Carlos glanced around quickly and saw with relief the Martinez' jeep was not there. He wanted to secure the horses and leave as soon as possible.

"Buenos dias, Carlos. How good to see you. It seems so long since you have been up this way."

Carlos jumped from his horse and grasped the outstretched hand, "Buenos dias, Manuel. Yes, it's been over a year I believe."

"You are no longer working with the Martinez family I hear," asked Manuel.

"No, I'm with the Hacienda Hermosa. This is my companion, Fausto Tipantiza. We're looking for stray horses," Carlos explained and then he described them.

"Yes, one of our workers brought them up here a couple days ago. I'll have someone show you where they are. If the two of you wouldn't mind accompanying him, he will be glad to capture your horses," he smiled, his dark face lighting up with friendliness and put out his hand again. "I will charge only for the feed they consumed. Come to see us again, Carlos."

Turning he waved farewell to Fausto, who was shyly hanging back with his horse.

"Thank you, Manuel. You are always welcome at my house," said Carlos as the broad-shouldered man disappeared into the barn.

Shortly, a disgruntled peon pulling a horse walked toward the driveway motioning them to follow. Carlos smiled to himself knowing the worker had been denied an early lunch and siesta. He winked at Fausto as the three mounted their horses and trotted to the opposite side of the road. They followed a worn trail down a gentle slope, across a valley, and up one of the many rolling hills. Alfalfa, grass, and scrub-brush covered the landscape as far as the eye could see, each small rise dipping into a valley and gradually rising ever higher. Behind them, miles to the west, Quito sat small and sparkling in the palm of Mt. Pichincha's hand.

Horses and cows grazed in clumps, feeding off one pasture, allowing other sections of land to rest. Several hundred feet from the road they approached a fenced enclosure and stopped while the peon dismounted and opened a crude gate. Motioning for them to wait, he prompted his horse into the pasture as Carlos jumped from his mount to shut the gate after him. The peon spurred his horse into a fast trot as he entered a shallow gully leading to a high plateau. Fausto directed Carlos' attention to two strays grazing in the distance. They watched the peon's careful approach, his lasso ready. Carlos

Chapter 21

grabbed a rope from his saddle and waited for the man's return with the errant horses in tow.

Within a short time both animals were secured and the small party headed toward the road home. Anxious to leave, Carlos paid the peon for the feed and added an extra amount for his help. He then motioned to Fausto and they gratefully started down the mountain, towing the two stray horses behind. Moving quickly downhill, they reached the crossroad and the Hacienda Tulcachi in the space of an hour.

Deciding to eat the leftovers for lunch, they returned to the same shady spot they had visited earlier. While the horses drank from the stream and fed on the abundant grass, the men shared bread, cheese and cola, refreshing themselves. Carlos felt better than he had in days. Now that he was returning with the horses, his heart felt light with remembrances of his visit with Eric Perez the previous day and plans for a possible relationship with Mercedes. He stripped to his waist and washed in the stream, drying himself with his shirt.

Turning, his legs weakened and his heart stopped momentarily. Hector Martinez' jeep passed, heading for the mountain. It happened in a blur, but not before he saw Elena with her family in the back of the vehicle. She hadn't noticed him until they were almost past, but from the jerk of her head and the mixed look of pleasure and surprise, he knew she had seen him. Their eyes met and time froze. A moment later he tried to move, but his limbs were shaking.

"Come on, Carlos. We must start back before it gets too late," yelled Fausto.

He looked at the boy, his mind in a whirl knowing he didn't have the strength to mount his horse. *I've never stopped loving her,* he thought. All the emotions he had buried raced to his heart. Passing his hand over his face, he returned to the stream to splash water on himself.

"I must rest a moment," he told a puzzled Fausto as he laid himself down on the grass. "Just let me lie here a moment, please."

"Hey, what's the matter?" Fausto asked, oblivious to what had happened. "We've got to get these horses back."

"Yes, okay. I just felt ill for a moment. I'm all right now," he opened his eyes to find Fausto bending over, looking at him.

"Here, help me up," Carlos asked extending his hand.

Walking to the horses, the familiar heavy sick feeling overtook him, "Oh my God, please don't let me suffer again. I thought my feelings for her were dead."

The rest of the day passed in a fog. Thinking of little else but Elena, his desire for food, the enjoyment of his family, and any thoughts of starting a relationship with another woman dissolved as though they were wispy clouds. Weary from the long day, he retired only to discover he couldn't sleep. Thoughts of a future with Elena pummeled his mind. The wracking pain hadn't died at all. It had been lying dormant, waiting to be revived.

"I can't go through this another time. It's unbearable," he cried softly into his pillow.

Throughout the long night he tossed and turned debating whether or not he should see her again. In the end, it was Rolando who pushed him toward Elena.

Chapter 22

One afternoon several weeks following Sandi's departure from Ecuador, Jillian went to the outpatient clinic where Marta was examining a man suffering from gastric problems. Amidst groans of discomfort, the nurse delivered a long lecture on sanitation when a loud knocking caught their attention.

Dark clouds had been forming over the mountains to the east since noon and now the rain was falling in torrents.

When Jillian opened the door, a man stepped inside and called to Marta apologetically, "Señorita Marta, buenas tardes. I'm so sorry but we need your help. There has been a terrible accident."

"Buenas tardes," she muttered over her shoulder. "I can't go with you. We are swamped with patients. Didn't you see the crowd on the porch?"

"I see them, but you don't have to go anywhere. The patient is in my truck."

He stepped back as Marta left her patient to peer over his shoulder, "He's dying. He was struck by a car. I saw it happen and brought him here."

Marta turned to Jillian standing behind her, "Go tell Flora and Elizabeth they will be responsible for the children all afternoon. I'll need your help."

She ran to the house with instructions for the girls and to grab a sweater. Hurrying back to the clinic Jillian was soaked within seconds, but that didn't concern her as much as the fear creeping through

While They Sleep

her body. She dreaded seeing the man but knew she had no choice but to obey Marta. Entering the main patient room, she crept forward and peeked into a curtained off area.

"Just when I need Lucia, she's stuck with a delivery in the maternity clinic," grumbled Marta. "Over here, Jill. I need you to bring two boards from the closet. We'll have to make a splint."

Swallowing her nausea, the girl hurried to the small door and returned with several narrow thin strips of wood.

"We'll have to straighten his arm. Lay one of the strips on the bed beside him," Marta instructed.

Trying to avoid the man's face, she laid the wood by him and looked at Marta for more instructions.

"Now, place his arm on it and I'll make the splint," she worked busily with the blood pressure device.

Reluctantly, Jillian picked up the man's arm and almost dropped it. The bones, broken in several places caused the arm to crumble in her hand. Bile rose in her throat as she fought the urge to vomit. Seeing her face, Marta stepped beside her and gently lifted the entire length of the arm, straightening it until she could lay it flat on the board and then skillfully constructed the splint. Jillian leaned against the wall and breathed deeply until her stomach settled. She then forced herself to look at the man. Noting the bloodied face and shirt, she could see nothing else wrong. In spite of the fact that he was unconscious, his breathing seemed normal. She decided his injuries were minimal.

"What happened? Do you know?" she asked Marta.

"While you were gone the man who brought him in explained," Marta was studying the man's eyes with a small penlight. "Apparently he stepped off the bus and walked around behind it to cross the road without looking both ways. A speeding car knocked him over and then took off. The man has gone to find the patient's family, but I'm afraid that we can't wait for them. You and I will have to take him to the hospital in Quito. Lucia will stay in the clinic."

"I'll be glad to go with you," Jillian assured her.

"We'll take the pickup since it's larger than the jeep and has a canopy. The trouble is you'll have to sit in the back with him because

Chapter 22

he needs to lie down. It's obvious he can't sit up. I have no idea how extensive his injuries are."

"Oh, Marta, please," she pleaded. "I don't think I can do that. How can I stay alone with him in the back? It's all I can do right now not to throw up."

"You have no choice. Let's just hope the rain has let up a little. I'm always afraid of landslides. Thank goodness the bridge is now crossable," Marta explained as she prepared the man to travel. Go get one of my raincoats for yourself and find one for me. We've got to go. This guy could die on us."

Jillian groaned and hoped fervently that Marta was exaggerating. It appeared to her that he had only a broken nose and shattered arm. She found two coats in the closet and brought them to Marta. The nurse rushed to the back door and called for help from two bystanders. Under her instructions, they placed the patient on a stretcher and carried him to the pickup. They stood in the diminishing rainfall until all was secure and Jillian climbed on board.

Thank goodness for a canopy, she thought. Shivering, she huddled on a wood bench built against the side. The unconscious man lay before her, a monstrous obstacle to her peace of mind. Unable to look at his gray face, she concentrated on the back of Marta's head. The streets of Pachuca were deserted. Everyone was inside their warm homes avoiding the wet, chilly afternoon. Jillian prayed with all her might that the canyon area around the newly constructed bridge was passable.

Marta carefully maneuvered the truck around each bend and across the new bridge. Occasionally the nurse turned around, reassuring herself that all was well. Once on the highway, speeding through the puddles and mud, Jillian tried to occupy her mind with other things. Philip was in her thoughts a lot these days. Thinking back to their first meeting in the plaza and his offer of friendship she had refused to acknowledge she was being too forward and had telephoned him at the government hospital on one of her biweekly trips to Quito.

Professing delight she had thought of him, he had met her for lunch. After that, they had made a practice of visiting together for a quick meal in between her errands and his trip to Yaruqui. Her feelings for him were growing as her need for a companion apart from Marta and Lucia were becoming pronounced.

Now, it seemed Philip was falling in love with her. She had been able to limit their visits to lunch once every two weeks, but he was beginning to insist that they see each other in the evenings. It mildly amused Jillian to imagine Marta's reaction to the idea she was dating. The nurse had made it clear that she didn't care for men. It was her strong opinion that men were out for one thing and one thing only and nothing good could come of such a relationship. It would particularly gall Marta to know she was dating an Ecuadorian much less a national doctor.

She was thankful she hadn't mentioned Philip after their first meeting in the plaza, but she would spend many agonizing moments trying to pacify her guilt. Several times she had been ready to tell him she would never see him again, but she needed his companionship and was reluctant to let him go. Her friendship with Lucia was developing slowly and she was frustrated because the Indian didn't seem to trust her enough to draw closer. Philip was able to assuage her growing loneliness.

Sighing deeply, she gathered her attention back to the road. It had started raining again, creating the appearance of dusk instead of daylight. A half hour passed before they began their ascent to the capitol city. Jillian was staring out the window when she was snatched back to reality by a terrible gurgling noise. The man was having difficult time breathing. She panicked not knowing what to do. Shall I turn him over? What about internal injuries? She tried to ignore the noise, her mind in a whirl of indecision. Shall I get Marta's attention? No, we're almost there. Any delay will make it worse.

Oh God, help me, she prayed.

The labored gurgle continued as they raced up the street where the American/European sponsored hospital was located. Lucia had telephoned ahead requesting the emergency staff to meet Marta at the door.

Jillian felt drained and shaky and slowly went into the empty waiting room to sit on a bench. Feeling despondent, she leaned her head against the wall. Visiting hours were over, but the bustle of activity kept her attention as aides appeared and reappeared in the

Chapter 22

hallway. Her mind replayed the sound of gurgling over and over. Somewhere she remembered reading that she should have turned him on his side.

The activity ceased and Marta walked out a door, a doctor accompanying her. Alert, Jillian tried to catch the rapidly spoken Spanish. Returning to the emergency room, the doctor disappeared and Marta walked toward Jillian. Jumping up from the bench, she waited breathlessly.

"What happened? How is he?" Jillian asked.

"He didn't make it. We tried everything we could, but he was too far gone," Marta said sadly.

With a groan, Jillian buried her head in her hands and burst into tears.

"Jill?" Marta moved to put her arm around the girl, but Jillian pulled away. Then deciding against it, she moved closer, glad for the comfort. They held each other for several moments.

"I understand," said Marta. "Sometimes I forget that not all people have been around sickness and death the way I have. Come now, dry those tears. In a few days you'll have forgotten why you were crying. You'll have to learn that life is cheap in Ecuador. People die all the time."

Pulling away, Jillian turned to the wall, "I think maybe I'm responsible for his death."

"Why would you say that?" Marta asked.

"When we were nearing the final ascent to Quito, the man started breathing erratically. I should have knocked on the window to get your attention, but it seemed more important that we get to the hospital," Jillian said as the weeping began anew.

"Oh, my dear, as far as the doctors are concerned, that man was already dead. His concussion caused extensive brain damage. Internally he was hemorrhaging so badly his lungs were filling with blood. There isn't a doctor alive in this country that could have saved him."

Jillian looked at her doubtfully until grief engulfed her again, "Really?"

"Really," Marta moved toward her again and smiled gently.

She wiped her eyes and sat down. Her head ached from the trauma and all could think about was going home.

"Can we leave soon?" Jillian asked.

"Right now. I'll say good-bye to the doctors inside. Just a minute," Marta said quietly.

Feeling ill, Jillian rubbed her temples and longed to shut out memories of this evening, but it was several days before she was able to shut out the sound of his breathing.

Chapter 23

The contradictions of Marta's personality troubled Jillian. The love and concern she had been shown at the hospital was in sharp contrast to her character's dark side. The harsh discipline meted out to the children continued and most of the time it seem without reason. Curiously Jillian wondered if Marta had such a need to be respected that she used her power over the weak and innocent to grasp it. Several times she fought the temptation to explain that the giving of praise and love would accomplish much more, but she knew Marta would stubbornly hold to her theory. Praise, Marta lectured only caused children to relax in their efforts, thwarting their development.

Jillian was at a point in their relationship where she was torn between mild feelings of affection and pure dislike for the woman. Without apparent reason the woman would explode either verbally or with physical abuse. Then she would be as gentle, soft-spoken and kind as she had been at the hospital.

It was on one of Marta's good days that Lucia wandered into Jillian's room at the top of the stairs and told her that the nurse wanted to see her and would be waiting in the maternity clinic.

"Why?" Jillian asked, laying a pen beside the letter she was writing, her eyebrows rose in question.

"How do I know?" Lucia gave her a knowing smile and left the room.

While They Sleep

Curious, she followed. Glancing in the playroom to ensure the older children were caring for the babies, she walked the distance to the clinic. Marta was in the main ward speaking with a young mother.

Realizing that Jillian had arrived, she brightened and took her by the arm, "Come with me."

Perplexed she followed as Lucia trotted behind. In the private ward, Marta reached into a bassinet and placed a bundle in Jillian's arms giving a huge grin at the girl's shocked face.

"He's yours. I thought you'd like a little boy to take care of and to replace the loss of your nephew, Russell. Well, he's yours," Marta said smiling broadly.

Jillian's mouth fell open with pleasure and her eyes quickly filled with tears, "Marta, thank you, thank you. Where did you get him?"

"The lady out there didn't want him. I just told her that we'd find a good home for him," Marta explained patiently.

She stared at the little face and then beamed at Marta, "I'll name him Andrew if that's alright with you."

"Whatever you like," said Marta gleefully.

Jillian could not believe her good fortune. Andy was a joy. Caring for a child as her own over the next three months brought out a motherly instinct that helped her better understand the other children's needs. However, she was not prepared for what happened next.

One afternoon Marta sent for her and after putting Andy down for a nap, she walked to the clinic wondering what awaited her. Opening the kitchen door, Marta called to her from the private ward. A woman stood in the middle of the room holding a dirty blanket. With a bow of her head, she smiled at Jillian.

"Come here and look at this," Marta motioned.

Hesitating, the girl walked to the bed where a small, naked baby lay looking up at the ceiling. Jillian's stomach lurched. From the tip of her toes to the top of her head, the infant was covered with scales and open sores.

"She has the skin of a snake. What's wrong with her?" Jillian whispered in horror, glancing at the mother.

Throwing up her hands, Marta shrugged as her eyes widened, "I have no idea. I've never seen anything like this. I suspect staph infection. The mother wants to leave the baby here. She doesn't want

Chapter 23

it with her anymore. She's not married and has three other children at home. The neighbors are probably talking. At least she brought it here instead of leaving it in the ditch somewhere."

"What do you think? Can we take her in?" she said as a sudden desire took hold of Jillian. "We have room and I'd love to have a little girl right now."

"I'm not sure. I have my doubts about taking in a child like this," Marta said as she leaned toward the baby to rub her skin. "What if it's staph infection? We had our problems with it in the past and it was a long time before we were able to get rid of it."

Looking again at the quiet mother, Jillian pleaded with Marta, "But it doesn't look like this is contagious. Her mother doesn't seem to have the same problem."

"You don't have your hands full enough now? You told me that you were satisfied with Andy and my children, remember? Now you say that you want to take on a medical condition that may keep giving us problems for years to come? Jill, you're just going to have to learn that you can't say yes to everyone," Marta said as if she had made up her mind.

Marta turned toward the mother, but Jillian grabbed her arm, "Then why did you call me? Please, Marta. Let's talk a little more. We can talk to Lucia."

"I called you because I wanted you to see this," Marta explained. "Besides, Lucia has already seen the baby and she said no. She's not interested in taking this baby when we don't have to."

The three women stood in silence. Jillian looked imploringly at Marta until the nurse threw up her hands in resignation.

"Go and see for yourself. Lucia is upstairs in the attic."

Jillian took the steps two at a time and found Lucia bending over her work-bench measuring a piece of plywood.

"Why don't you want to take the baby? If we don't take her she'll die," Jillian asked desperately.

"So what?" Lucia grunted without looking up.

"Lucia, look at me," Jillian pleaded.

Lucia lifted her eyes for a moment, "Who's going to take care of her? Marta won't. That leaves you and me, and you're busy with

While They Sleep

the children. So it's me who will be stuck with her. I just don't want to get involved."

"Since when don't you like challenges? You're always searching for a new project. You love difficult situations, Lucia. This would be the perfect one for you," Jillian said as she watched the Indian hunched over the workbench. "Lucia, please, I think we should help this little girl. I really do. Isn't that why we're here? Shouldn't we take care of children who can't live with the day-to-day conditions out there in the village?"

"You won't help me a bit. I know that," Lucia challenged her.

"I promise we can work together. Maybe she just has a very dry skin," Jillian speculated.

Snorting, Lucia shook her head and straightened up slowly, "That may be part of it, Jill, but she's sick from the inside out."

Sighing dramatically, she smiled, "Okay, let's go talk to Marta. You know that she still has the final say."

"Yes, of course," Jillian admitted.

They walked into the room expecting an argument, but to their surprise they found the nurse cradling the clothed baby in her arms. With a sigh of resignation, she placed the bundle in Jillian's arms.

"She's yours. You will be primarily responsible for her, but I'll be willing to do what I can," Marta said.

"What happened to change your mind?" asked Jillian stunned.

"I knew that you could persuade Lucia. I also know this is a good challenge for you. Worse, I know that the mother would probably drown the baby before she got home. That we can't tolerate," Marta said with uncharacteristic compassion. "We'll manage somehow, although I don't know how."

The mother scarcely looked at her daughter as the infant was carried to the main ward. Lucia followed close behind then took her from Jillian's arms. Placing her on a bed, she carefully opened the clean blanket Marta had wrapped around her and surveyed her condition.

"Where can we start? Jill, go find a bottle of baby oil, medicated lotion, and a supply of cotton balls stored in the hall cabinet," Lucia said as if thinking out loud.

Chapter 23

Coating the cotton with oil, she gently spread it on the baby's feet, then her legs.

"I've never seen anything like this," she said as she removed the clean diaper and stood shaking her head at the skin underneath.

She cleansed and covered the child with medicated lotion and oil and then dressed her in a clean, soft outfit.

"I must say she's quiet. She went through all of that without as much as a whimper. Here's your daughter, my friend," smiled Lucia. "Perhaps you should name her unless you want her to keep her given name, Blanca."

"If I have the right to change it, I'd like to call her Anna," suggested Jillian.

"Do what you want," Lucia said as she shrugged her shoulders.

"I can't thank you enough, Lucia. She looks better already," Jillian said with a smile.

In the days that followed, Jillian gratefully accepted Lucia's help. She could not have handled the workload without her. Now she was caring for two infants, plus Marta's infant and children. To her delight, Andy was gaining weight and beginning to recognize her. Anna's condition seemed to remain the same. In spite of their care, the baby showed no improvement. Lucia took a bus to Quito to consult a doctor, who prescribed a medication that eased the inflammation and sores, but the scaling continued. Jillian cried and prayed for her little girl, and Marta searched the medical books.

Chapter 24

One afternoon when Anna had been with them for a month, Jillian completed the baby's feeding and put her down for a nap. An hour later when she returned to check on her, Anna wasn't in her bed. She searched the clinic frantically and finally ran to find Marta who was in the main house kitchen.

"Where's Anna?" Jillian's heart pounded with fear. "I went to check on her and she's not there."

After a lapse of several seconds, Jillian took a step toward her.

"Where's Anna, Marta?" she asked bewildered.

The uncomfortable woman licked her lips and shrugged, "Now listen, Jill. I can explain. I've been watching you. You haven't been getting enough sleep. Look at yourself. You're so tired that I felt I should step in."

"What did you do with Anna, Marta?" she asked again in dismay.

"I waited until you were in your room after lunch. I knocked, you didn't answer, so I knew you were probably asleep...." Marta tried to explain.

Jillian sighed loudly with impatience, "Tell me where she is."

"No, I won't tell you where she is. Honestly, I couldn't talk with you because you would have caused such an uproar. Someone came and took her to Quito. She's staying with an acquaintance," Marta frowned defiantly. "Now, don't get angry with me. You must still remember that I'm in charge and I'll not have any outbursts from you."

Chapter 24

"How did she get into Quito without my knowledge?" Jillian asked, her teeth clenched, eyes wide with anger.

"I made arrangements yesterday afternoon by telephone," Marta said calmly.

"Why didn't you tell me then? You know I always try to rest a little after lunch while the children are napping. You could have talked to me yesterday. You planned to deceive me," Jillian accused with a shaking voice.

She glared at the woman, "I think that I hate you."

Storming up the stairs, she slammed her bedroom door shut and sat on the bed. Hatred burned in her heart. Hearing a soft knock she turned away.

Marta opened the door and walked in, "Can't you understand why I couldn't say anything? I was just thinking about you and your health."

"And you can't understand how this has affected me? She's my little girl. Why don't I have a say in how we treat her?" Jillian asked, still filled with anger towards Marta.

"Because no matter how many children you have in this house, they are still my responsibility. These children are really mine and I have the final say," Marta reminded her.

Clenching her teeth, Jillian stood and walked to the window.

"The thing that really makes me angry is that you didn't discuss this with me. I didn't even have a chance to see her before she left," Jillian continued through a veil of tears. "And you say that you care for me. I certainly haven't seen much love in this case. No, don't touch me."

She stepped back as the woman approached.

Without another word Marta turned and walked out the door, but not before Jillian noticed tears in her eyes. With a stab of guilt, she lifted her fist and hit the wall. Soon the anger turned into frustration and helplessness and she collapsed on the bed.

Sitting in stony silence through dinner, she went to visit with Lucia afterwards instead of staying with the children and Marta in the living room.

"Did you know that she had taken Anna?" Jillian asked Lucia.

"I knew but Marta told me not to say anything," Lucia admitted. "I told her how you would feel."

"Why is it, Lucia, about the time I feel friendly toward her, she does something like this?" Jillian asked and hit her forehead with the palm of her hand. "I would like to feel some kind of affection for her, but it's too hard for me."

"I've known her for many years and I still don't understand her very much, but she has always been my friend," Lucia explained. "Just let her do things as she wishes. It's hard but that is the only way you will have peace."

They looked up and saw Marta standing in the doorway of Lucia's bedroom, "I'm sorry for intruding, but I wanted to tell you that the children are in bed now. You don't have to worry about Andy because Flora is taking care of him."

"I know. I asked her to care for him," Jillian said stiffly as she stood and started for the door. "Excuse me but I must be getting home. Lucia, I'll see you tomorrow."

"Jill! Wait!" Marta exploded. "You may not believe this, but I sent Anna to Quito for your sake. I don't care if you hate me or if you walk all over me. Go ahead, spit on me. Do whatever terrible thing you can think of, but I do love you."

Scorn gripped Jillian's heart, "Then tell me where Anna is and I'll go get her."

"I can't do that," Marta said firmly. "She is to stay in Quito."

"I can't stand this," Jillian said shaking her head. "If you love me as you say, then you'll tell me where Anna is."

"I won't," Marta declared.

Jillian walked out the door without looking back. She had a hard time sleeping. Almost a year had passed since Sandi's departure from Pachuca, but in that time she still had not overcome her first impression of Marta. The woman's insecurities and hunger for power had driven away any desire she had for a relationship. There seemed to be no way to quiet her hatred for the woman and she was passed feeling sorry for her.

Philip had begged her to leave the orphanage and move to Quito, but the thought of living without Andy, Anna, and the children was unbearable. Marta had covered all her bases by giving her the

Chapter 24

children and guaranteeing Jillian's loyalty. There would be no chance of her leaving now.

"Oh, God, help me," she prayed. "Is Marta right? Am I wrong? If she is, why do I feel such contempt for her?"

Jillian was able, finally to persuade Marta to reveal where Anna was staying. Happy to learn two nurses were caring for her in an apartment behind the hospital in Quito, she left Pachuca early on her next shopping trip to visit Anna. Betsy Wagner and Emily Shoemaker had emptied a dresser drawer to make up a small bed. It grieved Jillian that in spite of the attention they could lavish on Anna, they were not able to love her as she did. With great care she examined the baby's body and wondered if she had improved at all. Her skin appeared scaly, puffy and red.

Forfeiting her luncheon with Philip, she stayed with Anna most of the afternoon and then hurried to complete her errands. With a start, she realized it was dark and Marta would worry at her delay. She burst through the orphanage door several hours past her usual homecoming concerned about Marta's reaction. Lucia and Marta met her in the hallway, visibly relieved. After Jillian sputtered a few apologies for her delay, Lucia marched off, disinterested in any explanation. Marta lingered only long enough to question her about Anna and to take her mail.

Checking to see if the children were asleep, she then changed into her pajamas and gave herself a sponge bath. Remembering she had eaten little since a sparse lunch with Betsy and Emily, she decided a sandwich and cup of coffee were in order. Grabbing a book, she padded through the darkened house to the kitchen depending only on the moonlight streaming through the windows to show her way. Entering the room, she jumped in fright. Lucia was sitting in the shadows at the kitchen table.

"What are you doing here?" Jillian asked. "You scared me half to death sitting in the dark like that."

Lucia sat silently.

"Listen, I'm really tired. I know you are angry at me for not returning on time, but tonight I just don't feel like explaining any further. We can talk tomorrow," Jillian said quietly as she walked to the table to touch Lucia's shoulder.

Suddenly Lucia reached out and slapped her across the face.

Jillian stepped back in surprise and put her hand to her cheek, "Why did you do that?"

"I'm your special friend," Lucia said angrily. "I don't like it when you have other friends."

"I still don't understand. Who are you talking about?" Jillian asked.

"You know who I'm taking about, Betsy and Emily. Someday you will leave Pachuca," accused Lucia.

"You didn't have to slap me," Jillian replied in disgust. "Betsy and Emily are new acquaintances. I hardly know them. They are taking care of Anna, that's all."

The Indian melted back into the shadows while Jillian mulled the situation.

After a long silence, she said, "Lucia, you and I are friends in a special way. I've told you over and over how long I waited and prayed to be able to come to Ecuador. For many years I dreamed of the day when I could come and live among the jungle Indians. I ate, slept, and breathed for the day I could just look at a jungle Indian. Then I was given an opportunity to live here, not in the jungle after all, but here with you. God brought you from the jungle to me and I'm thrilled that we have become good friends. Can't you see how very special you are to me?"

She waited in prolonged silence and then turned around to switch on the light and started banging in the cupboard for a pan.

"How about having a cup of coffee with me?" she asked as she worked at the stove, she relaxed with a yawn, familiar with Lucia's silences.

"Okay, Lucia?" she asked as she turned for an answer and stopped midway.

Lucia was holding a small gun in her hand. Shock turned her blood to ice water.

"Where did you get that and what are you doing with it?" Jillian asked with fear in her heart.

Lucia looked down at her hand and slowly pointed the gun at herself. Placing it at her temples, she said softly.

"If I thought that you would change your feelings for me, I would kill myself," Lucia threatened.

Chapter 24

"Are you crazy? Is that gun loaded?" Jillian asked as she walked to the table, her eyes focused on Lucia.

With a strange glint in her eyes, Lucia smiled and pulled the trigger. Horrified, Jillian heard the click.

"Of course not," she chuckled.

Angrily, Jillian prepared her coffee, grabbed a piece of bread, her book, and stomped out the door.

"I was just kidding, Jill," Lucia's voice trailed after her.

Jillian locked her bedroom door and leaned against it waiting for her heart to stop pounding. The next day when Jillian told Marta about the incident. Marta reacted only by clenching her jaw, but the matter was never mentioned again.

Chapter 25

Several days later, Marta made a general announcement at lunch that a patient expecting twins had been assigned a bed in the maternity clinic and that she would probably deliver sometime that afternoon. Jillian made a point of seeing the children's care was covered by Elizabeth and Flora and spent two hours watching her first delivery of twins. During dinner, an elated Marta told Jillian that the mother had decided to keep only the firstborn.

"We discussed it at length and feel it would be better for the second child if I take her since the majority of twins don't survive because the mother can't care for both of them. Anyway, the second baby is so small that she probably wouldn't last a month."

The next morning Marta showed Jillian a piece of paper with a typewritten message. On it the mother and father consented to turn the baby over to the orphanage and should they decide to take the child back, they agreed to pay Marta six hundred sucres a month for her care.

"Six hundred sucres? That's twenty-four American dollars. Were they able to read this?" Jillian asked, shocked.

"Of course not," Marta scoffed. "If they could read it, why would they have to put an 'x' for a signature? I told them that she'll be mine to keep here, but after thinking about it, I may put her up for adoption."

"Adoption?" Jillian asked. "Can you deal in adoptions?"

Chapter 25

"Why not?" Marta said. "I have so many friends who would love to have a child."

"Really?" Jillian asked. "That's wonderful. I can think of a few friends in Oregon who might be interested."

Marta frowned and adjusted her glasses, "Why don't you come over and see the baby after the children are napping this afternoon?"

Hours from the birth stress, Jillian saw how pretty the child was with her small perfect features. Marta seemed to take a particular interest in the infant spending hours doting on her. Therefore what happened next changed the peaceful atmosphere they had been enjoying for several weeks.

One evening, eleven days after the twin's birth, Lucia, Marta, and Jillian were discussing the day's happening and watching the children play, when the parents returned to the clinic steps. A dog's barking alerted Marta to the couple signaling from beyond the fence and she left the house to greet them.

A few minutes later Marta suddenly burst through the living room door weeping.

"They want the baby back," she sobbed. "They decided that they will be able to care for her. They said that the local church is upset with them and they've been the brunt of gossip and speculation."

Sinking on the sofa, she wiped her streaming eyes.

Then, with a sudden cry, she jumped up and yelled at Jillian, "Run! Run to the clinic! You've got to protect the baby in case they get into the building. Get going!"

Marta grabbed her arm and pushed her toward the door.

"Stop that, Marta," Jillian frowned, disgusted with the woman's theatrics. "They are not going to break into the clinic."

"Don't be a fool," Marta yelled. "Yes they will and if you don't get going, you'll be at fault."

Shaking her head, Jillian reluctantly wandered to the clinic.

The front door opened behind her.

"Go! Walk faster!" Marta shrieked. "Oh, God! Oh God!"

Quickening her steps, Jillian found the infant sleeping contently in her crib. Peeking out the window, she saw no one in sight. Her mind was in turmoil. Did Marta have reason to worry? It seemed only fair to give the child back, yet she remembered how she felt about losing Anna. Well, it served Marta right. Talk about your chickens coming back to roost.

Through the kitchen window she saw the nurse walking briskly toward the clinic. With eyes red and puffy from crying, Marta stood in the center of the room and pounded a fist into her hand.

"What shall we do?" Marta asked sadly. "I will not give that baby back."

"Are you sure that we can keep her?" Jillian asked. "What rights do the parents have?"

Marta gave her a look of annoyance, "Those parents have no rights as far as I'm concerned. I've cared for their baby eleven days and now I love her as my own. I'll never give her up. They'll take her and neglect her until she dies. Don't you see? They only want her because the neighbors are talking. It has nothing to do with love."

She paced the floor, arms waving wildly, "Oh, I'm so upset."

Jillian went to the hallway window and peeked out. Returning to the kitchen, she shook her head.

"You'll have to do something because the family is gathered around our door and I have a feeling they aren't about to leave," Jillian said.

"Just a minute, I have a plan," Marta turned abruptly and walked outside.

She remained only a few minutes, but watching from the window, Jillian saw the group angrily waving their hands in her face. Then, each one turned and walked off the property. The disheartened nurse returned to the clinic.

"What happened? What did you say to them?" asked Jillian anxiously. "And wasn't that the magistrate with them?"

"Yes, the old fool. I just told them that they couldn't have her until they paid me one thousand sucres a day for her care. I figured that with all the night feedings and hourly attention, I would raise the fee higher than the amount they signed for in their contract," Marta said.

"That's forty dollars a day," Jillian exclaimed. "What if they find a lawyer or someone to help them? That signed paper might not stand up in court, not with an 'x' for their signature. The judge would know they couldn't read."

Chapter 25

Bowing her head sadly, Marta lowered her voice confidentially, "I will just have to see that doesn't happen. Actually my hope is that the people are so stupid that they won't think about going to court. If they did, I would lose for sure. If all these people knew that I have no legal right to keep any of these children right now, but what they don't know is my gain. My biggest fear is that the government will come out here and look into this work and check my papers."

Jillian froze, "You told me the lawyer said all of this was legal when Sandi's parents tried to take the children."

"I think I can trust you for the sake of your little Andy," Marta replied with a small smile. "But I must say there are many ways of getting around problems like those that Sandi's parents handed us, believe me."

Marta whirled around, "We'd better check on the baby. I think instead of sending her to the United States, I'll keep her for my own. That means I'll have to name her. I've been thinking about calling her Julie. Julie is the perfect name. Now we can lock the door to her room and go back to the house."

Jillian could not forget what Marta had admitted. For a moment the woman had opened up, like a door briefly left ajar and then slammed shut. In her eyes, instead of a woman simply desiring to take in children to meet their needs, Marta had become an enigma. Why should Julie be so important to her? Wouldn't it be better if the baby was returned to the parents? Why should Marta put herself in jeopardy with the authorities? Why didn't she want the government checking on the work? What had she done to keep Sandi's lawyers at bay? Was it true that her papers weren't in order?

Never again in the years to follow would Marta confess anything amiss, but Jillian would not forget those troubling admissions.

Chapter 26

During the next few days Marta remained on the property, passing the time in tears or in lying about the house. The baby dominated her thoughts and actions until one morning her mood reversed and she decided to go to Quito. After her departure Jillian discovered that Julie was gone. When she asked Marta later about the baby, the nurse merely replied that a friend in Quito was caring for her. No other explanation was forthcoming and Jillian never again saw baby Julie.

Nothing was quite the same after that. Marta became edgy, Lucia was unhappy and the children were fearful all the time. On a shopping trip to Quito she poured out her heart to Philip over an extended luncheon. He pressed her to leave the orphanage after she revealed the events surrounding Julie's disappearance, but she convinced him that for the sake of the children, her place was in Pachuca and he would have to continue to be satisfied with a few stolen moments together every other week. Reluctantly, he agreed and they parted, her spirits lifted after confiding in him.

After spending an hour with Anna, she rushed home. It was quiet except for a radio softly playing national music in the kitchen while Flora hummed along. Walking into the playroom the children were delighted to see her. She hugged and kissed them, holding the babies close.

"Where's Andy?" she asked as she looked around, Lydia still clinging to her neck. "Elizabeth, where's Andy?"

"I think he's in bed," Elizabeth responded.

Chapter 26

"Flora, do you know where Andy is? Is he asleep?" Jillian yelled into the kitchen.

Wiping her hands on her sweater, the young maid peered into the dining room, "I don't know. I haven't seen him all morning and I don't ask questions."

"Goodness, I hope he's not sick. He was fine before I left this morning," Jillian said as her heart sank. "I'll go and check. A year old baby doesn't have to be in bed all the time. He should be up and you children should be outside in the sunshine. Why is everyone cooped up in the playroom? Who is taking care of you anyway?"

"Flora and Elizabeth," they chorused.

Opening the door to Andy's bedroom, she expected him to cry out with delight, but instead silence greeted her. She turned on the light and saw that he lay awake on his back, not moving. Alarm shot through her. What was wrong with him? She pulled the window curtain back and walked toward him. Eyeing her, he screamed out in fear. Bending over the crib, she saw a black eye and a large hand print covering his face. Choked with rage, her chest tightened. Tears sprang to her eyes as she picked him up and held him screaming in her arms. He was terrified of her.

"He just wouldn't stop crying so I had to spank him," Marta explained softly from the doorway just as Andy began to quiet.

Jillian whirled around hatred tearing at her heart, "Wouldn't stop crying? And for that you slapped him? What kind of monster are you?"

"You know how I feel about crying children. It just shows they're spoiled. There was no reason why he shouldn't be calm. His stomach was full and he had dry diapers," Marta's chin began to quiver and tears came to her eyes.

Jillian glared at her.

"Please don't start. It makes me sick to see you cry. Babies get beaten for what you seem to do all the time, whine and cry," sighing with disgust, she quieted Andy again. "I despise you. I can't bear to be near you."

"Please understand that I don't know what happens to me sometimes. It's almost more than I can stand to hear a child cry and if he doesn't stop I lose control because I understand what's happening. I know if a child is allowed to do what he wants, even at Andy's age we'll not be able to handle him when he's older," Marta said with conviction. "I can't tolerate that in this house."

"For Pete sake, he just turned a year old," screamed Jillian, causing Andy to jump and begin crying again.

"I'm sorry, Sweetheart," she crooned and held him to her heart.

"Don't you dare yell at me," Marta stomped to Jillian's side and grabbed her arm. "I won't put up with that either. What if the children or Lucia heard you talking to me that way? I'm the boss in this family and in this house. Don't ever forget it. No one yells at me."

"Take your hand off of me," Jillian demanded.

The two women stood facing each other, neither one wavering until Marta released Jillian's arm and looked away.

Speaking in a softer voice, Marta said, "Don't forget that this is my work and I'm in charge. If you remember that, we'll get along fine without any complications. If not, we'll never accomplish anything. We must stand together. And another thing, I've had years of experience with children. Don't you know that you can spoil a child in its first three days of life? Just the way you are holding Andy now and the way you held him when during his feeding when he was an infant proved that. He'd pretend he was drifting off to sleep so you would keep him in your arms. I didn't want to tell you this then, but I'm going to give you a lesson on how not to spoil a baby. If you hold a baby close to you he will refuse to eat his food quickly. His smart little mind tells him that he'll be held a lot longer. Don't forget that. You are to hold his neck in your free hand and gently shake his head to encourage him to stay awake and drink faster."

"Oh, then tell me why God created women with breasts full of milk. How do you expect them to feed their children from an arm's length away?" Jillian asked, disgusted.

"You are rude and hopeless," Marta said angrily. "I am talking about the children in this house, my children."

Turning to leave, Marta paused at the door, "I'm sorry you hate me. You'll never know how much I care for you."

Jillian walked Andy until he fell asleep and then returned him to bed, covering him gently. She descended the steps quietly and searched for Marta and Lucia. When she was satisfied they were out of the house, she walked quickly toward the gate and up the road

Chapter 26

toward town. She passed the plaza and entered a narrow road that led to the main telephone office.

Climbing a hardened mud stairway built onto the side of an ancient building, she entered the top floor. The room was long and bright with windows facing the street. Chattering, laughing Indians filled the wood benches lining the pale blue walls. Surprised to find so many people, Jillian stepped inside hesitantly and immediately all conversation stopped and all eyes turned to her.

A pregnant woman rose from behind an antiquated switchboard and smiled as Jillian walked across the creaking wooden floor. She stopped beside the board.

"Buenas tardes, Señorita," smiled the pleasant operator, resting her hand on her belly.

"Buenas tardes, Señora. Con permisso...."

A loud ringing interrupted their conversation as the woman sat down to pick up a jack and push it into a hole on the board. She smiled an apology to Jillian and spoke into a phone piece centered on her desk.

"Buenas tardes. Si. Un momento, porfavor," she pushed in another jack and dialed a number on a scratched battered instrument.

In a moment she announced the call into a headset and flipped a switch.

"Someone calling the Hacienda Cielo," she explained to Jillian with a smile. "Now, how may I help you?"

Glancing around the room, Jillian saw that everyone was watching her so she lowered her voice and spoke in careful Spanish, "Pardon me. I would like to speak with Dr. Philip Rios in the medical clinic in Yaruqui."

Showing intense curiosity, the operator nodded, made a few deft movements and shortly she was connected with the Yaruqui clinic. She motioned for Jillian to take the receiver of a telephone hanging on the wall opposite the switchboard.

Jillian quickly picked up the receiver and spoke into the telephone. After waiting for a moment, she heard Philip's familiar voice.

"Buenas tardes."

"Philip, this is Jill. You will have to listen to me in English. Can you hear me?"

"Si, why are you calling? Is something wrong?" he replied in Spanish.

She turned toward the wall, the silence in the room more stifling than the still air.

"I hope that I didn't disturb you," Jillian said urgently. "It's just that I have to talk to you."

"I do have a patient in my office," Philip responded professionally. "What's the matter?"

"She hurt Andy," Jillian said almost breaking into tears.

"What?" Philip asked incredulously.

"Marta hit Andy," Jillian said in a shaky voice.

"You say that she's always spanking the children. Why did you call about this?" Philip asked impatiently. "Did she injure him? Do you want me to come?"

"No!" her voice rose and she turned to see all eyes still riveted on her. "No, please don't come."

Tears stung her eyes, she swallowed against the lump in her throat, and she said, "Maybe it's time for Andy and me to move to Quito. I don't think I can live in her house any longer."

Silence greeted her, "Philip, are you there?"

She sensed reluctance in his hesitation, but then he lowered his voice and began speaking to her in English, "Maybe you haven't thought enough about the consequences if you leave now. She will be very angry."

"Yes I have. Why have you changed your mind? You acted like you wanted to this afternoon," she felt like screaming at him, instead she breathed deeply and calmed herself against the deafening silence in the room.

Hoping that no one understood English, she dropped her voice, "I can't speak here. Please meet me."

"How?" Philip asked. "I can't just leave my office now."

"Please meet me tonight after dark. The children will be in bed around seven o'clock. We can meet below our property down at the entrance to the new highway. I'll just tell Marta I feel like going to bed early," Jillian asked earnestly.

"All right," Philip agreed. "Tonight at seven at the entrance to Pachuca by the new highway."

Chapter 26

"Thank you," Jillian sighed with relief.

She hung up and turned toward the switchboard. Avoiding the operator's bright curious eyes, she dug in her skirt pocket and withdrew several sucres, dropping them on the wooden surface. Smiling she thanked the woman.

"Hasta mañana, Señorita."

"Hasta mañana, Señora," Jillian responded as she turned she gave a slight bow to the rest of the room.

The men removed their hats, while the women smiled shyly. Echoes of conversation followed her down the steps to the intersection. She decided that she would wait a week or so until Philip could find a room for her. Then she would take Andy to Quito where in a few days she could marry Philip and adopt both Andy and Anna. Marta would never be able to bother her again. The rest of the children would just have to get along on their own. Never again would she tolerate Andy being abused. Deep in these thoughts, she walked passed the marketplace and around the corner.

"Will you tell me where you have been, young lady?" Marta said stomping toward her. "We've looked everywhere for you."

"Why?" Jillian asked angrily as she tried to brush passed her on the narrow road.

"Where have you been?" Marta demanded as she grabbed Jillian's arm.

"I've been walking and now I want to go home," Jillian responded as she shook her arm free and started toward the compound leaving Marta with a troubled look on her face.

She quickly caught up with the girl and again took her arms, "Wait a minute."

Jillian glared and again shook her arm free, "Will you please leave me alone? I want to go home."

"You weren't just walking, were you?" Marta demanded. "You met someone in the plaza. I can sense it."

"No, Marta," wearily Jillian shook her head. "I didn't just meet someone in the plaza. I needed to get away."

"Away? You've been away to Quito most of the day. You've hardly spent a moment with the children and now it's almost time for dinner," Marta accused.

Could it be possible the woman had forgotten what she'd done to Andy? Puzzled, Jillian made it this time to the compound gate.

"Jill, do you have a friend in the plaza?" Marta asked.

The girl stopped and felt the blood drain from her face.

"I do not have a friend in the plaza that I visit," she said trying to remain composed and looked pointedly at Marta. "Why don't you leave me alone? I've had a very tiring day and I want to see if Andy is up from his nap and feeling better. He is the only person I am interested in right now."

Marta set her mouth in a straight line and studied Jillian's face carefully, "Once Lucia had a man friend who lived in the plaza. This was several years ago. For some unknown reason he began to seek out her company when she ran errands in the plaza, or who knows, maybe she sought him out. I caught him visiting her at her bedroom window one evening. Can you believe the audacity?"

"I can't see the harm at all. I think it would be wonderful if Lucia could find a man, get married, and have her own children," Jillian said ruefully.

"Oh!" the nurse clutched her breast. "You fool! You are such an idealist. You have no idea what marriage to one of these animals would be like, do you? The men in America are bad enough. They cause nothing but turmoil and heartache, but here in South America they cause such agony of heart that women die of despair. I saved Lucia from a terrible fate."

Jillian closed her eyes against the outburst, gaining a new compassion for Lucia.

Reluctantly she asked the question, "What did you do about it?"

"Nothing really. I merely told Lucia that she could go with him. I would let her go, but never again would she be welcome here. Never again would she see the children, and above all, never would Leah hear Lucia's name mentioned again. I would see that Leah hated her in time. You see if Lucia married a drunken heathen, she would lose all rights to everything she has here," Marta said smugly.

"I think the whole thing is disgusting," Jillian marched to the house and leaned on the door.

Did she know about Philip? One could never tell what this woman would do to protect those she claimed as her own.

Chapter 26

Marta looked at her hand and rubbed at imaginary dirt, "Why don't you stay home for a few Tuesdays? I'll do the errands in Quito. You can spend more time with Andy and Lucia that way."

"What about Anna?" Jillian asked realizing what Marta was doing. "I don't want to be away from her that much."

"I'll take your visits. She has enough attention anyway," Marta moved toward her, but Jillian opened the door and fled up the steps to Andy's room.

She listened at the entrance to his soft breathing and decided not to disturb him. Carefully shutting the door she went to her room and sat on the edge of her bed.

Oh God, she knows about Philip. What am I going to do? I'll never get away tonight to meet with him. She'll be watching my every move, Jillian thought to herself. Rising to her feet she looked out the window toward Oyambarrillo not caring how freely her tears flowed. She would miss Anna desperately. What would Philip think as he waited for her? Oh, I hope he doesn't try to come here. Tearing at her hair, she tried to calm herself. No, he wouldn't do that. He knows the trouble here. He'll just wait until he knows I can't get away and then go home.

She sat on the bed again feeling calmer. But when I don't come Tuesday, he'll become worried. *Maybe I should try to call him again.* She paced. *No, I can't do that. I can't leave the property and I surely can't use the telephone here.* She stopped. Maybe Lucia will help me. She's been through this before. *No, I can't do that either. I remember how she reacted to my friendship with Anna's two nurses. What would she do if she heard about Philip? No, I'll just hope he knows better than to come here. Lord, please help him to stay away. I can't risk losing the children. What am I to do?*

She sat in a daze until the soft afternoon sun sank in the distance and darkness covered the valley.

Chapter 27

During the last days of January the town of Pachuca celebrated its birthday. Village officials hired out-of-town brass and drum bands for street dances and parades. Large collections of firecrackers tied to gigantic wooden frames were carried by brave men through the streets as drunken bystanders stood and hollered, ducking pieces of flying fire.

Throngs of people came from miles around on foot, buses, trucks and horseback, jamming the streets, sidewalks, and door stoops. Noise from bands, firecrackers, yelling, and carousing filled the air. Echoes bounced from the mountainsides casting sounds to the far reaches of the valley.

Carlos joined the celebration wandering with the crowd until he found himself at a street dance. Watching from the top step of a nearby house, he felt disgust at the happy reveling. Unable to find joy as in years past, he was aware his attitudes had darkened and soured, causing everything to appear ugly and unappealing. He noticed Mercedes watching him from across the street, a frown replacing her smile as he turned from her without acknowledgment. Knowing he had left her puzzled and hurt, his conscience smote him, but all he wanted to do was escape to the peace of his home. How could he have considered a relationship with another woman?

Why am I here? he asked himself as he turned homeward fighting his way through the thickening throng. Because of the drunken crowd, heavy traffic and flying fireworks he had left his brothers and sister

Chapter 27

home. The thought of returning to them became a refuge for his troubled mind. To his relief, the noise inside the house was subdued. After shedding his jacket, he sank onto a bench.

"Let's make popcorn," he suggested to the delighted children.

"Oh, yes," they chorused as Joel scrambled to stoke the fire.

Jerman dug a pan from beneath the table and Yolanda opened a small cupboard searching for a handful of corn wrapped in newspaper. Within a few minutes the four gathered around the fire munching on the popped treat. Begging stories from their big brother, the three youngsters crowded close as he related again his visit to the Hacienda Tulcachi, a tale of which they never tired. In time the children became drowsy and Carlos sent the boys to bed and tucked Yolanda into his mother's bed in the front room.

He took off his clothes, knowing there was nothing left to do but retire. He dreaded the long nights when he had to face his thoughts and desires for Elena. Despite the drum beating and booms from the fireworks, he dozed. There was silence in the streets when he woke with a start. Listening carefully he heard muffled laughter and talk from outside the house, then the front door opened. In horror he realized the loud whispers were his mother and a companion. Jumping from the bed, he peered into the outer room and was taken back by the strong scent of liquor. Embers from the fire allowed enough light to see his mother leaning against a man. As quickly and quietly as possible, Carlos moved to Yolanda's bed and struggled to pick her up before the drunken couple tumbled on top of her. Placing Yolanda in his bed, she snuggled down in the covers unaware she had been moved.

For an hour Carlos sat in the darkness of his bedroom until all grew quiet in the next room. Lighting a candle, he walked to the door and into the main room. He wanted to know who was with his mother. There was little doubt, but he wanted to know for sure. Carrying the candle to his mother's bed, he looked down at Rolando for a long while. Even in this condition Rolando was handsome, weak, and filthy. Dried vomit stained his shirt. The stench of liquor and vomit was more than Carlos could bear.

"This is the man who said I wasn't good enough for his sister," he whispered. "Well, I'll not stay here to find out if my mother has conceived another child. It's time I find my own happiness."

Chapter 28

He would plan well. He must meet with Elena. Seeing Rolando in his mother's bed erased all fear of him. Now his concern was the state of Elena's feelings for him. She must despise his cowardice. Why had he submitted to Rolando so quickly without fighting for her love? He had to see her and explain why he had stayed away. His only hope was that she would understand. He discarded the idea of walking to her house. During the day chances were she would not be home. His worst enemies would be innocent people in the plaza who carried news as fast as a small child could run. What if tales of his relationship with Elena had grown out of proportion? No, he would use the utmost caution knowing a surprise encounter would be the most productive.

He chose the day carefully. During the month of February, the country of Ecuador would celebrate Carnaval, a time of frivolous fun, scores of water-filled balloons heaved from passing vehicles onto hapless pedestrians. If in some cases, water didn't create enough havoc, vessels of flour would be showered on a friend, or lard and chimney soot smeared on family members. During the final fiesta day, the day before Lent commenced, all businesses closed and people gathered in the plaza for dancing and drinking. Carlos decided this was the best time to carry out his plan.

Three weeks after finding his mother and Rolando together, he calmly ate a small dinner and waited until the children were in bed. His mother had left the house earlier using the excuse she was going

Chapter 28

to visit a friend. He shook his head in disgust at the thought of her probable date with Rolando.

Careful the children were sleeping, he prepared to leave the house. Finding it chilly, he drew his jacket around him and glanced up at the sky. The moon had yet to appear, but the sky was filled with glimmering, glowing stars that dimly showed his way. For a moment he hesitated realizing he would soon see Elena again and suddenly he began to shake violently, his stomach churning from nervousness. With teeth chattering, he tried to relax alarmed at his lack of control now that he was putting the plan into action. Should he return home? No, if he didn't go now, he might never go.

Leaving the main road, Carlos chose the road which led directly ahead. A quarter of a mile later he followed a narrow trail set between mud walls. Most of the pathway was in deep shadows, but the stars lent enough light for him to feel his way. He walked toward the mountains, away from Pachuca until he came to a crossroad. To the right lay a large hacienda, faint lights showing through the central building's small windows. Squelching his fear of guard dogs, he moved ahead. If he remained quiet and stayed close to the inner mud wall, they should be no bother. He paused, listening for any approaching footsteps. Tonight's dance was centered in the town proper, leaving the suburbs quiet except for the faint beat of music echoing off the mountains and the swishing noises of bats and nocturnal birds.

To his left lay a small deserted building, old and crumbling, but he knew the land was in use. Poor families living in the plaza who were unable to afford land of their own grew crops, claiming half and relinquishing the remaining half to the landowners.

Aware that the landowners paid a small salary to a caretaker who would be watching for trespassers and thieves, he had no desire to meet with the man as he didn't have a good explanation for what he was doing. Thankfully, cornstalks were standing tall and he was able to move easily between the rows. His plan was to follow the mud walls behind Pachuca's properties until he reached Elena's house and wait for her to retire, then call her to the window. Thinking of their reunion spurred him to walk swiftly into the black shadows until he reached the property's edge.

While They Sleep

Now he had to think of how to climb over the wall. With his attention on this obstacle, he suddenly found himself in the irrigation ditch. Cold water rushed up to his waist and the silent current pulled him off his feet. Startled, he grabbed for the shrubbery growing against the wall. Pausing to catch his breath, he reached for the bank and pulled himself up.

Nursing a sore ankle and ribs, he gritted his teeth in anger, "What a fool I am. How could I have forgotten the irrigation ditch?"

He rubbed his ankle vigorously cursing himself for this oversight.

Now he had to regroup his thoughts. Resting for several minutes, he began shaking with cold. Should he go home or continue on his way?

Covered with mud, his clothes dripping with water and filth, he knew he'd have to return home. Sick with disappointment, he stood and limped on numb feet. The mud and water weighed him down as he plodded dejectedly through the cornfield. Unable to see clearly, he tripped and fell across a large soft object. Yelping with alarm he jerked to his feet as the mound began moaning. Staring in fright, he was able to make out the form of a body lying face down in the shadows. It was all his taut nerves could take and Carlos began to cry hot tears. Fear and the cold air were beginning to take its toll until reason returned and he was able to gather some composure. Turning the body over, it began to groan in protest. Liquor fumes wafted over Carlos and with relief he realized it was the old caretaker indulging in his own party. Resisting the temptation to giggle, he saw the man was merely sleeping.

Weakened by his pounding heart and shaking body, he sat and waited until his strength returned. The bone-numbing cold, overwhelming fatigue and futility of his efforts were more than he could bear. He had no choice but to go home and try another day.

All that night he laid thinking and planning, sick with frustration, but more determined than ever. At dawn as he heard the first movements of mountain Indians on the road below and the crowing of the rooster behind his house, the idea hit him. What a fool I am, he thought. It is so simple. Smiling to himself, he sat up in bed. The very talebearers who would carry the news of his appearance in town would be the ones who would bring Elena to him. He relaxed knowing all would be well.

Chapter 29

Physically he didn't feel well until Monday. Deciding he could no longer wait to see Elena, he would go into the main plaza today for the first time in almost a year. To his dismay, three peons didn't appear for work, forcing him and Fausto to rush in order to complete their own chores plus the extra work. He remembered belatedly that most of his workers had celebrated Carnaval and would have continued drinking throughout the weekend, although officially the Lent season had begun.

During the siesta hour Carlos told Fausto of his idea. They must wait until the townspeople were about their afternoon duties before they could put their plan into effect. Most importantly they would need to find someone with a horse. His biggest problem would be finding someone sober.

He and Fausto sat on a grassy knoll beside the road patiently waiting for a good prospect. Several drunken men passed with their wives and children in tow, crying or sleeping babies strapped to the mother's backs.

After an hour's wait they saw a man in the distance leading his horse toward them. Strapped across the animal's back were two burlap bags of grain bound for Pachuca.

Carlos rose slowly and approached the man, holding out his hand, "Buenas tardes, Señor. How are you and your family?"

"Buenas tardes, Carlos. We are getting by. It's been awhile since we have talked. Your family is doing well, God willing?"

While They Sleep

They conversed at length on nonessential topics until at last Carlos requested the man's help, "I will pay you twenty-five sucres."

The Indian's eyes lit up with enthusiasm. Twenty-five sucres would more than pay for the corn grinding he was taking to the town miller.

"Yes, I will help you get to the main plaza if I can," he agreed.

Carlos counted out and placed silver in the man's extended hand. Then they solemnly discussed the plan until everyone nodded in agreement. Carlos turned and located a paper sack he had placed in the tall grass. Opening it, he pulled out a penknife and without a second thought jabbed a hole in his oldest pair of pants. Grabbing the material at the ankle he ripped to just below his knee. He paused to look at Fausto and the man, but both men had averted their eyes.

Gritting his teeth, Carlos laid the blade of the knife on his leg. As if reconsidering, he hesitated a moment, then with purpose pressed the sharp instrument into the side of his calf and around to the back of his leg. A stream of blood oozed down his leg and he involuntarily moaned as drops of sweat formed on his forehead and upper lip. Again he drew the knife through the wound; the blood now flowing in a steady stream. Deliberately he smeared the sticky red substance on his shirt, face, and into his hair

"Where are the rags? Get some from the sack," Carlos yelled to Fausto, who was covering his face and looking as though he was going to be ill.

Fausto fumbled with the bag until he located two clean, faded cloths, and bent to wrap the leg. Blood soaked one immediately and Carlos leaned forward to press the other rag firmly on the wound and tied it securely.

"Now I must get on top of the horse. Can you place the burlap bags back a bit further?" he asked as he waved an arm attempting to keep his balance on his one good leg and wondered why he hadn't had the rags and horse ready before he had injured himself.

The man adjusted the bags of corn, looking as if he regretted his part in the scheme and then reached out to help Carlos onto the horse's back, "We'd better go or you will really need a doctor."

Fausto tugged at the reins while the horse protested, balking and snorting nervous with the added weight on her back.

Chapter 29

Jumping behind, the man slapped the animal's rump, "Go! Get going!"

With another loud slap, the horse leaped into action, running in confusion. Fausto hung onto the reins trying to steady her until the man took over, calming the mare.

"Now, Fausto, go with the news," commanded Carlos triumphantly. "Ask for help, do whatever you must do to spread the tale."

The boy grinned and started running, yelling for help. Indians visiting in the street and storefronts turned to look in astonishment at the laden horse being pulled by its worried-looking owner.

As Carlos had predicted, the news reached town before the small procession and people waited in the doorways and windows. It was a sight to behold. Slumped on the horse's neck lay Carlos, his mouth open, blood oozing through the red-soaked rag and tried to appear as though he had fainted. His matted hair stood on end, his torn clothes saturated with blood. His bandaged, wounded leg was purposely exposed.

By the time they reached the main plaza he began to feel faint and had barely enough strength to hang onto the horse. They had been traveling for half an hour and even though the heavy blood flow had stemmed, he could still feel drops trickling down his leg.

He could not have hoped for more attention. People stood on the restaurant's long porch, store proprietors stepped to the streets, and patrons peered from behind doors. Residents of the mud homes watched from doors and balconies. He knew the story of his injuries had grown out of proportion as it was passed from house to house. Despite his growing worry that he was going to faint and fall from the horse, he had to smile to himself. His plan was working better than he could have imagined.

Squeezed between the grade school and registrar's office sat the clinic. It was a long one-story building constructed by the government for the purpose of supplying medical attention to the rural community. The doctor commuted from Quito to serve her last year of schooling before she could set up her own practice. She was accompanied by an assistant, who lived in the village and was hired to be on-call twenty-four hours a day, although Olivia seemed to be habitually absent after office hours. To the rear, past a small patio, an addition had been built to house a dentist and assistant working with the same program.

As they approached, Carlos noticed several women with babies sitting on the doorstep in the entrance, awaiting their turn. Through blurred eyes he saw Fausto pacing impatiently on the cracked sidewalk. He knew that people along the way had asked too many questions Fausto would have been unable to answer and the look on the boy's face revealed his fear and doubts.

Apprehensively, Fausto stepped to the horse's side as it drew to a stop at the curb. Helping the man pull Carlos from the animal, the boy steadied his friend as he attempted to walk into the building.

Through a fog of pain, Carlos saw the crowd of women with children scatter to make room and he tried to understand why there were no men in the group. Then a terrible thought gained a foothold, there was a flaw in his plan. He had forgotten there was no doctor in attendance on Monday. Sick patients were forced to find rides to the next town, wait until the doctor was on duty the following day, or hope that the American nurse, Señorita Marta would have time to see them. He would rather die than ask for help from Marta Brewer after hearing how she had mistreated Elena's mother.

Don Eduardo's daughter, Olivia, worked as the doctor's aide. A country girl with experience of sorts, but with no official training or schooling, she opened the clinic alone on Mondays solely for the purpose of vaccinating children against common childhood diseases.

What was I thinking of? Carlos thought through a cloud of pain and faintness. A pathway opened. Hopping on his good leg, he leaned heavily on his accomplices. Entering the waiting room they paused to look for an empty resting place among the benches filled with mothers and their children.

"Please make room for this patient. He is near death," panted the Indian, trying to shift the dead weight lying on his shoulder.

Without a word the room's population shifted all cramming against one wall, gasping in horror. An inner door opened and the heavy-set doctor's aide appeared in the entrance, her face blanching.

"What happened?" astonishment held her motionless.

Chapter 29

With a leap, Fausto was at her side, "Señorita Olivia, he has been hurt. Someone attacked him in the road up above the hacienda where he works."

The older man nodded his head nervously, hat in hand.

"I can't take care of a problem like this," Olivia said shaking her head. "You'll have to find a truck and take him down to the American clinic or over to Yaruqui."

"I don't think he'll make it that far," said a brave mother, a small child clinging to her skirt moved forward for a better look at Carlos, who by this time had slumped over.

Olivia squatted on the floor and studied him, feeling his clammy face, "I could contact Señorita Marta, but I doubt if she'd do much for us. Her outpatient clinic has been closed down."

Sighing in concentration she bit on a thumbnail, "Perhaps I should clean the wound and give you something for the pain, Carlos."

Standing up, she announced in a loud voice over the chattering of the other patients, "You'll have to wait until I finish with Carlos. He is too sick to send on to Yaruqui."

Guiding him to his feet, she led him to the doctor's office, as some of the waiting patients rushed to those gathering around the front door to relay the latest news. Fausto and his companion scrambled behind Carlos, helping him up to an examining table.

"Take off his shoes," she motioned to Fausto, while she cut the rags covering Carlos' wound. "It's a deep cut, but it's much cleaner than I expected."

Stammering, the Indian tried to explain, "I cleaned him before we put on the bandage."

Olivia gave him a questioning look and then set to work, filling a small metal basin with warm water, "Who did this to him? Do you know?"

"Ah, we don't know," said Fausto, looking to his companion for help. "We found him this way."

"Yes, he was up against a wall when we found him," said the man, backing toward the door.

By this time, Carlos' face was a sickly grey color and he could hardly stay awake. The blood loss had been severe and Olivia's movements were slow. She watched him anxiously and made her decision.

"Actually, I've helped the doctor many times and I've cleaned wounds for him. I can at least try to sew the cut and then try to get you to Yaruqui," she offered.

Carlos didn't care any longer. Through unfocused eyes he could hardly see her and suddenly realized he had made a dreadful mistake and was now dying. His throat contracted and tears welled up in his eyes. He was dying and would never see Elena after all. By the time she heard he was in the clinic a mere few meters away from her house, he would be dead. Feeling a pinprick as Olivia administered a local anesthesia, he felt blackness envelop him.

Chapter 30

Something cool was gently wiping his face and he drifted upward to consciousness. Struggling to open his eyes, he looked into Elena's face as she bent over him, a damp rag in her hand. Behind her stood a short, bearded man wearing a spotless white doctor's coat. Through cloudy vision, Carlos saw he was in a large back room of the clinic, an IV strapped to his arm. As his mind cleared, his attention was drawn back to Elena who spoke not a word, but clung to his hand.

"My name is Dr. Philip Rios. I live in Quito, work in the government hospital, but I also have a clinic in Yaruqui. Señorita Olivia telephoned me because she felt you were too ill to travel to Quito or Yaruqui. It's a good thing she did. You could have bled to death. She had your blood type on record and called me in Quito to bring a supply of blood for a transfusion. It probably saved your life."

Giving them a friendly, quiet smile, he pulled on his beard. Carlos thanked him and tried to smile as Elena bent over him, continuing to wipe his face.

"Where are Fausto and the man from Palugo?" Carlos asked.

"They left yesterday afternoon after the doctor arrived," Elena told him.

"I've been here all night?" Carlos asked, trying to raise himself.

"Yes," she calmed him. "You've been very sick. Your family was here for a while this morning, but they had to leave."

Olivia entered the room and Dr. Rios walked to meet her, "Señorita, you will have to keep him here overnight again. As long as someone stays here in case of a relapse."

"Our janitor will stay if I ask him and promise him a few extra sucres. If anything happens he will call me immediately," Olivia assured the doctor.

Somewhat satisfied, Dr. Rios re-examined him, "I was very concerned because obviously you have not been taking care of yourself. You are underweight and your lungs sound like you have an infection."

Carlos smiled, "Yes, I recently fell into an irrigation ditch."

Philip frowned, puzzled, "You must rest or you'll be back in bed in a short time."

He patted the young man's head and then left the building with Olivia escorting him to his car.

Content they were left alone, Elena leaned down and whispered in his ear, "I'm so glad you are all right. How I worried."

Tears rolled down his cheeks and he tried to wipe his face, but weakness overcame him, "Elena, before Olivia returns, I must talk to you. I want to go away so we can be married. Do you think we can manage that? I just can't live without you any longer and if you're willing, we can make plans."

He searched her face, "Can we meet again? Can you get a message to me without causing yourself a problem?"

Watching his face, she hesitated a few moments, "I'm only here right now because my brothers are still at school and Rolando hasn't returned from a party he went to on Sunday. I heard yesterday afternoon that you were injured, but because I had to wait until the news had died down and the maid was away, I can only remain for a few minutes. I live in fear someone will find out I still love you. Even my aunt and uncle are against us being together. Things have been very difficult at home. Rolando isn't the sweet man he used to be. He's always in a vile humor and I'm afraid of displeasing him. If he knew we were talking now, I'd fear for you and for the misery he can bring to my life."

Chapter 30

She brushed back his hair and wiped his eyes, "I am miserable. I've not been happy since we parted. I thought you didn't care any longer."

"Oh, my love, if you only knew how much I love you," he grimaced in pain.

Concerned, she asked him, "Are you all right? You know, you will have to report this incident to a magistrate. I'm sure Olivia will talk to you about it when you are feeling better."

"No! I will not report this to anyone. We must leave it alone, Elena. I just want to leave Pachuca with you," Carlos begged. "Please, consider what I say."

She turned to see if Olivia was out of earshot and lowered her voice, "If I can manage, we will meet again and make plans, but only one time. Do you know that sometimes I think my brother has lost his mind? We will have to plan quietly so no one will suspect."

"How do we know we can trust Olivia?" Carlos asked.

"We can't. We will have to take a chance. She has a boyfriend in Quito and drives to see him almost every evening even though she is supposed to remain nearby on-call," Elena told him. "Perhaps that will occupy her mind."

He closed his eyes for a long while and in a moment of impatience she reached out to gently shake him.

"What are you doing? I'm not asleep. I'm thinking," he frowned. "How would it work if I leave a note for you with all the plans?"

Weakly, he raised his hand against her protest, "Wait a minute, Elena. Remember the mud wall beside your aunt's house on the left side as you leave the front door? Unless they have repaired it, a piece of the mud brick has fallen out and left a hole. I'll have someone pass by the wall and leave a note. When you visit your cousins you can remove it. I'll leave it ten days from today after my leg is healed and strong and the stitches are removed. I'll figure a plan and write it down."

Groping for her hand, he grabbed it with all the strength he possessed, "Tell me if you will do it, Elena. If someone else finds the note there may be trouble for my family. They may have trouble anyway."

"Shhh, here comes Olivia," Elena said quietly. "Pretend you are sleeping. I'll tell her I've been watching you until she returned. Carlos, yes, I'll go with you. I love you."

She stood and turned, "Oh, Señorita, you're here. He's asleep and since you have returned, I will leave. I was concerned because as you know, Carlos once worked for my family."

The big woman nodded with a knowing smile on her lips, "Of course, I understand. Well, don't worry about him, Chica. Now that he's been under a doctor's care he will recover rapidly."

"Oh, thank God and thank you for calling Dr. Rios. How terrible this has happened. I wonder who attacked Carlos. Was there a chance to question Fausto?" Elena asked.

"No, he and the man left as soon as possible, saying they had other things to do," Olivia admitted. "The entire incident is very puzzling."

Chapter 31

❧

Carlos sealed the envelope and held it in his hand for a moment, thinking back through the past week. Soon he would be leaving his family and the thought made him sad, but he knew they would be alright without him. Yolanda amazed him with her sense of survival. He felt that Rolando was more talk than action and the man's bluster and fury were nothing more than a ploy to frighten and dominate him. With a sigh of joy he quietly acknowledged the fact that he and Elena would soon be together.

He had seen her only once since that day the previous week. The next morning he had left for home, shaky but able to walk without much difficulty. No one had spent the night caring for him, but Elena had brought food then quickly disappeared. Olivia, despite her promise for care, must have gone to Quito for the evening without hiring the janitor to watch him and he had not seen her since. Leaving a small pile of silver on the bed, he had left early in the morning before the clinic opened.

Tapping the envelope, he looked now at Fausto sitting across from him at the family table. A warm glow emanated from the fire curling around a soup pot. An aroma of chicken stew caused the boy to lick his lips. It seemed he made a concentrated effort to keep his attention on Carlos.

"What do you want me to do with the letter?" asked the boy.

Affectionately, Carlos smiled at his friend, "I need your help. I know you've helped me a lot lately, but this is the most important favor you have ever been asked to do and one with more secrecy. You'll have to be careful, but I'll pay you as much as you make in an entire day. Just don't ask a lot of questions, for your own good."

Fausto's eyes brightened at the mention of money. Carlos noticed and then studied the child who appeared years beyond his age. Hungry, unwashed, with thick, dirty hair, it was no wonder people living a better way of life would look at the neglected, filthy boy, and be repulsed. They would never understand that for his large family to bathe it would be necessary to carry many pails of water to their home. They didn't own a container large enough for a bathtub causing the impoverished family to bathe in the streets, fully clothed and shivering in the dusty wind. His heart went out to the boy.

"Does the letter have something to do with Elena?" Fausto squinted up his eyes in an attempt to understand the mystery.

Turning to see if they were still alone having purposely sent his three siblings to collect wood, he said, "Yes, but you don't need to know what. Listen to what you must do."

Acting as though he were hesitating for pride sake, the boy nodded desperately needing the money, "Please don't send me to Rolando's house. He's wild."

"You don't have to go to Elena's house, just to her aunt's. No one will see you if you go at night. Walk to the house and stay close to the mud wall and when you notice you are alone or when the family is asleep, slip over next to the house. About three meters up from the ground and six meters back, there's a spot where part of a brick has fallen from the wall. Feel in there and gouge out a bit more dirt. Fold this envelope and place it inside. No one must be able to see it. Do you understand? It must be put there tonight. Tomorrow may be too late. After you return, I'll give you the money," Carlos instructed. "Are you frightened?"

"No, I guess not," shrugged the boy. "Just so no neighbors see me. Oh, what's the difference? Who would care?"

"Possibly no one, but I still don't want any curious passersby to see this letter. It's only for one person and only she knows it will be there," Carlos sat back, pleased. "Are you hungry?"

He knew the boy was half-starved.

Chapter 31

"I'll get a bowl of soup for you," he said as he found two metal bowls and spoons on a shelf and limped to the fire. Dipping deep to find several potatoes, carrots and chunks of cabbage, he filled each bowl and placed them on the table.

"Go on, eat," Carlos said as he placed a plate of bread and cheese in front of the boy and stared in amazement as Fausto wolfed it all down and accepted seconds.

Swallowing the last bite, the boy grabbed the envelope, wiped his mouth on his sweater, and headed for the door.

"I want you to come back here tonight when you have finished," said Carlos. "Just knock on the window."

He followed the boy to the door, favoring his sore leg and laid a hand on his shoulder.

Grinning up at him, Fausto boasted, "Don't worry about anything. I'll do exactly as you asked and will return in a few hours."

Carlos lay most of the night without sleeping waiting for the knock that didn't come. His mind in frenzy, the next morning, he dressed, preparing to leave the house against his sister's protests.

"Your leg still hurts you. Stay home with me one more day. I don't want you to leave," she pleaded.

He stooped beside her, "Mi cariña, I must get out and walk on this leg or it will never heal. I'm just going down to Fausto's house. If he's there, perhaps we will work for a while today."

Throwing her arms around his neck, she hugged him tightly. Gently he released her and messed her hair.

"I'll be back for lunch. Fausto may be with me," Carlos told her fondly.

Walking toward town, he tested his leg and found it was more stiff than wounded. Reaching the shack where Fausto's family lived, he knocked on the weather-worn entrance. A small girl opened the door. He shuddered involuntarily and turned his face away as a horrid stench greeted him. Taking a deep breath, he returned his gaze. A fire burned on the floor in the corner, detailing shadowy figures on the ugly mud wall. A scrawny dog with watery, pink eyes sniffed at him as a pig grunted and hens clucked. Animals slept with the family as a prevention against thievery and because they owned no space out-of-doors.

The thin girl looked ill. Sadly undernourished, her bony legs and bare feet added to her look of hopelessness. It seemed her crumpled dress had been slept in. Stringy and unkempt, her hair was colored the unusual blondish red that accompanies malnutrition. Her skin was blotchy and her lip parched. She rubbed her dull eyes against the brightness of the morning sun.

"Buenos, Carlos," she muttered unenthusiastically.

"Hola, Lolita. Is Fausto home?" Carlos asked.

She turned and peered into the darkness as Carlos stepped out of the sun's glare and looked over her shoulder. He saw the straw mats lying on the floor, one lone piece of furniture, a bureau standing in the corner, the top overflowing with various objects. Sitting in the middle of the floor, a large can, one source of the overpowering stench, their indoor toilet.

Carlos' stomach lurched and he turned his head, breathing deeply. He pitied this family knowing Lolita's father swept the streets in Pachuca's plaza, each morning taking the village wheelbarrow and a broom to sweep the refuse from the front of each house. A notorious drunk, the few sucres he earned each day paid his way of escape into an alcoholic oblivion.

The child placed one dirty leg across the other and scratched her calf with the heel of her foot as she looked up at him and said, "No, I think he's already left for work."

From behind Lolita a woman approached, wincing against the bright sunlight, "Buenos dias, Carlos. You are looking for Fausto? I don't think he was here last night. He wasn't with you?"

"Buenos dias, Señora. No, I was home all night. You are sure he has not been home?" Carlos asked concerned.

"Well, I don't know. I guess he's left for work," she said then lost interest.

He watched her, wondering if she still remembered he was there. At times he puzzled at his people's short attention span. He failed to realize that poor eating and unsanitary habits seriously damaged both body and mind. Almost everyone he knew ate a diet of bread, rice, pasta and potatoes, anything that would fill their stomachs. He and his mother were able to afford meat once or twice a week because both of them worked, but some families like Fausto's rarely ate

Chapter 31

protein. The animals that shared their lodging along with eggs their hen produced would be sold to buy more starches to eat.

She yawned showing a toothless mouth. Her hair had been freshly combed, but from appearances had not been washed as he could see lice moving along her scalp. A dark skirt caked with dirt hung to her ankles. She, like other peasant women living in homes without plumbing purposely wore long flared skirts in order to squat in the streets and relieve themselves in a modest manner. Her sagging breasts were partially covered by a frayed sweater. He wondered if perhaps Fausto had failed to mention he had a new brother or sister.

Out of kindness he offered her a silver sucre, thanking her for her help. Her eyes brightened and she bowed her thanks, as she took the coin. He turned to leave determined to compliment Yolanda when he returned home. His own house was never completely clean, but it didn't have the stench and filth of this house. He was proud of the orderly way his young sister kept their lodging.

"I should go to work myself," Carlos said as he turned to leave. "Buenos dias, Señora."

She stood in the doorway, not noticing his departure in her haste to deposit the coin in a skirt pocket.

Where had Fausto gone? Hurriedly passing his own house he rushed toward the hacienda. Suddenly he slowed down. Maybe the note hadn't been delivered. Maybe Fausto had been discovered by Rolando and injured. Maybe Elena was again being persecuted by Rolando's fury. Could this be a sign that he should not leave Pachuca? After all, could he bear to live in the big city or in another valley away from the familiar sights he loved? Was a life with Elena worth this? What of Yolanda and his brothers, or the security of a home and job, and of course his mother. True, he seldom saw her because of their work schedules and her social life, but he still loved her. With a sudden premonition, he felt perhaps he would never see his family again. If that were true, was a life with Elena worth it?

As he slowly walked the road to Hacienda Hermosa, he watched Quito awakening far to his right across the wide expanse of Tumbaco Valley. Sun rays caressed Pachincha's mountainside, engulfing the capitol city. From this distance it looked quiet and serene, but he knew even at this hour people were struggling to find room on the hundreds of buses passing through the traffic-choked streets. The mere idea of joining the hordes of people rushing to earn a living repelled him. Passing the hacienda's first pasture, he breathed in the youth of the morning and looked to the mountains. Perhaps he couldn't leave. A wave of panic engulfed him. If Fausto had encountered trouble delivering the note, he would accept this as a sign he should not marry Elena.

In the distance he saw Fausto sitting on a fence near the driveway, chewing on a bun. Waving, the boy jumped down to wait.

Carlos quickened his step, "Fausto!"

"Hola, Carlos. You are late," scolded Fausto.

"Late? Where have you been? I was almost sick from concern. Why didn't you knock on the window last night and where were you this morning? I was at your house looking for you."

Fausto shrugged. "Sometimes I don't go home. There's not much room."

"What happened to the envelope? Did you deliver it?"

Snorting, Fausto wiped his nose with the sleeve of his dirty, holey sweater and turned, walking up the driveway.

Carlos followed with a questioning look. "Well? What happened?"

"Nothing happened," Fausto said between bites. "I sat in the dark against a wall all night. There were people at the Martinez house until late, probably people from Quito because some of them had cars. Lights were on and I was afraid someone would see me and think I was a thief. So, I waited."

"Did you leave the envelope?" asked Carlos as he flung out his arms in frustration.

"Yeah, yeah it's there," Fausto scratched his head. "I'm not sure what time everyone left and the lights went out, but I was sleeping when I heard the cars starting up and people talking. I just stayed all night and put it in the wall before daylight. Now I'm tired this morning."

Feeling a twinge of conscience, Carlos softened and smiled. He playfully hit the side of the boy's head as they reached the yard. Reaching into his pocket, he grabbed a handful of sucres and released them into Fausto's outstretched hand.

Chapter 31

"Thank you for doing this for me. Also I want you to know that I'm seeing that you have a position here at the hacienda permanently, starting today," Carlos told the boy.

The boy, stunned with pleasure stammered his thanks.

Recently built of wood and glass windows, the principle house sat in a grove of eucalyptus trees. A garden of roses surrounded a man-made pond boasting a large family of ducks. Chickens scattered in every direction scolding the thoughtless intruders as a little brown and white dog ran from the barn dancing about the men's feet in excitement.

Fausto laughed and patted the mutt, "The note is safe inside the wall. At dawn I passed and couldn't see it."

"Good," Carlos said as an uncontrolled joy flooded through him.

He forgot his indecision and knew only that his desire was to be with Elena.

"Good work, Fausto," he said to the tired boy. "Now I must wait five long days."

Those five days crawled by but finally it was Sunday night. The villagers of Pachuca were at evening mass or in the crowded saloon as Carlos carefully made his way to Elena's house. He tapped on her bedroom window at the appointed time. It opened quietly and a canvas bag was tossed to the ground. He reached to protect her as she dropped to the high grass lining the house. Within minutes they were running in the direction of the American nurse's compound and down to the Pan American Highway.

Chapter 32

For a week the atmosphere in the house was gloomy. Jillian stayed to herself, caring for the children. She refused to pay attention to Lucia, who by process of elimination, she now suspected as the one who had suggested to Marta that she had gone to the plaza the previous week to meet with someone. Even Marta came and went in silence, not showing any concern that Lucia had retreated into one of her dark moods. She stayed in her bedroom and the clinic whenever possible.

On Sunday Marta attempted to make amends by planning a special dinner. Four chickens were pressure cooked before frying to ensure tenderness. Sweet, young peas were topped with fresh butter, and potatoes were mashed to fluffiness and placed beside gravy bowls brimming with rich, creamy gravy. Flora made a giant green salad while Marta cranked out homemade vanilla ice cream.

The children gathered eagerly around the table.

Looking about with a frown, Marta asked Jillian, "Where's Lucia?"

Jillian shrugged her shoulders and helped the little ones into their chairs, tying bibs around their necks.

"Go over to the clinic and see if she knows that dinner is ready," Marta commanded Jillian.

She looked around the table, "Has anyone seen Lucia at all today?"

"No, Mommy," Elizabeth smiled, biting into a piece of chicken.

Chapter 32

Without a word, Jillian walked quickly to the clinic, sensing something wasn't right. She hadn't seen Lucia for several days. Opening the door to her bedroom, she found it dark and stuffy.

"Lucia, are you asleep?" she asked softly.

"No," replied a muffled voice.

Jillian drew back the curtains.

"Close them," Lucia stormed. "Close those curtains."

"I won't. There's a beautiful dinner waiting for you," she said placing her hands on her hips. "Why are you still in bed? Are you sick?"

The Indian grabbed her stomach, "Yes, I'm sick."

"Why is it that I don't believe you?" Jillian said. Sitting on the edge of the bed she peered at Lucia's face, thinking she looked perfectly healthy. "Tell me what's wrong. Are you vomiting? No? Then what's wrong?"

"I'm sick," she repeated, rolling to her side. "I've already taken pills to settle my stomach, but they don't help."

"Why don't you come with me and try to eat something?" Jillian coaxed. "You'll feel better. You've hardly eaten anything at the house this week."

"No. It's because Marta said you were tired of looking at me. I asked her to send you over because I was sick, but when you didn't come I knew that she was telling the truth," Lucia said.

"What?" Jillian asked. "I don't understand what you're saying. Marta didn't say anything to me about you until ten minutes ago. I would have been over here a long time ago if I had known you were sick."

"No, you wouldn't have come," Lucia whined turning to the wall groaning. "You wouldn't have come because you don't like me any longer.'

"Don't be silly," Jillian said as if she was speaking to a child. "Come, get up and eat with us. We can talk later."

"Leave me alone," Lucia moaned again. "I'm sick. I'm sick of everything."

Jillian pulled on her arm, "Please. I'll feel terrible if you don't eat with us."

Lucia pulled her arm back, "Go and leave me alone. You don't like me."

Throwing her arms up in frustration, Jillian yelled at her, "Okay, I'll go. I'm getting so tired of everything going on in this place. Stay here and rot in your dark room because I'm going back to the house and eat my cold dinner."

She slammed the door behind her. Back in the dining room, she found Marta eating with relish.

"Why did you tell Lucia I was tired of looking at her?" Jillian asked Marta.

The woman's mouth closed over a heaping spoon and her tongue pushed mashed potatoes into her cheeks.

"What?" Marta asked as she swallowed the food in one gulp. "I didn't say any such thing."

Jillian gave her a dark, knowing look, "Well, that's what Lucia just told me."

"I said no such thing," Marta said as she slammed down the spoon. "After the delivery last night, she told me she wasn't feeling well and wondered if you could go over to see her for a while. I merely said that you were tired and probably wouldn't be able to look in on her until this morning. Then I forgot all about it."

She hit the spoon against the table again and sighed in self-pity, "Leave it to that Indian to mix up what I say. You'd think she'd understand English by now."

She took another bite, "That really upsets me. Now I see that Lucia is trying to turn you against me even more."

"Marta, I'm sick and tired of this whole thing. In the first place you shouldn't have told her I was too tired to see her. You should have just dropped the whole thing. I'm not angry at either one of you anymore," she turned to Andy and cleaned a blob of mashed potatoes from his highchair tray.

A feeling of relief swept through her when the front door opened and Lucia walked into the room. Without a word or glance around, she sat at her place and reached for the potatoes.

"Susana, do you want more salad?" asked Marta, still in a huff.

"No, Mommy. Please may I have some ice cream?" she asked.

"Me, too," chorused the children.

Chapter 32

"Flora, bring the ice cream," Marta yelled toward the kitchen.

"Mommy, what's wrong with Lucia?" asked Paul.

All heads swung toward the woman, where she lay face down in her plate of potatoes.

"Help me! Help me! Flora! Flora!" screamed Marta.

Startled, Andy and Lydia began crying, the other children sat in stunned silence.

Jillian hushed the babies, while Marta pulled Lucia up by her arms and Flora caught her legs. Running to the living room they dropped her on the sofa where Marta began wiping mashed potatoes from her face. She slapped her but there was no response.

"Jill, put Andy down and go to Lucia's room to see if you can find something that will explain this," called Marta.

Jillian plopped the baby into Flora's arms and whispered, "See that the children have ice cream and Flora, see that Leah is all right. She must be very frightened right now."

In Lucia's room, she searched her desk and bed. Nothing could be found, but when she looked in the wastebasket she found a syringe. Picking it up, sick with fear, she thought of the access Lucia had to drugs and medicines. She remembered her threat to kill herself with a gun and suddenly realized Lucia believed Marta's tale that she was meeting someone in the plaza. All of this started to make sense as she was digging through the basket and discovered several tablet wrappers and a small flask. Gathering the evidence, she stuffed it in her pocket and left the room.

Fear escalated into terror and she ran as fast as she could to the house. The living room was empty, but hearing noises from above, she took the steps two at a time and rushed into Andy's room. Marta was hovering over an unconscious Lucia who was now lying on a cot in the corner.

"What did you find?" asked Marta without turning.

"I'm scared. Look at this," Jillian pulled the pile of wrappers and flask from her pocket.

The nurse dropped a damp cloth to the pillow and grabbed the articles, studying each one carefully.

"The shot was valium. She frequently uses it because when she was a child, she contracted a serious case of hepatitis. Now every time she eats greasy foods she says she suffers from cramp attacks. For some reason valium helps," Marta explained. "I gave this to her early this morning before I came to the house for breakfast, but she knows better than mixing it with all these pills. Why, they could kill her."

Jillian was speechless. Walking to the bedside, she looked at Lucia's sprawled form, her closed eyes and slightly opened mouth.

"Why would she take pills along with the shot? With all the experience she's had, she should know better. I just don't understand," Jillian said.

"Don't you?" Marta asked.

Jillian swung around to face Marta, "Why did you ask that?"

"Well, look at how you've been treating her. I told you not to get her too interested in you. You've been acting as though you hate us both all week," Marta pointed out. "I try to help you, Jill, and all you have done is act like you can't wait to get away from here. Now that she seems to be captivated by your friendship, you drop her from your life. Why is it you never listen to me?"

Guilt and shame struck Jillian with a blow. Turning back to Lucia, she reached out to touch her forehead.

"Yes, you're right," Jillian admitted sadly. "I've ignored her and right now she's the most important one. Do you think she'll die?"

"I need a good stomach pump. I was going to pick one up when I go to Quito this week. I had to toss our old one. Let's get her to her feet and walk her," Marta said. "Come and help me."

"You need a stomach pump?" Jillian asked. "Isn't it too late for that?"

"I don't know, probably. We have so few good instruments," Marta said as she pushed past Jillian and began to pull Lucia to her feet. "Here, take her other arm."

"Wait a minute. I'm going to find Flora. I need her to care for the children," Jillian said as she headed out the door.

Leaving an impatient Marta behind, Jillian dashed into her bedroom and fumbled in her purse for a small card. Pocketing it, she ran down the stairs calling for Elizabeth and Flora. She found the maid in the bathroom washing Peter's face.

Chapter 32

"Go upstairs and help Señorita Marta. Elizabeth, you finish washing Peter's face," Jillian said quietly. "There is something I must do."

Leaving Elizabeth with the boy, she paused in the hallway listening for any sound of Marta descending the stairs. Satisfied there would be no encounter, she grabbed the telephone receiver. Carefully she cranked the handle at the instrument's base alerting the main switchboard in Pachuca that she wished to place a call.

Thankful when a male answer instead of the curious operator from last week, she hoped that Philip was home.

"Buenas tardes," she replied. "Will you please connect me with the home of Doctor Rios in Quito?"

She quickly withdrew the business card Philip had given her in the plaza, "His number is 5459. Gracias."

After listening to a few cranks and bells, she heard a distant woman's voice, "Buenas tardes."

"Buenas tardes. May I speak with Doctor Rios?"

"Doctor Rios? Si. May I ask who is calling?"

"Si. La señorita Jill de Pachuca."

"Gracias. Un momento."

Jillian heard a conversation in the background and then another woman's voice came on.

"Buenas tardes. May I help you?" she asked in a mature, cultured voice filled with dignity.

Feeling inadequate with her unpolished Spanish, Jillian replied, "Yes, I would like to speak with Doctor Rios, por favor."

"Doctor Rios does not live here. I am his mother."

"Oh, he told me one time that if I ever needed to speak with him, I should call this number."

"The doctor does live in an apartment adjacent. If this is an emergency, I will wake him from his siesta."

"I'm so sorry to disturb him, but this is an emergency. Please tell him that Señorita Jill from Pachuca is calling."

"One moment, please."

Jillian wiped sweating palms on her dress and breathed deeply.

Then she heard Philip's voice, "Jill, what's wrong? Mother said you have an emergency."

While They Sleep

"I do. Please come to Pachuca. This is Sunday and there is no doctor in the plaza," Jillian tried to explain, "Lucia is very ill. We need a stomach pump."

"Wait. Be calm," Philip asked. "What's wrong again?"

"Lucia took too many pills. She's dying," Jillian said near tears. "We need help here."

"I'll come right away," Philip promised.

She replaced the receiver and pondered how she would tell Marta what she had done. Perhaps it would be better not to say anything until Philip arrived.

Thirty minutes passed as Marta and Flora dragged Lucia up and down the hall. Marta's wailing and moaning was pathetic, and Jillian tried to hide herself away with the children. She held Lydia and Andy tightly, soothing their frightened questioning looks and tried to assure Leah that Lucia would be all right. She was frightened herself. Watching Lucia's feet try to make contact with the floor and listening to her garbled attempt to talk made Jillian realize how much she cared for her, but listening to Marta was more than she could bear. The nurse loudly summoned Jillian, ordering her to make strong coffee, to bring damp washcloths, and to pray for God to spare Lucia's life. If Lucia had any doubt how Marta felt about her, Jillian hoped that she sensed her concern now.

After another fifteen minutes had passed, she began a standing vigil at the window. A stomach pump was probably too late now, but just having Philip here would bring a stabilizing effect to an atmosphere in turmoil. She saw his car at the gate and left the children, running down the driveway in a surge of relief. Unlocking the padlock, she threw back the gates and bounded to the driver's side. I'm so glad to see you. Please hurry."

"Get in the other side. Are you sure Marta wants me here? Why on earth doesn't she have a stomach pump in this clinic? Of all things she should have is a stomach pump," he asked as she perched on the seat.

"I don't know. I think she recently tossed the old one and was going to pick one up on her trip to Quito. She has no idea I called you, but I have little doubt she'll be thankful," Jillian said.

Chapter 32

The car braked to a stop before the house and Philip gathered his doctor's bag and equipment.

At the door, he turned, "You know we must talk before I leave. I waited two hours for you the other night."

"Yes, before you leave," Jillian promised.

They ran up the stairs where Lucia again lay on the cot with a tearful Marta bent over her.

"Marta, I asked Dr. Rios to come from Quito. I hope that you don't...."

The woman turned and ran to grab Philip's hand, "Oh, thank God! Doctor, please help my friend. She has taken too many medicines and is near death even now."

She wrung her hands and wailed without constraint.

"Jill, please take the Señorita into the next room so I can do an examination on the patient," Philip said calmly.

He noticed Flora trembling in a corner and beckoned to her, "Please stay with me in case I need help."

Jillian led the subdued nurse down to the dining room and pulled out a chair for her, "I'll check on the children and be right back. They haven't had a nap. They are quite bewildered by all of this."

When she returned, she found Marta dry eyed and in control, "Thank you for sending for the doctor. As many times as I've spoken against the medical profession in this country, I know Dr. Rios by reputation is far above the rest in his qualifications."

She turned in her chair, "Why did you think of him?"

The girl hesitated. This would be a good chance to tell about her relationship with him. Maybe, in this mood, Marta could admit Philip was not like any other man.

"The day that Sandi left Pachuca, I took a walk to see the town plaza. While I was sitting in the park Philip saw me, introduced himself and gave me his business card. I remembered it when Lucia became ill," Jillian said truthfully.

For a long moment, the nurse watched Jillian and then replied, "I'm glad you did."

Footsteps from above caught their attention and both women hurried to the bottom of the stairs to see Philip and Flora descending.

"I don't think you have a thing to worry about. Her heartbeat is good, breathing is normal. She may not have taken all the tablets you think she did," Philip said.

They stared at him, a frown furrowing Marta's brow as she brushed past him on the stairway, "Thank you, Doctor. I will get my purse and pay you well."

"There is no need. Perhaps we can help each other through our clinics. I would like to see us working together in this valley," Philip suggested.

"Yes, that's a wonderful idea. Please contact me soon. Now I will sit at Lucia's bedside until she awakens fully," Marta said as she hurried on up the stairs.

Philip thanked Flora for her help. The girl gave him a small bow and retreated to the living room to be with the children.

"I will get them ready for bed," Flora said to Jillian. "Because this was a difficult day, they are tired. Jill, I'll heat leftovers, feed them, and put them in bed."

"Thank you, Flora. I don't know what we would do without you," Jillian said sincerely.

She waited until the flushed maid had disappeared behind the living room door, then turned to Philip, "I'll walk with you to the car. We must talk."

Nodding his head, he took up his satchel and other equipment and led the way out the door, "Where shall we go?"

"I don't think it matters. Marta will be with Lucia for several minutes," Jillian said. "She'll think I'm with the children."

"It'll be dusk soon," he looked toward the west and sighed deeply. "Come, let's park the car on the road and then we can walk a little."

Jillian glanced back at the house, got into the car and relaxed knowing that Marta could not see her from Andy's bedroom window where Lucia was resting.

Parking the car on the road below the property, Philip cut the motor and reached for her hand, "I've been very worried about you."

"Yes, I'm sorry for not meeting you on the new highway the other night," Jillian said apologetically.

Chapter 32

"I was very upset," he said though his eyes softened behind his glasses and he smiled sweetly. "I think I understand why you couldn't come. It must be difficult living here."

"You'll never really understand," she shook her head. "I mustn't stay out here too long. She'll soon go downstairs and wonder where I am. Did you look for an apartment for us?"

"Yes," Philip answered.

"I almost told Marta about us this afternoon," Jillian admitted. "She seemed so pleased with you."

His face looked troubled, "Don't do that, Jill. It would be a terrible mistake."

"Oh, I wouldn't. I want to take Andy with us. I'll wait until she's in Quito then leave with Andy and pick up Anna on the way," Jillian told him.

"Are you sure you want both babies?" he asked, seemingly concerned.

"Of course, we can't leave them with her. Philip, I wish you could have seen Andy. His eye was black and her handprint covered his cheek, all because he cried," Jillian said shuddering as she remembered her shock when she saw the boy.

"You're right. The apartment I found will have enough room for all of us," his smile returned. "Now, let's get out and walk."

"No, I must go back," Jillian said with regret.

"I'll see you Tuesday at the same time?" Philip asked hopefully.

"No, she doesn't want me going to Quito for a few weeks," Jillian explained.

"Why?" Philip asked.

"She thinks I'm meeting a man in the plaza," Jillian giggled. "If she only knew how close to the truth she is. There's nothing quite as bad as that in her opinion. I'll call you when I'm ready."

She opened the car door and stepped into the gathering darkness. He met her halfway and pulled her into the shadows of the high wall.

"I'm glad you didn't suggest we live at your mother's house, Philip," Jillian admitted. "I don't think I'd be ready for that."

He stiffened, "Why would you think we would live with her?"

"I talked with your mother on the telephone this afternoon, remember?" Jillian reminded him.

He swept his hand over his face and tugged the end of his beard, "What did my mother say to you?"

"She told me that you don't live in her house, but in an apartment beside the house."

She looked at him closely, "Why does that matter? I don't want to live there."

"Oh, nothing really," he laughed and grabbed at her playfully. "I just know that I love you very much and want to take you away."

He leaned over to kiss her when suddenly a voice rose in anger behind them, "Don't touch her or I will put you in your car myself and see that you are on your way. I could do it you know, you little worm."

Marta marched toward them as Philip jumped away from Jillian in alarm.

"I knew what was happening the moment I heard you two address each other with your first names. Jill, a short encounter with Dr. Rios in the plaza over a year ago does not give him the right to call you by your first name. He was too familiar with you. What a fool you are standing here in secret with this heathen."

"Heathen? How dare you call him a heathen?" Jillian defended him. "He's a well-educated professor of doctors, Marta. I really resent you speaking of him that way."

She stormed at the woman, hating her sneakiness and eavesdropping.

"Why didn't you tell me you were meeting a man away from home? I already suspected it, but you continually denied any relationship. Then this afternoon you finally admitted you had talked to him in the plaza. The good Lord only knows how many other times you've met up with him."

She shook her head sadly, "Nothing good can come of this, Jill."

"Oh, you think not?" Jillian started. "Well, I'll tell you that Philip and—-"

"Jill, please," pleaded Philip.

"Why can't I tell her?" Jillian asked.

"Tell me what?" Marta stepped closer, her mouth working in agitation.

"Jill, don't say anything now," Philip pleaded.

Marta took Jillian by the shoulders and shook her, "Tell me."

Chapter 32

"Philip and I are going to be married," Jillian announced.

"Married?" Echoed Marta and Philip in unison.

Doubt crept into her voice, "Yes, married. Why do you act so surprised, Philip?"

"I'll tell you why, Jill," Marta said with a smirk. "It's because he's already married."

Jillian's hand flew to her face in horror, "You're lying. Tell her she's lying, Philip."

"I'm not lying," Marta interjected. "I didn't go up to see Lucia at all because I had such a strong suspicion that you were meeting the doctor in the plaza and who knows where else, that I stood at the top of the stairs until you left the house. You see, I know a little bit about your doctor friend, but I wanted to make sure before talking with you, Jill. I made a phone call to Doctor Rios' assistant in Yaruqui and asked him if the doctor was in. He said no, that he normally spent Sundays with his family. I followed a hunch and said I wouldn't disturb him at home, but that I was interested in how the doctor's wife and children were feeling. I had heard they were ill with a virus. Of course, the man was puzzled. He hadn't heard that doctor Rios' family was ill at all. They were fine the last time he and the doctor had worked together. He was very concerned."

"Oh," Jillian turned toward Philip in pain. "It's true, isn't it? The very fact that you are silent proves that it's true. How could you have made me think that you wanted to marry me? What if I had gone with you?"

The starlit night exposed his grief-stricken face, "I never said anything about marriage. You thought that's what I meant. I couldn't tell you the truth because I really do love you."

"Humph," snorted Marta. "You're just like the rest. Well, why don't you go ahead, get a divorce and marry Jill? If you care so much, divorce should be the answer."

Philip touched Jillian's arm, "I've thought of doing it. I even spoke with a lawyer, but he talked me out of taking such a step. The consequences would be very difficult to face."

"Yes, like losing your family's money and your good standing in the community. Love, as you call it, isn't worth it, huh, Doctor?" Marta's voice dripped with sarcasm.

Turning to Jillian, who stood with her face in her hands, she said gently, "He would never give up his family or his reputation to go through a divorce and then marriage with you. Remember, this is primarily a Catholic country and divorce is frowned on by the majority. I know about his parents. They are highly regarded in this country. His father holds a high position in the medical community and they have invested much in the success of their son. This is well known among those who work in medicine. They would never allow their son to obtain a divorce. I have a feeling that the doctor would never jeopardize his status, no matter what he says he would do for you."

"What would I have been to you then?" Jillian screamed at Philip in English.

After a moment's silence, Marta answered for him, "His mistress, of course."

"Never," Jillian declared as she backed toward the house.

He started after her, but Marta stood in his way, "If I ever see you near this property again, I will ruin your reputation. I promise that you will never work in this valley again and that your parents will hear of your actions if I have to knock on their door myself. Now leave so I can repair the damage you've caused."

Clearly shaken, Philip climbed into his car and started toward Quito. The nurse watched until he turned the corner then, with a satisfied smile, she accompanied Jillian to the house. With a quick step in order to leave Marta behind, Jillian went to the kitchen and made herself a cup of coffee, then turned off the light and sat in the darkened room staring out the window at the stars.

Marta waited until she was settled and in a voice tinged with compassion, said, "I'm sorry, Jill."

Jillian waved her arm without emotion, "I'm all right. It's funny but all of a sudden I don't care. When I think of the mistake I almost made, I shudder."

"You will believe me now about the men in this country. I've been here so many years I know what they can do to a woman," Marta said.

Jillian turned to face her, the woman she hated and wanted to love, "Yes, I believe you. Thank you for caring. I just didn't realize that you wanted the best for me."

Chapter 32

"My dear girl, how could you ever doubt? I told you that I care for you very much. Everything I've done to this point has been for your good," Marta said with compassion.

"I don't think I really loved him. I just wasn't happy here after what you did to Andy. I wanted to punish you by leaving," Jillian finally admitted.

"I'm sorry about Andy. The minute it happened I wanted to take it back. Please forgive me," Marta admitted as she started crying, her voice rising to a high, nasal pitch.

The stirrings of love Jillian felt toward her dissipated in the face of her irritating self-pity. She rose, patted Marta on the arm and wandered to her room.

Staring up at the ceiling, she muttered, "I sort of took things in my own hands, didn't I? I'm so sorry, Lord. You can believe me that I'll never let another man turn my head. From now on it's just You and me and the kids."

Chapter 33

She rolled groaning out of bed the next morning. Pain followed faithfully on the heel of her shock. She had slept little. Thankful to see Lucia at the breakfast table helped lift her dark mood and she greeted her warmly.

"You can't imagine how relieved I am to see you this morning." Jillian said.

"Yeah, I'm all right," Lucia replied gruffly.

Jillian sensed her embarrassment, "You really didn't take that many pills, did you?"

"Did you worry?" the Indian looked at her sideways.

"Of course, and you'd better not do it again," Jillian warned.

Lucia shrugged, smiling, "Who knows?"

Wanting to get away from the house and see Anna, she asked Marta if she would change her mind and let her run the errands. Surprisingly the woman seemed to forget that she'd volunteered for Jillian's weekly trip to Quito, or maybe she was showing some sympathy for the occurrences of the previous evening so on Tuesday Jillian went herself as usual.

After running a few errands, she stopped at the hospital hoping to catch a glimpse of Betsy. Climbing the stairs to the second floor, she walked to the nurse's station. A young national nurse was filling small white paper cups with medicine while an American nurse and national doctor joked in fluent Spanish.

Chapter 33

It didn't take long to hear Betsy's giggles and Jillian turned to see her emerging from a patient's room. Waving to one another, they met halfway. Betsy was prim and proper, her blonde hair combed perfectly in a bob. Blue eyes bulged slightly behind thick glasses. Her nose was short and set above a protruding jaw. Though physically unattractive, her face glowed with contentment and she radiated compassion.

"Oh, Jill, it's so good to see you. It seems like a long time, but it's probably only a couple of weeks since you were here," she said as she threw an arm around Jillian's shoulder. "Please come to lunch. We're having leftovers like we always seem to have when you come over, but please come."

"Sure. I'd love to. I've been to the market, so I have some food in the jeep that we can eat if you want. How's Anna?" Jillian asked. "I can't wait to see her."

Betsy stopped in her tracks, "Anna? I don't understand. Anna isn't with us. Marta came for her a few days ago."

She searched Jillian's face, "Oh, Jill, I'm sorry, you didn't know."

Sickness rose in Jillian's throat and she felt behind her for the wall. Sighing deeply, she said, "No, I didn't know. Where is Anna?"

Cold anger settled in her heart.

"I think that since we found out what was wrong with her, Marta felt she was ready to be put up for adoption. She's probably already on her way to the United States or at least in some half way place," Betsy explained. "I had no idea that you didn't know."

Jillian stood in the hallway grasping her purse and feeling faint, "You found a cure for Anna and I wasn't told?"

"Yes, and it was so simple. We experimented and discovered she just had a terrible allergy to milk. We began giving her other liquids along with calcium and her skin cleaned up beautifully," Betsy said proudly.

"I can't believe this. It's my fault not making her my first priority. I should have come to see her more often," she said, thinking of her luncheons with Philip.

Betsy patted her hand, "We know how busy you are."

"No, Betsy, I found plenty of time to do other things," she admitted sadly.

She passed her hand across her eyes, "I can't believe this. She was sent to the United States? It's impossible. How could Marta have done this without consulting me?"

She felt her voice rising.

"Shhh," admonished Betsy gently, glancing around while holding Jillian's arm. "This is a hospital. I can understand how you feel, but don't get excited. Marta said she was sending her away because she may need further medical help. Are you all right?"

"Sometimes I think Marta is crazy or else I am. Something is so wrong. How could she have done this to an innocent baby or to me?" Jillian looked at her friend incredulously. "Do you have any idea how I feel about this?"

The nurse put her arm around the girl, "Anna is much better off in the United States. She'll have a good family life, so much better than she would have in an orphanage, Jill."

Jillian felt weak, "She was mine."

"Come and have lunch with us," Betsy urged her. "You'll feel better."

"You don't understand at all, do you? I can't eat lunch. I'm much too upset," Jillian shook her head sadly as she pounded her thighs. "Thank you for the invitation, but I must be on my way to Pachuca right now."

Marta was sitting at the table sipping lemonade when Jillian walked into the house. From the expression in her eyes, she knew that Betsy had telephoned ahead with a warning. She stood for a moment in the doorway as the children yelled greetings from the playroom. Walking to the inner doorway, she picked up Tommy and kissed his cheek. Several ran forward to hug her neck and she spent a few minutes with them to give her anger time to subside.

On the drive between the hospital and Pachuca, her fury became overpowering, but now Marta's presence dulled it. To quell her anger, she poured out her love and emotions on the children.

"I know that you're mad at me, but let me explain," Marta's chin quivered.

"Don't you dare cry," Jillian said in a low, menacing voice, gritting her teeth. "I'm going to my room because I don't want the children

Chapter 33

or Flora to know how I feel. If you want to know, then follow me. If not, that's fine because you may already have an idea."

Stomping from the room and up the stairs, she waited, but Marta didn't follow. In a way she was glad. It was too late for words.

For several days they avoided one another except at meals. She visited only with Lucia, afraid that another misunderstanding with the Indian would cause more problems. It wasn't until much later that she heard a young family in the eastern United States had given Anna a good home.

Chapter 34

Marta knocked at Jillian's bedroom door one sunny afternoon in January, "May I speak with you for a moment?"

"Sure," replied Jillian showing little interest. "Move those things off the chair."

"I'd rather sit with you on your bed," Marta said.

Jillian frowned with resentment, but moved over, "Is it real important? I'm getting ready to take a little nap. I was up with Andy during the night as he's having nightmares."

"He's just spoiled. I wish you wouldn't get up to coddle him," Marta said shaking her head.

"Don't start that or we'll have trouble," Jillian threatened quietly.

Marta waved an arm to dismiss the subject, "I'm here to talk something over with you. I've decided that perhaps a lot of our problems have stemmed from the fact I don't talk over my decisions with you."

"I should say that's a good part of it," Jillian agreed sarcastically.

"I resent your hatred for me. I resent the fact you don't remember all I have done for you these past years," the nurse set her mouth sternly. "You won't relent and frankly I'm tired of it."

Her shoulders sagged in resignation and she stared at a spot on the floor. Suddenly she grabbed at a fallen white anklet, pulling on it.

"Isn't there any way we can be friends? I'd like to make an effort," Marta asked hopefully.

Chapter 34

A leaden feeling forced Jillian's eyes closed. She didn't want to face this encounter; she just wanted to take a nap.

"Marta, I can't help my feelings. I have no control over my emotions. I appreciate what you've done for me. I've told you many times over the past months that I'm thankful for letting me know that Philip is married, but if you were truthful with yourself, you'd have to admit you did it for your own benefit," Jillian said as she fiddled nervously with her hair.

"There have been so many things you've done to make me dislike you. If it weren't for the children, I'd leave right now," Jillian looked up and her heart sank when Marta's chin began quivering. "Now, don't start crying. I can't stand to see and hear you cry. You asked me how we can become good friends. Can you understand that you don't trust me and I don't trust you?"

"I trust you," Marta tried to assure her.

Jillian's eyes drooped, knowing the woman too well to believe her, "I'm here to help you and Lucia with the children. We're working together, isn't that enough? Please, don't pressure me for anything more."

"I don't like it when you talk about leaving," Marta shared as she rubbed her hands down her thighs, smoothing her nurse's uniform. "So I won't bother you anymore. It's just that you seem to love Lucia no matter what she does."

"Lucia is so different from you. She would never hurt me like you have," Jillian frowned. "Why are we talking about this now?"

"I need you," Marta said candidly. "Everyone needs friends."

"You don't need anyone. That's your basic problem. You are so independent that you can't open your heart to anyone. So when you make an attempt like this, I become suspicious. This is why you've never been close to anyone. Who is it that has been a best friend to you? Lucia can't be one because of your need to dominate her. What about a male friend? Have you ever thought of marriage?" Jillian asked.

The nurse shuddered and stood up, a red flush rising from her neck to her face, "The last thing in the world I need is a husband, but for your information I did have a boyfriend once."

"You're kidding," Jillian burst out in shock.

"There's not much to tell. He was a friend I met one summer at camp. He seemed to like me and asked me to go horseback riding with him," Marta shared then sat quiet seemingly mulling over what she was going to say next. "I shouldn't have gone."

"Of course you should have," Jillian said. "Didn't you like him?"

A sense of melancholy settled on the older woman, "Yes, I did like him a lot. He was so nice looking and I just couldn't believe he had a crush on me."

Marta had Jillian's full attention and she swung her legs over the side of the bed to face her, "What happened?"

"You won't understand this," she said fidgeting with a loose string on her pocket. "I know you won't because you seem worldlier than I am."

She peered up from under lowered lids and became still, "We stopped to walk the horses and when he helped me dismount, he continued to hold my hand."

"Yeah?" Jillian asked.

"It made me sick," Marta admitted.

"Why?" Jillian asked. "It sounds rather nice to me."

"It would," she said bluntly and lowered her voice. "When he held my hand it stirred some emotions in me that made me ill."

Jillian threw out her hands wondering where on earth this conversation was going, "Why? Why should they make you feel ill? Those emotions are normal."

Abruptly, the nurse jumped up startling Jillian, "No, they're wrong! We weren't married! I'll never allow myself to feel them again. It was not for my benefit that I saved you from making the worst mistake of your life. It was for you. The feelings I had were wrong and that's why I saved you from that doctor."

Jillian felt a desire to hurt Marta, "Perhaps I do want to get married someday, but I've just not found the right man."

The woman's face winced in pain as the words hit their mark, but Jillian felt no pleasure.

Moved by compassion, she remarked, "Don't worry. I'm not going to make a mistake."

"That's right because as long as you're here you won't have a chance," Marta declared firmly.

Chapter 34

Jillian's compassion evaporated, "Was there something else you wanted to talk about because I need to take a nap?"

"Yes, I've decided that since you've been with us for over three years and you will probably stay for the rest of your life, you need a house of your own. I'm going to build one for you and your future children," Marta declared.

Nothing could have surprised Jillian more. Rarely was she rendered speechless.

Marta smiled triumphantly, "We'll begin as soon as possible. Are you happy with the idea?"

"You certainly never fail to surprise me," Jillian exclaimed, shaking her head.

Giggling excitedly, the woman waved her arms describing the imaginary house, "It will be larger than this one with an attic and basement. It will be perfect for the children," Marta explained. "I've already drawn up the floor plans and I need to know if you care to make any changes."

Overwhelmed with emotion, Jillian was dumbfounded. Marta's incongruities challenged her. How can she love the children so much that she would sacrifice money and her own comforts to build them a home and at the same time discipline them so severely? She was willing to provide for their physical needs, but not their emotional needs. She would do all of it knowing how Jillian felt about her. How could Marta entrust her with more babies in the future, build her a home, and keep on loving her?

"Why are you doing this? Why don't you raise the babies you have and stop there? By expanding you think I'll possibly stay with you the rest of my life. What if we can't adjust to each other?" Jillian asked as she shook her head again. "I just told you that we could have nothing more than a working relationship, yet you continue to make ways to further our commitment to each other. It's hard for you to understand this, but I can't turn to you as a best friend just because you're giving me these things. I can't. We are too different."

The nurse bent forward to look at her levelly, "There will come a day when you will want this friendship as much as I do."

Jillian swallowed against the fear that Marta knew something she didn't and smiled, "I don't think so. I must say that I appreciate your thoughtfulness. Does this mean that I can take complete responsibility of my own family along with Andy?"

"Yes. You'll be responsible for all the children during the day, but at night I will take over care of my children in this house. Flora is going to move in. Her family's home is so small. Here, she can room with Elizabeth. They seem to care for each other. Lucia will rig up a better bell system from the clinic to this house in case of deliveries. Lucia is going to move into the outpatient clinic."

"It sounds like you've planned this in detail," Jillian said impressed.

"Sure, and we'll see if we can find another baby for you," Marta said firmly. "Now, does that prove how much your friendship means to me?"

Jillian didn't answer as uneasiness cautioned her that there seemed to be something still unspoken. Though thrilling, Marta's plans made her uncomfortable.

"Not only that," continued the woman. "I think it's time that we sell the jeep and buy you a new car. The jeep needs so much work done on it. I think we can sell it for a reasonable price and buy a smaller pickup. Maybe we'll be able to do this before you leave."

Jillian stiffened, "Leave? Leave for where?"

Marta cleared her throat and walked to the bureau, leaning on it to look out the window. Focusing on some distant object, she spoke slowly carefully considering each word.

"Jill, please don't be offended. I know you have made wonderful progress in Spanish these past three years since coming to Ecuador. I understand everything you say, but some of your grammar is terrible. I catch you speaking English with Lucia and Flora because you are still insecure with Spanish. When you are angry, like you were with the doctor that evening, you can't seem to get your thoughts across in Spanish. What you need is an advanced course in the language that will establish your grammar and give you an ease when speaking Spanish," turning, she planted her feet firmly. "I have already begun the paperwork on your trip to Costa Rica. You'll be there for a three-month course in the language school."

"I'm not going," exclaimed Jillian, shaking her head. "I should have known you had something planned for me."

Chapter 34

She stood, eyes smoldering, "I should know that you just don't hand people gifts without wanting something in return."

"This is for your own good. I contacted Sandi who, as you know, lives in Costa Rica. She would love for you to come. You'll leave the last part of April, so you have about three months to plan," Marta declared as though it was already decided.

"You're running my life for me again. How many times have you done this? First Lucia, then Anna and it goes on and on. You see, Marta, that's my point. Why didn't you tell me what you had in mind when you first came here today? This is my life that you've been playing with since the day I met you. Why do you obsess about dominating me?" Jillian asked as she pulled at the bangs on her forehead.

"I'm well aware of my difficulties in speaking proper Spanish. You have no idea the nights I've cried myself to sleep over this shortcoming. Now I have a little boy and it's not proper to leave him. Just think of how I feel. You want me to leave Andy after I've lost Anna? The problem you have is thinking everyone should speak Spanish as you do. Well, that may never happen," Jillian said firmly. "I just won't go."

"I'm aware of all the problems your absence will bring. I ask you to have patience. Please don't hate me more. I've already made the arrangements. Need I remind you again that what I say in this house is final?" Marta threatened. "You'll obey orders or have to leave for good."

"What is the real reason you took Anna away?" Jillian asked. "I've heard all your other flimsy explanations."

Marta frowned in surprise, "I've told you. She had a wonderful opportunity for a good life with excellent parents. It was for the best."

"Why didn't you tell me before you sent her?" Jillian pressed. "Why didn't you tell me she was feeling better?"

"We've discussed this over the course of these past several months, Jill," Marta said sighing heavily. "You would have begged me to bring her back here and we would have had a terrible argument. The way I did it was the better way. It was all finalized when you finally found out and that diffused most of your disappointment."

"It took a long time for me to think about you without feeling terrible anger. I'm not like you. When I think back to how you wept over Julie or whatever you named her when her parents wanted her back and then seemingly without an afterthought, you sent her to the States," Jillian exclaimed. "I don't understand that. My attachments to the children are permanent."

"You've got to learn not to hold onto things too tightly in this life, my dear. You're still such a novice. You can't possibly understand that yet," Marta said as she smiled sardonically and turned toward the door. "Well, you did it again. I try my best to do what's right for you and then you dig up problems we've had in the past and make me feel in the wrong. I can see that no matter what good I try to do for you, you only see it as evil."

She was leaving and nothing had been resolved.

"Please, before you go, couldn't I learn Spanish from Lucia in the evening?" Jillian asked hopefully.

Marta chuckled, "All you two do is play games."

"Please, Marta," Jillian begged. "Maybe you can teach me. I just don't want to leave."

The woman walked out and shut the door, and Jillian ran to open it, "Marta, there's one more thing I must ask."

Pausing at the top of the stairs, Marta turned.

"Would you tell me how you put these adoptions together? Where do the babies go? Is there a half-way point where they wait until the papers are ready?" Jillian pushed.

Marta's brown eyes turned black and a familiar red flush spread from her neck and all over her face. In a tone that emanated cold fury, she declared, "You are here to care for my children. Whatever other business goes on is none of your affair."

Jillian returned to her room confused. *Maybe the whole thing is my fault*, she thought. With a mind in turmoil, she sat on the bed. *I just want to know where these babies are disappearing to. Why is she so angry? It has to be my fault. She came here in a good mood, offering me a new house, a new car, and more babies. Somehow I upset her again.* Then a horrid thought brought her to her feet. Maybe Marta wanted her gone for good and wouldn't let her come back. Maybe this was an excuse to get rid of her.

Falling to her knees, she prayed in earnest, "Lord, I don't want to go to Costa Rica and leave the children and Lucia. I don't want to

Chapter 34

leave Ecuador. This is where I belong. Am I wrong? Are my attitudes displeasing to You? Why does she always make me feel guilty in the end? When I think back to how independent I was when I first moved here and see what changes I've already made for her, it frightens me. I'm a prisoner in this house most of the time. I'm even afraid to make friends on the outside because I don't want her to find out. Should it be this way? For some reason, I can't feel this is right in Your eyes, Lord. I dislike her so much. Just about the time I start having feelings of affection for her, she ruins it all. Is she wrong or am I wrong?"

Jillian pulled herself up and lay down because her head was aching from the confrontation, "All I know is that I must stay with Andy. I must learn to live in peace with Marta for his sake. Somehow I must learn to bend. I crossed the point of no return when I accepted Andy as my own, and everything else is secondary."

Chapter 35

"Y ou'll have to slow down, Carlos. I can't go any further," panted Elena, as she stopped in the middle of the road and pulled on his arm. "Please, slow down. I'm so tired."

"But if we do, someone might realize you're gone and then we'll have your brothers looking for us," Carlos pointed out urgently.

"No, don't worry. They won't notice anything until tomorrow," Elena tried to explain.

Out of breath, she struggled to speak, wiping her face with the sleeve of her jacket, she refused to move, "Please, Carlos, I can't run any farther."

He placed two ragged canvas bags on the road, "We're only one kilometer from your house. You've got to try."

"It's dark. No one can see us. Please," Elena begged. "I'll be ready in a minute, but I've got to rest."

Relenting, he smiled, "All right, Cariña. Here, let's sit down on the grass. We have to talk anyway."

"I'm sorry. It's just that I'm not accustomed to running in the dark," Elena apologized. "It's hard to see where we're going."

"We just go straight ahead. There aren't any turns until we get down to the new highway," Carlos explained, familiar with the road.

"It may be straight, but there are a lot of holes in the road and I keep tripping," Elena pointed out.

"That's why I've been holding your arm," Carlos assured her.

Chapter 35

He made sure she was comfortable and then sat beside her. Reaching for her hand, he laughed.

"What's funny? I can think of a lot of emotions I feel right now, but gaiety is not one," Elena asked as she peered at him through the darkness.

"I guess nothing is really funny, but I was thinking of the look on your brother's face tomorrow when he goes into your bedroom," Carlos admitted.

Solemnly he patted her hand, "I hope you are sure they will wait until then."

"I'm positive. I told our maid not to bother me at all, that I had a headache and needed to sleep. Besides that, Rolando and my brothers are out somewhere."

Looking at him hopefully, she asked, "We'll be far away by tomorrow, won't we?"

"Yes, but truthfully I'm not quite sure what we're going to do now. When I planned this, it was hard deciding which way to go. Perhaps we can walk up to the old highway, but then we'll have to walk through pasture land. We can go on to the new highway, but it's not completed yet and is muddy and difficult to walk on in parts, especially in the dark. We could go through town, but we both know that wouldn't be a good idea."

He released her hand and put his elbows between his raised knees and pondered the situation a moment, "Of course we could go back up by my house and walk to the old Pan American highway by way of the Tulcachi Hacienda which would take most of the night. There's always Yaruqui, too."

He expelled a loud sigh, "We have many choices and none seem too good, so I thought I'd wait until we talked to see what you want to do."

She reached to squeeze his hand, "Let's not worry about it this very minute. I want to enjoy you a little bit, Carlos. This is the first time we've been alone for such a long time. It's so good to be with you."

Leaning her head on his shoulder, she sighed as he slipped his arm around her, "You know, I've dreamed many times we would be doing this together."

"Have you?" Carlos asked. "I thought perhaps you didn't care for me anymore. That was my greatest fear."

"I've never stopped loving you, not for one day, but I have to admit I was beginning to wonder if you hadn't found someone else," Elena admitted.

Shaking his head, he said, "I haven't had one girlfriend since we parted. Oh, there was a girl living near my house I considered taking to a dance, but only because I was tired of being alone."

"Do you think that God meant for us to be together?" Elena asked him seriously.

"There's never been a doubt," he assured her as he kissed her lightly. "Now, we must start down toward the new highway."

He lifted her to her feet and then grabbed the bags in one hand. Placing his other arm around her waist as they walked past the maternity clinic owned by the American nurse, they glanced through the main gate to see lights shining from various buildings.

"I was almost born in that clinic," exclaimed Elena. "Rolando told me he tried to get help from the nurse when my mother almost delivered me on this very road. Of course you know the story, the whole town remembers. I've wondered at how much my brother has changed from those days. Of course I wonder how different my life would have been if my mother had been well enough to raise me."

Carlos released her waist to adjust his hold on the two canvas bags now hanging heavily from his shoulder.

"Elena, you're going to have to forget all of that. The moment you decided to go with me, you closed the door on your past. We may never see our families again," he reminded her.

Stopping, he put the bags down and turned to her, "You don't have to doubt their love for you. I know in his own way, Rolando loves you, but perhaps before we go any further you should examine your feelings. Can you go through with this? I love you enough that I'm willing to take you back if leaving your family is too difficult."

"Living with my family was becoming unbearable, or perhaps I was unbearable to live with," Elena said sincerely. "One way or the other, I can't live with them any longer and I can't live without you."

"That's all I need to hear," Carlos said happily as he reached out in the darkness and touched her cheek. "Let's go."

Chapter 35

They reached the highway which ran east and west across their path. In the process of being graded, it was strewn with piles of dirt. Fearful of tripping, Carlos stopped and pulled a flashlight from his bag.

"I guess we can use this now," he told her.

Taking a firmer grip on the bags, he flashed the light ahead as they picked their way across the mounds, "It's time to make our decision, Elena."

"Could we travel on this unfinished part until we reach the old Pan American highway?" Elena asked. "Wouldn't that be better?"

"I don't think so," Carlos answered. "The heavy rain we had yesterday turned part of the road to mud. Also, about one-half kilometer from here, there's a large ditch in the middle of the road where they're going to place irrigation pipes. I don't know if they've filled it up yet. It might be too dangerous to try and get passed it in the dark."

"Well, we can't go through town. Don Eduardo always stands in his doorway and I'm afraid the neighbors might see us," Elena reasoned. "No matter what area we pass through, someone would see us."

"Shall we try running through the pastures?" Carlos asked her.

"Maybe that is the best way, if we avoid the irrigation ditches," Elena said.

He laughed, "I'll tell you about my experience with a drainage ditch later."

"If we go through the pastures, when we get up to the old highway, how will we get to Quito?" Elena asked him.

"We can go by truck or bus, but we will have to be careful not to flag down a truck belonging to a friend. Perhaps we stop a bus or truck from the jungle," Carlos said thinking out loud.

"How will we know the difference?" Elena asked.

He shifted the weight of the bags, thinking of each direction they might go and the dangers each presented. All of a sudden he hit his head in exasperation, "Of course, I know what we can do. I'm so stupid."

"What?" she asked as she grabbed his arm tightly. "What?"

"Let's take the road leading north. We'll go to Quito by way of train," Carlos declared happily.

While They Sleep

"Go by train? But the train doesn't pass until tomorrow morning," Elena pointed out. "The station is a long distance from here."

"We'll just have to walk. No one from Pachuca would travel by train because they are so close to buses and other means of transportation and the best part is that the station is straight ahead on this old road. We won't have to pass anyone we know and we won't have to worry about turning off somewhere," Carlos pointed out, feeling more and more this was the way to go.

"Come to think of it, the train might be fun," Elena said excitedly. "I've never ridden on one, although friends at school have traveled up north and said it's quite uncomfortable. Here, let me carry one of the bags."

Handing her the lighter of the two bags, he grabbed her arm and said, "Let's do it."

Stumbling around the mud holes, they searched for the narrow entrance on the opposite side of the new highway. Finally they stood panting on the cobblestone path.

"Do we have everything?" Carlos asked.

"Yes," she checked her bag that she had taken from him and felt for her handbag that she had stuffed inside her jacket.

On this side of the highway under a canopy of trees, the darkness was denser. Carlos flashed the light occasionally to make certain they had not strayed from the pitted road.

"I would guess if we rest once in a while, we will arrive in about two hours," Carlos told her.

"How will we know when we get there?" Elena asked impressed with Carlos' knowledge of the road.

"Because across the road is a small hacienda and they usually shine a few lights close to the house," Carlos told her. "When we see that, we'll know we are there."

"Have you thought of how we must spend the night?" Elena asked.

"Do you mean, where will we sleep? I don't think it will be too much of a problem," Carlos said thoughtfully. "I doubt it will rain tonight, so we can sleep either under a tree or perhaps close to the station."

"There must be a family living in the station," Elena pointed out.

Chapter 35

"Of course, there would have to be someone to guard the building against thieves and vandals," Carlos said, admiring the wisdom of Elena. "We'll just wait until we get there then we can decide what to do."

In just under two hours they saw the hacienda's lights and across the road loomed the dark shadows of the train station.

"Wait here, Elena," Carlos suggested. "I want to talk to the family who lives here."

He left her standing alone as he walked around the side of the building. Carefully he searched until he found a door with a faint light shining from beneath. Knocking, he heard a small movement and slowly the door opened.

"Who's there?" a short, heavy bosomed woman peeked through the cracked opening.

"Buenos noches. Please, we would like to know when the train leaves for Quito," Carlos inquired politely.

"It doesn't pass by until tomorrow," the woman told him.

"What time does it pass?" Carlos asked her.

"Six o'clock," she told him.

"Is there any way we can rest here tonight?" he asked her.

"I don't care. You can sleep on the other side of the porch," she said and shut the door.

"Elena," he whispered. "Come this way."

She appeared as a shadow and he led her to the vacant cement porch. There was no bench.

"I'm sorry, Amor. We'll have to make ourselves as comfortable as possible. I'm sorry you have to sleep on a porch in the cold instead of in your bed," Carlos said sadly.

"I would sleep on a cement porch the rest of my life to be with you," Elena told him softly.

He squeezed her hand and then shined his flashlight the length of the porch, checking for filth. There was none.

"Here, put your things down," he said.

They gathered their belongings and sat on them.

"We have until six o'clock tomorrow morning. Are you tired?" he asked her.

"A little," she admitted. "I'll lay out some clothes. I have a poncho and both of us have jackets."

Feeling in the bags, she drew out the poncho and some other articles of clothing saying, "We'll be comfortable."

Folding sweaters for each of them to use as pillows and improvising a mattress from their clothing, they were soon huddled under the wide poncho. He found her hand.

"We may have to do this more than once," Carlos told her. "I don't know what the future holds."

"I'm concerned only about what we will do tomorrow," she laughed.

"My mother's brother lives in Quito," Carlos told her. "I'm sure he will help us. I have saved some money, so I hope he can do something about getting permission for us to marry."

"I'm not eighteen yet," Elena wondered. "Will there be a problem?"

"Maybe. That's why I want to talk to him. He's a professional man, a lawyer so he will know," Carlos assured her.

Silence covered them as they lay without speaking for several minutes. In the distance a dog barked and a baby cried from within the station. Suddenly a low chuckle burst from Carlos and Elena followed with a giggle.

"I'm so happy," she laughed with pure joy.

"Can you believe we finally did it? We did it," he said as he joined in with her laugher.

They talked excitedly for more than an hour, and then drifted off to sleep.

Chapter 36

The chattering from a group of waiting passengers on the other side of the train tracks awakened Carlos. Sitting up, he found he was stiff and cold.

Elena opened her eyes, wondering for a moment where she was, "Who's that talking?"

"Over there by the road, there's a small group of men. They haven't seen us yet," Carlos whispered. "It's still pretty dark."

"It must be close to six o'clock, though," Elena deducted. "You can see daylight above the mountains."

"Yes, let's get our things together," Carlos suggested. "We can sit here like we've just arrived and are waiting for the train."

Elena shivered, snuggling in her jacket.

"There must be a water faucet on the road," Carlos said. "Do you want to wash your face?"

"Yes, and brush my teeth," Elena responded. "I'll be back in a minute and then you can have your turn."

She wandered to the front of the station and watched the occupants of the road. A few children straggled by, heading for school. She waited until the way was clear, and satisfied that she recognized no one, ran to the faucet to splash water on her face and then quickly brushed her teeth and hair. Ducking into nearby bushes, she relieved herself and ran back to Carlos. In a few minutes both were washed and refreshed. They repacked their belongings and were sitting on the edge of the porch as daylight approached.

While They Sleep

A woman appeared at the end of the building. Carlos recognized her as the woman he had spoken with the previous night. With a greeting she thrust a large wooden tray at them. It was piled high with empanadas, a treat made of pie dough filled with sweets or cheese or meat and then fried in pork lard. Carlos pulled several silver centavos from his pocket and purchased four empanadas filled with cheese and handed two to Elena.

"We'll drink water until we pass a town where they sell colas," Carlos told Elena.

As the sun rose higher in the sky several new passengers arrived, mingling with friends and acquaintances. A few people gathered at the porch to buy empanadas from the eager vendor who relied on the few centavos she earned each day to feed her family.

The train arrived with a roar. To Elena's disappointment, it was nothing more than a long bus. The wheels had been replaced with round discs that moved freely on tracks. The steering wheel controlled the brakes rather than direction; but other than this minor change it was nothing more than a bus.

Carlos guided Elena inside the train lugging their baggage with him. He found a seat halfway to the back and both of them sat nervously. Slowly the train began to move, the driver changing gears until soon they were passing through the familiar beautiful countryside. Carlos thought he would feel sorrow with this farewell to his past, but he failed to sense any remorse. Both of them sat rigidly in hard, lumpy seats, willing the train to hurry from the area where they would be more vulnerable to encounter acquaintances.

Eventually they stopped in Cumbaya, a town halfway between Quito and Pachuca. Knowing this was the last stop the train would make in their hometown area, they relaxed with big grins. Carlos forced open the train window and called for two colas. Running to stand below the window, a woman held out two warm bottles for him to grab as he handed her two sucres. Sitting back on the hard seat they drank, thirsty from the hot, difficult ride. Polishing off the last sips, they slumped toward each other, dozing.

Despite a long wait in a forest of eucalyptus trees while the driver carried buckets of water from a stream to feed an overheated radiator, they arrived in the southern section of Quito by midmorning.

Chapter 36

The quaint city bustled with merchants, beggars, vendors, and wandering people. Balconies projected above store fronts facing the traffic-choked streets.

The avenues of the old city crawled up Mount Pichincha's sides, which has one of the largest bases of any mountain in the western hemisphere. Neither had a desire to live here, but to visit was a pleasure. Elena attended school in the center of town, and was taken aback when she realized they were to pass within a block of the building.

"We can't go this way. My school is down that street," Elena said worriedly. "If we walk past with our bags someone may see us."

"Caramba, I didn't think," Carlos exclaimed. "Let's walk over two blocks and get something to drink."

They stopped, searching the street for a cola sign.

"Walking up these hills takes my breath away," Elena said as she exaggerated her breathing, holding a hand over her chest. "Let's find some place to sit."

They found an open café containing three tables. The entrance was partially barred by a large metal trough filled with chunks of potatoes and pieces of pork sitting over a kindled fire. An elderly woman standing inside the door wearily fanned the flames to create more heat.

"Do you want something to eat, Elena?" Carlos asked. "I'm hungry."

"Please," Elena responded.

She chose a table against a wall in the darkened room, hoping no one from school would look in and see them. Carlos soon returned with two pieces of paper filled with hot potatoes, meat and large hava beans. Placing the food on the table, he then searched for a cup of salt. Finding one, they pinched enough between their fingers to sprinkle the food liberally. In a bowl they found aji, a hot sauce and began dipping the steaming food into the fiery liquid. The old woman plodded over, two glasses and bottles of cola in hand. In a short time they felt refreshed and Elena sat back, excitement filling her face.

"It's becoming real to me that we're together and running away. I don't have to leave you and go back home. We're together for the rest of our lives, aren't we?" Elena asked happily. Half the time I can't believe it. It seemed to happen so fast."

"I'm glad you're not sorry," Carlos said as his eyes softened, watching her. "Yes, we're together and if we can get to my uncle's house, nothing will separate us again."

"Where does he live?" she asked as she sipped at the warm cola.

"He's not far from here, but the streets are confusing, so we'll have to catch a bus that leaves the main part of town and then find our way," Carlos explained becoming anxious. "Do you want anything else to eat?"

"No, I feel satisfied. Perhaps we won't have to worry about meeting someone from school since classes have started, but I think we should avoid the building," Elena suggested. "We can catch the bus closer to the Plaza de Independencia, even though it means we must walk further."

Nodding together in agreement, they gathered their belongings and walked uphill away from the school to the large plaza facing the Presidential Palace. Just as they reached the bus stop, Elena let out a small yelp.

Carlos stopped as she grabbed his arm, "What's the matter?"

"There's Geoff. He just walked down the street where we were. He must have come from Pachuca by bus and now is heading to the school. What if Rolando is here with him?" frozen in fear, hysteria threatened to overcome her. "What if Geoff has already been to the school and is looking around the plaza for us?"

"Why would they think us here?" Carlos asked calmly though his heart pounded.

"Maybe they're trying to find some of my school friends to see if they know where I've gone," Elena said worriedly. "Perhaps they think I confided in some of them."

"Did you?" Carlos asked concerned.

"No, of course I told no one about this," Elena assured him.

"You asked me not to in the note. Remember?" she answered with a touch of contempt in her voice.

He saw the panic in her eyes and couldn't deny the fear growing in him, "I'm not going to put up with this. We'll take a taxi. I don't care how much it cost."

It wasn't difficult to find a cab in the traffic-lined streets as it seemed every other car was a yellow taxi cruising, the driver prowling

Chapter 36

for potential passengers. Without much effort he flagged one down. Helping Elena in, he dumped the bags beside her and opened the front passenger door to sit beside the driver and give directions. Within a few minutes they were away from the activity, noise and smells of the old city, entering an area unhampered by heavy traffic. Quickly rolling past a main street, they made a sudden turn uphill, riding toward a suburb built on a ridge overlooking the valley where Carlos and Elena had lived all their lives. The taxi moved along the edge of an immense canyon covered with flimsy matchbox houses clinging precariously to the sides. Finally the driver found the sloped street where Carlos' uncle lived. He descended with care, stopping the car at a slant. Paying the man, Carlos and Elena were left standing in front of an old house.

"Which one does he live in?" Elena asked.

"They live behind that big door over there," Carlos pointed toward two large wooden doors drawn together and latched from the inside.

Carrying the bags to the other side of the street, he knocked loudly. There was no response.

"Maybe they aren't home," Elena said, shifting her tired feet.

"There's no padlock on the outside of the door so someone has to be here. Anyway, the siesta hour has begun so it's probably difficult to hear from inside," Carlos reasoned

He pounded until the door vibrated. A minute later they heard running footsteps and the heavy door opened. A teenage boy peered out, pleasantly surprised at the unexpected visitors.

"Hola, Carlos! It's Carlos!" he yelled. "I can't believe it. Come in. Come in. Hey, Momi, Popi, look who's here."

A dark stout man appeared, running on short legs. He grabbed Carlos in a hug and reached up to kiss his cheek.

Elena stood back, ignored until the excitement of first greetings passed and Carlos stepped back to pull her forward, "Uncle Jose, this is Elena."

The little man reached out to grasp her hand, "Con mucho gusto. Come this way. Come into our house. Our house is your house. You will always be welcome here."

Beaming with pleasure, he led them behind the double doors into semi-darkness and pointed to a woman standing in the upper doorway, awaiting their arrival.

Carlos waved and yelled a greeting as Elena looked around and saw they were standing on an old, worn stairway landing that led up to the entrance of the house. Another stairway behind them led down to an enclosed patio where she saw a cement tub built for the family laundry and for gathering water. It was dim, grey and damp, the only filtered light provided was from a hole in the roof.

Climbing the stairway, they walked across a narrow landing until reaching the door of the house.

An attractive middle-aged woman with bright black eyes and pudgy cheeks greeted them with a wide, white smile and a hug. Self-conscious, Elena was overcome with her show of affection as she was introduced to her as Aunt Carlota.

"I was named after my Aunt Carlota," laughed Carlos with pride.

Elena was offered a place on the davenport as Carlos sat with his uncle on two chairs pulled out from the dining room table. High windows looked over rows of houses sitting below them following the canyon's ridge. In the distance, Elena could see the old city of Quito resting at Mount Pichincha's base, white buildings with red tile roofs clinging to their neighbors as if dependent on each other.

A sudden touch of homesickness brought a knot to her throat. She missed her mountains and wide-open spaces; the smells of home; her mother. Momi. There had been no way to explain to her mother why she must leave. Her greatest pain would come later when she allowed herself to think of Aunt Mariana, Uncle Hector, and her cousins. Carlos was right when he said that they may never see their families again. Perhaps after this, they would never be welcome in Pachuca. Blinking against tears threatening to fall, she looked toward Carlos who was explaining to his uncle the need for temporary hospitality.

Carlos, sweet gentle, handsome Carlos. Think of it! Here she was, with Carlos. This had been her dream, her fantasy for years. If all worked well, he would be her husband in a few days. Her husband. Now the promise of a home, of babies, of love, of security all lay within her reach. Pride dissolved the lump in her throat and dried her tears. There was nothing in Pachuca that could compare to

Chapter 36

Carlos. Nothing would make her return to that life. In that moment a spontaneous joy sprouted as from a seed in the center of her being, its roots spreading like fire and bursting into a full flowered garden. It was more than she could contain. Her cheeks blazed pink, her eyes shined brightly and her red lips threatened to burst forth with gleeful laughter.

Uncle Jose had been deep in conversation with Carlos, somewhat troubled with the proposition confronting him. Always impressed with the boy and his level headedness despite tremendous problems at home, his feelings were divided, desiring to help the two young people and yet not wanting to betray his sister. He was tempted to offer the comforts of his home for the day and then send them back to Pachuca to think about their future for a few years. Both were so young and what Carlos was asking bothered him a great deal. Perhaps he, as a professional would know how to get them a marriage certificate without trouble, but first he had to know that he was doing the right thing.

At this moment he turned to look at Elena sitting on the davenport and caught the look of joy and pride on her face. Quickly all doubts fled and he knew that no matter how many years these children waited, they belonged together. Understanding touched him. He had felt that love long ago. He still dearly loved his wife, but there was nothing more beautiful than unfulfilled love about to be consummated.

"Elena, are you sure this is what you want? Won't you miss your family and home?" Uncle Jose asked merely for the pleasure of being fatherly.

"Oh yes, this is what I want and yes, I'll miss my home and family in Pachuca, but now Carlos and his family are my family. This is what I want," she assured him with a smile.

Jose sat back in his chair, folding his hands over a protruding belly and sighed with a feeling of importance.

"You will let me think a little. Mama is in the kitchen preparing a bit of food for you. Then I must get to the office," Uncle Jose said to Carlos.

Turning to Elena again, Jose explained, "Perhaps Carlos has told you, but if not, I am a lawyer. That is why, if I choose, I leave for work late, early or not at all."

He chuckled, revealing a nice smile, "I'm getting older and don't have the energy I once had. When I was young like Carlos I was on my way to work before the sun had a chance to roll over your mountains in Pachuca. Now I like to stay home and enjoy my beautiful wife."

They looked up as Carlota entered the dining room with a tray of cups and plates of cheese and bread.

"Come, all is ready," she beamed.

Uncle Jose escorted Elena to the dining room and held a chair out for her at the table as Carlos replaced the two chairs he and his uncle had removed earlier.

He seated himself to Elena's right and indicated Carlos to sit opposite her. Carlota wandered from the kitchen to the table, puttering with odds and ends, although a place had been set for her. Alfredo, Carlos' cousin had retired to his room after the excitement had died down and Elena could hear boys' voices, laughter and music, and she decided he must have guests.

As they drank a hot cinnamon-flavored drink and snacked on fresh bread, sweet butter and salty cheese, the conversation turned to matters other than the marriage. A sincere effort was made to include Elena in the talk about family and she spoke freely of her own home, family, and schooling.

It was late evening after Jose returned home from work before they talked again of the impending marriage, "How much money have you saved, Carlos?"

"I have enough to pay someone to marry us without asking questions," Carlos assured his uncle.

Fatigued from the day's stimulation, Uncle Jose wiped his face with a handkerchief and refolded it, playing with the edges.

"It may take a bit of work, but I think we can do something to pass as Elena's parents or at least her legal guardians," he explained to Carlos.

Standing, he placed the handkerchief in his back pocket and walked to a side table. Opening a drawer he pulled out a pad of

Chapter 36

paper and grabbed his briefcase from where he had left it by the front door. Clearing a place on the davenport, he invited Carlos and Elena to join him and for the next hour they made plans. Not one to be left out, Aunt Carlota continued making trips from kitchen to living room, insisting they must be hungry and tempting them with offers of after-dinner snacks.

Jose would handle the legalities of a civil wedding while Carlos would be responsible for running the many errands to hasten the wedding day. After much pleading on the part of Carlota, it was decided that Carlos and Elena would spend a few days with the family until they were able to find an apartment of their own. The busy days flew by and a week later they were married in a civil ceremony.

Chapter 37

The nagging memory of seeing Geoff in Quito troubled them and they decided to leave the capital city. Guayaquil became a possibility but tales of the dirty, humid seaport caused them to reject the idea. They had lived in clean country air all of their lives and they knew they could not abide the filth and smells of Ecuador's most populous city. Even the lesser populated city of Quito was becoming claustrophobic to them.

One night as they were lying in their Cousin Alfredo's bed, the boy having been expelled from his room to stay at a friend's home until the young married couple found their own apartment, they discussed the possibility of returning home to Pachuca.

"We can't go back, Carlos, not yet. There's a chance we'll be welcomed, but I have doubts. As far as they are concerned what we did was wrong and I fear Rolando will separate us again, especially if he finds out we were married with your uncle's help and his fraud," Elena said.

"I'll never feel we are married illegally," Carlos said with deep conviction. "No two people love each other more than we do."

"That may be true, but in the eyes of God, I wonder, and certainly in the eyes of my family we are not legally married," Elena pointed out. "Rolando would go to the authorities and they would eventually discover how we were able to get married without my true parent's permission."

Chapter 37

"No, think about it. The only thing that is questionable is the signatures of our aunt and uncle instead of your parents, but tell me this. How would your father and mother ever sign permission papers, even if they did agree? Your mother is too ill and your father too intoxicated. Elena, we were married by an official of Ecuador and he pronounced us husband and wife. That made everything legal Cariña. We had to do it this way; otherwise we might never have been married, don't you see,?" Carlos asked.

"Perhaps, but oh, please don't think I regret this," Elena assured him. "I love you so much. It's just that we have been living here for two weeks, causing your cousin to leave home, eating your family's food and taking advantage of their hospitality. I guess I feel guilty."

Slipping his arm under her, Carlos held her close, "They love you. Can't you see what it means to Aunt Carlota to have a young girl in the house? She has only the one son and taking care of us has made her happy, I know that."

He kissed her cheek, "I know what you mean, though. I can't live in the city and living in a part of town that overlooks our valley almost makes me sick. I miss the mountains while here all you smell are fumes from cars, buses and garbage trucks. How I would love to smell a morning in Pachuca."

"Perhaps we could try living in another valley. There is one on the south side of Quito. Have you been to Conocoto?" Elena asked.

"Yes, once and all I could think of was getting back to my valley," Carlos said with a smile.

Pulling himself up on his elbow he looked down at her. The pale light coming from the window gave her face a faint glow.

"The other night someone suggested we try living in Guayaquil. We could never do that, I know, however it gave me an idea. Have you heard of Salinas?" Carlos asked her.

"Yes, because one of my friends visited there for a vacation," Elena answered.

"Well, further south below Guayaquil there's a small town named Playas located on a stretch of beach that is quite beautiful, they tell me. Many wealthy vacationers from Guayaquil stay at a hotel located on the beach front. I thought if we could live in Playas for a while

I could find a job in the hotel or one of the restaurants," Carlos explained.

She sat up and propped a pillow behind her, "Where did you hear about this?"

"Actually my uncle mentioned it by chance. I know they want us here in Quito with them, but he knows we could never live confined in a small apartment. I feel too that he doesn't want us going back to Pachuca because of what he did for us. That may cause some problems for him," Carlos answered.

Thinking for a moment, she absently rubbed her hands across the blanket, "You're not accustomed to working like that. All you know is farm labor."

"I can learn how to do anything, Amor. Maybe I won't have to work in the kitchens. Perhaps I can find something else more suitable," Carlos assured her.

"It's close to vacation time from school, what if someone from Quito goes there and sees us?" Elena asked still worried they would be discovered.

"Almost everyone goes to the beaches at Manta or Bahia, or as you say, some of your school friends may on occasion go to Salinas, but few people will go to Playas from Quito. It's too far away, or at least we can hope they feel that way."

He rubbed his hands together in anticipation, "We can't take up room in my uncle's home much longer. I think we should leave as soon as possible."

"Do we have enough money?" Elena asked.

"Don't worry about that because I have been saving part of my pay since you were twelve years old, just for this day. Even when we were separated, I saved. I guess part of me always knew we would be together," Carlos said with a smile.

Shaking her head in wonder, she hugged him hard, "I'll go anywhere with you. I didn't know I would be so happy being married. If someone could have made me believe this sooner, I'd have run away with you when I was twelve."

"You think you have family problems now," he laughed, returning her hug.

Chapter 38

Rolando woke with a start, pushing away the hand shaking his shoulder. Opening a bleary eye, he saw the young maid standing nervously over him.

"What's the matter?" he muttered irritably, the effects of last night's party still clouding his mind.

"Elena's gone," the maid announced worriedly.

"Gone? Elena? Gone where?" he asked as he attempted to rise to his elbow and sank back.

"Her bed hasn't been slept in. I went to wake her for school and she's not here," the young girl apprehensively scratched her head.

Rolando groaned and put his face in the pillow, "She probably went to the store for something."

Pulling at her long hair, she said, "No, I would know that. I think she ran away."

"What?" he asked as his head came up sharply. "What did you say?"

"I think she ran away," the girl repeated, stepping back.

Rolando stared at her and sat up straight, "Why would you think that?"

"The window is open and some of her things are missing from on top of the bureau," she said fearfully, her voice trailed to a whisper.

"Where are my brothers?" he asked as his eyes swept the unmade empty beds.

"They are getting ready for school," the maid answered, still keeping her distance.

"Leave me. I'm getting up. We will see about this," Rolando said angrily as he crawled out of bed, his heart thumping hard.

Hurriedly dressing, he headed for the back of the house. His three brothers were finishing a breakfast of bread and coffee as he entered the kitchen.

"Have you seen Elena?" he demanded.

Geoff set his coffee cup down and shook his head, "Not me. I thought maybe she was at Aunt Mariana's."

Roberto and Pablo shrugged their shoulders and elbowed each other smiling mischievously at their brother's tousled hair.

"She probably is, but the maid says she thinks she ran away," Rolando glared, ignoring their teasing.

The three sat stunned for a moment and then all eyes turned toward the young servant who had just appeared, out of breath in the doorway.

"I ran up to your Aunt Mariana's," she declared. "They haven't seen her."

"Madre mia," exclaimed Roberto.

Rolando found a chair and sank onto it before saying firmly, "Roberto, you and Pablo go on to the University. Geoff, before you go to class today, hurry to the school and see if by chance she is already there or if anyone knows where she may be."

"What are you going to do?" asked Geoff, nodding.

With jaw set, Rolando pounded one fist into the palm of his other hand, "First, I'm going to visit Carlos' house to see if he is there. I'll find out if his family knows where he is. I'll be able to tell in a moment if he has left home. I have a terrible feeling that they may have run off together."

"Oh no," cried Pablo jumping to his feet nearly knocking his cup of coffee to the floor, "I'll help you find him."

"The best way to help me is for you, Geoff to go to her school," Rolando said as a terrible look of hatred glazed his eyes. "I want to find Carlos myself. If it's true they have run away together, they have probably gone to Quito and if that be true, I will search every street, every house, and every alley until I find them, even if it means I have to move to Quito myself."

Chapter 39

Time passed quickly because of all the activity. Jillian, Lucia, and Marta talked of little else but house plans. A contract was signed with the same construction crew that built the other buildings on Marta's property. Ground breaking was scheduled for the following week. Bags of cement, sand, wooden cross beams, nails, and large rocks for the foundation were delivered.

Saturday dawned bright and beautiful. Jillian loved the mornings with air so pure that clumps of needle-thin trees could be seen miles in the distance. Dazzling, puffy white clouds punctuated the deep blue sky.

Immediately after breakfast, she led the children to the playground. Yelping with joy, they ran energetically, flopping and rolling on the green grass. She sat in the large sandbox, removed her shoes and wriggled her toes in the cool sand. The boys coaxed Elizabeth into joining them in a game of hide and seek. An hour later a light breeze picked up and Jillian wrapped a sweater around her shoulders.

"Look behind you, Jill," Lucia yelled from the clinic as she ran down the steps to gather the wash hanging on the clothesline.

Jillian whirled around and saw dark, rolling clouds. Already the mountains were concealed by the curtain of rain racing toward them.

"Get in the house! Elizabeth! Leah! Get those kids in here right now! Right now," Marta screamed in her high nasal voice, leaning out the door.

Everyone made it to the house as the first drops fell. In a moment a sheet of water deluged the clinic blotting it from view. The walkways became rivers of water. The children ate their food with little interest, dispirited by the sudden onslaught of rain. Jillian hurried to put them down for their naps. She too, longed to get into a warm bed to escape the chill of the house.

Several loud raps on the front door woke her with a start.

"Oh no," she groaned, rising to poke her head out the bedroom door.

Hearing Flora muttering in the hallway below, she walked down the steps and stood behind the maid.

"May I help you?" Flora asked.

"Yes, please help me," a muffled male voice replied from beneath a soaked poncho.

"You'll have to walk to the clinic behind you. There is no one here who can help you," explained Jillian.

"Please, you help me. My wife needs help. I knocked on the clinic door but no one answered. Por Dios, please help me," the man begged.

"Wait a minute. I'll go with you and find someone," she said as she grabbed a poncho and put on her boots, grumbling to herself. "There goes my afternoon."

Outside, she was drenched before she slouched five feet through several inches of water on the sidewalk. The rainstorm now diminished to a steady downpour had transformed the play area into a lake of water.

Opening the clinic door, she called out, "Lucia, are you here?"

No answer. The building was oddly deserted. Reluctant to muddy the spotless floor, she closed the door and ran to the outpatient clinic where a light shone through the drawn curtains. Standing in the doorway, she yelled for Marta and Lucia. There was no answer.

Irritated, Jillian ran back to the clinic, ignoring the impatient man. Bursting through the door, she trailed water into the kitchen and stopped short. Hysterical laughter sounded from behind Lucia's door. What was going on? She pounded again. Lucia opened the door, still giggling.

"What in the world are you two doing?" Jillian shouted. "There's someone out here that needs help. I've been calling everywhere."

So choked was she with anger that she could hardly talk.

Chapter 39

Marta came to the door gasping for air and wiping her eyes, "I'm sorry, Jill. We were just talking about some of the stupid, ignorant things that go on in the government clinic and it got us laughing."

Jillian stomped through the clinic kitchen and back to her house. Feeling distraught, she changed out of her wet clothes. By then her anger was abated and she felt childish and foolish, hating it when Marta and Lucia spent time together because they shared a friendship and mutual love of medicine that she could never feel a part. What did they talk about? They seemed to have so many secrets. But on the other hand, never could she believe that Marta really cared for Lucia in the purest sense of the word. There were too many factors involved with Marta's need for power and domination and her dislike for the lower class.

Maybe I'm just feeling left out, she pondered. I need companionship. I'm so lonely. Maybe I'm frightened that Marta might be sending me to Costa Rica to get me out of the way so she can have more time with Lucia. I'm not sure I could bear to lose Lucia's friendship. All three of us have been so isolated planted behind these walls and gates. No wonder we are all needy.

It was too complicated for her to understand, so as she had done so often in the past three and a half years, she swept all her concerns from her mind. With a sigh, she picked up a book.

Lucia opened the door, poking her head inside, "Are you mad at me?"

"No," Jillian replied weakly. "I just couldn't find you."

"We didn't hear you," Lucia smiled hopefully and raised her eyebrows. "Please, don't be mad at me."

"Really, I'm not. Do you want to come in for a while?" Jillian invited.

"I can't. Marta sent me over because we've got to go get someone. Come on," Lucia said now with an urgency in her voice.

"What? Are you crazy? I don't want to go out in this weather. It's cold," Jillian exclaimed.

"You've got to go. Marta said so," Lucia declared.

"Why is it we have to jump every time she says something?" Jillian said angrily.

"You're still upset because we didn't answer the door. We were just resting and talking after lunch. I asked her to give me a backrub, nothing more. Put on your clothes. We have to pick up a woman who is about to deliver a baby on the roadside," Lucia explained quickly.

"Why doesn't Marta go?" Jillian asked.

Lucia shrugged, "I didn't think to ask her."

"Why should you ask?" Jillian grumbled, slowly stepping out of bed to dress.

They sloshed through standing water on the sidewalk and entered the clinic. Marta was waiting for her and gave Jillian an apologetic smile.

"You rang?" Jillian asked sarcastically.

"You'll have to go pick up a woman," the nurse replied, missing the sarcasm. "She's on the road a mile from here about to have a baby. Her husband will go with you and Lucia.

"Why don't you go? What if she needs a nurse?" Jillian asked.

The woman hesitated and coughed dramatically, "Because you know how susceptible I am to colds and sore throats. Anyway, Lucia is with you."

"Marta, that's why I was in bed because I was soaking wet from searching for you and Lucia. Now you want us to go out again?" Jillian complained.

"I already feel a tickle," Marta grabbed her throat and her voice cracked convincingly. "Oh dear, where's my cold medicine?"

In a foul humor Jillian motioned to Lucia, who stood against the wall amused by their carping and they made their way to the jeep. The long-suffering husband followed them and climbed into the back. Splattered mud and dwindling rain smeared the windshield as she strained to see the road. Driving slowly across the newly paved highway, she entered the narrow road heading north. Jillian carefully avoided the potholes for fear of bogging down.

They drove a mile beyond the train station and stopped, "Where do we go now?"

"Look! Look up the road. Something is coming," Lucia called, pressing her finger against the windshield.

Jillian could make out the indistinct shape of a vehicle crawling toward them in the distance. She moved to one side of the narrow

Chapter 39

road, carefully bypassing a ditch. Gradually she discerned the object was a tractor with a man bent over the steering wheel. It had almost passed when, suddenly their passenger almost climbed into the front seat.

"Pare! Pare! Stop! There's my wife. My wife is sitting behind the driver on the tractor. There's my family running behind," the man yelled.

Jillian jerked the jeep to a stop, "I must find a place to turn around on this narrow road."

By the time they returned to the clinic, the pregnant woman was stripping off her clothes for a shower, while her waiting family huddled on the clinic's porch.

"You realize, Lucia that we made this trip for nothing?" Jillian gave her a wry smile and made a grand exaggeration of wringing out her skirt.

"I thought it was fun," Lucia said with a smile.

"You would," Jillian said ruefully.

Now too curious to leave, Jillian with Lucia following close behind walked to the labor room where Marta was setting up her instruments.

"She got here before you, huh?" the nurse remarked without looking up.

"Yes, and we're wet and cold," Jillian shivered and patted her wet hair.

"It's good for you. You're much too independent Jill, and I intend to help break your will," Marta said firmly. "I was pretty sure the patient would get here one way or another."

"And you sent me anyway," Jillian stated angrily.

Marta shrugged, "I just wanted to prove that you will do what I tell you. You should thank me as I was doing you a favor."

For a moment Jillian glared at the nurse, stifling a sharp retort and then whirling around, she walked into the patient's room. Sitting on the bed's edge, she counted to ten under her breath.

"……nine, ten. She was doing me a favor? Whatever can that mean?" Jillian said.

Lucia chuckled as she watched Jillian struggle with her emotions, "Why don't you just accept her as she is? She'll never let you win. You should know that by now."

"I guess you're right," Jillian admitted as she studied the Indian's damp, unruly hair and giggled. "Where's a mirror. You look funny, like a chicken with its feathers dragged through soup."

"Ha! What about you? I think the cook took one look at you and tossed you out the back door right into a mud puddle," Lucia teased back.

They hooted with laughter falling backwards onto the bed. Then trying to talk, another wave of humor hit them and they grabbed at their stomachs, rocking with convulsions. Lucia dropped to the floor, wiping tears from her eyes while Jillian lay doubled on the bed.

Marta came to the doorway and stood sadly, mutely watching the scene. Then shoulders drooping, she slowly returned to the delivery.

There had been no danger of the baby being born on the road. The woman had a slow delivery with her twelfth child. The routine deliveries in the past had broken down the muscles of her uterus leaving her with little ability to aid Marta. Jillian stood on a stool and leaned over the patient, pushing on the infant's buttocks as it slowly moved through the birth canal.

A baby girl, perfect in features was finally born. While Lucia bathed her, Jillian ran to the house to change into dry clothes and check on the children. Flora and Elizabeth had gathered the children, just up from their naps in the playroom.

Sitting on the floor with them, Jillian tried to participate, but a strong restlessness drove her back to the clinic. She stood in the hallway ready to call out when she heard Marta talking softly with the patient. Quietly, she walked toward the patient's ward and peeked around the door. Sensing she shouldn't interrupt, she decided to look for Lucia, but Marta's lowered voice caught her attention.

"It's a shame you had to deliver another baby, Señora. Think of it, now you have seven children still at home to care for," the nurse giggled and slapped her knee. "Your house must be so full. I just couldn't take care of that many children without help."

Caught up in Marta's undivided attention, the patient joined in the laughter, affectionately rubbing the top of her baby's head.

Chapter 39

"But, Señorita, think of how blessed I am to have so many living children. God has been good to me," the mother said softly.

Leaning forward, Marta took hold of the infant's tiny hand and looked earnestly into the mother's eyes, "I've been thinking about your heavy burden and decided to give you a solution. Since you first arrived, I've been wondering if you'd like to give me your child. I can care for her in my home."

Surprised, the mother shook her head, "Oh no, Señorita. Thank you very much, but my husband and I want to take our baby home with us."

"But think about the hardship you'll be facing with a new baby in the house. If the child stays with me, she'll have much better food than you can provide and I'll give her beautiful clothes. She'll be educated, even be sent to a university when she is older. Can you and your husband do that much for her?" Marta pointed out.

"I can't give you my baby," the mother replied, but standing at the door, Jillian caught her hesitation.

"Why not?" Marta pressed her. "Can you give her a better life?"

"What will my family say? I'm sure my husband wants her," the woman's voice took on a pleading tone. "What will the neighbors say?"

Raising her eyes to the ceiling in frustration, Marta retorted, "I'm so tired of people asking me what the neighbors will say. What's the difference? Would you rather see your baby grow up in a filthy house, with insufficient food when I can give her so much?"

With effort, her harsh tone softened and she leaned forward again, "I can give her so much more."

"My husband and mother won't let me," the mother pointed out.

"I'll speak to your family," Marta said sensing her victory.

Again the patient hesitated. Marta moved her chair closer to the bed.

"Will it make any difference if I tell you that every year on her birthday you can come to visit her? I'll give you a photo taken at that time and on Christmas I'll give you a box of food. I'll not charge you for your delivery and stay in the clinic either," Marta offered knowing these were things that would worry the mother and family.

"Well...," the mother started, obviously wavering and considering the offer.

"Listen, you'll have no problems with your family. You can just tell the neighbors that the baby died," Marta coaxed the mother.

Suddenly Jillian felt a strong urgency to leave the clinic for fear Marta would catch her listening. She carefully shut the clinic door and hurried toward the house.

Chapter 40

At dinner that evening Marta brought up the subject of the mother and baby. Jillian noticed an excitement about her and decided that the patient must have decided to give up the baby. When Marta turned away, the children took advantage of an opportune moment and mimed playfully. Lucia carried on about her aching back, while Marta, oblivious to everyone else rapidly spooned food into her mouth. Jillian was torn between pity for the mother and knowledge that Marta was indeed capable of giving the child a more comfortable life.

Just as Marta opened her mouth to speak, the phone rang.

Flora answered and then called out, "Señorita, the telephone operator in Pachuca's central office says your awaited call is ready."

In the hallway, Marta grabbed the receiver from Flora's hand as Jillian strained to hear the conversation spoken in Spanish.

"Hola. Buenas tardes, señor Fernando. Is that you? Hola. I'm so glad I caught you before you left the office. Si, I have a little girl that was born this afternoon. Yes, it's all right with the mother if we take her. Si. In fact she almost begged me to take her. Do you think that you can start the papers soon? Oh, that is wonderful. No, at this point I think the prospective parents living in the United States will be willing to pay anything we need. I have just enough money to care for her here. You know maybe it would be better if I drive into Quito tomorrow and talk with you about this. What? Tuesday is better? Fine. Sure, I'd love to have lunch with your family. I'll see you Tuesday. Hasta luego," Marta said as she ended the call.

Jillian sat in shock, food stuck in her throat as a beaming Marta returned to her place at the table.

"The mother gave up her baby for adoption, Marta?" Jillian asked.

"Isn't that wonderful?" Marta confirmed, stuffing her mouth with bread. "You can't believe how she begged me to give her child away to someone in the United States. That means we're going to save another baby from death."

"Death?" Jillian asked recalling the conversation she had overheard. "What do you mean by death?"

"You know how it is for babies living in these terrible conditions here," Marta pointed out. "They live in filth."

"Lots of babies survive in these conditions," Jillian responded.

"Half the babies in Ecuador die before they are five years old, according to a Quito newspaper," Marta said knowingly.

"And the mother was willing to give her up just like that? How could she do it? How will her husband and family feel?" Jillian asked.

"Jill," Marta groaned impatiently. "These people are not romantic like you are. They meet the sorrows of life with reality."

She glanced around at the children and her face reddened, "You know what happens...you know what I mean? Then there's the birth of the child nine months later. Since it takes nine months for the birth of the baby, these people just aren't educated enough to know there's a connection between both incidents. Can't you see what I'm saying?"

"I hear what you're saying, but no, I can't imagine a woman not realizing that a child is the result of a love union between her and her husband," Jillian exclaimed.

"Oh!" wailed Marta. "Good grief, Jill, do you have to be so blunt?"

Lucia snickered.

"What's wrong with what I said?" Jillian asked, confused.

"Forget it," Marta replied as her voice rose in anger. "Apparently this mother doesn't care because she gave up the child without a second thought."

"Then you're going to take the baby to Quito to see Señor Fernando?" Jillian asked.

Chapter 40

"Were you listening to my telephone conversation?" Marta asked angrily.

"How could she help it?" Lucia piped in laying her chin on her cupped hand. "The telephone is in the hallway right outside the door."

"Alright, yes, I'm sending her to the states and I think it's wonderful," Marta turned quickly and noticed Peter dabbling in his food.

Abruptly, she slapped him. Immediately the atmosphere was charged. Everyone paused knowing if he cried out, he would be punished. Shock and fear froze on his face as he looked to Jillian for consolation. Desperately she pleaded with her eyes that he remain quiet. The boy slowly looked at Marta, relaxed, and put his hands at the sides of his plate.

"Stop playing with your food, Peter, and eat it. When I think of all the time and effort we put into making dinner for you children and all you want to do is play in it," Marta said angrily.

He bent to nibble at a spoonful and Jillian breathed a sigh of relief. Peter had learned well.

"Anyway," continued Marta, as if nothing had happened. "I'm merely going to visit with Señor Fernando who understands the paperwork connected with adoptions. We'll see what he says about this baby."

"Is he the same attorney who has helped you with the other adoptions?" Jillian asked.

Eyeing her for a long moment, the nurse replied scornfully, "This is not the first time you've questioned me about adoptions. What is it you're after?"

"Nothing really," Jillian answered.

"Then I'll forget you even brought it up," she declared as she peeled a banana and pushed half of it into her mouth.

Swallowing a huge mouthful, she struggled to talk, "Sometimes I think you forget you're here to watch my children, not every other little beggar running around the countryside."

In went the other half of the banana, "Anyway, since you have to know, there have been lots of problems in Ecuador with adoptions. I heard about an attorney who has worked with legal adoptions so I thought I'd call him. After all, it's not like we're doing anything illegal."

Lucia began making small, annoying noises on the table with her fingertips in an effort to draw attention to herself. Suddenly Jillian found it difficult to follow Marta's conversation, keep an eye on Andy and ignore Lucia. It had been an exhausting day and she had a premonition that something terrible was about to happen.

What was Marta up to? Several times in the past the nurse had mysteriously disappeared without notice. Could it be that this wasn't the first time she had dealt with the attorney? Had he helped Marta with Julie's and Anna's adoptions? How many other children with less emotional ties to Jillian had been shipped off to the States? She had overheard the nurse's conversation with this baby's mother and not a word had been said about adoption. Now she wondered if the nurse had taken other babies by deception.

Noticing the children had finished their meals she excused herself and helped them into the bathroom. After they were in bed for the night, she was able to think more clearly. Standing at her bedroom window, she watched the night lights of Quito in the distance and pondered what she had learned that day. Her thoughts were interrupted by a knock at the door.

Lucia peeked in, "May I visit with you?"

"Sure," Jillian answered inviting her in.

She entered carrying a tray laden with a steaming teapot, cups and a saucer piled high with animal cookies. Placing the tray on the desk, she plopped on the bed yawning.

"Are you real tired like me?" Jillian asked.

"Yes and I decided that if I made the tea, you could serve it," Lucia said with a smile.

Smiling back at her, Jillian poured tea into the cups and handed one to Lucia as she moved her legs against the wall to make room for Jillian.

"I am so tired and my back hurts. Did you know we had another delivery come in last night? You must not have heard them. I had just gone to sleep when someone knocked at the clinic door. Anyway I checked her but she wasn't ready to deliver yet, probably sometime this week. By the time I had sent her off, I had a hard time getting back to sleep," Lucia explained with a yawn.

Chapter 40

"No, I didn't hear a thing," Jillian admitted. "Lucia, maybe it's because you're tired, but I have a feeling that something is bothering you. I wish you would tell me how you feel about everything that's going on around here."

"No, there's nothing bothering me, just my back," Lucia answered as she put her hand out for a cookie and dunked it in her tea.

Jillian tested the dark Ecuadorian tea and leaned back against her pillow waiting for her friend to speak. The moments elapsed and she leaned forward to study Lucia's face.

"Is it something you can't tell me?" Jillian finally asked.

"I don't want to talk about it," a dark frown covered the Indian's face.

"You know better than that. You want to say something and as usual I have to drag out each word," laughed Jillian, but she quickly turned somber when she saw how serious Lucia was. "What is it?"

"It's settled that you leave for Costa Rica in April," Lucia said sadly. "Right now I don't think I can bear that."

Jillian's temples tightened in a knot, her heart beat faster and a nauseous wave rose in her throat, "I thought she had forgotten."

Lucia snickered bitterly, "She never forgets something once it's stuck in her head. She will never give up on something she wants. Learn that lesson, Jill. No matter what it is, whatever she wants she will get it. She may put it aside for a while, but she won't let it go."

Lucia's emotions surprised Jillian and she saw how defeated and dominated her friend had become under Marta's grip. With sudden clarity, she recognized that the same fate had befallen her. With every passing day she was becoming more and more submissive to Marta's will. Where would all of this lead? Frighteningly, she knew she was willing to do whatever she must to live in Pachuca with her children even if it meant giving in totally to Marta.

Chapter 41

The next morning she was so thankful to discover that Marta was gone for the day she didn't question the mysterious absence on a Sunday. Perhaps her appointment with Señor Fernando was changed to today instead of Tuesday. It didn't matter. This was going to be a day to treasure. Without the nurse present the children were able to play outside to their hearts content. The ground was still damp, but the sidewalks had dried. There seemed to be no lack for something to do. When noon arrived and they were called to lunch, a feeling of gaiety remained in the air. After the blessing was said, Jillian looked around the table with a bright smile.

"Elizabeth, you and Leah dish up the food for the older children and I'll see that Andy and Lydia have theirs," Jillian instructed them with a smile.

Spooning peas onto Andy's plate, she glanced up and saw Paul sitting motionless at his plate.

"What's wrong, Paul? Are you sick?" she asked the boy.

He shook his head.

"Why don't you eat?" Jillian asked concerned.

He shook his head again, a look of bewilderment crossing his face.

"What's wrong with you?" she asked again with dread.

She walked to his place at the table and asked, "What's in your mouth?"

"Nothing," Paul said looking down.

Chapter 41

"It's obvious that you have something in your mouth. I just saw it when you spoke," Jillian said firmly. "Now, what is it?"

"Nothing. Nothing," Paul said with tears welling up in his eyes.

"I promise that you won't get into trouble if you just show me what it is," Jillian promised.

The boy slowly opened his mouth, eyes wide and fearful.

"Why, it's gum. Now where did you get gum?" Jillian asked the frightened boy. "You know that you aren't allowed gum except when Mommy hands it out."

She had mixed feelings. Anger that he had spoiled this nice day and put the responsibility of discipline on her, yet she couldn't help but feel sorry for the boy. Only on special occasions did treats come his way. Marta, quite correctly knew that if the children ate too many sweets, she'd have tremendous dental bills. But now, she found it difficult to explain this concept to a child who craved gum and candy.

Paul was having a hard time finding a place to hide the gum, so she offered him a paper napkin. Throwing it into the garbage, she decided to wait until after lunch to discuss it further. She was relieved that Lucia had been delayed for lunch and knew nothing of the incident. As soon as possible, she led him into the living room, positioned him at her knees and seated herself. He stood nervously blinking his eyes and jerking his shoulders.

"Honey, I'm not upset at you and I promise you'll not be hurt. I just need to talk with you about the gum," Jillian said calmly. "Maybe we can clear this up in a hurry, but you must tell me where you got it because if you found it outside, I need to know if a patient threw it away after chewing on it."

"I don't know," Paul said fearfully.

"You don't know?" she repeated in surprise. "Paul, if Mommy gave it to you she would have left me a note or said something and the other children would also be given some, but if she didn't give it to you, then I need to know if you found it somewhere and were chewing somebody else's gum. If it was from a patient, then it could make you sick."

He looked at her.

"Where did you get it, Paul?" she searched his face.

"From Lucia," Paul said. "She gave it to me this morning."

"Lucia?" Jillian sat back thoughtfully.

She believed him because Lucia would do almost everything she could to make the children happy when Marta was gone. Despite the Indian's harshness, she loved them dearly and found it especially pleasurable to grant favors behind Marta's back.

"Yes," he looked down.

"Okay, honey, you go to bed. Take a nice nap and I'll see you later. I love you," Jillian said as she pulled him down to her and gave him a kiss.

Flashing a playful grin, he ran through the doorway and up the stairs.

She made sure all the children were in bed and wandered into the dining room where she discovered Lucia eating a late lunch. Sitting down beside her, she nodded a greeting.

Lucia looked up, her fork stopping at her mouth.

A frown gathered on her brow as she closed her mouth over the food, "What's the matter?"

"Why in the world would you give Paul gum? If you must sneak the children sweets, give them candy. At least it would be gone in a few minutes. He didn't have enough sense to get rid of the gum before he came to the table," Jillian reprimanded mildly. "I'm just glad he didn't swallow it."

"I don't know what you're talking about," Lucia said as she placed the fork on the table.

"The gum you gave Paul this morning," she explained patiently. "You know what happens to Marta when she doesn't approve of what the kids are doing."

Shaking her head stupidly, Lucia replied softly. "Jill, I don't know what you're talking about. I didn't give Paul gum. I haven't seen him all day."

Her voice rose, "The condition the clinic was left in with all the deliveries we had last night and this morning has kept me very busy, especially since Marta took off and left me alone."

Her eyes grew blacker, "This makes me mad. Why did he say that?"

Jillian pursed her lips, "He's probably scared. Now I wonder where he did find the gum. Shall I just let it go or what?"

Chapter 41

"Are you kidding? With all the diseases these patients carry around? We can't take a chance that he picked up the gum in the grass that some idiot threw over the fence," Lucia said confirming Jillian's own thoughts.

Groaning, Jillian rubbed her forehead, "I'd better let him sleep now. Do you know where Marta went? Did she go to Quito?"

"She didn't say," Lucia said shaking her head.

"I thought she was supposed to go on Tuesday? Didn't she talk to you?" Jillian asked.

With a shrug, the Indian reached for her dessert.

"Lucia, what did she say? Did she take the baby with her?" Jillian pressed.

"Will you leave me alone? I'm tired," Lucia whined. "She didn't say one word about what she was going to do in Quito."

"Oh, so she did go to Quito and I bet she took the baby with her. You'd know because the baby wouldn't be in the clinic. You do know," Jillian discerned sadly, the day thoroughly ruined because she was certain Lucia was lying and her heart was sad because of Paul.

This coupled with the mysteries surrounding Marta's activities was enough to make her want to seek out a place to hide.

When she faced Paul again, he was frightened.

"I'm just a little upset with you. Lucia says that she didn't give you that gum. Please, tell me who did," she paused for an answer.

When none came, she continued, "Did you find it on the ground when you were playing? Paul, please tell me."

"No! No, I didn't. Honest, Auntie Jill, Lucia did give it to me," Paul insisted.

"Why are you lying?" she closed her eyes against the frustration she felt. "I'm not going to hurt you. I promise."

"Will you tell Mommy I lied?" Paul asked fearfully.

"No, not if you tell me right now where you found it. I'm just scared that it might make you sick. That's all," Jillian assured him.

He shifted nervously from foot to foot, his hair rumpled from sleep.

She waited, irritated by his hesitation and the nervous twitching of his eyes.

Her voice raised a notch, "Where did you get it?"

Silence.

"Okay, maybe I can find a way to get you to tell me," she headed for the door.

"No! No, not the belt. Don't spank me," Paul pleaded. "I'll tell you. Mommy gave it to me."

"What?" yelled Jillian. "Mommy didn't give you anything."

"Yes, she did," he wept in frustration.

Lucia stood in the doorway, drawn by the loud voices.

"He says Marta gave him the gum," explained Jillian, placing her hands on her hips.

Walking over to the boy, Lucia shook him, "You lied about me and now you're lying about Mommy. Go up to your room. We'll let your Mommy handle this."

"No," he pleaded.

"Go on and get out of here. I don't want to see your face," she pushed him out the door. "I'm telling Mommy the minute she gets home."

Jillian moved to touch Lucia's arm, "Maybe we shouldn't say anything to Marta. He's so scared anyway."

Standing face to face, the two women waged a battle of wills and the outcome troubled Jillian. If she pushed her authority, she would lose her equal standing with Lucia. Already familiar with the consequences of her friend's insecurity, she was pulled between loyalty to her and to the boy. After all, what is a piece of gum? Nothing. She wasn't even sure chewing something a patient had had in their mouth would bring illness, but the principle of this situation was too large to ignore now. Marta hadn't given him the gum and he wouldn't have been anywhere in the house where gum was kept. She knew that. Finally, she backed away from Lucia's dark glare and left the room.

Her heart ached when she heard Marta's truck pull into the carport.

The nurse stomped into the kitchen yelling orders to Flora, "Bring me a glass of water and a lemon."

Jillian and Lucia sat at the end of the table watching the children romp in the playroom.

"Isn't anyone going to ask me how I am?" Marta demanded.

"How are you?" Jillian asked obediently.

Chapter 41

"Tired, of course. I'm so tired, I'm numb. What traffic?" she tossed her purse on the table and grabbed the lemon from Flora's hand. "You forgot a knife."

"Weren't you supposed to go to Quito on Tuesday? Did you take the baby to the lawyer? Are you going again on Tuesday?"

Marta stopped cutting on the lemon, "Why? Do you have plans for Tuesday?"

"No," Jillian shook her head.

"Why don't you believe me when I say I completed some errands and leave it at that?" she sighed, then perked up with a laugh. "Hey, Lucia, listen to this. I stopped at the Pachuca's town market to see if they had eggs left and that little Señora Baptista told me some great gossip."

"Yeah?" Lucia replied slowly still miffed that Marta had left her with the clinic work.

Taking a huge gulp of lemonade, the nurse sputtered, "You'll never guess. Elena Martinez took off and got married to Carlos Tapia. At least they think they're married. More likely they're living in sin somewhere. Carlos Tapia, of all people. Why, he's nothing more than a low life Indian. I bet that was one marriage the family didn't approve. If they had, the two would have gotten married in the church. Can you believe she actually ran off with that no good Indian?"

A slow burn crept up Lucia's dark face, a reaction to Marta's jabs at Indians.

"Just think how Rolando took all this? I laugh to think about it," she polished off the lemonade, set the glass down and seated herself at the table. "Rolando took off, too. The Señora thinks he's in Quito."

"Maybe the marriage is a good thing," Jillian interjected innocently. "Maybe Rolando knows where they are and is visiting with them."

"Hmmph! I suppose you don't remember how possessive he was toward her that day in the plaza. Now tell me he's taking her elopement with pleasure. I told you something was strange there," Marta said and then sucked noisily on the lemon rind. "No, he's upset and you can believe me, he's not visiting them."

"He'll probably find her and bring her back home," chuckled Lucia, her anger dissipated as she rose to check on one of the children.

293

"You know what makes me mad," continued Marta. "I've been waiting years for her to get married and pregnant so I could turn her down in case she came to my clinic. I'd love nothing more than to pay back her family for all the gossip that has been spread about me, saying I caused her mother's stroke, especially when I was in no way at fault."

Knowing better than to mention Sandi's version of the story, Jillian began thinking about Paul's situation again and knew they would soon have to discuss it.

"Anyway, that was my laugh for the day," Marta laughed as she spread open the fruit and ran her tongue over the lemony flesh.

Squinting up her face at the sourness, she stretched, "Actually, Jill, I'm working on an adoption."

"The baby who was born yesterday?" Jillian asked.

"No, this one was born last night. Betsy is taking care of him, so I don't think we'll have to worry about him. I'll probably have to do a good share of the paperwork, but there again I have the most ability in speaking Spanish," Marta paused with a smug smile, giving someone a chance to agree.

When no one offered, she yelled again into the kitchen, "Flora, please bring some more water and a couple lemons, and this time a little sugar."

Twisting to get a good view of the playroom, she asked, "How are my kids?"

"Paul's in bed," mumbled Lucia.

Jillian burned with anger. She wanted to break the news to Marta herself.

"Really?" Marta came to attention. "Why?"

With dread, Jillian saw a familiar gleam in the nurse's eyes and her heart sank. Putting down a lemon, Marta stood to go upstairs.

"Wait a minute," Jillian put out her hand. "Don't you think I should explain what happened before you see Paul? The boy is frightened enough."

"Well?" Marta asked impatiently.

With a heavy heart, Jillian wished this had never happened. Why hadn't she just let the child alone? She explained the morning's events, leaving out Paul's admission that Marta was responsible

Chapter 41

for giving him the gum. Lucia, who was still angry with the boy for causing the quarrel between her and Jillian had no intentions of keeping quiet. She related the entire story.

Marta was horrified to learn that Paul had incriminated her. With slow, deliberate steps the nurse climbed to the second floor. They heard her enter Paul's bedroom and within minutes the house was filled with her screaming and his shrieks of terror that soon subsided into gasps and whimpers.

Jillian grabbed the guesthouse key and ran out the back door. Beside herself with grief, she walked behind the small building and stood limp against the warm bricks until she no longer had strength. Hobbling to the front door, she entered and fell to the floor in agony. Tears flowed down her face. She opened her mouth and screamed at the top of her lungs. Pressing her clenched fists against her head, she wept until at the end of an hour, exhausted, she returned to the main house. She had made a grave error exposing a young child to unnecessary torture because of lack of wisdom. Never again would she do it.

The house was quiet except for water running in the bathroom. It was bath day; the children were taking turns. Sick at heart, she wandered to the kitchen for a cup of coffee. Vegetable soup was simmering on the stove and bowls had been set out, ready to be filled.

Her longing to see Paul was more than she could bear, but she would have to wait until dinner. She was not only angry at herself but with Lucia. Why couldn't that Indian grow up? Why must she be so self-centered? Why did she have such a strong desire to please Marta? Worry nagged her that soon she would have to leave Ecuador for language school. How she hated the thought of leaving the children alone with Lucia and Marta.

I can't leave them, she thought. *I must protect them and never allow any harm to touch them again.* Jillian made a resolution. *I will beg Marta to let me stay in Pachuca no matter what I have to do.*

At dinner, Paul was subdued. The atmosphere had changed since the morning playtime when laughter and talking surrounded the children. Now the children sat in silence, refraining from the secret smiles and quietly mouthed words that were in evidence during a normal meal. Jillian sought Paul's eyes, but he avoided her. She was heartbroken.

At last the terrible silence was broken by Marta, "Paul said that I gave him the gum, Jill, but he lied. He picked it up from the filthy ground by the clinic where someone had tossed it."

She glared at the boy and sighed with exaggerated despair, "I can't believe it. He's begging to get sick. Think of it. Chewing disease-ridden gum that's been sitting in somebody's dirty mouth. To think that I forbid gum in the first place, but he goes out and chews it."

"Oh!" she exclaimed, infuriated. "I can't bear to think about it. Well, he'll think twice when I start giving him antibiotic injections."

"Hasn't he been punished enough? Pills will do the same thing," Jillian replied tartly as Lucia walked into the room.

In disgust, she left the table and walked into the kitchen searching for something to do-anything to avoid looking and listening to Marta. Her protruding teeth, reddened eyes, and enlarged neck veins were more than she could tolerate. Lucia's depressed, downcast eyes, a familiar act to gain attention made her sick. As soon as she made her exit Marta quieted.

When she returned to her seat, she looked at the back of Paul's neck. Rising from his collar to the base of his ear was a large, angry welt covered with dried blood. Sickened, she walked out of the room begging the beleaguered Flora to care for the younger children.

Her first opportunity to check on Paul was the next day when Marta was called to the clinic for a delivery. Both Lucia and Marta had stopped by Jillian's room to speak with her, but the girl turned her back on them both and finally they left her alone.

Still subdued, Paul played in the corner of the playroom. Jillian climbed the barrier and walked to him, longing for a smile. She wasn't surprised when he didn't offer her a glance.

"Children, let me speak with Paul for a minute," Jillian asked as she gently pushed the clamoring little ones away.

She turned to the boy, "Honey, can you believe that I'm so very sorry?"

"Why?" Paul asked in surprise. "It's not your fault, Auntie Jill."

She looked out the door to check for any other adults and satisfied, she returned, "Turn around. I want to see your back."

Chapter 41

Gingerly pulling up his shirt, she saw four short stripes. Standing him on his feet, she pulled down his pants and saw other wounds that laced his buttocks.

"You were spanked on your legs also?" she asked.

He nodded his head and his eye twitched, "It hurts to sit down."

She lifted his pants and he leaned toward her so that his chest lightly touched her face. Tears sprang to her eyes and he smiled.

"What did she use to spank you? It doesn't look like marks from the belt and there was blood on your neck last night. Did she use something else?" Jillian asked.

"Mommy washed my neck and back before I went to bed and told me not to tell anyone what happened just in case they asked. She told me to say that I fell down outside, Auntie Jill," the frightened boy told her.

Gritting her teeth, she paused as nausea washed over her. How many times Marta had used this excuse for beatings she had administered?

"Did she use the belt or what?" Jillian asked again.

"She said not to say, but I'll tell if you promise not to say anything," Paul pleaded.

"I hope that you can still believe my promises after yesterday, but I give you my word," Jillian assured the boy sadly.

"It was like the thing we use to wash the truck," Paul said quietly.

"The what?" thinking quickly, she sorted through several objects in her mind. "I don't understand, honey. A towel?"

"No, Auntie Jill," Paul said shaking his head. "The thing the water comes out of."

"The hose?" Jillian asked, shock filling her heart.

He nodded and his shoulder jerked nervously. Dropping her head, she pretended to wipe something from her skirt. Marta had whipped him with a hose.

"What was it like? Was it long?" Jillian asked, trying hard to control her anger.

"Like this," he spread his arms wide.

"Thank you, darling for telling me," Jillian said as she stood and leaned over to kiss him, caressing his cheek.

"Am I going to die for chewing the gum?" Paul asked her fearfully.

"No, sweetheart," she smiled. "Why don't you go and play with the others? You got to stay home from school today, but tomorrow you'll have to go."

He walked gingerly to the other children looking as if a great load had been lifted from his shoulders.

Chapter 42

Leaving Carlos' family created mixed emotions in Elena. She cared for Aunt Carlota and Uncle Jose and appreciated the help they had given them, but living in Playas with her husband was a dream come true. Carlos called a taxi and when it arrived there was a flurry of kisses and hugs, tears, and groans.

In no time they arrived at the bus station and bought tickets. Following the barking voices of drivers, they quickly found the bus to Guayaquil. Depositing Elena inside the large vehicle, Carlos checked to see if their bags were tied securely to the racks on the roof. He then ran off to buy something to eat. Shortly, he returned with a sack full of oranges, tangerines, chirimoyas and hard-boiled eggs. Leaving these in Elena's lap he left again in search of empanadas, hot potatoes, and fried pork. Despite the breakfast Aunt Carlota had prepared, they settled back in their seats eating the hot food, giggling, and licking their fingers like children.

Exiting Quito, the road climbed higher than the capital city, passing Mt. Cotapoxi and on to Latacunga, the highest village in Ecuador. From there the road descended and the style of living changed. Thatched roofs adorned small huts, instead of the sun baked mud tile coverings common in the Tumbaco Valley. As the road took them further from the equator, they noticed the Indians wore thicker, heavier ponchos than the Indians of Pachuca to ward off the chill. The small differences in custom, dress and home styles amused the two young lovers for a time, but soon weariness overtook them and they drifted off to sleep. At noon they were awakened as the bus pulled into an area designated for passengers to refresh and relieve themselves.

Stretching, Elena and Carlos made their way to the front of the bus. A low, flimsy building constructed of long uneven pieces of wood stood open facing the highway. Several benches had been placed under cover. The men gathered around tables laden with bottles of whiskey and beer before finding a place to sit. Several women stood beside metal boxes filled with smoldering kindling cooking troughs full of potatoes, beans and meat sitting over the embers. One table was laid with several types of colorful fruit and cooked grains, such as havas, a large meaty bean, toasted corn and chochos, a small white rich legume. One table held nothing but roasted pork skins including the pig's heads, legs, and hoofs.

"Look, Elena! Tripa! Let's buy some for lunch," Carlos pointed, delighted with his discovery.

"Oh, yes!" cried Elena, pulling on his hand.

At the end of the row of tables a woman sat on a wooden stool, skirts billowing. Between her legs sat a bucket filled with white and brown objects. Carlos took a few coins from his pocket and the woman pulled two pieces of brown paper from under a plate. She reached into the bucket and brought out chunks of beef intestines.

"This reminds me of home. I've been hungry for tripa since we left Pachuca," Elena moaned contentedly, savoring every bite.

After buying second helpings, they wandered to a vendor selling colas. Sipping their drinks, they watched their fellow travelers lay aside their heavy ponchos as the strong noontime sun grew warmer.

"Are we far from Playas?" asked Elena, drinking the last of her cola and setting the bottle on a nearby table.

Oh, cariña we have a long way to go. We may arrive in the middle of the night," Carlos told her wiping his mouth with the back of his hand, he shook his head. "If we encounter any problems it will be sometime tomorrow. I hope you don't become too weary."

"Of course not. This is fun for me. Aren't you glad we came?" she exclaimed as she stood and threw out her arms as if to capture the beautiful scenery, the warming air, and the distant white-capped mountains.

Chapter 42

Carlos gave her one of his rare bright smiles that she so loved, and said happily, "Yes, I'm glad we decided to do this. I feel we are doing the right thing. Somehow, everything will work out all right. Perhaps we will never want to return, Elena. Perhaps we will be so happy on the coast we will be able to buy a home and raise a family there. Why do we need anyone else? You are the only one I really need."

"And you, my husband, are the only person I will ever need," Elena said joyfully.

Seated on the bus again, Elena handed him a chirimoya, a scaly, green fruit shaped like a large apple. Filled with sections of white meat, covering several large black pits, it was soft, sweet and tangy. She giggled and wiped his chin when he popped too much in his mouth.

As the hours rolled by, they lost interest in the scenery except for the hour it took them to pass Mt. Chimbarozo, the beautiful lofty mountain of the southern Andes Range. As the sun began to sink they noticed the road was in continuous descent and their surroundings were changing. The mountains and their lush green luster were exchanged by hills and tropical bogs. An occasional village appeared with houses made of wood sitting high on stilts placed over swamp land. A few scraggly trees and thick grass decorated the landscape. Men were wearing the same styled baggy pants and shirts of the mountain Indian, but the women wore lightweight cotton dresses. Most children were attired only in shirts, their bottoms uncovered. Bored with the monotony of travel, Elena was thankful that darkness was approaching and she snuggled close to her husband for sleep.

They arrived in Guayaquil and searched immediately for a bus to Playas. Discovering one would be leaving in a few minutes, they waited for their baggage to be thrown down from the bus top. At the same time they noticed nervously that the coastal bus was filling rapidly.

"Elena, you must take these tickets and find two seats. I'll get the baggage," Carlos told her.

Hesitantly, she walked to the bus and found two seats in back. Fearful that Carlos would not arrive before the departure, she decided to return to him. When the bus motor kicked over, she readied herself to yell at the driver to wait, but at the last minute he left the bus for luggage adjustments and she strained her eyes, watching for Carlos. He appeared and the bus driver followed him on board.

"I was scared you'd not be here on time," she sighed with relief.

"They had a hard time finding your bag on the other bus. It was at the front of the rack, but we have it and it's now on this bus," Carlos said, breathed deeply and gave her a weary smile.

"I'm tired of riding, Carlos," Elena agreed tiredly. "I hope it doesn't take long to get there."

"I know. I'm thankful we didn't have to spend the night waiting for this bus. Now we can arrive in one or two hours," he told her.

Looking concerned, he brightened a moment, "Are you hungry?"

They ate hard-boiled eggs, oranges, and finished the cold empanadas.

"We'll probably get there after midnight and will have to look for a cheap hotel," he said.

"We can sleep on the beach. Wouldn't that be fun?" Elena suggested happily.

"We'll see," Carlos smiled. "Since we don't know what to expect, we may have to."

As the bus pulled into Playas, they could see the small town was closed for the night. Locating the big tourist hotel, they found only a solitary light shining in the lobby. After talking with the clerk they decided since the night was almost over the expense of a room was more than they wanted to pay. In front of the building flood lights illuminated a sea wall below the flowering gardens. Following the wall until it ended, they found their way behind a long sand dune and laid out their clothing for warmth. Despite the thrill they quickly fell asleep in each other's arms.

In three hours dawn broke over the town behind them and they sat upright, tired but eager to look around.

"Look at those houses, Carlos. Why are they sitting on legs up off the sand?" Elena asked curiously.

Carlos turned to see they had been sleeping in front of three wooden houses built high on stilts, "I guess to keep pests, rats and perhaps high tides out."

Chapter 42

Elena gasped and smoothed her skirt, "Rats? What if there were rats here while we slept?"

"There's a chance, I guess," Carlos suggested. "But we have nothing of interest since we ate all our food."

After shaking the clothes free of sand and carefully folding them they replaced them in the bags and moved from behind the dunes to stare in amazement at the ocean. This was the first time they had seen this much water. The beauty and salty smell intrigued them and they strolled for a few minutes enchanted by the shoreline while Elena explained what she knew from reading her school books about the shells and sea animals. Small boats dotted the horizon and a few early risers from the hotel sat on the seawall. Elena and Carlos stared at the white building with red trim for a long while, discussing his approach for a job.

"Before we do anything we should go into town and eat breakfast," Carlos declared putting his arm around her waist. "Are you sorry yet?"

"I've never been happier," Elena declared happily. "Never."

They found a small clean restaurant. Using the tiny restroom, they washed and changed clothes. The waitress was friendly and interested in their sierra accents, willing to help them find a place to spend the night. She directed them to a modest hotel off the main street. After inspecting the entrance, they decided it was better than the prospect of spending another night on the beach. The hotel was old, but clean and included a dining room where they could take their meals.

After settling in a room Carlos begged her to take a nap while he walked back to the Grand Hotel to look for work. He returned an hour later with a job. When his key sounded in the door Elena sat up and swung her feet to the floor. He ran across the room and picked her up in a hug.

"I got it," Carlos smiled. "It was easy."

"You have a job? Doing what?" Elena asked amazed at her husband.

Setting her back on the bed, Carlos kissed her before he said, "I went to the tourist's hotel. When they heard I'm from Quito they were very interested. I guess they think someone from Quito has more experience than local folks. Anyway, they were interested, but said they didn't have positions open. I told them I would do anything, clean the rooms, work on the grounds or help in the kitchen. When I told them I have worked on farms most of my life they changed their minds and I got the job. They had been looking for someone who has worked with plants, trees, and in fields of crops. I'll be grooming the grounds and taking care of all their flowering plants."

His eyes sparkled, "I'm so happy."

He jumped up, clapped his hands together as her eyes followed him, then he reached down to take her face in his hands and looked at her, "I love you so much. I feel I can't contain any more happiness."

"I love you, too," Elena smiled happily. "Now all we're missing is a home and after we find a home to live in we can start thinking about having babies. Wouldn't that be wonderful?"

"Babies," Carlos laughed. "Yes, we'll have dozens of babies."

They looked for a room to rent and discovered that one of the three houses they had seen that morning was empty and owned by the hotel. The hotel manager told them if they would invest time and money in repairs, they could have it rent-free for a year. Jubilantly, they walked to the center of town that afternoon and bought nails, boards and paint, carrying them back in several trips. Damaged planks were replaced, holes filled, and loosened boards tightened with fresh nails. A saw, paint brushes and small tools were borrowed from the hotel so Carlos could make wooden shutters to cover the windows. Painting would have to wait until another day.

The brilliant sun was sinking into a golden sea as the daylight fishermen bearing heavy nets made their way home. Unable to work in the darkness, Carlos and Elena walked back to the small hotel. Over dinner and throughout the evening they made detailed plans for the house.

After Carlos' first morning at his new job, they spent the siesta hour scrubbing the inside of the two room house. They scoured the neglected walls with hot, soapy water carried in borrowed buckets from the Grand Hotel.

"We're fortunate the roof is in good condition," said Carlos. "We'll not be bothered by heavy rains, rats or pests since we have sealed the house well. The door is old, but heavy enough."

Chapter 42

He inspected both rooms carefully, "Now, we must think about mats to sleep on. I hope you won't mind, but it will take a few days before a carpenter can complete a bed for us. Besides I feel we have been spending too much money. We need to keep savings aside so we can buy our own house. Before we can start having children we need a home. Right?" Carlos asked Elena.

"I don't mind," she said. "We can sleep in our clothes until we can afford blankets."

"Blankets are no problem. There's a man who sells them on the street. He traveled here all the way from Otavalo. Can you imagine?" Carlos said as he shook his head in wonder. "We need blankets more than a bed, so I'll buy two before I go back to work."

Standing at the window facing the restless blue ocean, he told her, "We can move in today if you can find some other furnishings. I'll go to our hotel and pay our account. Would you like to sleep here tonight?"

Turning, he gave her a mischievous smile, for he already knew the answer.

"Oh, yes, yes! I can have the house ready by this evening," she danced in the center of the room, her ponytail flying behind.

He chuckled contentedly and grabbed her waist as they danced together. She accompanied him to buy the blankets and mats. After depositing them in the house, Carlos left for work and she returned to the town's center to buy a few pots and a bucket. An old discarded table that had been placed in a hotel storage room was salvaged and Elena took it home. Lopsided, it sat pathetically under the window. She put a small block of wood under the short leg and pulled a bright scarf out of her bag, covering the scarred top.

A warped bench that had been sitting under an open window in the second room was brought into the front room and placed opposite the table. There, she carefully folded their clothes and put them in small stacks.

Satisfied, she walked down the leaning wooden steps of the stilted house and went to the beach searching for rocks. Finding several, she placed them on the sand close to house, then dug a shallow well and gathered scraps of paper and pieces of dried driftwood to build a fire. Lining the well with stones and filling it with the driftwood, she lit a fire. The head waiter had given her an old grill that had been stored away when modern kitchen equipment had been bought for the Grand Hotel. Elena now placed the grill on top of the rock well as the fire took hold. From a basket she withdrew a few vegetables and meat bought on one of her visits to town. She simmered the meat with onions and garlic all afternoon. An hour before Carlos returned from work she would add the potatoes, carrots, and bouillon cubes for more flavor.

Since it would be awhile before her husband returned she decided to walk into town by way of the beach front. Leaving the soup inside the house until she returned, she stuffed a few sucres into her skirt pocket in case she found something she needed. Gazing down the south beach she saw several people on the shore and on impulse walked toward them to see what they were doing. Since Carlos had suggested she buy spoons and bowls, she wondered if perhaps the crowd was a group of merchants selling wares. But as she drew nearer she saw they were fishermen clad only in swimsuits sitting on logs mending their nets. Walking past them she was alert, watching and listening to their strange coastal Spanish, the rapid swallowing of words, the small hint of the letter 's'. Beyond the cluster of men and nets she saw an open market sitting on a small rise overlooking the ocean and a slow-moving river. Several long tables had been set side by side and covered with the day's fish catch. A busy group of men and women stood behind the tables serving the milling patrons as they called out their preferences. The merchants would then grab a fish and deftly chop off its tails and fins. Kept intact were the heads which coastal residents believe is the best meat of the fish for making a delicious savory soup.

Elena wandered among the tables not knowing one fish from another, but she decided on a medium-sized white one after being assured it had fewer bones than the others. The merchant cut off the tail and fins, removed the intestines, wrapped the fish in a newspaper and handed her the package. He threw the garbage into a pail which later would be dumped into the passing river where swarms of flying sea birds were hovering hoping for a meal. Some of the intestines would be used for fish bait.

Chapter 42

Elena walked behind the market and up a block to the central plaza. Discovering a store providing a variety of products, she found plates, silverware, and a sharp knife. Pulling out a wad of money she approached the clerk, a thin girl with hair stringing down her back.

"Buenas tardes, may I also purchase a pound of rice, a bunch of bananas, and a chunk of lard?"

"Buenas tardes. Si, I will help you," the girl said taking a large sheet of brown paper from below the counter.

She shyly studied Elena and asked, "Are you from Quito?"

"Yes," replied an interested Elena. "I'm from a small village east of Quito. How did you know?"

Folding the brown paper around a mound of rice, the girl smiled slowly, "My sister recently married a man who was raised there and they decided to move to the mountains to be with his family. You sound like him."

Elena was immediately drawn to the smiling girl and hungry for a female's companionship decided to do most of her trading in this store. They exchanged names hesitantly, but with the intrigue of new friendship.

Anita spooned pork fat onto butcher paper and put the package alongside the rice while Elena was choosing the ripest bananas. Noticing that Elena's arms were too full, she found an old basket and offered it to her. With a promise to visit soon, Elena stowed her purchases in the basket and walked back to her new home. After stoking the fire, she dropped more vegetables into the soup and sat down to wait for Carlos.

Chapter 43

"After the children are in bed this evening, Marta, may I see you for a few minutes?" Jillian asked.

Turning swiftly, the nurse stopped rocking her chair and stared at Jillian, clearly pleased.

"If no deliveries come in before then, yes," she glanced at Lucia, who tried to mask her disappointment behind a dark scowl. "How about we meet in my room? We can boil some tea water in the clinic's kitchenette."

"Well, it's time for me to go and clean up the patient's beds," growled Lucia, swiftly marching from the living room.

As the door slammed, Marta smiled knowingly, "That's one reason I tried to warn you about a friendship with her."

"Where did Lucia go?" Sara hung on Jillian's neck.

"Sara, don't drag Auntie Jill down like that. Sit up like a young lady," barked Marta.

"She had to go to the clinic. Maybe she'll be back before you go to bed," Jillian explained playing with Sara's hair.

"Humph," Marta said. "We'll probably not see her for three days."

Jillian waited for several minutes until Marta settled in her bedroom before she was able to build up the courage to see her. She wanted to stop by the clinic and reassure Lucia that it was in their best interest she talk to Marta about Costa Rica, but she knew it would take too much time to battle it out with her friend. Her departure date was fast approaching and she had delayed this encounter with

Chapter 43

Marta too long. She did not want to leave Pachuca and was hoping she would be able to strike a bargain with the woman.

Poking her head into Elizabeth's bedroom, she found the girl bent over a makeshift desk doing her homework, "I'll be at Mommy's for a few minutes. Ring me if you need help."

"Okay, Auntie Jill," Elizabeth smiled sweetly.

Glancing at Lucia's darkened bedroom window, she sighed and knocked on Marta's door.

"Quien es?"

"Jill."

"Come in," the door swung open and Marta beamed at her. "Come on in."

Jillian walked into the cluttered, small bedroom and glanced around. She decided it wasn't so cluttered as it was crowded. After a double bed, bedside table, bureau, portable closet, desk, and chair had been pushed into the room there was little space for anything else. The strong smell of alcohol antiseptic mingled with the smoky odor from patients filled the air, but they were not unpleasant odors. She looked for a place to sit.

"Why don't we go into the clinic area and boil some water for tea? I've set up a card table so we'll be more comfortable," the nurse led the way into the next room and pointed to a table and two folding chairs.

While she turned on a hot plate under a pan of water, Jillian sat down and glanced at a scrabble game and dictionary on the table.

"If you have coffee, I'd like that," Jillian said.

"Sure," Marta reached into a small cupboard and brought out a jar of instant coffee and a bowl of sugar and placed them on the table.

A glass of milk was taken from a small refrigerator, crammed with vials of medicine and poured into a creamer.

Nervously, the woman tried to make small talk and likewise, Jillian was struggling with her own nervousness on how to broach the subject of her visit to Costa Rica. When the drinks were ready, Marta gave her a secretive smile and left the room. Jillian heard her rustling around in the bedroom and waited, wondering.

"I've been saving this for a special occasion, Jill. Look what I have," she held up a can of mixed nuts and then proceeded to open it.

Pushing the can toward the girl, Marta's eyes shone at her reaction.

"Wow! When was the last time I ate a salted nut from the United States?" eyes wide with pleasure, Jillian dipped in and withdrew a handful of cashews, peanuts, and pecans.

There was a moment of silence as Marta followed suit and they chewed in bliss. Giggling together, they licked salt from their fingers and took another handful.

"Do you want milk and sugar in your coffee?" Marta asked.

"Just milk, thanks," Jillian answered beginning to relax a little.

"Have you ever played Scrabble?" Marta asked her.

"Sometimes on Christmas Day at home," then a poignant sense of loss brought tears to her eyes.

She smiled, embarrassed, "Sometimes I miss my family. Memories like that can make me cry easily."

"Your Christmas holidays must have been special," Marta commented. "I have a hard time remembering a happy Christmas in my youth."

Jillian paused, wondering suddenly if an unhappy childhood could account for Marta's stormy adulthood, "My family is very special."

"Do you ever think about going home?" Marta asked wiping her fingers on her skirt and leaning forward, her brown eyes soft. "This has puzzled me as you see, Lucia and I really don't have a family left to speak of, so we have made each other family, but your family is so far away."

"Yes and I dearly love each of them, but now you and Lucia and the children are my family, too," Jillian said sincerely. "The emotional roots I have here in Pachuca are as strong as those I have in the United States."

"I believe you," Marta nodded and then changing the subject, she asked. "Well, how would you like to play a game of Scrabble?"

"I've been told you're pretty good," Jillian smiled.

"I've won my fair share," Marta admitted.

"Yes, I'd like to play a game," Jillian answered.

She helped set up the board and letters wondering what was happening. For the first time in her memory, Marta was not irritating her. She was actually having a good time. The nurse won two games and

Chapter 43

kept Jillian laughing at her methods of throwing in Spanish slang when she couldn't think of English words.

"Hey, this isn't fair. I have a hard enough time speaking Spanish, let alone slang," teased Jillian and remembered why she was here.

She suddenly sobered and stood, gulping nervously, "I don't want to go to Costa Rica. I can't bear to leave everyone."

"Everyone?" Marta asked.

"Yes. I really had fun tonight," Jillian answered with tears in her eyes. "I don't want to leave the children, Lucia or you either."

"Sit down," thoughtfully Marta licked her lips. "I've enjoyed this evening too. You know, you've never given us a chance to be friends. You've been so wrapped up with Lucia and the kids that I haven't had a chance. I know I do things that irritate people. There are probably a lot more things I don't realize. I have needs, too."

She crossed her legs, "But Jill, to be honest I need you to leave Pachuca just to give me a respite."

"A respite?" pain stabbed at her stomach and she held her breath. "You want a respite from me?"

"You're not an easy person to get along with. I never know from one moment to the next if you're going to be angry or happy. Every morning I wonder what kind of mood you're in. When you moved in I told you I was strict with the children. You accepted my position fully aware that I'm not easy to like," smiling gently, she patted Jillian's hand.

"I admire your strength, spunk and abilities, but you are much too independent. I've learned that we all need each other. I realize this more every day. I want you to think about the burden I carry. Think about how many people depend on me. If I make one wrong decision it could mean death, and believe me, we're not in a position to call for help on a p. a. system," Marta said ruefully.

"True, we're not as bad off as some jungle clinics, but we are on our own if an emergency comes up. I've never told you how many babies have died in this room. Does that surprise you? I didn't think you would be that interested. Most parents bring their sick children in at the last minute and expect me to perform a miracle. Usually their eyes are rolling back in their heads and they want 'la Señorita' to heal them," Marta shook her head sadly.

"Don't forget the demands on me to see that no mother or baby die during childbirth. To date, no mother has died and I've delivered over a thousand babies. We've had only one or two babies die because they were breech," she continued.

"I'm not trying to get your sympathy. I just want you to know that besides all the patients, I'm really the one responsible for the children, you, Lucia, and the homes, including the new one under construction. On top of everything else, you're angry at me most of the time. This is why, sometimes I can't bear the way you treat me," tears formed in her eyes, but she blinked them back.

"I'm determined not to cry tonight because I know how you hate that, but there are times when I sit here in my room and know that you and Lucia are having fun together. Lucia used to be my companion, but you came along and stole her away. I know that she and I were never as close as you two are now, but at least I saw her sometimes in the evening. There are times when I am jealous because you two have secrets and laugh together while I'm left out," Marta admitted squeezing her eyes tightly, two big tears dropped. "Sandi had no desire to be with either Lucia or me, and really I didn't care because she never meant that much to me."

Never had Jillian felt more shame. Everything that Marta said hit home like a sledgehammer. It was like taking off blinders and seeing Marta not as a blustering bully, but as a woman of patience with needs of her own. Sitting back the girl was speechless.

"Jill, it's too late. All the arrangements have been made and you must go to Costa Rica. I wish we had talked earlier," Marta said sadly. "If we had maybe something could have been done, but right now we'll have to go ahead with plans. I think some time apart from each other will do all of us good."

Jillian's antipathy for the woman melted in a moment and she realized how much she had counted on her. Now instead of guilt, she felt fear.

"Please, Marta, I don't want to go. This is my home. I don't want to leave the children. I don't want to leave you. You can spend evenings with Lucia. I'll stay alone or else you and I can be together," she stood, full of new plans. "Maybe every night we can trade off. Please."

Chapter 43

Dissolving into tears, Jillian took the nurse's arm.

"I just don't think I can. Sandi is planning on your coming. I've bought the tickets and we have your exit papers. The school is expecting you; the classes are paid for. The home you'll stay in is waiting and ready," Marta declared as she patted the girl's hand again. "I really do feel a separation will do us more good than not. Perhaps during this time I can reevaluate how I discipline the children. When you come back, we'll discuss it again."

"What if you decide you don't want me to come back?" Jillian asked fearfully.

Leading the girl toward the front door, Marta paused, "Go home now. I have to go to Quito tomorrow. Who knows when the two women in the clinic will deliver? I may be up all night."

With her head hung low, Jillian walked home without looking back. Marta closed the door and leaned against it, a satisfied smile on her face.

Chapter 44

With a sense of detachment, Jillian watched the construction crew place stakes in the ground and wind thick strings from one pole to the other until the length and width of her new house was measured. For Lucia, however, only an occasional meal or baby delivery could tear her away from the construction site. It was as though new life had been breathed into her. Each truckload of sand, rocks and pebbles was selected by her, each bag of cement inspected, every detail discussed with the foreman. She was there when each shovel of dirt was lifted and the foundation leveled.

Jillian's heart was heavy as the departure date for Costa Rica drew near. The relationship between her and Marta had been different since that night the previous month. Either Marta was making a greater effort to improve or Jillian was now able to excuse many of the nurse's irritating habits. Due to the work on the new house and in the clinic, Lucia seemed too busy to notice that Jillian was spending more time with Marta. Around the house everything was relaxed. She herself was making an effort to be more congenial and less moody. With limited strain in evidence among the adults, the children, perceptibly began to laugh and play with more freedom, all of which made her upcoming trip more difficult to face.

So when Marta appeared distraught at lunch a few days before Jillian's departure, everyone was surprised. Worry lines etched her brow and her hand played nervously with a crumpled handkerchief as she took her chair.

Chapter 44

Jillian looked up, her heart contracting. What had happened? Even with the small step the two women had taken toward each other in the past month, she still feared her. Despite her curiosity, she was reluctant to question Marta and decided to ask Lucia later.

They proceeded with the meal in silence, interrupted only with a few barking commands from Marta to the children and when Lucia appeared in the doorway. Finding a place at the table, she seized a piece of bread, buttered and folded it over and took a bite.

"It's your fault, Marta," Lucia said softly.

In amazement, Jillian eyed the Indian in hopes of getting her attention. What was going on? Deliberately Lucia ignored Jillian and grabbed her plate. She walked into the kitchen and returned in a few minutes with it piled high with rice, green beans, and a pork chop.

"Who asked you?" yelled Marta.

"I'm just telling you," yelled Lucia in reply.

Jillian and the children held their breath.

"Don't you dare talk to me like that in front of the children and Flora," bellowed Marta.

Without warning, Lucia flung her dish to the floor, the food bouncing on Flora who was cowering in the corner. She leaped across the dining room, hauled Marta up by her arms, turned her around, grabbed her by the ears and threw her against the wall. Banging the woman's head hard, she then turned and walked out the door, slamming it behind her.

Andy and Lydia began to cry while the other children sat in stunned silence. Marta, obviously shaken, straightened her glasses and returned to her chair. Reaching up to arrange her hair, she touched the back of her head. Then bending forward to fork a piece of meat, she suddenly set the utensil on the plate and looked at Jillian.

"Did you notice if anyone brought pipes for the plumbing yet? We need to get those laid before we have another big rain," Marta asked Jillian.

The discrepant question surprised her.

Jillian tried to match Marta's coolness, "I don't think so. We may have to drive to Tumbaco to buy them ourselves."

How can she be so calm? She thought as she searched Marta's face.

Finding it passive and unruffled, she asked, "Do you want me to go for them?"

"No, I may go myself after a nap," her chin quivered a little. "Perhaps I need to get away."

She put down her fork again and stood, "I wonder if anyone realizes just how much I do care about all of you."

She exited with Jillian right behind her, "Marta, wait a minute. What's wrong?"

"Why don't you ask your friend Lucia? Let's see what you think of me then," Marta said sarcastically.

"I know that you care about all of us. I just wish you would talk to me," Jillian said in frustration

Standing in the warm sunshine, Jillian watched the nurse disappear into the outpatient clinic. Confused she returned to the table and wished the children were in bed napping so she could visit with Lucia.

When finally she was able to get away, she went to the maternity clinic where she found Lucia bent over her sewing machine, a Christmas gift Marta had brought from the United States.

"May I come in?" Jillian asked softly.

"If you must," Lucia answered, shrugging as she bit off a thread and smoothed a dark blue skirt.

Lucia's capabilities ranged from sewing, knitting, construction work, and wood-crafting to baking tasty cakes. Jillian marveled that somewhere in the distant Ecuadorian jungles, a missionary had cared enough for the Indian child to teach her how to be creative and independent.

"Whose skirt is that?" Jillian asked pushing aside a pile of cotton scraps so she could sit on the end of the bed.

"Susana's," Lucia answered.

As usual when Lucia was upset, she retreated into herself. The chances of getting answers to her questions would be slim.

"What's wrong?" Jillian asked as she moved closer to Lucia.

"Who said anything is wrong?" Lucia asked in return pressing the pedal sending the sewing needle whizzing up and down along the skirt's waistband.

"Lucia, what's going on? Please tell me," Jillian begged.

Silence.

Chapter 44

"Lucia," she implored, reaching out to touch her arm.

Recoiling, Lucia glared, "Leave me alone, will you?"

Infuriated, Jillian jumped to her feet, "I sure will. I will leave you alone with pleasure. I can't wait to leave this awful place. Everyone is crazy and I can't stand to stay here one more day!"

She raced through the kitchen, slamming the door so hard the windows rattled and pounded angrily down the sidewalk.

The door opened behind her and Lucia yelled, "Thanks a lot for waking up the patients. That's all I need."

In her room Jillian seethed all afternoon, counting the days until she could see Sandi who would provide the perfect dumping ground for all her problems. Quiet, peace-loving Sandi. Even the sorrow of leaving the children couldn't change her mind now. She desperately needed the reprieve.

Marta sent a message that she had a severe headache and would not be at dinner. That was fine with Jillian. After putting the children down for the night she just wanted to crawl into bed with a book and forget everything and everyone.

It was late when her bedroom door slowly opened, "Jill, are you asleep?"

"Yes, I always sleep with a book propped open in my hand," Jillian responded sarcastically.

"Can I come in?" Lucia asked softly.

"What do you want, Lucia?" Jillian asked barely looking at the woman.

"I can only stay a minute because one of my patients is about to deliver, but I want to say I'm sorry for the way I treated you this afternoon," Lucia said sincerely.

"That's okay," Jillian replied without looking up from her book.

"Are you still mad?" Lucia asked.

"A little," Jillian admitted sitting up in the bed and placing a bookmark in the paperback.

Shuffling her feet, Lucia made a move toward the door, "Well, I guess if you're still mad I'll go. I just wanted to say I'm sorry."

"Hey, you didn't come here to say you're sorry," Jillian accused. "You could have done that tomorrow."

"Maybe, but I do have a delivery ready," Lucia said continuing toward the door.

"Shall I go with you?" Jillian asked raising her eyebrows questioningly, feeling about for her slippers with her bare feet.

She wasn't about to lose this opportunity to discover what ailed Marta.

"If you'd like," nodded Lucia, failing her attempt at nonchalance.

She sounded relieved.

"You go on. I've got to check on the children first," Jillian stepped through the door and moved room to room down the long hallway, listening for any sounds.

Satisfied that all was well, she descended the steps and found Lucia waiting. Together they walked the long sidewalk, Lucia shyly taking her arm.

"Do you want something to eat?" the Indian asked as they entered the clinic kitchen.

"No thanks," Jillian shook her head. "I just want to know what's going on."

"Okay, okay," Lucia said as she led the way to her bedroom.

Jillian eased backward on the bed, leaning against the wall.

"Do you really want to go to Costa Rica as you said this afternoon?" Lucia asked with an earnest, worried look in her small, black eyes.

"Yeah, I really do," Jillian answered sadly. "I'm tired and I need some peace and quiet."

"You think you're tired," Lucia responded rubbing her eyes. "I wish you could be in my shoes for just one week."

Lucia waved her hand in irritation, "Do you know how much sleep I get? Marta's able to sleep a little more than I do, but she's up half the night, too."

"I know that there have been a lot of deliveries lately," Jillian acknowledged impatiently.

"A lot?" Lucia exclaimed as she shook her head, her shiny black hair reflecting light from the bulb overhead. "We have at least one a night. If we hadn't done the prenatal work on them, I'd turn them away."

She lowered her head, tears glistening in her eyes, "I don't want you to go away."

Chapter 44

Jillian shrugged, "I didn't think you'd notice that it's almost time for me to leave. You've been so busy I've hardly seen you in the past month."

"Sure, because you've been with Marta every minute," Lucia pointed out angrily.

"Oh, Lucia, that's not true," Jillian objected. "By any chance is that part of the problem you and Marta were having this afternoon?"

"Part of it, but it really makes me mad how she's taking all your time," Lucia said still seething with anger.

Jillian closed her eyes, tired of all the drama.

"I wanted to talk to you about this sooner, but you were always occupied in the clinic or at the construction site."

Opening her eyes, she leaned forward, "Lucia, I don't think we have any choice right now. You'll just have to understand that part of my time must be spent with her. For a long time Marta was willing for you and I to be friends without including her. Now things have changed. You know that she'll want to spend time with you, too."

"Do you love her more than you love me?" Lucia asked like a wounded child.

"You will always be my favorite and best friend, no matter how much time I spend with her," Jillian told the Indian sincerely. "Please, never forget that."

Lucia sat slumped over on the edge of her bed, head in hands.

"I hate her," she said, muffling the words.

"What? You don't hate her. I'll never believe that," Jillian scooted over to sit by the Indian. "Haven't you noticed how much calmer Marta is since she and I have worked out some of our problems? It's ironic that now you are having trouble with her. Why did you hurt her this afternoon? What happened?"

"I'm still upset how she punished Paul for finding that gum," straightening up, she sneered trying vainly to cover her emotions.

"We were all to blame," Jillian pointed out.

"Don't you think I know that? That's why I've been staying away," Lucia said sadly. "I couldn't bear to see Paul's face. Did you know she used a hose on him?"

"Yes I know," Jillian said. "Paul told me."

She looked at her quizzically, "How do you know?"

"I was at the outpatient clinic this morning. We were talking about the three of us and our relationships when I noticed the piece of hose," Lucia said angrily.

Running her hand through her hair, she faced Jillian, "It was sitting on her bureau. When I asked why it was there, she told me she had used it on him. I was shocked and since I've been so depressed this past month over the part I played in his punishment, when I saw what she had used something in me came apart."

"But you could have seriously hurt her, Lucia, and in front of the children, too," Jillian said accusingly. "I was horrified."

Lucia jumped up and paced, "You think that's all? There's more. She's been working on all these adoptions. That's alright with me. We have babies coming out of our ears right now and they'll go to good homes somewhere, but I'm left with all the explaining."

Every fiber in Jillian's body quickened and she held her breath, "What explaining?"

"Do you remember last month during lunch when Marta talked to that attorney on the telephone?" Lucia asked.

"Yes, it was about the little girl who went to the attorney's home," Jillian answered. "What about it?"

"What else do you know?" Lucia put a hand on her hip.

Clasping her hands, she shook her head, "Nothing much. Marta said the attorney had room for the baby in his home until the papers would be ready and then she'd be sent to the United States."

"Do you know how many babies are living in his house right now?" Lucia asked.

"A lot?" Jillian asked wondering where this was all headed.

"At least five from our clinic. His teen-age children and wife are busy taking care of them while he works on the papers," Lucia explained.

"It's all legal, isn't it?" Jillian asked again wondering why Lucia was so upset.

"I guess but that's not the problem. The little girl's mother went home after the delivery without a backward glance, but when her family heard that she had left the baby with us, they were furious. They've been back at least once a week since then and I have to put them off because Marta won't talk with them," Lucia explained.

Chapter 44

"Today when I was cooking the patient's lunches, I heard someone calling for Marta. When I opened the door there stood the parents, grandparents, uncles and aunts, and of all things, a policeman. The mother had come back and she wanted her baby. I explained to her that the child was on her way to the United States, but they didn't believe me because Marta had told her that the baby was going to stay here with us. The policeman said he wanted to come in and look around. I was really upset and I told them to wait while I went next door to tell Marta."

"What did she do?" Jillian asked.

"She yelled at me. She told me never to talk to anyone like that without her being with me. Can you imagine?" the Indian's eyes smoldered. "She said I was a fool to have told the policeman that the baby had gone to the United States. Jill, she was more upset than I have ever seen her."

"Did she talk to them?" Jillian asked.

Lucia stopped her pacing, "Oh, yeah. She came right over and told them I didn't know what I was talking about and that I was merely one of the helpers. She said the child I had been talking about didn't come from this clinic at all and that the patient's baby they were asking about had contracted a fatal disease and died."

"Died?" Jillian couldn't believe her ears. "Died? That baby is alive and healthy. Did the policeman believe the lie?"

"You should have heard her. She even had papers," Lucia said getting angrier by the minute. "They looked official enough that they asked no further questions."

"How can the baby be sent to the United States if the parents didn't sign for her to go?" Jillian asked, confused.

"She merely writes that the child was abandoned in the clinic," Lucia said. "After all, it had been left by the mother."

Jillian thought back to the conversation she had overheard between the mother and Marta and slowly shook her head, "That sounds like the patient's buzzer."

"One of the patients may be ready. Her water has already broken. I'll go check. Do you want to come?" Lucia asked as she headed out the door.

"Why not?" Jillian answered knowing she would never be able to sleep now.

Lucia hastened her steps as the buzzer rasped for attention, "Si, si, por favor callase! Be quiet! There are other patients here."

"My pains are worse," the woman lying on the bed was twisted in agony.

"Watch her. I have to wash my hands," Lucia told Jillian as she trotted to the sink.

"Here, let me check," Lucia told the patient. "Oh, oh, the head's right there. We've got to get her on the table."

Moaning, the woman slid off the bed and padded into the labor room. Jillian eased her onto the delivery table as Lucia deftly tied her legs in the stirrups.

"Wash your hands, Jill and then I'll help you put on gloves," Lucia told her. "You're going to deliver this baby."

Jillian stopped in her tracks, "Are you crazy?"

"Sure, but I'll be here to watch your every move. It's time you learned how to do this," Lucia grinned. "Now, wash your hands and get over here."

Lucia grabbed a gown from a metal bureau and held it up for her to slip into.

"Hold out your hands," removing two powdered, sterilized gloves from a plastic lined box, she slipped them on Jillian's outstretched hands.

She pushed a bucket to the end of the table and positioned Jillian at the patient's feet.

With her heart pounding, Jillian faced the patient. Her eyes were riveted to the vertical opening where with each push she caught glimpses of the baby's head. The force of the patient's pushing spread the woman's pelvis and thinned the perineum. Water spurted with each effort and Jillian slipped her gloved fingers inside to massage the skin, hoping it wouldn't split. As the baby slid downward and closer to freedom, at last, with a final thrust from his mother, he poked his head out. Her heart quickened at the sight of his thick black curly hair. As he lifted his head, she saw the long, curling black eyelashes.

"He looked at me, Lucia. He looked at me," Jillian cried excitedly.

Chapter 44

The Indian slapped her leg and laughed, "Don't be foolish."

To the patient, she instructed, "Now, one more push to free the shoulders. Push. That's the way."

As he emerged, Jillian grabbed the child, taking his ankles while Lucia clamped the umbilical cord, pinned the other end and then cut it. Jillian suctioned his mouth until he bawled with displeasure. She carefully laid the baby boy in a bassinet.

"Now, Jill, the placenta," Lucia instructed. "Gently pull it out and check it carefully for tears."

A small tug produced the large soft bloody tissue. She took it in her hand and checked each side, "All in one piece."

"Great," Lucia said. "Drop it in the bucket and go care for the baby. I'll clean up the patient."

"Lucia, he's beautiful. Look at all that hair," Jillian smiled as she wrapped him in a flannel blanket. "I sort of wish I could have another baby now that I see him."

"Just bathe him," Lucia exclaimed over her shoulder as she gave the patient a shot of vitamin K to help clot the blood flow.

Jillian filled a small metal basin with lukewarm water and took it into the patient's ward and then returned for the baby. Dressed in a white flannel gown he was the prettiest baby she had yet to see. Holding him on her breast, she sniffed deeply of his freshly bathed newborn smell. The yearning for this child was as strong as she had felt when Andy and Anna had come into her life. Already she sensed a wrenching loss knowing that soon she would have to lay him in his mother's arms. A thought crossed her mind. If Marta could beg for a baby, why couldn't she? Then she thought of how cruel that was and rebuked herself.

"Can you believe this is the patient's fifteenth child? Look at her. She's only forty-two years old but looks like she's sixty," announced Lucia without compassion.

The woman smiled as if it were a compliment.

Jillian came close and returned the smile, "You have a beautiful little boy."

"Que lastima!" she smiled but didn't look at the child.

Lucia pulled the stirrups out of their holes and straightened the patient's gown.

"Come, let's go to bed," she lifted the table's wheel brakes and pushed it alongside the clinic bed.

After tucking her in, she crossed the room to check on the other patient who had remained asleep through all the noise.

"When you live in a crowded house like she does, you can sleep through anything," she chuckled.

Following on her heels with the baby still in her arms, Jillian whispered to her, "The woman acts like she doesn't want this baby."

"Maybe she doesn't," Lucia said. "If you want him, take him."

"Don't be silly. I can't just take a baby."

"Why not? Everyone else does," Lucia took off for the labor room with Jillian still behind her.

A smile played at the corners of her mouth, "No matter to the mother if the baby was a girl or boy, she had already planned to give him to us. Marta says the woman cannot care for another child. I believe her because I talked with the patient myself. They simply can't afford this baby."

"Will Marta send him away like the others?" Jillian's eyes opened wide, the makings of a new problem lurking nearby.

"Ha! The way Marta feels about you right now, you could probably ask for the moon and get it," Lucia exclaimed, her jealousy filtered through. "Ask her in the morning."

Disappointment lowered her voice to a whisper, "Oh Lucia, what about Costa Rica? She'll never let me keep him."

"Maybe I can offer to care for him while you're gone," Lucia offered.

"But you're so busy," Jillian answered thinking of their previous conversation.

"No matter what you think about me, I really care for you," Lucia said sincerely.

"You're the most special friend I've ever had. Marta could never mean as much to me as you do," Jillian said with emotion. "I tell you the truth."

Embarrassed, yet pleased, Lucia took the infant from her and placed him in the private ward.

"I must try to feed him, but you should leave. Get some sleep because you will need to be here for his six o'clock feeding," Lucia instructed Jillian. "We'll wait until morning to see what happens."

Chapter 45

Early the next morning Marta found Jillian in the clinic cradling the infant in her arms. Stopping in the doorway, she stared at the scene.

"What is this?" Marta asked.

"Oh, Marta, I'm so glad you stopped here before going to the house. Look what I have," Jillian placed a baby bottle on the table and wiped the baby's mouth with her finger.

Bending over the bundle, thick hair falling around her face, Marta frowned, "Why are you feeding it?"

"So much happened last night. I was here with Lucia and..." Jillian tried to explain.

"You were here last night?" Marta interrupted stepping back.

"Yes," Jillian answered, hesitated a moment, then launched into a breathless explanation. "I just wanted to visit for a minute because I see so little of Lucia. She asked me if I wanted to deliver the baby because...."

"You delivered this baby?" Marta asked, obviously shocked.

"Yes, because Lucia said I should have the experience. Marta, the mother didn't want the baby, but you knew that already. Lucia said you talked to her. She's the one who has had fifteen deliveries," Jillian tried to continue but she was out of breath.

She looked up hopefully, "I want him. He's just beautiful. Look at all his hair and his perfect little face."

She lifted him up for Marta's benefit before placing him over her shoulder.

325

"Yes, he is very pretty," Marta said, rubbing her hands against the chill in the room.

She stood back thoughtfully, "What about Costa Rica?"

"I knew you'd ask that. I don't really want to go, but if you'd let me keep him, I'd not complain once more. You said you wanted me to have more children for the new house," said Jillian pleading. "Marta, I'll spend time with you. I'll not complain about going to Costa Rica. I'll do anything to keep him."

Soft brown eyes surveyed her, "Who's going to care for him?"

"Lucia said she would," Jillian explained.

Her eyes hardened, "No, she's much too busy."

Peeking down the hallway, her voice dropped to a whisper, "Where is she, by the way?"

"Still asleep. She was really tired after last night," Jillian explained.

"My point exactly," Marta said pulling on her ear, deep in thought, she shook her head a little. "Are you sure you want a boy? You already have one."

"Oh yes," Jillian replied earnestly. "I don't mind two boys a bit. I'll take a girl next time and think up a real pretty name. Then my next little boy will be named...."

Marta interrupted and pointed in the baby's direction, "What will you name him?"

"I've already named him Ryan," her eyes watered. "Please let me keep him."

"I suppose I can have a girl come in from Pachuca each day until you return. She and Flora can manage the house and baby together. Lucia and I can feed him in between deliveries at night," Marta said.

"Thank you! Oh, thank you!" Jillian exclaimed.

"Just one thing. I have a favor to ask of you," Marta said.

"Anything," Jillian answered without even thinking about it.

"You are to leave next Tuesday morning, but I don't want the children to know which day. Let them think it's a week later or even next month. This way the shock won't be so great. I don't want them to go through what they did when Sandi left. We'll put your suitcases in the truck Monday night. We can have them think you're simply visiting someone in Quito for a while," Marta explained.

"What about Lucia? Won't she talk?" Jillian asked.

Chapter 45

"I'll take care of her. Will you do it?" Marta asked.

"Of course," Jillian answered, joyfully kissing Ryan's cheek.

Marta shook her head over the affectionate display, but refrained from speaking her mind.

All too soon Tuesday morning arrived. As the sun rose over the mountains, Marta's truck nosed its way onto the newly paved highway. Jillian sat in the cab's corner too tearful to speak. Seemingly unaware of Jillian's distress, the nurse kept up a cheerful banter, reporting on everything she saw. Under different circumstances, Jillian would have loved this drive. Marta's past in the Tumbaco Valley was filled with interesting and intriguing stories, but today her heart was heavy. She had kissed the children and Ryan good-bye the night before and hadn't been able to tell them that she'd not see them for three months. Three months. Ninety long days. How could she live without them? Without Pachuca? Without Ecuador?

As they climbed around the winding, narrow highway to the capital city, Jillian looked back at the valley, "This was the view that convinced me I belonged here. On my first trip I had all but decided to scurry back to the United States, but something about this valley convinced me to stay. Does that make sense to you?"

"I know exactly what you mean and I know how you feel about the country," Marta said with a smile. "I could never live in the States again."

They turned at the familiar intersection where Jillian had stood with Lucia and Leah several years before. She had passed it many times grinning to herself, but now it brought tears to her eyes. If only she had known that day how much Lucia would mean to her in the future.

Following the Avenida Dias de Agosto, they arrived at the small airport. It had been constructed years before when Quito's north side population was sparse, but little by little the suburbs had expanded until now they surrounded the airport. Homes, schools and heavy traffic flowed beside the long runways. Marta turned the truck toward the entrance and with a big grin pulled over to the curb.

Jillian struggled to return the smile, "I guess this is it."

"I want to tell you how much I appreciate your efforts to be my friend, Jill. These past few weeks have made a big difference for me, especially with all the additional pressures I've been carrying. Now I feel that we can really start working together in our little village. Think of what we can accomplish," Marta's grin broadened, displaying her protruding teeth and narrowed her eyes behind black, horn-rimmed glasses.

Surprised, Jillian realized she no longer felt ambivalence toward Marta. The dislike that had plagued her in the first years was gone. She felt affection for the woman. Her questionable activities that periodically surfaced no longer bothered her. With a small start, she suddenly recalled the times Marta had promised her that she would someday want to be her friend. It had happened.

"Jill, I have some news for you. A week ago I sent a telegram to Sandi and told her you wouldn't be coming. Now, don't look so shocked. The school has been notified, along with the family you were going to live with. I just wanted to see if you would be willing to go. That is why I didn't want you to say anything to the children," Marta giggled at the girl's stunned face. "I don't want to see you go away. We need you here in Pachuca."

The news boggled her mind but slowly it started sinking in.

"Oh my, what wonderful news! I can't believe it!" Jillian leaned forward and hugged the nurse. "But what are we doing here? Why did both of us come to Quito? Couldn't you have told me this at home?"

Still laughing, the woman started the motor, "Because we have never been able to go anywhere together. I decided that today is our day and because I want to see something. I need your opinion and since we had to go this direction anyway, I thought, why not look at it together."

"Why did you change your mind about Costa Rica?" Jillian asked.

"A lot of reasons. Your Spanish isn't too bad. It's adequate for the situations around the orphanage. If you need more experience, I'll give you lessons. I really wanted you to go to school up until last month, but when things started improving between us, I changed my mind," Marta explained.

"You can't imagine how surprised and relieved I am," Jillian bounced a little on the seat. "I can't wait to see Andy and Ryan and all the kids. Won't Lucia be pleased?"

"Lucia knows," Marta said flatly.

Chapter 45

"No wonder she didn't come to say good-bye," Jillian remarked.

"Humph," was Marta's only reply.

They drove several miles north until Quito's suburbs started thinning out. After checking a few scribbled notes on a notepad she turned onto a narrow dirt road and Marta eased the truck through a forest of eucalyptus trees.

"Where are we going?" Jillian asked as the scenery changed.

"I'm not sure," Marta said concentrating on her driving.

Finally, after driving a mile east over ruts and mud holes they reached a cobblestone path which ended at the entrance of a hacienda. A plastered low mud wall enclosed a large yard where a group of children played with a rubber ball. A woman stood over to one side dipping water from a large cement vat onto a slab while another briskly scrubbed clothes by hand. Behind them, a man pushed on the handle of a water pump, filling a narrow pipe that led to a large barrel placed on a platform above the two women. As more water was needed, one of them turned a faucet to refill the vat. When the woman finished scrubbing, she rinsed the cloth and placed it on the grass to dry while the other woman took her place and continued the scrubbing.

Marta moved the truck ahead until they reached a long, low lying building behind a cement wall.

She turned the key to stop the motor and opened the door to step out, "Come with me."

Jillian looked at the clutter throughout the yard, the old building and the disinterested children. Even those working with the laundry paid them no attention.

"What is this place?" Jillian asked.

The nurse leaned in the window, "I heard about this orphanage the other day. The American man who runs it takes care of children until the papers are completed for adoption. My lawyer has run out of room and I think this might be a good place for our babies."

Jillian had already made up her mind that she didn't like this place. There was a strange atmosphere surrounding the complex. As they walked through the entrance in the wall, the main house door burst open and a large man ran out. He was tall with a belly that hung over his belt. Every one of his features was accentuated, huge face, huge lips, and huge ears. His enlarged head seemed to be growing up through thinning brown hair that was plastered down in hopes no one would suspect he was balding. He extended a fleshy palm and grasped Marta's. Flashing a wide grin in Jillian's direction, he grabbed her hand.

"Hi. I'm Clint Marshall. To what do we owe this privilege?"

Jillian glanced at Marta, too overwhelmed to speak.

"My name is Marta Brewer and this is Jill Townsend," she spoke up courageously. "We're from an orphanage in Pachuca. I heard about your work the other day and decided to drop by."

"Well, we're more than happy to see you," he beamed. "Come on in. Where are you from Jill and Marta, I mean, where are you from in the States?"

"I'm from Oregon and Marta's from North Carolina," Jillian answered.

"God's country, huh? I mean Oregon. I'm from Montana myself. Never been to North Carolina, so who knows. Could be that's God's country, too," laughing, he winked at Jillian and placed his hand on her back.

Frowning up at him, she arched her back and moved closer to the nurse.

Winking again, he stepped ahead and guided them into a hallway that was in total darkness. They entered a room just inside the entrance that was filled to capacity with tables, bunk beds, dressers, and babies. Two large windows in one wall provided the only light. In an attempt to ignore the stench, her attention was drawn to the gray, dingy baby clothes laying on the dressers and to several rows of long wooden boxes placed on the tables. Each box held an infant lying on its back with folded blankets elevating bottles to their mouths. A group of girls gathered at one end of the room.

Clint was enthusiastically explaining the operation while Jillian wondered how a tiny infant could drink milk from a propped bottle. Watching the man more closely, she saw that despite his attempt at excitement, he was nervous. A layer of perspiration formed into droplets and began to crawl down the sides of his face. He continually wiped his hands on his pants.

Chapter 45

"We don't have very good facilities yet. No running water or electricity, but we're doing the best we can. I'm waiting for support to come in. We don't make a lot of money from all this effort, just what prospective parents send from the States. If we don't find parents for the kids, we have to support them ourselves."

Jillian couldn't bear to look at him. Turning away, she watched the group of young girls sprawled on bunk beds, chattering and laughing among themselves. Longing to ask them why they couldn't feed the babies by hand, she had just about talked herself into approaching them when a slender, blond-haired woman appeared at the door. Visibly nervous she was introduced to Jillian and Marta as Clint's wife Regina. Immediately she made apologies for the clutter and lack of help. Again Jillian wondered what the young girls were doing there. For one brief moment when Clint wasn't talking, she was able to catch Marta's eye and with understanding, the nurse excused themselves and they made their departure.

"Let's get out of here," exclaimed Jillian, slamming the truck door.

"What's wrong with you?" Marta asked as she got behind the steering wheel and started the motor.

"I don't know, but something is wrong. The atmosphere, those people or something. Did you see how those babies are being neglected?"

"Yes," Marta admitted. "I don't like that very much."

"You wouldn't think of leaving any of our babies there, would you?"

"I would look at every other alternative first," Marta explained. "But I'm afraid I don't have many options right now."

"Anything would be better than with the Marshalls," Jillian said with feeling, secure she had seen the last of that dreadful place.

Between normal Tuesday errands, Marta treated her to a lovely lunch in one of Quito's major hotels overlooking the Tumbaco Valley. They chatted and fellowshipped like good friends and discussed ways they could help the neglected babies they had seen that morning. The drive back to Pachuca was pure pleasure. Never had she imagined when she left home that morning that she would be returning the same day. Jillian decided life had turned a corner.

Chapter 46

The days passed swiftly and soon they had lived in Playas for more than a year. Any concerns of not adjusting to the new culture seemed distant now. Carlos had been accepted by his co-workers as competent and talented, while Elena made herself busy keeping house. A month before their living arrangements in the stilted house had ended, Carlos approached the hotel owners with an idea. He would be willing to restore the two neighboring houses making them livable if they would allow him to live in their house free of rent one more year. The manager readily agreed and in a short space of time the houses were ready and rented out by two local families. Their neighbors were friendly and on occasion Elena shared light conversation with the women.

She never tired of watching the small fishing vessels. The rugged fishermen seemed worldly in a way the men of Pachuca could not. Each day several paddled out to sea standing on their vessels, several logs strapped together to gather fish in small nets. Another form of fishing took place on the shoreline. A band of fishermen walked the beach using the ancient method of throwing a net from the sea's edge and drawing it back with captured fish.

Each afternoon Elena walked to the beach with a few coins to select a one. Taking the squirming fish in hand, she would run to the hotel where the cook would kill and clean it for her. At first Carlos and Elena had little taste for seafood, but grew to love it as her neighbors taught Elena various ways to cook sea life.

Chapter 46

Several varieties of bananas grew plentifully a few miles inland. She learned to fry one variety, stuff others with meat, boil them in soup or roll them in a bread mixture to fry with cheese. Their favorite, however, was a small banana called an Orita, three inches in length, meaty and sweet.

Another coastal treat was coconut milk. One hot afternoon, Carlos and Elena noticed a local native standing on a corner selling the large globes. For a few centavos the man pounded two holes in the coconut top with a hammer and large nail and then placed two straws in the holes. He handed one to Elena. Not fully ripe, the fruit had little meat, but was filled with coconut milk and offered a hearty drink they found refreshing and thirst quenching.

Little by little their house had become homey, much to Elena's delight. Carlos bought another small table and a four-burner kerosene stove. A local carpenter had built a simple bed and matching bureau for the inner room, which completed their bedroom suite.

Yellow cotton curtains on the shuttered windows sparked both rooms with color. It became the young couple's delight to pull them aside each morning to watch the sun spread her golden beams on a sparkling sea while eating breakfast.

Elena was happy and thought little of her family. Pachuca was a world away and only when special incidents occurred did her mother and brothers come to mind. Then she would feel a twinge of guilt over her lack of concern. Never did her father enter her mind.

Carlos had written his Uncle Jose during their first month in Playas, informing him of their location and suggested he keep in contact with his mother and siblings to see how they were faring. Begging him not to let his mother know of their whereabouts, Carlos urged Uncle Jose to write soon with any news. With each letter they were informed that although Laura and her children missed Carlos very much, his sister knew Carlos had done the right thing. Never did they receive news of Rolando and Elena's family. He worried that lack of news would affect her.

"Are you alright not knowing how your family is doing?" he asked.

"Not as bad as I thought I'd be," Elena admitted. "I'm still convinced we did what was right moving to Playas. How do you feel?"

Carlos held her close, "Happy we came here. I'm so pleased we're married and don't live in Pachuca any longer. May our lives be as happy as they are today!"

Epilogue

Jillian decided life had turned a corner for her once she dealt with her relationship with the often volatile Marta. She and Lucia had become good friends just as she had hoped back when she first came to work at the clinic in Pachuca. With the disappearance of old resentments, the construction of a new house, Andy and Ryan, new understandings, new projects, and an entire lifetime ahead of her, what could possibly go wrong?

And what of Carlos and Elena? Their love seemed deeper than ever even after leaving their families behind and seeking a new life on the ocean shores of Playas? Was their love for each other deep enough to overcome the trials and tribulations ahead of them? Would Carlos' Uncle Jose keep their secret? Would Elena's obsessive brother Rolando give up looking for his sister?

You won't want to miss the second book in the Ecuadorian Trilogy as Edie Livesay skillful continues this compelling story of the colorful residents of Pachuca, Quito, and Playas in ***Book Two: Beyond Mud Walls***